IN THE SHADOW OF THE SUN

IN THE SHADOW OF THE SUN

POLI FLORES JR.

To Goyo and all the magnificent military vets
who sacrificed too much for the rest of us.

Every man is presumed to be sane, and…that to establish a defense on the ground of insanity, it must be clearly proved that, at the time of committing the act, the party accused was laboring under such a defect of reason, from disease of the mind, and not to know the nature and quality of the act he was doing; or if he did know it, that he did not know what he was doing was wrong.

—House of Lords, 1843

When thou goest out to battle against thine enemies…be not afraid of them…What man is there that is fearful and fainthearted? Let him go and return unto his house, lest his brethren's heart faint as well as his heart…

—Deuteronomy 20:1–9, King James Version

Since Vietnam, we have learned that even when we hate a war, we can still love our warriors.

—Justice Eileen C. Moore, Associate Justice of the Fourth District Court of Appeal. Formerly Lt. Eileen C. Moore, combat nurse Eighty-Fifth Evacuation Hospital, Qui Nhon, South Vietnam, 1966.

PROLOGUE

I cannot think of anything I have loved more than baseball.
I cannot think of anything I have hated more than baseball.

With unbridled confidence, I slowly swaggered to the batter's box in the final game of my last Little League season, the championship of Allen County Little League at stake. Slowly adjusting my helmet, I heard the snare drum in my heart beating under my uniform, heavy with creamy sweat, dirt, and grass. Consciously taking deep breaths from the bottom of my gut, I felt my muscles relax, and my heartbeat slowed to a steady rhythm.

My father reminded me, "Never go into the batter's box until your breathing is calm…control that breathing, *mijo. Then* you're ready…" My pulsating heartbeats didn't tell me I was scared, just excited. We were losing in the last inning, 2–1, and we had a runner—the slowest runner, Miguel—on third. I was the best hitter in the Allen Valley, and I knew the chances were good that I would tie or win the game. And if I failed, my teammates behind me would undoubtedly bring in the win. I blocked out the shouts from parents, players, and coaches, as if I were in my small, insular world, just the pitcher and me as he was nervously pacing the mound, glancing toward me, both jittery. We were the only two who could feel what the other was feeling at that moment. I could sense he was also trying to control his breaths. At that moment, I admired him. He had pitched six innings in unbearably hot weather—110 degrees with the kind of humidity seen only in Costa Rica—and he showed little fear as he glared at me from the mound. Proud. Unflinching. Angry.

On deck was Jimmy Torres, an imposing twelve-year-old lefty, almost six feet tall, swinging an enormous club—thirty ounces of maple hardwood. He looked primal, like a caveman holding a weapon. One of our best hitters, he smirked at me with his slanted green eyes, confident that he would win the game if I failed. He was probably thinking, "Shit, I want this guy; I own him. Just get me to that batter's box…" His green snake eyes glanced at the pitcher as if he were an assassin looking at his target, smelling blood on that dying animal languishing on the lonely mound.

I knew the pitcher had little left in him. If he were a car, he would have been running on fumes and a depleted battery, petering out any minute. But he was still determined to win this one with his last ounce of will. I had to admire his courage. Our symmetry of movement—him, pacing the lonely mound, looking at his catcher's sign, and me, pacing the batter's box like a caged animal—was sheer beauty that we both shared. Soon there would be a symphony of wood, soft leather, and a baseball playing the sweet melody of this game.

As I slowly approached the batter's box, walking behind the umpire to loosen up, my rigid concentration snapped because the umpire, a skinny, old drunk named Skeeter, was peering up at the sky, mesmerized. I squinted up at the pale-blue sky, which was slowly darkening with the approaching cool evening, to adjust my sight. I noticed other parents in the stands also glancing upward. Some rose, almost respectfully, focusing on an object in the lazy afternoon sky. I could see one parent with his hat across his chest and another saluting.

Slowly emerging from the dry clouds gliding above, I could see a glimmer of a fat gray airplane. I could barely read "US Army," with the American flag emblazoned on its side.

Removing his mask, the umpire drawled softly in his lazy southern accent to no one in particular, sounding reverential: "Look, boys, that's an army plane heading east. And ya know what they got in there? They've got dead American boys, coming back home to rest…from Vi-et-nam. Let's wait till it passes, OK?"

The game paused serenely until the fat mechanized bird disappeared into the dusty haze of the eastern horizon, slowly crossing over the bleached-dry, brown mountains. I removed my helmet and instinctively placed it across my heart. My heartbeat then slowed to a gentle pulse.

My baseball world disappeared into the shadows of my thoughts for that one fleeting moment, and I thought only about my brother Curt "over there"—in Vietnam.

Nineteen sixty-seven was the twelfth summer of my life.

PART ONE

THE BOSTON LAWYER AND
THE GREEN BERET

In the summer of 1967, I would see one of my two older brothers returning from Boston, where he worked as a lawyer, and the other from "over there" …in Vietnam. I didn't know much about what Enrique (Hank) did as a lawyer, but my mom told me it was very complicated, *muy duro*. Something about "corporation and litigation" and "mergers," whatever the hell that was. Even after looking up those words in my mom's old Spanish-English dictionary, I could not precisely understand what Hank did. He was our family's pride, the first to attend and graduate from college since our family's roots could be traced to Texas in the late 1800s. He graduated first in his school class of 1957—West Side High—then went to Harvard and Boston University Law School.

Hank moved away to Boston when I was three years old, and I hardly saw him after, except during brief visits, like during my grandpa's funeral or holidays. He never missed Thanksgiving and would always pat me on the head and say how much I had grown to make sure I studied hard in school.

My nana proudly recounted stories of Hank when he was a kid about my age. I enjoyed listening to Nana recite family stories on those long summer evenings when the rhythm of life comfortably slowed down a bit. She had time to recount our family history slowly, with warmth, humor, and deep affection, like her slow-cooked meals. I would listen and devour those precious stories, savoring them with a sweet aftertaste. According to my nana, the family knew Hank was different when he entered kinder. He seemed more curious than most young children his age and began reading comics before he entered school. Nana and my parents thought he was a childlike nuisance because he always asked questions: "Why does the sun move? Why are ants and spiders mean? How come those birds fly like a V? What makes the car move?" Habitually a loner and unemotional, he incessantly asked questions about the world around him as if he had entered an alien universe. My mom thought he was only looking at the colorful comic drawings but quickly realized he was reading the comics.

Superman and Flash Gordon were his favorites. By first grade, he began reading books my mom borrowed from the local library. The library was on the other side of town—the "West Side"—and she had to take a bus. But she brought books home for Hank, and they read together. My nana also joined their book reading, and Hank absorbed them like a starving child. Once he learned a new word or phrase, he would never forget it. My nana said, "His memory is like a photograph that he never forgets…a photographic memory…"

My dad would buy the local newspaper to read the sports page, dutifully following the Dodgers' box scores. Meanwhile, Hank began to read the paper daily by the time he was three years old, primarily the comic section. My mom and dad would sometimes circle articles he might find interesting and test him later to see if he understood. His insatiable thirst for reading never waned. He knew more Dodger trivia at an early age than even my father did. My father vividly remembered the following conversation with Hank in 1947, when Hank was seven:

"Son, how do you think the Dodgers will do this year?"

"Better, Pops. I think."

"They might get a negro player, some guy named Jackie Robinson."

"He should play third base, Pops."

"Why, mijo?"

"Well, because Cookie Lavagetto only hit .236 with three home runs and twenty-seven RBIs. They need help at third base. Robinson might even be better than Pee Wee at short."

My father only stared at Hank and said nothing for a while. Thinking Hank's statistical review might be an aberration, he tested him. "Son, Lavagetto did get on base a lot, didn't he?"

"Only thirty-eight times."

"Strikeouts?"

"Seventeen, Pops."

"Maybe this Robinson kid might steal more bases than Lavagetto did last year. Do you know who led the Dodgers last year in stolen bases?"

Hank was busy drawing with crayons, almost as if he wasn't listening. "Pete Reiser…thirty-eight."

My father shook his head and smiled quietly to himself. Hank continued drawing,

Shaking his head with a smile, my father replied, "Yeah, mijo, I guess that Robinson guy might play pretty good at third."

My dad bought him his first book and a used Webster's dictionary that Hank kept in his room and later took to college. Its brown binder was loose paper taped together by the previous owner, probably an old English teacher. He was probably a coffee drinker, judging from all the blotches and stains. My father began playing a game with Hank: my father would give him a nickel for every new word he learned. After a few years, the game took a financial toll on my father's pocketbook and was changed from nickels to candies.

Hank entered West Side High School in 1953. Nana recounted the time our family received a visit from the principal of West Side High, Mr.

Roberts—a tall, thin man in his early fifties who spoke somberly with a laconic southern drawl and was to the point. He met them prior to Hank's entry at West Side.

Mr. Roberts: "Mr. and Mrs. Mendoza, I want your son to transfer to West Side High this fall. I have seen his test scores and spoken to his teachers, and he would rank as the top student as compared to those kids entering West Side High."

My mom: "Mr. Roberts, we know Enrique's a smart boy, and he sure loves to read. But all his friends from the neighborhood are going to Rockwood High, and I—we—don't think he would be happy at your school. No offense, sir. And he has no friends there."

My father: "We know our high school is old and run down. The buildings were built in 1920, and they never get fixed. The plumbing is broken, there are no working drinking faucets, and the classrooms seem crowded. We know West Side High is a prettier and newer school…nice green grass, all new. Hell, it looks like part of a country club and golf course. I cleaned the toilets one time as a part-time job…the cleanest bathrooms I have ever seen. But we know he will have a good education here on the eastside, and he'll be happy around his friends. We help him with his schoolwork, and he knows it's important. We just want him to be happy."

Mr. Roberts: "He will make lots of friends in no time. Are you worried because there are few Mexican kids at West Side High?"

Mom, choosing her words carefully: "Well, we never thought of that. We teach our kids to make friends with everyone, no matter where they come from. And besides, we have kids in the neighborhood from all backgrounds, and Enrique—Hank—knows them all. Anglos, Filipinos, Asians, and Black. But now that you mention it, would he be treated well by the other kids?"

Mr. Roberts: "To be honest, Enrique—Hank—doesn't look, act, or talk Mexican. He will blend in very well. He is a gifted student who can excel in our school. Our teachers are looking forward to having him in our school. You have brought him up well; we know he is a good, well-mannered kid, and we would really love to have him with us."

Dad: "Maybe we can try it for a while, but if there are any problems with him, we will bring him right back. We know he will do well in any school, but we also want him to be happy with the other kids."

Mom: "He is also very shy. Some of our relatives think he is strange because he never smiles or laughs much. He likes to keep to himself. Even though he has friends his age, I think he prefers to be around adults and have adult conversations. I hope you understand."

Mr. Roberts: "Yes, I do. Thank you for your time and hospitality. Those empanadas were delicious, Mrs. Mendoza. You know, my maid, Teresa, makes those during Christmas, but yours are much better."

"We will talk about this with him. We just want what's best for him."

Thus, Hank transferred to West Side High in his second year of high school.

Hank was thin, about 140 pounds, and of average height. Although strong and physically quick, he did not look like much of an athlete, although my father said he could hit the baseball and tennis ball as hard as anyone. His ironic nickname was Gordo—Fatso—even though he was wafer thin. The irony was never lost on him, and he seemed to relish the name, although the mean kids from both schools whispered other epithets behind his back. Whether he ever heard them no one ever knew for sure. According to my mother, when he was six months old, he ballooned into a fat child "like a happy tick full of blood for a few months." Then he quickly returned to his normal weight and has been thin like a green bean ever since.

Everyone in this town was blessed with an ironic nickname. And the nicknames stayed with most kids well into adulthood. Nicknames were conceived, gestated, born in childhood, and aged to adulthood: *Guero* for the darkest kid, Tiny for the largest kid, and so on. Thus far, I had avoided any label, but it was a matter of time. However, I did hear whispers of *Nalgon* uttered behind my back. The provenance of most nicknames is rarely traceable, but once you had one, it stuck with you far into adulthood.

Always quiet and sometimes distant, Hank had an emotional barrier that most could not penetrate. He spoke softly and carefully, and many of his words I did not understand. He would think about every single word and syllable before he even uttered anything out loud. Not pretentious or vain, he impressed others with his impeccable manners and intelligent speech. He liked things most of his peers didn't. As a kid, he preferred reading over sports, chess over checkers, but he excelled at marble competitions, which required hours of practice in isolation. As an adult, he favored live theater to movies, dress pants to jeans, and Chopin to the Rolling Stones.

He was often mistaken for an Anglo growing up. The brutal summer sun turned his face bright red, whereas most of us in this valley had skin that turned brown, like leather discarded in the desert. His eyes were light, an intense pale gray like a coyote, and his hair was light brown and thin with a hairline that showed hints of receding into his broad forehead. He got his looks from my mother's side; her great-grandfather from Jalisco had French blood. He jettisoned his valley accent as the years went by, whether by design or natural progression. Eventually, he spoke like an outsider—like someone from Boston.

Five years younger than Hank, my other brother was named Curtis, or Curt. My father forsook other conventional Spanish names and named him after a marine buddy. They both survived physically, and my father spoke about Curtis Wellens throughout the years.

Curt was a star athlete in three sports, but football was his best. Even though he was only 5'8," he weighed about 160 pounds and was, according to his coach, "a wild animal on the football field." He had powerful and intimidating forearms, much like my father's, an ex-marine, with arm muscles that were well defined. His thick neck made him seem larger, but he had soft facial features with an easy smile. I noticed that girls would often give him that second look when he was around, and he made them feel comfortable. His football moniker was Wild Boar because of the way he ran untamed around the football field, looking for his prey—anyone from the other team with the football. On defense, he was in the thick of the action, nose guard, and would block for the running backs on offense. Although he didn't spend as much time preparing for classes, my father often said he was "street smart, not book smart," with a keen instinct for judging people quickly, assessing situations intelligently, and finding answers pragmatically.

For as long as I can remember, Curt was my hero, and he let me tag along with him. He taught me how to fish, how to throw a football, and how to throw a curveball, and sometimes, with a wink of his eye, he would tell me secrets about girls and what they liked.

Throughout high school, he was dedicated to only one girl—Sally—who grew up a few blocks away. He told me he knew in first grade he would marry her. But he waited until the fifth grade to even speak to her. I also had my first crush on her, and who wouldn't? She was tall with beautiful olive skin, pale-green eyes, and shiny black hair, and she was always happy. Sally's mother was from Jalisco, Mexico, and her father was from Arkansas. He had come to the valley to work for the US Border Patrol. She and Curt "made plans" after graduation for a future together and enrolled at the local junior college.

"As long as we have one another, we can do anything," she often reminded Curt. "I don't know what I would do without you," he confided to her in their quiet moments. Beneath his tough and confident exterior was a young boy who feared his future without Sally. She was his driving force in their future, and their road ahead was paved with hope and joy. Both couldn't wait to get to the destination, hoping to settle in Allen County for the rest of their lives and grow old and fat together in the cool shadows of the Western Mountains.

The provincial and conventional attitudes of the mid-1960s strangled Sally. These rigid attitudes dictated an intelligent young lady's only career options: nurse, secretary, or happy housewife. She, no doubt, had the drive and intelligence to do anything she wanted. She chose nursing and wanted to dedicate her life to a stable career and her true love, Curt. I think Curt felt as though he was in Hank's shadow and wanted to focus on school, with aspirations of becoming a teacher. With Sally in his future, he maintained good grades at the local junior college, interestingly, better than the grades he had in high school.

My childhood memories often take me to those times from not so long ago, and it still hurts.

PART TWO

"MAN, NAM IS BEAUTIFUL FROM UP HERE"

Two years earlier…

May 20, 1965

Tactical area of operations: five kilometers north of Long Xuyen, near the Mekong Delta, South Vietnam

1530 hours

"Damn, it's beautiful from up here."

Matt Bradley was exhausted. After three days of recon "humping the boonies," he was glad to be in a chopper returning to base camp twenty kilometers due south. Maybe he could finally get some sleep and warm food. His best buddy, Willie Harris, was snoring loudly next to him near the door. Looking at him, Matt just smiled to himself. Willie was going home to San Francisco in twenty-one days and could now sleep like a baby. How could someone sleep so soundly in the middle of this shit? After two tours in country, Willie's restless nights were over. Matt would miss him.

Willie was his bunkmate in boot camp and was one of the gentlest men he had ever met, even though he was 6'3" and weighed 230—all muscle.

He was the only Black person he ever actually knew. There were not too many in Allen County, except those he had seen as a kid, picking cotton back at home, and a few on the football field in high school, but only across the scrimmage line. Some in high school were Matt's distant friends, but they usually hung out only among themselves. Willie was a good friend, and he and Matt knew each other well out in the bush. At some point in their friendship evolution—from boot camp to Vietnam—Willie's skin color evaporated. Matt thought of him only as funny, gentle, intelligent, respectful, a solid marine, and one of his best friends.

"Hey, Matt, when I get back, the first thing I want to do is to have a few cold ones at Candlestick. Ya know, my dad named me after Willie Mays, and he promised to take me to see him at the stick. After I get fat and stay drunk for a few months, then I'll be a real job. Maybe a cop or maybe even college. I like history, all that stuff from the Civil War." They were headed back to base camp, and Matt thought the jungle was peaceful for a change—quiet except for the usual sounds of the wilderness under the lazy hum of the chopper.

"Bullshit. When you get back to the world, you're gonna get drunk like you never have before and go find some female companionship. I know you, Frisco, and you'll have *buku* babes after your big Black ass."

"Shit, maybe I'll do both," he said with a wide-toothed grin.

"Hey, Jeff, watdaya think about our main man here, Frisco, going back to the world?"

Jeff was on their recon team. He was a quiet guy with thick-rimmed glasses and large buck teeth who had soft cheeks that still had no hair. He wasn't too big, just about 5'6" with sandy-blond hair, and he was from Minnesota. But he was calm and focused in the field, a solid marine.

Jeff leaned against the door of the helicopter clutching the M60. He smiled lazily and said, "Frisco's one lucky son of a bitch. You're the only short-timer in this fuckin' chopper. Don't jinx us, man. You *dinky dau* motherfucker. I've got six months and ten days in the country. I'm here for the long haul. Willie, you take good care of yourself, bro. When you're back in the world, drinking and whoring every day, think of us once in a while, man."

All three smiled, quietly lost in their thoughts.

Matt peered out the helicopter's open door down into the rich vegetation of the jungle carpet. He always asked himself how such a beautiful country could be in the middle of a shitty war. Some places looked like the proverbial Shangri-La, and its unparalleled beauty often mesmerized you even in the middle of a combat zone. He had never seen such lush colors in the hills and mountains, sunsets, waterfalls, and wild animals, which were in sharp contrast to the arid desert of his home in Southern California. The helicopter floated heavily, like a giant mechanical hummingbird, low over the jungle canopy, at what the pilots called "cruising speed." Matt usually felt uncomfortable in that iron death trap; it was just a slow floating target for the VC, but that day it was his protective shield after three days in the boonies. He was so glad to see a helicopter and was always amazed at the astonishing bravery these pilots exhibited in hot combat zones. The cool air from the open doors refreshed him like a shower. His body crevices were caked with jungle soil, sweat, feces, piss, and dried blood. He began to doze off, and images of home seeped into his thoughts—his mother, his girlfriend, the smell of desert soil, his green VW in the garage, the smell of Mom's cooking, especially the cobblers.

"MAYDAY…MAYDAY. We're hit!" The pilot's frantic message slapped Matt out of his daydream as the helicopter began to spin helplessly out of control. In helicopter parlance, they "were circling the drain." Panic… shouts…a lifeless soldier blasted out the door fell to the jungle one thousand feet below… "Jeff!" "Mayday…" Smoke…grease spilling inside…pain on the face…marines trying to maintain their balance…the copilot's head vaporized in a pink mist, only a bloody pulp above the shoulders. "Oh God!" … "Shit, man, shit…get the control…" Matt felt tossed around like a scared puppet without its strings, tetherless and helpless. The pounding sounds of the metallic beast slamming onto the jungle floor. He thought he heard Willie's low voice. Small arms fire crackling in the distance. Frantic yelling, panic, pleas, crying… "Fucking dinks…" Bleeding marines like confused children crawling back into the protective womb of the motherly Huey, now lurching on its side, engulfed in flames.

An explosion of darkness…a vague floating sensation…brief snapshots of Mom…a whisper from Dad…a glimpse of Willie smiling at him… pain…voices…then darkness met him again…fleeting recollections of childhood…summer swims…football…making out with his girlfriend.

Subdued light. Muffled voices. Moments of endless darkness. Pain throbbing throughout his body and spreading deep into his nerves, muscles, and bones. Then darkness and silence.

"I think he's doing better, Doctor. We were able to save this one," whispered a female with a soft, thin voice, perhaps an accent from New Jersey.

Matt opened his heavy eyes and looked up from the bed. His body painfully pulsed all over, and he felt something on his legs and hips that was hard. His head and face pounded as if he had a massive hangover. He had cracked lips and was craving water.

"Hi, soldier, you look good!"

He looked into the soft pale-blue eyes of the nurse at this bedside. She was about twenty-two years old, with strawberry-blond hair and a wide, inviting smile, and she gave him a motherly welcome.

My God, he thought, she is beautiful. "How long…how long have I been? And where am I?" It was a struggle for Matt even to speak since he was weighed down with pain, fatigue, and morphine. The left side of his face felt like fire. He saw the IVs, which looked like long worms sucking his arms, and slowly realized that morphine was flowing throughout him. His senses slowly sparked to life. The sterile whiteness around him told him he was in a hospital. Maybe hell was colored in white. Whatever crap he had been through, he was alive.

"Well, it's June second, and you're in a hospital in Saigon. After a few days, you might be shipped to Hawaii. You will be just fine, and I am pretty sure you're going home soon."

"What the hell happened? Do you know?" he asked.

She nodded her head demurely, offering nothing. "I can give you information regarding your injuries, and they were quite substantial. You sustained a concussion, a broken pelvis, two broken legs, and a partially fractured neck. But you have no permanent injuries there, and you will walk just fine. Oh, and…you suffered some first-degree burns to the left side of your face, probably from the hydraulic fluid. The medical team conducted grafts after two surgeries."

"Grafts? Can I get a mirror?"

She handed him a small white mirror, and he slowly raised his head from the bed and saw his face.

For a moment, he thought he was looking at another person; his father's vague features came into focus. There was another person on the other side of the mirror. "Pops?" Slowly his consciousness regained its focus, and he began to recognize himself in the mirror. He had a full beard with new white hairs, sunken dead, bloodshot eyes, high cheekbones that suggested extensive weight loss, and gauze covering the left side of his face. He let the mirror image sink in so he could accept that it was indeed him at the other end. The mirror felt heavy, and he quietly returned it to the nurse, trying to force himself to remember his recent past.

Hours later, his sergeant stopped to visit. "Hey, Sarge, how ya doing?" Matt asked meekly.

"All right, kid. You're going home, back to Allen County, back to the fucking world, man. You lucky son of a bitch…how do you feel?" Matt always liked that guy, who had been no-nonsense and was a mentor when he arrived six months ago. Matt paid attention to the vets, which enhanced his survival in that shit hole.

"Do you know what the fuck happened out there?" The morphine was working as the pain slightly abated. His veins felt warm, and his senses focused on his immediate surroundings: a sterile white hospital room with stale, cold air that settled like desert fog. Matt felt stronger. His memory returned to fleeting snapshots of the crash, the awful screams of the doomed soldiers. Deadly wails of pain and anguish would be forever embedded in his memory. He heard Willie's voice: "Hold on, little guy; we'll get us out of this fucking mess. I'm all messed up, man, but we're going home. I'll see you on the other side of the world…" And the image of Willie's sweating Black face faded into a gray shadow.

"The VC hit you guys with an RPG. Shit, they're using more sophisticated stuff now to shoot at the choppers."

"How's Willie? That big Black bastard always said he would beat me back to the States." Matt was eager to see him and share their latest war story.

"Oh…uh…you haven't been briefed. Sorry, Matt. You were the only survivor, and all the other guys on the Huey didn't make it. Except for you and Willie, most died on or before impact."

"Jeff?"

"He got hit in the chopper. Probably didn't feel a thing. He's going back home."

"And Willie?"

"He survived the fall as the VC zeroed in on your position. You were receiving small arms fire from a nearby tree line about three hundred meters away from the point of impact. With his left leg shattered below his knee, your buddy managed to get at that hog, the M60, pulled it from the copter, and blasted suppression fire at those gooks in the tree line. Then he pulled you into the bushes. The dust-off guys in the rescue choppers could see all this unfolding; it was quite a sight. The big boys then flew in and wasted them with napalm. Man, that big colored guy deserves a medal."

"His name was Willie," Matt said, correcting his sergeant.

"Yeah. Willie…he must've greased a few gooks as the second evacuation team came in for the dust off to get you guys out of that hot LZ. That M60 went to work on those fucking gooks, man. Victor Charlie got to meet Big

Willie that day. Motherfuckers. He probably even saved our asses."

"By the time we landed to pick you up, the LZ wasn't too hot…shit. The big colored guy cooled it off."

"His name was Willie."

"Yeah, OK, Willie. You got picked up about twenty minutes after impact, but Willie didn't make it. He got it in the head and was probably KIA before hitting the ground next to you. He was losing a lot of blood anyway and wouldn't have survived. Even if he had, he probably would have been a fuckin' vegetable anyway. We picked up his body next to you. He took about six rounds. We also thought you were dead with that big gash on the side of your face. Shit, you looked worse than him. No offense. Sorry, man, I knew you guys were close. They did get all the other guys out of the field. Marines never leave our brothers behind. Semper Fi, mothafucka! HU RA!"

"Yea…OK. Semper Fi…"

Matt slowly regained his senses. Heavy tears poured from his body, and he shrank into a fetal position like a newborn, sleeping for fifteen hours. Mild pangs of guilt began to throb deep down in the hollow caverns of his gut, but the morphine trickling through his veins soothed that feeling.

■ ■ ■

Matt continued to slowly improve. Strength and lucidity greeted him in the following mornings. The food tasted better, and the sun splashing through the windows restored him. The increase in his strength was proportional to the decrease in his pain. He would soon be home, and he could live with this facial scar—a battle scar—but it was no consolation for losing his best friend and those fellow marines in the crash. They were his brothers who would never be forgotten.

He tried to recall those conversations with Frisco Willie, especially on that last day before they boarded the helicopter. "Hey, Matt, you think those muthafucking gooks hate me more 'cause I'm Black?"

"No, asshole, they hate you 'cause you're one ugly bastard, and they like you 'cause you make a big fucking target. Those big fuckin' white teeth of yours are like a lighthouse. Hey, man, do me a favor. Don't get next to me and smile during a firefight, all right?"

Willie just laughed and shook his head.

Willie made Matt feel safe and protected. Nothing could touch Willie, and he would return to the world looking for something we all wanted: a sense of normalcy, to feel like we did before we were there. Matt hoped to get rid of the smells, the sights, the nightmares, the food, and the people and completely erase those memories from his mind, as if he could simply switch off a TV channel.

"When I get back, I just wanna walk…just walk around the neighborhood and soak things in…ya know? No place to go, just walk. Feel normal."

"Yea, Willie, I know, man. I know."

In the early morning, after breakfast, an orderly in the hospital handed him mail from home. The first he anxiously opened was from his girlfriend, Belinda, who would be waiting for him. He recognized her delicate handwriting on the envelope because she always dotted the *i* in her name with a heart. They met his sophomore year in high school, and he thought she might be "the one," even though nothing formal was promised from her except that she would "wait" for him. They had dated for a year before he enlisted, and even though they never consummated their love, he knew they would both be patient. He couldn't wait to squeeze her in his arms when he returned to Allen County and returned to a normal life. Damn, Belinda was so beautiful, so simple, so loving.

April 2, 1965

Hi, Matt:

I hope you are doing well. I'm sorry I have not been writing to you as often as I promised, but things have been busy. I got a part-time job at the theater. Right now, I'm only selling entry tickets, but I think I might have a chance as the assistant manager pretty soon. Better pay and hours, I hope. I get free popcorn and flicks candy, and I can see all the movies in my free time. They showed *A Hard Day's Night,* and the theater was packed, like it was a live concert. All the girls in the county were here just screaming their heads off. I could not hear a thing, but John, Ringo, Paul, and George were all funny in the movie. My favorite is Paul, but my sister likes Ringo the most.

Well, you know things never change here in Allen County, but we do have a new department store, Sears, in the north end of Rockwood. It's a pretty neat store, and they have almost everything. My parents bought one of those new TVs without those rabbit ears. And they all have color now.

My parents say hi. I have been worried about you. I don't read the paper too much, but I know things over there in the war must be difficult. My cousin Peter returned last month from Vietnam, and he has not been doing too well. I don't understand too much about why he's like that. My dad just shrugs his shoulders and says, "It's the war." My daddy also told me to avoid him, and I think I will. He's not like he was before. It's hard to explain. Please take good care of yourself. I don't want you coming home like that, and I know you'll come back the same: sweet, smart Matt.

Matt, things for me have changed in the past year. I have matured and taken more responsibility for my future. I have been thinking a lot more about what I want to do. You and I hardly got to know each other before you left overseas. You promised to write to me, and you hardly did. A few letters came from you, but you hardly ever said anything in those letters. You sounded so stiff, as if you didn't really want to write. You didn't sound very affectionate toward me, and I thought we had something special going before you left. I thought you lost feelings for me, and I assumed it was because you were so far away. So I was confused and sad.

I met a guy, Brandon McDonough. He's a bitching guy. He was about a year ahead of us in high school, and he's planning to become a teacher. You might remember him because I think you guys played Little League together. He told me he got lucky and was not drafted because he's in college, and he mentions you with great respect. It happened so quickly, but I really like him, and I think you will understand because you're such a nice guy. If anyone is to blame, it is me.

I think Brand and I are getting serious in our relationship. When you meet him, you will like him.

I will probably see you when you return, and I still do not want to lose your friendship because it is so important to me. Take good care of yourself, Matt, over there, and it's OK if you don't want to ever speak to me. I hope you do.

Always, peace and love,

Belinda [dotted with a heart]

Matt read the letter three times, searching for any nuanced words or phrases that might suggest she wasn't dumping him like the morning trash. He shredded it, turned to his side, and fell asleep. All he had left was the pain. The face was throbbing. But the morphine felt good.

The last time he and Belinda were together was at the bus station before he left overseas. He remembered the look on her face: pain, angst, and profound sorrow. Neither one said it, but both knew things would never be the same when he returned, and they both grasped onto this naive fantasy that they might be together and live forever as a couple...in a nice home with children and happiness forever.

"Nurse, more morphine. I wanna sleep."

■ ■ ■

From the *Sonora Desert Review*, November 13, 1965:
The War Department announced that twenty US soldiers were killed last week in heavy fighting along the Mekong Delta in Vietnam. This marks an escalation in the Viet Cong's efforts to control this region. The enemy sustained 380 casualties, primarily from heavy bombers assisting the troops in the Lei Ming Valley. President Johnson continued his upbeat assessment that the war would soon end in victory and that progress was being made on the ground and in the air. General Westmorland echoed those sentiments and expressed confidence in a decisive victory in the near future now that we have more troops on the ground.

■ ■ ■

Matt Bradley arrived at Clarktown, the county seat of Allen County, on December 24, 1965, by Greyhound bus close to midnight. Not too many folks were around the station that Christmas Eve. He did not tell his parents his arrival date so he could surprise them on Christmas, and they did not expect him for another week. His parents had already been briefed on his injury and the scar on his face, which would possibly require several more surgeries.

He was their only child, and both parents had quietly advised him against signing up to go to Vietnam. While both were highly patriotic in an old-fashioned way, they harbored mixed feelings and had unanswered questions about Vietnam. Matt's parents were apolitical, and they saw no interest in national or even local politics. They were not like the antiwar protesters they saw on TV. Matt's parents hardly mentioned Vietnam to their friends and relatives. They simply could not see the reasons for sending young men like their son across the world for a distant war that lacked the clarity and urgency of World War II. What they did not realize was that the sentiment lingering beneath their thoughts was common throughout the country but was only overtly expressed by the antiwar protesters exploding on the college campuses. Now their son was wounded, and he would recover with their help. They couldn't wait to smother him with constant love and support. For Matt, operations and doctors could wait. All he wanted was his warm bed, good homemade food, and quiet.

After he departed from Saigon, he was transferred to Hawaii for more skin grafts. The left side of his face had improved. He wanted to vomit when he first glanced at his injury in the mirror. From the left side of his jaw up to his ear, there was a mass of purple jelly, pus, and shreds of skin. The doctors worked on him in Hawaii, telling him the scars would improve but would not disappear. He never felt sorry for himself, since he always thought of the brave soldiers in the helicopter who didn't return to their homes, to their families, to their girlfriends.

And Willie. Hopefully he could see and meet his family as a matter of respect. Matt knew he owed him something for his loyalty—and his life. There was no object on earth that could fully repay Willie, and Matt simply accepted that fact. The scar would be a lifelong reminder of that horrible day when the chopper went down with all those soldiers. Why did he survive? An act of God? Matt placed little value on the idea of divine intervention after Vietnam. God could not—should not—have allowed the kind of human grief he witnessed.

He was probably one of the lucky ones, with only a bloody scar on his face. Matt's sensibilities left no room for self-pity, and he would just see the ugly purple blob as a badge of honor. Some of the vets got tattoos as a matter of pride. His repulsive facial scar was his tattoo, but not for pride—partly for the shame of surviving.

He recalled the odd encounter he had had several hours earlier on his bus trip. As he entered the Los Angeles station, a teenage couple sat across the aisle from him. They looked thin and hungry—probably runaways. The girl gawked at his facial scar and looked away, embarrassed, when their eyes met.

The boy was about seventeen and the girl no older. He had unwashed blond hair, shoulder-length, and his face had shadowy bags drooping under his bloodshot eyes, which were empty and sad. He let out a hiss when he spoke through a wide gap where two upper front teeth should have been. Matt could see lines of blood around the gums. This kid had recently gotten his ass kicked; somebody knocked out his teeth. He wore a Micky Mouse T-shirt with pale yellow stains around Mickey's eyes, making Mickey look as hungover and sad as the couple did. Micky didn't look like he was from the happiest place on earth.

The girl had a face without any striking features, except there was sadness and despair in her pale-blue eyes, which were framed by dark shadows underneath. Although Matt knew she was a teenager, she looked much older, with thin hair, specks of dandruff, and old arms. Her skin sagged like leathery Jell-O and reminded Matt of his grandmother's arms...dry, leathery, and bony. She had dried mucus under her right nostril and couldn't have weighed more than eighty pounds. A filthy T-shirt adorned with a large peace sign draped over faded bell-bottoms. She said nothing and appeared uninterested in the discussion. Probably still stoned.

"Where ya going?" the boy asked with a deep southern drawl, scratching a bloated pimple on his right cheek with his bony finger. Blood and pus oozed out, dribbling slowly downward. His eyes were sunken with dark shadows underneath the lids. Matt thought, Christ, these kids are in worse shape than I am. They need to go home, back to their parents, wherever the hell they live. The vile stench of West Hollywood came with them: urine, cigarettes, stale beer...hopelessness.

"Home."

"How long ya been away? We've been in West Hollywood, but it got too messed up, man. We just wanna go home too, like you. We just lived on the streets. Too much shit out there, man, too much heavy shit we can't handle. Some fucker wanting drugs or pussy from my girlfriend beat me up, but we got away. So how long you been gone again? Too much shit, man…too much shit. So how long you been over there, soldier-man?" He squeezed the pimple harder so that blood began to harden on his cheek. His skinny companion moved to scratch her neck, and she began dozing off, curling up on the seat like a lazy cat.

"A long time."

"Were you in Nam? I noticed your bag."

"Yep."

"What's it like over there?"

"Hot."

"How's the pot over there? I hear they have some really good shit, man."

"I wouldn't know, man."

"Groovy. Did ya see any action?"

"Nope."

"Kill a lot of gooks?"

"Nope."

"Kill any babies? Rape any VC bitches?"

"Go fuck yourself, man." Matt squeezed the armchair with both hands, bit his lip hard, and inhaled. Matt turned and fell into a long slumber.

When he arrived in Clarktown a few hours later, the kids—and their stench—were gone, and Matt wasn't sure if the odd encounter had been a bad dream. He laid his bag over his shoulder and decided to walk home, about ten blocks away from the station. Peach cobbler awaited.

Matt heard the church bells at midnight announcing Christmas morning. Midnight Mass was just beginning.

The bells were loud…and they frightened him.

PART THREE

THE FUTURE IS STOLEN

In the winter of their first year in college, Christmas 1965, Curt and Sally announced their engagement at our family's house. We must have had over one hundred neighbors, cousins, and uncles packed into our tiny house. Sally and Curt announced that they would not set a date for the wedding, only that it would be sometime after they earned their degrees. Curt wanted to teach, and Sally was planning on a nursing career. One of our uncles from Texas—the "old country," as my nana would say—even came. I secretly sipped my first beer.

Curt pawned everything he owned for the engagement ring, and my parents also pitched in some of their savings. The summer, he had worked washing cars, picking tomatoes, cutting lawns, and cleaning out the modest savings he had squirreled away in his drawer. He spent $200 on it and put it on layaway at Abby's Jewelry Store on Fifth Street. Curt thought it still wasn't enough. He wanted to wait until after the party to give it to her, when they would have a chance to be alone in the coming days. He wanted to avoid a public spectacle, so he had the ring in his pocket all night during the engagement party. All night long, Curt and Sally were beaming. Although Hank could not come from law school, he called Curt and Sally during the party to wish them the best of luck.

"Hey, Enrique, how's that cold in Boston treating you?"

"Hey, brother, I'm proud of you. I will see you later this year, and we will party like we never have. What can I get you guys for your wedding? I know you will say you have everything next to you."

"Just bring plenty of yellow roses—her favorite. We're going to plaster the wedding with wall-to-wall yellow roses. You know what's weird? Yellow roses are also Nana's favorite. She always talks about her yellow roses from Texas. That's why she has a bunch of them in our backyard—'cause she says it reminds her of Texas. Yellow roses at the wedding will make both Sally and Nana happy." Curt giggled and passed the phone to Sally.

"Hey, Hank, how ya doing?"

"Sally, you don't know how happy I am. You guys were born for each other, and I will see you guys in a few months." He sounded lonely and misty.

"Hey, Hank, before I forget, can you be our best man? Can you?"

"You really have to ask?" Hank said proudly. "Listen, I'm glad you're on the line. Please listen carefully." Sally tensed a little since the tone of Hank's voice quickly changed, as if he were speaking in court or with a client about an important legal dilemma. "As you know, President Johnson is elevating the troop levels with the draft. LBJ—thank God I voted for Goldwater—wants half a million troops." Sally thought this political conversation and legal treatise could wait, but Hank continued on the phone. "Curt will be the first they draft. This war is not going to end soon. Our law firm has handled a couple of these draftees pro bono, and the political and military situation will only get worse. Now listen, I'm not some radical, and I'm as red-blooded American as anybody, but Curt has several ways to seek legitimate waivers to circumvent the draft. Please tell him to stay in college full-time if possible because he can qualify for a draft deferment. No matter what LBJ says, we might be in Vietnam for a long time. But please make sure you keep him in school until this thing abates, OK?"

"Hank, I appreciate that legal advice. You won't send us a legal bill, will you? Haha. Did you hear the one about the client who asked her lawyer what he charged? The lawyer says one hundred dollars for three questions. She asks him, 'Isn't that a lot?' And the lawyer responds, 'Yes, it is. Now, what's your third question?' Haha…"

"Yes, that's a good one, but in reference to your question, no. I fully realize this is an awkward moment to engage in this discussion, but it cannot be deferred…no pun intended." His voice returned from the lawyerly voice to the normal voice Sally knew. "Give my two brothers a hug for me, and I will see you all soon."

Later in the evening, Curt whispered to me, "Hey, buddy, when I leave, you and I won't have to share our bedroom, and you can have all my baseball cards." It was the best night of my life. Curt's collection included signed baseball cards of all the Dodger infield: Wes Parker, Jim Lefebvre (rookie of the year), Maury Wills, and Jim Gilliam. And the two prizes were cards signed by Don Drysdale (the "Big D") and Sanford "Sandy" Koufax—the greatest baseball player who ever lived. I could not wait until they were married because the collection would be all mine.

Our family partied until 4:00 a.m., until Sally's parents and she were the last guests to leave. Curt escorted them to their car, and they all took a deep breath of the cool desert air that never smelled sweeter. The polished diamonds above the western horizon glittered like flickering lights, as if the heavens joined the happy event.

He quietly took out the ring and placed it on her finger as she was leaving. Both had never been as happy in their lives as they were at that moment. For the first time, they envisioned their lives in front of them, a future to share with someone, to live out their lives together, to grow old and fat together, to share their pain together. Together.

■ ■ ■

There are specific incidents that frame your life in terms of the past and future, a plaintive moment that defines, clarifies, and separates the chapters in your existence on this earth. It's like a snapshot of a bad photo that remains locked up deep inside you forever, one that you cannot ever suppress when you're awake or, worse, when you're dreaming. The morning after Curt's engagement party was that moment for my family and me. I often look at stages of my life as simultaneously ending and starting that early morning because nothing, as I remember it, was the same after that phone call.

I heard it about 6:00 a.m. as I was about to finally fall into a deep sleep. It sounded shrill, mean, and sharp like an impatient banshee waiting for an answer. Curt answered the call in our kitchen, listened for a few minutes, said nothing, dropped the phone line, and sprinted full speed out of the house without saying a word. I never saw him run that way outside the football field.

My father later told me he spoke with the paramedics at the accident scene. Sally's father, a nondrinker, was taking his family, after the engagement party, for breakfast when a drunk driver T-boned their car at the far northern edge of town. Sally's mom received the full brunt of the impact and was dead in a millisecond. Later, at a court hearing before the trial, some guy said the defendant's speed at the point of impact was eighty-five miles an hour. When Curt arrived at the scene, the mangled bodies of Sally's parents had already been removed. Sally was tragically pinned in the back seat of their Ford sedan, her body intertwined with metal, glass, and leather. The paramedics could not pry her loose and were using some new kind of large metal instrument to extract her, ironically labeled the "jaws of life."

She was whispering to herself with stiff lips, and her fading eyes were blinking indifferently as the paramedics continued to work frantically to free her. She was drowning without air and gasping for life itself. When Curt arrived, he used all his strength to pry the metal apart, and he delicately removed her. He cleaned her bloody face and gently kissed her before placing her in the ambulance waiting nearby. The city hospital was only ten blocks away. Her face on the outside remained beautiful; her insides, however, were mangled and twisted beyond repair.

After regaining consciousness at the hospital for a few precious seconds, she faintly smiled at Curt, who had been at her bedside. Her left arm was shredded in the accident, but her fingers were still intact; Curt gently kissed their engagement ring and whispered goodbye. She was pronounced dead shortly before nine that morning.

■ ■ ■

She left me quickly
To another place,
Somewhere past those gleaming stars,
Somewhere past my outstretched arms,
Somewhere past the heavens,
And all my grieving nights she calls to me,
In the blackness of the desert sky,
There among the stars, waiting among the clouds,
For her,
The soft desert winds are her whispers to me,
in the solitude of early winter mornings,
The softness of her lips I caress,
The sweetness of her breath I embrace,
Where I reach to hold her tight,
Where soon I will join her again,
Somewhere among the clouds,
We will be one day be one forever,
Somewhere past the heavens,
Beyond the doleful memories of our stolen future.

■ ■ ■

From the *Sonora Desert Review*, December 31, 1965:
Jim, Maria, and Sally Lewis were laid to rest on December 30, 1965, at the Courtney Cemetery. Jim is survived by two sisters, Olivia Benton and Sally Smith, from Little Rock, Arkansas. Maria is survived by her mother, Imelda Gonzalez, from Guadalajara, Mexico. Sally is survived by her fiancée, Curt Mendoza, from Clarktown, California. The flag at Rockwood High School will be set at half-mast, and a nursing scholarship will be funded in her honor.

Matt Bradley left the Courtney Cemetery after offering his respects to the Lewis and Mendoza families. He only knew Jim Lewis, his boss at the US Border Patrol. Mr. Lewis hired him six months after Matt returned from Vietnam, and if Jim Lewis hadn't seen his potential, Matt probably would not have a job. His facial scar would never disappear, and he still heavily sensed the stares, whispers, and giggles. He was turned down for many jobs for a myriad of specious reasons, none of which were the ghastly scar. Mr. Lewis looked past the scar and hired him on the spot, recognizing his potential, discipline, and loyalty.

He kept to himself for the most part and hardly ventured outside his home. The scar turned from an ugly purple blob leeched to his face to a pale red. Jim Lewis felt Matt's military skills would be well applied to the Border Patrol. He could handle weapons, he could track, and he was calm under the pressures of battle. There was a marked increase in illegal activity coming across from Mexico into Allen County: drugs and human trafficking.

Matt was attracted to the job since he could spend much of his time in relative isolation, out of range of the derisive looks and questions. Work was a daily grind of patrolling the remote corners of the county, but it was exhilarating and challenging. This might be the career he had always sought, and he was profoundly indebted to Jim Lewis. And now he would pay him his final respects.

"Hey, Matt! How ya doing, man? I heard you were back." As he left the funeral, Matt heard a familiar voice and saw his old high school friend, Lucy Miller. He grabbed her in a bear hug and embraced her. "We got so worried 'cause we heard you got hurt over there, but you look good. No one knew you were back." She took a pained look at his burned face and bit her lips.

"I'm doing good, Luce. I got a job with Mr. Lewis at US Border Patrol, and I just started. I'm good, thanks. What's new with you? Haven't seen you since graduation." Matt could not understand why he felt deeply self-conscious around someone he had known all his life. Civilians were harder to relate to since he had returned to this world.

"I'm doing good, and I'll be transferring to state college next year. We all missed you, and I heard about Belinda. Shit, I hope you're OK."

"Well, that's life. I moved on. How's she doing?"

"She's gonna get married next spring. She asked me to be one of her bridesmaids…hope you're not mad at me. Matt, I can't see you and her apart, and I thought you would both grow old together once you came back. You guys were together a long time."

"What can I say?" Matt asked rhetorically.

An awkward silence formed between them.

"Matt, can I ask you a question?"

"Yeah, Luce, anything."

"Remember Tim Shafer? He used to hang out with us in high school. Kind of a quiet guy. Played trumpet in the band and a little bit of basketball."

"Yup. He and I played football our freshman year. Pretty good player, and he was the backup quarterback, I think. He had that cool Ford. What about him?"

"He lives a few houses down from us. Well, anyway, he enlisted in the marines a few months after you left and returned from Vietnam three months ago."

"How's he doing?" Matt asked, knowing the answer.

"He was one of my best guy friends. We grew up together, and he was so cool. Well, I know some of the guys coming back have problems…I don't know, adjusting to normal life." Matt said nothing; his nonresponse offered nothing to her. She pressed on, carefully forming her words. "Please don't take offense. Anyway, his mother tells me all he does is watch cartoons all day. A lot of the guys who are coming back have problems…mental problems of one sort or another." Lucy was now whispering as if she was sharing a long-held secret.

"What do you mean cartoons?"

"Yeah. He watches Looney Tunes, *The Flintstones*, and all that other shit. All cartoons. His mother says that's all he does and never leaves the house—cartoons, eating and drinking, and who knows what else."

"Is that all he does?"

She nodded yes.

"Damn," Matt whispered to himself.

"Well, his mom says the only other thing he does is cry at night in his room when he thinks everyone else is asleep. Is that normal?"

"Lucy, I don't know what 'normal' is anymore." Matt looked away, and his eyes floated away.

Lucy sensed that this was the right time to part ways, and she left the subject dangling in the air. "Matt, come by the house. My parents will be glad to see you. We'll hang out and maybe eat something…maybe those monster burgers at Oden's Drive-In. I would really like to see you." She carefully caressed his face and gave him a light kiss on his purple cheek.

He returned a warm smile to her, something he had not done in a long time.

Matt walked for three hours around his neighborhood, just looking at and smelling the sights as he had never done before. His senses returned to him, and everything around him seemed sharper and more focused. The lazy pace, the light redolence of sweet jasmine, the muffled sounds of laughter, and the quiet conversations from the porches slowly returned to him. He embraced these familiar senses, absorbing them—clutching them like an old girlfriend.

The Guadalupes to the west were sprinkled with a light snow, as if the gods had dusted sugar on them, and he could smell the wet soil of the desert, hinting at a light shower earlier. The western heavens were painted with broad strokes of blue and purple pastels from the sky down toward the horizon, as distant showers cooled the thirsty desert mountains below. The soil opened to welcome the rain like young birds awaiting their evening meal. He buttoned his army jacket, the only remnant of the war he still prized. Winters in Allen County were beautifully stunning. While many folks in other parts of the country faced blizzards, sleet, and tornadoes, Allen County's winters were gorgeous, sweet, and warm.

He noticed the local Clarktown library was open. It was at least fifty years old, built with solid brown flagstone and two iconic pillars at the entrance projecting power and respect. He had spent the summers of his youth in that library. His mother had sent him to the library to keep him out of trouble so he wouldn't be like other young boys who had too much time on their hands. She often told him "Idle time is the devil's time" or some bullshit. He first thought she sent him to punish him. But he soon continued going to the library of his own volition, and he read more in the library than he ever did at school when he was told to do so. Maybe he didn't give his mom enough credit for her common sense and wisdom for forcing him to go. He hoped he had not let his parents down by avoiding college and going to Vietnam, but he still had time.

He loved wandering through the endless book stacks. He preferred all the biographies of famous people, especially the presidents. Lincoln and both Roosevelts were his favorites, and he wished he could have met them and asked them a bunch of questions, maybe try on Lincoln's big fucking hat or ask him why he always looked so sad in photos.

As Matt climbed the stairs and entered, he spotted old Miss Grimes, the librarian who had worked there since the end of World War I. She heard him climbing the old concrete stairs and didn't look up to acknowledge his presence. Perched behind the large, imposing counter at the entrance, she was reviewing index cards.

When he was a kid, all elementary kids were terrified of her since she never smiled and always wore a perpetual frown on her face. A spinster, she seemed not to like children, and he never knew she lost a young child and her husband many years ago. After Matt spent many hours there during the summers of his youth, she warmed up to him and always helped him around the library, offering suggestions for good reads.

"Hi," he said.

Old Miss Grimes said nothing and continued looking down at her index cards. Matt could see her thin white hair, and her scalp reflected the bright lights above her.

"Son, please be quiet. This is a library and mind your manners. If you came to talk to those girls over there, I would warn you. The first loud yapping I hear, you're all out. Do you understand what I'm saying?" She still did not look up.

Miss Grimes might have been a frail old lady. But in this iconic two-thousand-square-foot building, her world, she was the sole authority, and she ruled it with quiet discipline and soft intimidation. She had aged a bit, but her stern glare remained the same.

"Uh, Miss Grimes, it's me, remember?"

She looked up from her thick reading glasses perched on her pointy nose and grimaced as she focused her eyes on him. The dark shadows of her old memory began to light up as she remembered him.

Zeroing in on his scar, she asked, "Bradley...right?"

Matt proudly shook his head affirmatively. "Yes, ma'am."

"Where ya been, young man?"

"Well, ma'am, to tell the truth, I've been overseas...in Vietnam, serving our country." Matt thought that sounded corny, but he was proud of his military service.

"Young man, you have had two books overdue for over two years. You know which ones: *The Old Man and the Sea* and *Huckleberry Finn*. That's over twenty dollars in fines you owe, and ya better pay it back! Is your address still current, or do I have to track you down over there…in Vietnam?"

"Yes, ma'am. I still live with my parents at 504 Hill Street. I'll get to it as soon as I can. I'm here to stay." He walked down the stairs toward the exit.

Behind him, Miss Grimes followed him with her tired eyes. "Mr. Bradley!"

"Yes, ma'am? Those are the only two books that I know of."

"Mr. Bradley, I'm glad you're home safe, son. Come back soon. And forget the fines…someone paid them. Have you read *To Kill a Mockingbird*?" There was a small smile at the right corner of her crusty lips.

■ ■ ■

The day after the funeral, I went with my mom and Nana to gather the Lewises' possessions for storage. Their surviving relatives asked us to do this as a favor. It was late afternoon when we slowly entered the Lewis home, a simple wooden craftsman surrounded by protective ash trees. As we entered the house, we were hit by its loud silence, which felt heavy and cold.

The living room was sparse, with a small TV and comfortable couches of mixed colors. The soft leather sofa had to be Mr. Lewis's. I imagined him falling asleep on it after watching TV with the newspaper in his lap. The local paper was strewn on the coffee table, and it looked as if someone had read only the sports page—Mr. Lewis, I guessed. Pictures were everywhere, a wedding photo of Mr. and Mrs. Lewis, probably in Hawaii, happily in front of a large wedding cake. Baby photos of Sally and her parents were scattered throughout. Shelves were crowded with family mementos: souvenirs of vacations to the Grand Canyon, camping, and Disneyland. I saw one of Curt and Sally holding each other with a snowy background, both blissfully smiling at each other.

The kitchen still had unwashed dishes in the sink, and a cup of cold coffee and Mexican sweet bread lay on the small wooden kitchen table. Someone had taken a small bite from the bread. The kitchen windows had been left open to let the sweet breezes flow in, and I felt refreshed. I could feel a presence in that kitchen from another world, and I felt self-conscious, as if I were being watched.

My nana and mom said nothing as they began carefully placing many items into storage boxes. My mother looked at me and grabbed me tightly by both shoulders: "Mijo, I want you to gather up Sally's things from her bedroom. Please be careful not to damage anything, OK?"

I entered her tiny room, trying to absorb the confusing moment. The bedroom was light blue and pink, with large pillows strewn about the bed. She had posters of the Beatles and James Dean on her wall next to her bed and had carefully placed a soft cotton yellow dress with pearl earrings on the bed, as if she planned on wearing them soon. Her lost future. An open book next to her nightstand was half-finished: *The Great Gatsby*, along with a stack of *Tiger Beat* magazines. Near the lamp on the nightstand, a photo of her and Curt stared at me like it was greeting me. I think it was the '64 prom. Curt had a dark tux, and she had a flowery yellow dress. Both looked happy and content as they held hands in the picture. They didn't look into the camera lens; they looked at each other. She had shelves full of trophies and ribbons: 4H, softball, swimming, student council. I saw a picture of her and Curt at Disneyland wearing Micky Mouse ears and laughing. I couldn't disturb anything, and I felt like I was intruding on someone's sacred ground. I ran outside and cried.

■ ■ ■

The cool winter months of 1965 quickly melted into spring 1966. The misty morning fog wrapped around the base of the Western Mountains and often dissipated to the heavens before the onset of the lazy afternoon. The Western Mountains slowly turned from soft white pastel to sharp shades of brown as the spring waters trickled into the Allen Valley, feeding the desert flowers, ocotillo, wild mesquite, and the rich Allen County farmland. The sweet fragrances of pink jasmine, rosemary, and mint offered a glorious bouquet to welcome our spring.

• • •

In the following months, I hardly saw Curt, even though we shared the same bedroom. After quitting community college, he would stay out late and constantly argue with my parents. Many of my buddies heard rumors about Curt around town, that he would be at bars, heavily drinking, using drugs, and getting into fights. It was a slow suicide, and I know my parents heard the same rumors. To this day, I still visit Sally's grave marker next to her parents. There are always fresh flowers and yellow roses, and her plaque never seems to gather dust. A part of Curt, and a part of all of us, was buried with her.

When I started playing Little League that summer, he never came to my games. He had never missed one since I started playing at age seven. I could see the strain on my parents, and they constantly argued in the privacy of their bedroom about what to do with Curt. Two months later, I saw him packing a large leather bag with his clothes. He said nothing to me, but he quietly gave me his baseball collection. "Take good care of Sandy and the Big D, OK? I love you, little guy. You take good care of Mom and Dad, and always be strong. You, little guy, are the man of the house next to Dad."

I was confused about what was going on with him, but he seemed like a different person from the one I had grown up with and worshipped. Grabbing me hard by my shoulders and bending down to my eye level, he told me with a severe tone, "I will be sending Mom and Dad money every month. They will give you ten dollars to always put fresh yellow roses on Sally's grave. I need you to do that for me. Can you? Even if I don't come back, but I will. Promise."

I nodded yes, sniffling, frightened.

He hugged me with all his strength, and I could still smell him long after he left. I didn't want him ever to let go. He kissed my parents goodbye, quietly walked out the back door, and caught a ride to the bus station. He had enlisted in the US Army and was heading to Georgia for basic training.

That night I looked at an old-world globe and asked my parents, "Where is Vietnam?"

■ ■ ■

I didn't know my father when I was growing up. He was a rather bland, average-looking man who would camouflage himself in a crowd. He was only about 5'8" and 160 pounds with sad features: droopy black eyes that looked like small olives and said nothing to the outside world, thin but muscular, high Indian cheekbones with rough brown skin that approached black. His nose was irregular, as if it had been pounded into his face with a mallet or someone's fist—a remnant of youthful boxing. Meaty forearms suggested a man who had been powerful in youth, and those arms still commanded respect in old age. My father was quick to smile at those around him, but his smile was a protective shield. Inside, he was sort of a ghost. Nana told me he returned from the Pacific and "changed a little bit down below," but I could not comprehend the meaning.

My nana sporadically gave me small snippets about my father before and after the war, telling me about how he was different after. Before: outgoing and gregarious. After: quiet and morose. Before: focused. After: often lost in thought. Before: patient, kind, and selfless. After: temperamental, sullen, and impatient. He often dealt with his mood swings by retreating to his bedroom or outside in the garden and going for a smoke. Often at night she would see him wandering the house, pacing; he told her he was "just getting something to eat from the kitchen." But it was clear to all around him that he adored my mom, and he seemed docile and submissive in her presence. I could see him focus on her whenever they were in a room together, and he always treated her with an astonishing level of respect and adoration.

I knew he was an alcoholic at an early age, and I accepted that fact. He usually drank alone in his room or, only during special occasions, outside his room. But even when I knew he was drunk, he always treated his family well, never raising his voice. As a drunk, he was almost childlike, and the drinking never affected his work ethic. I truly enjoyed those brief moments when we could talk baseball or boxing, and he always reviewed my school grades. "You will be going to college like your brothers; you are as smart as they are…unless you pitch for the Dodgers," he often said with a half-smile.

As a child, I had conflicting feelings about him: I loved him dearly, although I felt sorry for him for some unknown reason. I don't think I respected him as a good son should. He erected an emotional wall between him and the rest of the world, except for my mom. My father's persona seemed like it was made up of a few snapshots of a person, giving you an incomplete picture. My grandma often filled in the gaps and would tell me stories of the old days when my father and mother were young, and I enjoyed those stories. She would introduce her stories by saying: "Come here, mijo, and listen to your grandma…"

I know he dutifully went to work as a janitor every weekday at 5:00 a.m. sharp, and my mother told me with pride that he never missed a day of work in twenty years. During the summer, he would take me along to help him with his odd jobs, cleaning bathrooms, removing gum from the classroom chairs, and picking up trash on the playground. Most men his age found grueling work in the fields picking cotton, melons, okra, lettuce, and tomatoes. But my father considered himself lucky to have this secure job—a steady paycheck, vacation, and some medical insurance, all luxuries that were hard to come by in the 1960s for a man with my dad's background. He was adamant about our family never working in the fields again. I really didn't mind going to work with him, and I felt like my summers weren't wasted. He taught me how to take pride in my work. The bathrooms had to be cleaned a certain way and the floor mopped a certain way, and while, at the time, I thought it was drudgery, as an adult, I appreciated his proud work ethic. He did not complete high school because he married my mother when they were seventeen. Hank was born four months after. One year later, he joined the marines on December 8, 1941, and left behind my mother with a young child.

"Come here, mijo, listen to your nana. I think your father had to make a tough decision. He was already married with a small child, my Enrique, and he thought about not going to the war. He probably could have gotten out of it being a father, you know.

"You know who convinced him to go? Your mother. She told him he must go or regret it for the rest of his life. Your mom knew what she was doing. Most of his friends enlisted after December 7…pinche Chinos.

"Joey Sevillos from down the block, he came back all right. One of your father's best friends, Gustavo Bernal, joined the navy. His ship got sunk in the Pacific, but he survived and returned.

"Your mother convinced him to go and told him it was his duty, almost as important as his duty to his family. They attacked all of us, and your parents love this country as much as anyone else. Don't you ever forget that.

"Anyway, she told him she would be able to take care of the family, her son, and me…and that she knew he would come back so long as he promised to return. I think that's what kept your father strong and safe over there: coming back to his family. I lived with your mom during the war after your grandpa died, and we got close. She's a strong woman. Thank God your father came back alive after all that he went through in the war. Many of the Allen County boys are buried all over the Pacific, Africa, France, and Germany."

I knew nothing about his war experiences since he never spoke with me about it, except oblique hints about the savagery he witnessed. When he was very drunk one afternoon, he recounted hearing about Pearl Harbor on a beautiful Sunday afternoon while playing baseball out in Miller Park. Heck, I thought he was also a janitor in the marines. Most of his buddies signed up for the military after December 7, and many failed to return.

Allen County lost eighteen men to the war, two who were on my dad's baseball team: Freddie Ramirez, second baseman, somewhere in North Africa, and Ben Johnson, the catcher, on the beach at Iwo Jima. He had a framed picture in the living room of that team taken in 1941—all young boys with happy dreams waiting for them in the future, standing and kneeling for the team photo.

One quiet afternoon out in the backyard, as he laid down a bottle of scotch, my dad showed me the team photo and pointed to Ben Johnson standing in the back row and Freddie Ramirez sitting cross-legged in the front near the stack of bats. My father was in the back and looked like a teenager with a severe countenance. As I looked at his eyes, they reminded me of a flickering film projector. I was looking at his eyes, into the human film projector, and the picture played in his mind. He went back twenty years to another time…

"Steady Freddy, we called him. He was our smallest player—about 5' 7"—but the fastest. He could field anything near him and could hit in his sleep. He was also smart in school and probably could have gone to college. I know for a fact some colleges wanted him to play ball. I heard he stepped on a land mine somewhere in Tunisia. Damn Germans. Cowards. There wasn't much left of him in the coffin…probably a few body parts they found in the desert. They told his mom closed coffins were always required in military burials. She didn't know better. Everything but his hands and nose was left out in that desert." He slowly took another gulp from the bottle, savoring it and thinking carefully about what to say next. His eyes flickering. A little spittle of brown nectar slowly crawling down his lower lip. The movie projector resumed to another image.

"Benny Johnson…one of my best buddies. Damn, I had a crush on his little sister, but I never told him that. We even kissed one time behind the bleachers. She was beautiful. Bonnie, that was her. Pretty. Not as pretty as your mom. Never.

"He was a pretty good ballplayer. Strong arm, good contact hitter…

not too much power. But he was the slowest runner I had ever seen, like an old turtle with fucked-up knees. He turned many doubles into singles. And funny as hell, always cracking jokes on the bench. Couldn't shut him up. The other teams made fun of him because he was the only White guy on our team.

"He told us one day, 'Shit, I thought I was one of you Mexicans all this time. Had I known I was white, I would never have joined the fucking team. HOW COME NONE OF YOU MEXES NEVER TOLD ME I WAS WHITE?' We laughed every time he said that. We were brothers."

My dad added that Ben never even reached the shore at Iwo Jima. "The Japs got him before he even hit the beach. He ran too damn slow and probably swam even slower. Damn, Ben, you should've gotten off that beach at Iwo…" My father drifted away into sleep.

I picture the lifeless body of fat Benny Johnson, the catcher, face down in the dirty black, bloody sand of Iwo Jima, saltwater quietly lapping over his limp body as if the ocean gods were soothing him. Too slow to reach second base. Too slow to make it to shore at Iwo. I know Freddy and Benny visited my father in his dreams, shapeless phantoms waving at him to come along.

Guilt gnaws at you from the inside out.

■ ■ ■

From the *Sonora Desert Review*, May 17, 1966:
County Health authorities are issuing warnings of rabid dogs in the county's southern end. If you see a strange dog, do not go near it, and under no circumstances should you touch it. Contact the Allen County Health Department if you see one.
-Koufax/Dodgers beat Pirates at Forbes Field, 4–1. Pirates' lone run coming from a Roberto Clemente solo home run.
-The Rolling Stones release their new album: *Paint it Black*.
-Westside baseball drops doubleheader to Rockwood High.

Part Four

"EL BIG BOB"

Sheriff Robert Johnson was acutely pissed. He had just lost one hundred dollars on a cockfighting wager. He had heavily invested in one young import from Sonora, Mexico, who was as mean as they come. This feathered monster had literally torn all his opponents to bloody shreds, and Big Bob was confident that this one would make him enough money for an early retirement. He proudly boasted that he even gave the cock his nom de guerre: El Gran Diablo. El Gran Diablo was now making a name for himself on both sides of the border and commanding top fees for the matches. Big Bob was the absentee owner who kept this ownership discreetly confined among his trusted friends, fronts, and associates.

He had been the sheriff of Allen County for five years and on street patrol the five years before. Between the bloody hemorrhoids, back surgery, petty politics, and long hours, he was ready to find a quick way to retire. And squirreling away some extra money on top of his retirement would hasten his move to a quiet beach in Mexico with some anonymous nubile trollop by his side. Nothing complicated, just nice sex and some fun. El

Gran Diablo might be his ticket to retirement, and then he could hand over the reins to his next in command. Unfortunately, the sheriff had long ago cut the tether that connected him to any ethical guidepost and spent a lot of time "collecting and saving" for his "retirement" outside his regular paycheck. He kept money in his home that was beyond the scrutiny of anyone nosing around in his business. Nearing the end of his career, he was unsure who would replace him as the top cop in the county. His problem was that his next in command was Jaime or Jim Garza. Not that Garza was not fit for the job: a local boy and tough cop who grew up in a tough neighborhood, loyal to Big Bob and the department, discreet. Garza was the first Mexican-American in the county to rise in the ranks to captain. Garza probably was aware of Big Bob's many peccadilloes: the women; the alcohol; the small-town graft, thinly veiled bribes labeled as "donations"; and the cockfighting.

Under normal conditions, Garza was the logical choice. The only impediment that kept Garza from ascending to Big Bob's vacancy was that Garza was, as Big Bob eloquently put it one evening at a local bar, "a fucking wetback, and no fucking wetback is ever gonna be sheriff of this county as long as Big Bob is alive. Mexicans just don't have the stuff to be a sheriff." Garza understood Bob's sentiment and remained a loyal undersheriff who took pride in his work. But he never lost his clear, focused image of the odious human being known as Sheriff Robert Johnson, Big Bob.

Garza and Big Bob maintained a healthy—albeit distant—professional relationship. Garza wanted to be a good cop, and he liked Big Bob when he was first hired in 1958. Oblivious to the critics who called him a kiss ass behind his back, Garza only wanted to be an honest and good cop, which was difficult under Big Bob's tutelage and his assortment of peccadilloes.

Big Bob could quickly dispel the rumors floating throughout Allen County about graft and corruption in his department because he knew how to instill fear in the voters who returned him to the office every four years: robberies are on the rise; too many wetbacks crossing the border with drugs, disease, and violence; heroin; gangs; etc. He knew the voters felt safe with him in office. He would protect them from the vicious hordes of criminals, thieves, gunrunners, prostitutes, illegal aliens, and killers lurking in the shadows of the sun in Allen County. Thus, any rumors of corruption arose and subsided near election time. Fear kept him in office. His institutionalized mistreatment of criminals was overlooked by the voting citizens as long as they felt safe, safe from the hordes and drugs coming from Mexico, safe from dirty old men in the parks, safe from the local thieves ready to steal from their well-manicured homes.

Someone tipped off the US Border Patrol that an illegal cockfighting operation was thriving in the county's north end. The feds wondered why the local sheriff was unable to pierce the operation and dismantle it. Big Bob often lamented to the feds, "Well, you gotta know how those Mexicans and Filipinos run their operations for the cocks. They are loyal to only each other and no one else—especially law enforcement. It's in their blood. These wets have been doing this crap for generations, and they will continue doing it. All we can do is try to find them and shut down their operations whenever and wherever we find them." That evasive bullshit was good enough to mollify the federal authorities and draw any undue attention and suspicions away from Big Bob.

Since the death of his wife ten years before, Big Bob developed eccentric habits, one of which was eating breakfast every morning at Sam Wong's Chinese Restaurant on Main Street in downtown Rockwood. Garza and Big Bob were the first and only patrons on this warm morning, and Garza ordered only black coffee.

One of Sheriff Johnson's annoying habits was quoting John Wayne, in or out of context, if he thought the situation or discussion called for it. His fifty deputies watched most of John Wayne's movies as part of their initial training because of a veiled suggestion from the sheriff.

"Damn, looks like another hot one today—probably 105 degrees. Listen, Garza, I want to find out how these feds were tipped off. I knew some of those guys arrested, and it looks bad when folk around here think I'm not in control." Big Bob loosened his belt to make room for the kung pao chicken he had ordered. They were seated in a corner booth in the back of Sam's.

"Well, sir, I assume they were tipped off—at least that's what my sources say. You know how things run around this place. Sorry, sir," Garza lamented as he sipped the syrupy black coffee.

"'Sorry won't get it done, dude.'" *Rio Bravo.* "Damn, there was a time when I knew everything that was going down in this county before it even happened," he said.

Sam Wong brought the hot plate and carefully placed it in front of Big Bob.

The term "Big" was an ironic misnomer since Sheriff Bob was only about 5'8." He always brandished cowboy boots, expensive ones made of slaughtered reptiles, with high heels that added three inches to his height and ten feet to his ego. His costume was completed with a custom-made silver belt buckle with an inscription reading "Big Bob." No doubt a "gift" from an unknown acquaintance. His black Stetson offered a funny likeness to Yosemite Sam, complete with the large, dangling mustache. All his external accoutrements were symbols and confirmations of his manliness, which he took great pains to project to the outside world around him: symbols of strength, virility, and innate power, but really they symbolized insecurity, weakness, and smallness. Through the years, he had put on weight and, at thirty-one years of age, developed a soft beer gut that cascaded over his belt. Sporting a flattop haircut that had not changed since he was a teenager, he had specks of white on the sides of his head. His clear blue eyes with thick blond eyebrows curled up to his prominent forehead, and his callused hands suggested he was someone who was not afraid to get his hands dirty. His deep baritone voice could intimidate someone just by its very sound, and he was comfortable intimidating anyone.

"Thanks, Sam. You ever see *Bonanza*? Sam looks like Hop Sing, don't he? Damn, all he needs is to grow that chink hair long, don't you think, Garza?"

"Huh, not sure…but back to our discussion. This cockfighting thing will blow over. Hell, this kind of thing has been going on since long before you and I were born, and it will continue long after we're gone. Don't worry about it." Garza slowly sipped the coffee, staring closely at his boss.

"Damn. How about some breakfast? This Chinaman makes the best damn food outside of Peking. In the middle of these goddamn Mexican restaurants, and he makes Chinese food. Ha! Order a plate. Shit, he never likes me to pay for the meals, even though I always insist. I've been eating here for over four years, and he's never let me pay. That's his only condition when I eat here. So help yourself to anything on the menu. It's on me.

"HEY, SAM, get us some more hot coffee. Shit, this stuff is as cold as a Siberian toilet seat!"

Big Bob slowly lit up a fat cigar, never taking his eyes off Garza, and he gestured to Garza, asking if he wanted one. Most people felt uneasy with Big Bob's deep stares, but Garza was used to them and felt no intimidation. Garza shook his head. He didn't smoke or drink. "Sam's a good guy. I'm sure he knows you appreciate that."

"Yeah, you know I love these cigars—Cuban. I have a friend who brings them from Mexico and gives me some as a gift, you know."

"Sir, aren't those things illegal? The Cuban embargo thing…"

Big Bob ignored him and waved his hands dismissively. "That fucking Kennedy. What a damn hypocrite. Did you know he smoked Cubans? That SOB signed the cigar embargo in 1962, but he didn't sign it until his assistant, Pierre Salinger, got him one thousand Cuban Upmanns the fucking day before he signed the restrictions. What a bastard. What a hypocrite. Worse than his brother Bobby. He probably smoked one as he was dinging Marilyn Monroe. An Upmann in his mouth and his pecker in Marilyn. I bet the Upmann was bigger and sweeter…HA. Lucky son of a bitch. Eat something, Garza."

Garza broke into a small, forced smile. "Yes, sir. Well…uh…thank you, sir, but I hardly eat breakfast, and coffee's just fine. It's gonna be a long, hot day. Have a good day, sir." With deference, Garza excused himself and left two dollars for the coffee at the table. "Thanks, Sam. Good coffee," he said on his way out.

As he saw Garza exit, Big Bob quietly slipped the two-dollar tip into his pants. A few minutes later, Walt McCoy slipped into the booth across from him. McCoy was one of the wealthiest farmers in the valley and a staunch political supporter of Big Bob (who had run unopposed for the last two terms). At election time, he hosted a legendary barbecue for five hundred guests for Big Bob.

The sheriff had his hands in all sorts of grafts from the petty to the absurd: shakedowns of undocumented farmworkers and motorists, free meals and drinks at most local restaurants, "discounts" at local car dealerships and clothing stores. One strange rumor that floated around the valley was that he was involved in the black market for body parts. Those unfortunate souls who died or were killed in jail, leaving no surviving relatives, were chopped up by the local coroner under the pretext of conducting autopsies. Big Bob had a market for some of the organs. A middleman, only known as Repo Man, would occasionally visit Bob and take some of the parts with him. Livers, eyes, teeth, and hair were the most popular. Bob argued that it was "all legal since the donors all signed waivers upon entrance into the county jail." Repo Man would then distribute these bodily "donations" to the black market in Latin America. Rumor also had it that some universities were the recipients of the donations to promote research. This enterprise was not too profitable when supply met demand.

"Hey, Sam, how about some of those egg rolls? I'll wrap them up for the road.

"Hey, Walt, I wanna ask you a question. Last month, up in the foothills area on the Allen farm, our deputies found two bodies of some wetbacks in one of the small caves out there. They had probably been dead about a few days, probably wandered in during that thunderstorm we had back then."

"Yeah. You know, there are a lot of caves out there. Pretty dangerous.

Legend has it that a robber hid a lot of gold bullion out in one of the caves in the 1800s, but it's all bull. Some idiot gold seekers have gone into those caves looking for it, but no one ever found anything, and some died trying. Anyway, what's the big deal with these dead wets?"

"During the autopsy, the coroner told me that the official cause of death was hypothermia. But this is the interesting part: he also mentioned that he found traces of methane in their lungs, but he only mentioned that in a small footnote in the autopsy report. And he also mentioned that, several years ago, they found the body of a local kid trapped in the cave and that he died not of suffocation but of methane. What the hell do you make of that?"

"Well, I don't know too much about engineering, but that is interesting. There have always been rumors of natural gas deposits in that area. But nothing has ever been confirmed. Jimmy Allen is a great guy and a rich sonovabitch. He's never mentioned gas deposits before. I sit with him at the local farm board, and I've known him socially at the Ranchers' Club. He's never mentioned anything like that, but why would he? That damn family has the Midas touch; they always have. Besides, he doesn't need the money, does he? All that land is priceless with or without gas deposits."

"Yeah, OK, but if there was a source of natural gas, couldn't that make the land even more valuable?"

"Not necessarily. The process of converting natural gas is expensive as long as we have cheap coal. So maybe Jimmy Allen is aware of that potential source but doesn't want to pursue it. It might be more expensive to pump it out and process it, and it isn't cost effective. He might be holding onto the reserves for the future."

"OK, but those deposits would make that land valuable, or at least the mineral rights might make it a potential bonanza, don't you think?"

"Hard to say. Only Jimmy Allen knows, and I doubt he will divulge that info to me. He has a funny way of keeping to himself when it comes to his holdings and business, except when we have joint ventures. He has business all over the state. That's why he has his own damn airstrip on his property; he's hardly ever home. Anyway, I need to get going. Gotta check my fields. We pick tomatoes next month. But I'll check around for you. I know this guy who might give you more definite answers."

"All right. Thanks for your time." Big Bob's mind returned to that mystical lonely Mexican beach. He had learned that methane gas had no odor, but Big Bob could sure smell an opportunity. He tasted that cold beer, felt the warm Mexico sun on his face, and felt the soft, warm sand under his toes. *I wonder how much I could get for the livers of those two wetbacks,* he thought.

As Jim Garza entered his police sedan after leaving Sam Wong's, he felt satisfied that he had done a good day's work, and he was proud to be a cop. His military-clean and crisp short-sleeve shirt was soaked in sweat from the approaching morning heat. The rising sun in the east was bleach white that early morning, suggesting a punishing blaze in a few hours.

He looked at his polished boots to wipe them clean, thinking, *Even if I couldn't break up that cockfighting ring myself, at least I alerted the feds myself. El Gran Diablo fights no more and is probably the main meal in Sam's kitchen as we speak. Big Bob's kung pao chicken might be a little special today...go to hell, Big Bob. The sheriff has to live with the consequences he creates.* "There are some things a man just can't run away from" *Stagecoach.* Garza had a smug smile he kept to himself. *Fuck you, Bob; you are near retirement,* he thought. He tugged his white Stetson and started the ignition.

◼ ◼ ◼

From the *Sonora Desert Review,* June 13, 1966:
Residents of Rockwood are advised to be on the lookout for any suspicious persons, especially in the alleys and backyards of residences. Apparently, there has been a rash of stolen ladies' undergarments, which has escalated in the past months. The

suspect, or suspects, steals ladies' undergarments from the victims' clotheslines, usually in the late evening. If you see someone suspicious or have lost your undergarments, please call Rockwood Police Department.

■ ■ ■

Big Bob's lineage is not well illuminated, and he took great pains to avoid casting any sliver of light on his background. Family histories are often shrouded in the misty shadows of the past.

He was born on a humble farm—a dilapidated wood shack, nine hundred square feet on ten acres of rocky, barren land, somewhere south of Altus, Oklahoma—to a pious mother who was gentle in spirit and simple in thought. Born one month prematurely, Big Bob almost didn't survive the first three months of his fragile life during a brutal winter. His breathing was labored, and he rejected any forms of nutrition, including his mother's breasts. His mother clutched her Bible and prayed almost nonstop, coaxing her god to save this precious baby, and he did. She willed him to live.

As an only child, he was the only source of his mother's attention and affection and the only source of unmitigated physical abuse from his father—abuse of multiple degrees and dimensions: physical, emotional, psychological, verbal. Gleefully punching his son or wife without compunction or reservation, Wayne Johnson would curse his son without provocation or thought. And he would slap him without reason or care. In Bob's insular world on their Oklahoma farm, he thought such treatment was normal, and those daily beatings were merely a boy's rite of passage into the adult world. His father's beatings would only prepare Bob for his transition and entrance into adulthood, where he could apply their lessons.

The Johnsons barely scraped by. The physical demands and responsibilities of the farm were solely his mother's, and Wayne spent most of his time sleeping or drinking at the local bar, boasting about his war exploits.

She chopped wood and sold it to neighbors. She washed clothes. She tilled the parched soil of the Oklahoma countryside in a futile attempt to grow anything they could eat or sell. She kept herself busy mainly to avoid spending time with her husband, who found any excuse to beat her or rape her at the slightest whim. Every crevice of her body was battered, bruised, cut, pinched, slapped, bitten, and punched. The damage seeped below, into herself, and every square inch of her soul and pride was beaten into submission. Occasionally Bob's father would help make repairs around the farm, but he spent most of his time at the local American Legion sharing war stories with other vets.

The only happy times of their marriage were during World War II when he was thousands of miles away. She quietly prayed for him not to return from North Africa at times, which she thought would be the only way to salvage her son's soul. During the war, veterans' wives dreaded the visit from the War Department—faceless military personnel in gloomy, dark sedans arriving at their homes to deliver mortally bad news. Bob's mother quietly prayed to herself that they would visit her doorstep. That somber black sedan never arrived. But her husband did. He survived.

Wayne Johnson suffered a major nervous breakdown during World War II after a few days of combat in North Africa. He proudly landed with General Patton in Casablanca with the American forces in 1942 but was in North Africa no more than one month. He returned to the States after suffering, officially, heat exhaustion and possibly combat fatigue. Unofficially, he suffered from cowardice. Apparently, he was AWOL from his unit during a night patrol near Kasserine Pass. All twenty members of his unit were slaughtered or taken captive in a Wehrmacht ambush, and he had to explain to his superiors how the hell he got separated from the unit. He lacked the courage to tell them the truth: he intentionally disengaged from his company during their patrol and ran away from the sounds of the shooting once the slaughter began. He ran until he was safe behind Allied lines and never looked back. The army never bought the explanation, but there were no living witnesses that could prove or disprove desertion. He admitted the truth to Bob's mother years later after chugging two bottles of vodka, and strangely, his mother never conveyed this admission to her son until after Wayne's death—as if to protect her son from learning the pathetic truth of Wayne's wartime experience. He never fired a single shot in North Africa.

Wayne's final day on earth came on a scorching Oklahoma afternoon on May 12, 1947. Bob remembered the air's thickness that morning and the menacing black clouds hovering on the eastern horizon—tornado weather. The morning began with warmth and humidity, clear skies, and a blazing sun. Later, it looked almost like nighttime, as angry black clouds swallowed the sun by late morning. Anyone living in that part of the country recognized that tornadoes would certainly spring from the heavens like coiled snakes onto the ground. Bob was at school and was attuned to the blather of Mrs. Corfman's lessons on the Civil War when he got the news of his father's death.

On that fateful morning, Wayne decided to chop wood near the ranch. After a night of drinking and trollop hunting, he felt energized and sought to burn off excess energy that he could not burn off during his whoring and drinking. He was king of the world and wanted to work on the farm, his farm, his kingdom.

As he took an aggressive swing at a dead limb of a mature oak tree in the backyard, he noticed a beehive about twenty feet above, firmly embedded in the tree. Honeybees are generally docile creatures and don't like to be bothered. Wayne's primal instinct, however, was not to avoid the bees. That would be counterintuitive to his demented way of thinking. Instead, he approached the hive like he did his family: attack it into submission to remind the poor creatures who was boss. He was king of this universe and would remind these small subjects to respect him, to worship him, to fear him.

His hatchet cleanly cut the hive in two. For a few seconds, the bees failed to react. Wayne was gleeful. His testosterone was running on a full tank, going full throttle. He thought, God, that felt good. However, a handful of drones quickly scrambled within the hive for aerial combat, reacting in a way that only a war veteran like Wayne would fully appreciate—with military precision, with deadly discipline, and with suicidal alacrity.

First, the initial wave of two sacrificial drones exited the hive, and they scouted their giant adversary below, who posed a threat to their hive, their small empire, and their empress, their queen. During World War II, Japanese soldiers and pilots subscribed to the Bushido code: loyalty and honor until death. A warrior's code. The drones also demonstrated that code and then proceeded to sacrifice themselves like warriors, like kamikazes. (A beeshido code?) They bit Wayne on his right hand as if to neutralize the threat of the hatchet. Wayne dropped the hatchet in pain and cursed them. He squished the two suicidal bees embedded in his hands, leaving the stingers intact. Their venom slowly penetrated the defenses of his outer epidermis and quickly entered his bloodstream.

Sons of bitches, I'll show them, he said to himself. His growing fury matched the increasing anger from inside the hive; a battle between two armies was about to be waged in the backyard of the Johnson homestead. To fully dramatize the unfolding events, the gods in the heavens increased their fury with the impending storm. The winds began gushing, and the dark clouds started bloating. The rain quickly became more weighted. Funnel clouds could be seen on the western horizon, as if they were monsters uncoiling their ugly hands.

In these last moments of his life, Wayne began to see things with clarity and soon realized that he was allergic to bees. His arm quickly bloated; his breathing became labored. His body was going into shock due to an allergic reaction to the stings: increased pulse, lungs burning, the synapses of his brain going haywire like electrical lines during an Oklahoma thunderstorm. He tried to harness all his energies to prepare for battle as his body began to list portside. His knees buckled and quivered.

Hallucinations crept into his head as a swarm of at least fifty bees descended upon him in disciplined formation. In his warped mind, he saw German Stukas and was transported back to North Africa 1942. The Stukas blared as they attacked downward toward their target. They attacked him with impunity in his upper torso. They showed absolutely no mercy as wave after wave continued their assault on his body. By then, he was crawling ten yards from the safety of his back porch. He glanced up to the heavens, seeking God, but only saw menacing black creatures glaring at him from above. The soft sprinkles of rain soothed his aching body. Then the clouds above released solid hail that painfully pummeled him all over his now frail body.

As the second wave of attackers retreated to the hive, a final squadron swarmed down on him for the coup de grâce. As Wayne looked up to the heavens to make his peace with the Lord, he saw a fresh squadron of German Stukas. He marveled at their tenacity and sense of purpose as they pummeled him with hundreds of stings throughout his body. Wayne's last burst of energy triggered his innate sense of survivorship. He had survived North Africa and Rommel and knew he could survive a bunch of fucking bees. Just like he and Patton beat Rommel in Africa, he would win this battle as he crawled within five feet of his back door.

In Oklahoma, folks need to protect themselves from the wrath of tornadoes and mother nature in general. Wayne had built a rear double door of solid maple, reinforced with enough metal bars and wood to solidly protect the inside from the general wrath of mother nature. This door was the only decent thing he had built on earth. Good, solid craftsmanship that would withstand any storm—three inches thick, nine feet in height, with thick wrought-iron locks that could keep out an angry bear. This was the door that Wayne was now banging, pleading for his wife to open. She had secured it earlier at the onset of the gathering storm. He would beat these damn bees like he beat the damn Germans. He knew he was minutes from lapsing into cardiac arrest, but he could always depend on his wife to save him from his own mistakes. She was always dependable and would now protect him from this onslaught.

A good woman.

A strong woman.

A loyal wife.

And he knew she was right behind the door. Soon she would mend his injuries and take him to a warm bed where he would sleep it off.

The doomed man was relieved to see his wife peering through the window. Sucking in his last breaths, imploring her to open the heavy door, praying for God's redemption for all the sins he had committed during his worthless life. He lacked the energy to even break the window and slowly realized she would not let him seek refuge from the bees' onslaught. She only looked at him with dead eyes, nothing but utter contempt for him as he was sucking in his last breaths on that back porch. The left corner of her upper lip tightened into a light smirk. As his light was slowly extinguishing, he realized her light had been dead for years. With stark clarity, his epiphany made him look back at his pathetic life on earth. Those men he abandoned in the African desert came into view. In that last moment of his life on earth, he looked at her through the porch window and accepted his inexorable fate. At that moment, nothing was more evident in his mind than his impending death. In the wind and rain, he could hear her placing additional barriers behind the door. He could see her lips moving, reciting something to herself, praying. Reading her lips, he knew she was repeating one of her favorite passages from Matthew, 4:16: "The people dwelling in darkness have seen a great light, and for those dwelling in the region and shadow of death, on them, a light has dawned."

His heart and life finally stopped as he grasped the doorknob he had just installed for their protection. Wayne's heavy body continued to list portside and slowly sank to the wooden floor of the porch. He had been able to outrun the German Wehrmacht in North Africa. But on that afternoon in a tiny corner of Oklahoma, he could not outrun a nest of angry bees and could not outrun his fate.

After suffering only three casualties, the swarm exited the theater of battle and retreated to the safe confines of their warm, hive-victorious warriors.

"…and for those dwelling in the region and shadow of death, on them, a light has dawned."

· · ·

It took a long time for Bob to accept the truth about his father since he was always treated as a war hero, and he never corrected anyone who said so. Bob always bragged that "my dad kicked Rommel's ass" and helped "boot him out of North Africa." John Wayne was Wayne's favorite actor, and he often suggested to Bob, a highly impressionable boy, that John Wayne's exploits in the movies were not unlike his in the real war in North Africa. Bob believed his father was John Wayne in the flesh.

The only normal time Bob spent with his father, when Wayne wasn't drinking or abusing his family, was watching all the John Wayne movies. They would both mouth the dialogue. Bob often overlooked the abuse from his father since he felt his father was a war hero. That undeniable fact outweighed everything else: the slapping, the kicking, the bruising, the yelling tantrums, and the humiliation his father inflicted without any outward compunction or semblance of remorse.

The abuse from Wayne was transferred to Bob and seeped into his DNA. Most fathers pass on something of value to their sons: a sense of value and respect, humor, physical skills. Bob's father passed on an unmitigated hatred for the human race that Bob embraced. Violence was the norm in the household, and Bob carried that violence to school. Being the smallest kid in his class, he had to earn respect by being the most brutal and inflicting terror on his classmates—especially the larger ones. He learned to fear no one except his father. His father taught him not to ask for anything but to take—take everything he thought he was entitled to.

After his father's death, his mother doted on him as if she could erase all the years of brutality and degradation. They wandered the Midwest for the next five years until they moved to Allen County in 1956 in hopes of a new life. Bob was attracted to law enforcement and joined the Allen County Sheriff's Department. Its allure was the excitement of the job and the power of the title—power to wield unrestrained control over those who broke the law, Bob's law. He quickly rose in the ranks and was appointed sheriff in 1962 by local voting politic who wanted law and order in this California outback. And Big Bob was quick to oblige.

PART FIVE

THE JUDGE

"All right, counsel, let's get this case to a quick conclusion!" Judge Timothy Gates's baritone blast bounced off the mahogany walls with anger and impatience. He was seated in his chambers in his oversized leather chair that felt like an old baseball glove. His chamber was dark, and the blinds were tightly shut to snuff out the growing heat outside. The late-morning sun was high in the sky as slits of light crept into the chambers and illuminated his lifelong mementos: photos of his wife, now deceased; photos with local and state politicians; an autographed football from his days at Penn State; and law certificates. The local attorneys were perturbed by his crass habit of speaking and continuing conversations from the bathroom as he sat on his toilet, continuing discussions about case settlement and often meandering to matters unrelated to the proceedings. The only interruption was the sound of the toilet flushing.

For twenty years, Judge Gates was one of only three municipal court judges in Allen County who handled only criminal dockets. Although he did not grow up here, he thought of himself as a valley native but was unable to jettison his Arkansas accent altogether. He possessed an excellent grasp of border Spanish, and, unlike most attorneys, he could effortlessly discard any pretense of legalese when the occasion demanded it—like now. He wanted to make sure he was understood.

Everything about him seemed plump—his belly, his muscular fore-arms, his fat jowls around his neck, and his stubby fingers like ten plump hot dogs. He sported a flattop with specks of gray and had light hazel eyes behind horn-rimmed glasses with two vertical wrinkles above the bridge of his nose that gave him a perpetual sneer. Thick sideburns framed a plump face with a Karl Malden nose in the center. His crude social mannerisms and gruff manner of speech hid an intellect that few could appreciate or equal in his profession.

"Listen, Mr. Stein, your drunk client will rot in hell as far as I'm concerned, and he won't get any breaks from me. He killed three people 'cause he couldn't control his damn drinking. And he's going to pay at the Timothy Gates toll booth with some serious prison time. From here, I don't see too many mitigating factors, except that he's a drunken asshole. My mother didn't raise a fool, and I won't be taken for a fool now, counsel. The Lewises were friends of mine; we belonged to the same church. And my grandchild went to school with the girl. Shit, how can you expect me to show compassion?"

"Your Honor, with all due respect, I only ask that you keep your mind open and objective until you hear all the mitigating evidence I hope to sub-mit. Should I have some concerns about your objectivity?" Defense counsel Robert Stein was in control, but his anger percolated near the surface like bile trapped in his throat. He was currently assigned to People v. Thomas King, and Allen County Case No. F-2387 was one of the most important cases in the county in 1965. As the most experienced defense attorney in Allen County, he was assigned the case. Stein really had no choice but was guided by his ethical demands and the demands of paying his rent. Stein was a long way from UC Berkeley, which was in another universe, for that matter. He missed the cold blasts from San Francisco Bay, the lazy coffee shops, the jazz clubs, mingling with the intellectuals from Cal, the antiwar frenzy that was building, and the sophistication. The beguiling lure of San Francisco was put on hold until he found the right opportunity to escape from this simple backwoods community.

In the summer of 1963, after a night of smoking hash and drinking cheap mescal, he drove down to Allen County on a whim to answer an ad for a job opening for a defense lawyer. Bob Stein intended to stay in this foreboding backcountry only for a few months until he could find more challenging legal work in the Bay Area. When the hash haze finally lifted, he found himself working as a sole practitioner out of his apartment near the courthouse above a Mexican restaurant. That was almost two years ago.

The months turned into years, but he still yearned for an escape from this intellectual and cultural cesspool called Allen County. He wanted to be part of the revolution bubbling in the United States and to make a difference in society—especially with the Vietnam War growing and young kids like him returning in body bags. He wanted to take a stand and fight the good fight in and out of court! Stein ideally envisioned a day when he would storm the gates of the political establishment and help build a new society, a society that is ideal, just, and moral. But Allen County was not the place to start the revolution. Shit, this place hadn't changed much since their pioneers crossed this fucking desert in horses and buggies. He was getting tired of the heat, the boredom, the quiet, the slow pace, and some of the locals with whom he could not relate comfortably.

Dealing with this reactionary jurist was not something he had learned about in law school, and he had difficulty dealing with the judge at the professional level. This judge was from a different generation with an ingrained set of values that were foreign to him: stubborn, petty, ignorant of the progressive extensions of the law, temperamental, and not discerning of the subtle areas of gray between black and white. Maybe I should call some radicals, my SDS buddies, back at Cal and throw the bastard a few

Molotovs at his house, he thought, smiling.

"Something funny, counsel? Mr. Stein, do you see something funny here? Why are you smiling, Mr. Stein?" The prosecutor, Dennis Speck, turned his head away and sighed.

"And shouldn't we have a court stenographer memorialize our discussions here in chambers for a record in case of an appeal?" Stein asked, dismissing the judge's comments.

"Mr. Stein, I've always said you've got a hell of a lot of chutzpah. We'll get a reporter if you would like. Would that make you feel better? How about a cup of coffee, perhaps? A croissant? Bagel and lox?" The judge continued. "The voters of this county have placed their collective faith in me that I will protect and uphold the law, and this guy deserves no compassion from me."

"But, Your Honor, some elements in this case might lend themselves to viable defenses, and I can't divulge exactly what they are. But the evidence might show some problems with my client's vehicle—the braking system—and the blood sample taken was somehow lost." Stein still had not erased the thoughts of the Molotovs.

Judge Gates looked up from behind his massive chambers desk and turned his attention to the prosecutor. "Lost?"

"Well, Your Honor, the blood sample is not exactly lost. We just can't find it. The People are not too worried. Perhaps a bit concerned, but not worried. The People feel comfortable that the case is solid, and we anticipate an easy conviction." Speck relaxed, crossed his legs, and sat back in his leather chair, looking at his watch like he had a hot date. His smug attitude never fared well with jurors, and it did not fare well with this judge here in chambers.

"What the hell did you just say? Don't they teach you guys English at law school? Well, maybe 'The People' are not too worried. But damn, you, Mr. Speck, should be worried because you know these backwater juries sometimes lose focus. And they can easily be persuaded by some smooth-talk-ing defense lawyer"—he glanced at Stein— "through smoke and mirrors to ignore the facts and see things in a way they shouldn't. Some lawyers have gift of a verbally ambidextrous mouth and can talk on each side of it. Jurors might be dazzled by a slick attorney spouting multisyllabic words. We would not want that would we, Mr. Speck? This is a court of law, not some circus act. Let's call a couple of midgets and some court jesters for our entertainment."

Speck leaned forward on his chair in a faux dramatic gesture and gazed intently at Judge Gates. "Sir, we are confident of a conviction. The Clarktown police have worked diligently on this case, and it commands the highest priority. We won't take anything less than six years in state prison, with probation off the table. We want two-year terms to run consecutive to each other, two years for each victim. I don't see too many mitigating factors in this case, both in terms of his background and the case itself. He got drunk, got behind a wheel, and drove into that poor Lewis family. Case closed." He leaned back and glanced again at this watch. His hot date was waiting.

Stein rolled his eyes. "Judge, this guy is a family man with no priors. His wife and kids just left him, and he normally doesn't drink. On this particular day, he just lost it. He has three young children, ages five, seven, and ten. He has his own business, which is going bankrupt, a car wash up on the county's north end. His wife was gravely ill, and they had no insurance. Their bills piled up quickly."

The judge brushed his hand in the air and intervened. "Car wash? I never heard of his. I usually take my Cadillac to Sonny's Car Wash on Fifth Street. They do a great job. You know, they carefully hand wash it and treat my old Caddy like a young woman, nice and gentle. You know what their slogan is? It's Sonny's Car Wash: The best hand job in town. Ha-ha!"

Stein chimed in. "Well, Your Honor, I haven't had a good hand job in a long time. I'll make it a point to go there. If I drop your name, you think they'll give me an extra nice hand job when I bring in my old VW?"

"Well, Mr. Stein, I don't see why not. Please think of me when you're getting your hand job, OK?"

"I certainly will, judge." Stein felt an odd connection with the judge, and maybe it was just a matter of appealing to his darker side. Although they were worlds apart politically, they understood each other on crass levels.

Adjusting his tie, Speck looked befuddled and could not grasp the double entendres dancing in front of him. "Gentlemen, let's get back to the central issue. As I was saying, I feel we have a strong case against the defendant. My boss, District Attorney Richmond, has given me explicit instructions that I cannot go below six years in the joint."

"Your Honor, this is almost like the case I tried just two years ago. People v. Todd Johnson. Similar facts. The mitigating factors are very much alike. And Your Honor gave him probation with only six months in the local jail. He hasn't reoffended as far as I know. And that case had no plausible defenses," Stein said.

"Mr. Stein, I see and analyze cases individually. Didn't the Todd case involve a couple of old people in the car? They didn't have much longer to live anyway and left no relatives. Besides, the old couple may have been partially at fault if I recall." The judge leaned back and looked up at the ceiling as if he were about to take his afternoon nap. The stuffy air in chambers was beginning to thicken. Judge Gates slowly reached toward a fan and turned it on. The circulating air refreshed them as they gathered their thoughts.

"Your Honor, there's one other thing." Stein was now leaning at the edge of his chair as if the judge and DDA could not hear…as if he was about to let them in on a secret. "Our expert conducted his investigation and analysis. The police lost the diagram that included the measurements and skid marks. They cannot establish whether my guy was even speeding. There are no percipient witnesses, except for some old hobo two blocks away at the time of the impact. He's just some Mexican farmworker who is halfway to Sinaloa by now. Further, the prosecution might have a problem regarding who even had the fucking right of way. After I get through with the investigating officers, this jury might be angry at the People, and they might want to send a message to the DA's office."

"And the message is what? The DAs are legal nimrods?" Judge Gates turned to Speck for an answer.

"Your Honor, we're aware of some of the negative variables that might undermine the prosecution. On balance, the stronger elements will certainly outweigh those small negatives. We are still confident that we can sustain a conviction."

Judge Gates noticed a small blob of sweat forming on Speck's forehead. Not even the oscillating fan could not evaporate the sweat blob. Speck now sat up in the leather chair, and his smugness evaporated in the warm chamber air. His lower lip twitched nervously as he chewed his pencil like it was a fat toothpick.

"Well, Mr. Speck. Now I will send your boss a message. You tell your boss that perhaps a two-year concurrent sentence might be the better alternative to save the registered voters…er…taxpayers of this county the cost of a lengthy trial. I want an answer by tomorrow morning. Gentlemen, I will see you here tomorrow at nine o'clock."

■ ■ ■

Curt returned from military training in the early spring of 1966, and our family hosted a going-away party for him. The army selected him for Special Forces, the Green Berets, and he would be going "over there" a few weeks after. He returned about ten pounds heavier, all muscle. His meaty neck and shoulders were well defined. After years of lifting weights and playing football, he was already muscular, but when he returned, he looked unreal. He looked as if he could squeeze the life out of anyone and anything with an easy grip. The military gods had

quickly sculpted this mortal into a titan, a warrior, a killing machine. Titans ruled the earth in ancient times, and my brother was indoctrinated into thinking he would rule this earth in battle.

After the party guests left, only Curt remained with my father and my two uncles, Ray and Diego. My uncle Diego was a Korean War vet who had received a Purple Heart. He often showed me his bullet scar on his lower left hip whenever he was drunk. "That fucking sniper was a bad shot. Heck, I was only 150 meters away, and all he did was hit me in the hip. Fuck you, Commie *puto*…"

Curt said, "Tio Diego, you got shot in the butt."

"The hip, mijo, the hip."

"The hip…the butt…the *nalgas*…your brown ass…tomato tomahto…" Laughter.

Because of the injury, he walked with a slight limp that made him look kind of funny when he danced Mexican cumbias, dragging one leg, which threw off my *tia*'s dancing opposite him. His wounded hip locked into position facing outward, as if he were going to kick a football, and he danced in circles, sometimes stopping before the end of the song because he got dizzy.

But he was proud of the injured hip.

Opinionated, bigoted, and profane, he was still my favorite uncle. He gave me the strange nickname of Nikita, after the Russian Nikita Khrushchev, telling me I looked like Khrushchev when I was a baby: a large head, a white round face, and a permanent scowl. I grew up to hate Khrushchev, partly because he was a political tyrant but also because of that nickname.

They were huddled outside the backyard of our house on rickety wooden chairs in the early morning, and I could hear their hushed conversations as I peeked through my bedroom window. The morning sun would greet us in two hours, and the western breeze smelled moist. Adhering to an unwritten code that I could not be privy to these discussions, they were sitting on old patio chairs, smoking plump cigars and drinking cold beers.

"Those damn Dodgers better come through this year. Koufax and the Big D can't be beat this year. They just need more hitting." My father looked worried. He had followed the Dodgers since they came out to Los Angeles. One of the best nights of my life was when he took me to Dodger

Stadium the year before to see Koufax pitch against the Phillies. I wanted his autograph but never got it—only Jim Lefebvre's and Wes Parker's. My father always said Koufax had the "left arm of God."

My uncle Diego was stationed for a while in the Presidio in San Francisco and became a Giants fan. He tried his best not to start an argument in a house full of Dodger fanatics. He poked at my father: "Shit, Mays and Marichal will take care of business this year. Your Dodgers can't hit. That chubby kid Fairly's all they got…Wes Parker's OK. Hey, Nikita, I know you're there, mijo. Get me a *pinche* beer!"

I quickly went to the kitchen, returned with the cold bottles, and resumed my eavesdropping through the window screen.

"Diego, you're full of shit. When Koufax and the Big D pitch, all they need is one pinche run to win. Maury Wills can steal your fucking brown underwear while you still wear it, *baboso*. He'll score one hundred runs. Fuck you…" Muffled laughter.

"All right, *cabron*, a bet here and now. If the Dodgers win the pennant, you take me out to dinner in Hollywood. If the Giants win the pennant, you take me to San Francisco."

Uncle Diego blurted out, "Damn, that Ann-Margret is good looking. Shit, I wish I could meet her."

My dad joined in: "Then what? You wouldn't know what to do with her."

"You know, in Korea, I saw her with Bob Hope at a USO show. Damn, she looked good. She had this tight sweater on, and she could also sing. Jane Russel was also there. *Mamacitas…*"

Someone whispered, "Damn, they're both *buenotas…*"

My uncle Diego continued. "You know, it's funny, but in Korea, the soldiers named two mountains after Jane Russel. I don't think we ever bombed those fucking mountains…sacred pair…the military declared a no-fly zone over those pinche chi chis…"

Laughter. My nana only shook her head and puffed her cigarette.

"You men only think with your huevos! Ay…" My nana was rolling her cigarettes as she had done since she was fifteen. Her raspy cigarette voice sounded like a rusty tuba. A cold beer was waiting next to her. She did not like baseball and ignored their rantings about the Dodgers and Giants that had gone on for years. The dexterity Nana exhibited with her hands when she rolled her cigarettes belied her advanced age of sixty-eight.

"Ma, those damn cigarettes smell worse than these cigars—" Before my uncle Diego finished the last syllable, he was quickly whacked on the side of the head by my nana's right palm. Her palm had developed a thick patina of calluses after working hard every single day during most of her sixty-eight years on this earth, and the jolt felt like a wet, leathery baseball glove on my uncle Diego's head. "Damn, Ma, that hurts…you know? Ma, you got quick hands, pretty good jab, like Cassius Clay. Ma floats like a butterfly and stings like a beech!"

(Laughter.) I even laughed out loud at that one.

"That'll show you, *baboso*. Don't make fun of these cigarettes. I love them…almost as much as I loved your father. Show respect for your mother, or you'll get another sting, cabron."

Curt chimed in with a serious tone. "Dad, I'm scared. But we'll beat those Vietnamese. We're better trained with better equipment. They say we'll be out of there in a couple of years."

The others quietly nodded in unison.

My uncle Diego blurted, "Hey, Curt, whaddaya gonna say when you confront your first Viet Cong?"

Curt quickly chugged his beer and stood up with theatrical flair. "Mr. Victor Charlie, Mr. V fucking C, I'm a fucking Green Beret, and I've been trained to kill my enemy one hundred different ways. So…pick yo numba, muthafucka! Haha." Curt slurred his words as he tossed another empty bottle out into the yard. My uncles and nana laughed for a few seconds, and my father giggled quietly.

My father, with a subdued voice, said, "Mijo, keep your head down. Listen to those guys with experience, trust all your training, and come back safe…safe."

"Hell, we should have thrown the A-bomb at those funking chinks in Korea, but our president didn't have the balls like MacArthur told him. We won't let the same thing happen again this time in Vietnam," said my uncle Diego. "Just kill as many of those chinks as you can, and kill a couple of the fuckers for me, all right?" His eyes lit up as if he were in another place, in another time.

"Tio Diego, damn. We're here in Allen County, not near the thirty-eighth parallel," Curt interjected. "The nearest Chino is at Sam's Restaurant, and I think he's pretty safe except for that shit he calls kung pao chicken. That'll kick your huevos harder than some fucking North Korean. Probably harder than getting shot in the ass."

Laughter.

My grandma took a deep drag from her cigarette and said, "Why do those Chinos hate our family? They tried to kill your father in Okimammma—"

More laughter. "That's Okinawa, Momma. And they were Japs I was fighting, not Chinos."

"Okimmmmaaaaammmmmaa, don't interrupt your mother. Then the pinche Chinos tried to kill my other son, Diego, and almost did over there in Korea…shooting him in the ass."

"Those were North Koreans and Chinos, ma. And it was my hip… not my ass," said my uncle Diego, now more reserved as he tried not to interrupt my grandma, massaging his head. He moved beyond her reach.

"Now they gonna wanna kill my little Curt, Chinos *cabrones*…"

"Nana, they are Vietnamese and Viet Cong."

"Viet what? Cong, Bong, Fong, I don't care! They're still pinche Chinos," my nana retorted, slowly blowing smoke out of the left side of her mouth. "And they still are gonna wanna kill you. You better come back!" She began to cry softly, embarrassed.

The gentle laughter slowly drifted into the cool darkness of the evening as the group briefly retreated to the quiet comfort of their thoughts. The blackness of the eastern horizon was now a light blue with orange hues, and the air was slowly warming with the approaching day. Only a few stars glittered in the sky. Shapeless clouds hovered over the western hills and headed our way.

"Listen, son. Always listen and watch the *veteranos* out there, especially when the shit gets confusing. They are the ones you will learn from. Don't do anything stupid. All those guys that never came back were heroes. You don't wanna be a hero, OK? Please come back safe. I love you, and you have always made us so proud."

"OK, Pops. I promise I'll be back." Through the soft lights of the backyard, I could see both had tears slowly crawling down their cheeks. The only other time I saw my pop cry was the day they shot Bobby Kennedy.

My father interrupted, giggling, "Hey, watch this…OK, Curt, you ready?"

"Yeah, Pops."

Just then, my father and brother began their pre-rehearsed parody of an old Italian organ grinder with an imaginary pet monkey dancing to the organ music. My father played the part of the Italian, and Curt, of course, played the monkey's role, hobbling on all fours, grabbing his armpits, and scratching his privates. Watching a dancing monkey with a cigar wearing a polished Green Beret uniform was one of the funniest things I'd ever seen in my life. My uncles were rolling on the ground, laughing with their cigars. My nana started spilling beer all over Curt, the monkey, laughing hysterically. I think my uncle Ray even peed in his pants. Within the hour, they fell asleep on the cool lawn of our backyard under the protective canopy of the grand mesquite tree, the shimmering stars, and the misty sky above.

Fifty years later, I think about that funny incident in our backyard through the eyes of an adult. My father survived the savagery of World War II in the Pacific. Unlike most of us who never experienced combat, my father knew what Curt would ultimately experience in Vietnam and that Curt, if he returned, would never be the same inside…deep inside. I know my father was never the same after sustaining intense levels of brutal warfare, and his friends who returned from World War II were never the same. At that moment, in the backyard, I'm sure his paternal instinct was to grab Curt—his son, his blood, his skin, his hair—and beg him to not go and to stay there in our backyard, where it was home, where it was warm, and where it was safe.

Yet my father never discouraged him from going. In that poignant moment, my father proudly shared a cigar with him in that backyard as they joyfully danced to the songs and parodies of the old Italian grinder and his trained monkey in the park. All under the paternal protection of the old mesquite tree.

■ ■ ■

From the *Sonora Desert Review*, June 13, 1966:
Thirty men were rounded up last night after local and federal police responded to reports of illegal cockfights at a farm in the north end of the county. Sheriff Bob Johnson vowed to clean up this illegal activity, but "these Mexicans just can't stop what has been here for generations…it's deep in their culture."

■ ■ ■

"Ladies and gentlemen, please rise. Allen County Superior Court, Department Fifteen is now in session. The honorable Judge Timothy James Gates is presiding."

Judge Gates was imposing as he slowly approached the bench in all his regal splendor, panning the audience before him, soaking in the spotlight. He was like a Roman king slowly climbing his throne in the Roman Forum before his terrified subjects of Allen County. With his giant paws, he motioned the audience to resume their seats. The courtroom was packed, and several observers mingled outside in the hallways, trying to see and listen to the legal proceedings. The homicide case was one of the most significant cases in county history. Even some news outlets from Los Angeles and San Francisco had reporters in court.

"Mr. Stein and Mr. Speck, good morning. Let's call the case of People v. Thomas King, Case F-2387…Counsel, where's your client? How long do you expect me to wait? It's nine fifteen."

"Judge, probably quite a long time. My client is…dead." Stein let that sentence slowly linger in the packed courtroom to dramatize the moment. Once the drama of the last sentence settled like a waft of heavy fog, Stein continued. "Apparently, according to the sheriff's office, he committed suicide early this morning before breakfast. Regrettably, he never even touched his powdered eggs with moldy biscuits and stale waffles. The transportation unit found him in his cell with his wrist slashed." Stein spoke in a monotonous tone for effect. The savvy lawyer was composed and under control. His face registered nothing except the professional stoicism that was his trademark as a fine trial attorney—cool and detached, as if he were only a casual observer looking from afar. He glanced across the counsel table to Speck, who nervously peered down at his briefcase, and he began to clutch it tightly like a child with their blanket. "He probably should have been on a suicide watch. But I guess you need to ask the good sheriff of Allen County."

"Mr. Speck, what do you know about this?"

DDA Speck's voice shifted a few octaves upward whenever he was about to lose control. He went from a baritone to a soprano anytime he felt his testicles metaphorically squeezed, and Judge Gates was grabbing them with all his might. "Your Honor, this is the first time I've heard this. It does not matter—"

"What? What are you talking about, counsel? 'It does not matter.' You normally need a live guy to try, don't you? Mr. Stein here might have a hard time conferring with his client. How's he gonna do that? Through a court-appointed medium?"

Subdued giggles in the audience. Stein remained stoic, but he actually enjoyed the absurd colloquy that was quickly unfolding inside. The theater of the absurd was now in session.

"Your Honor, with all due respect…" Speck's voice continued to rise to unprecedented octaves that only dolphins could hear.

Now the judge was playing to the audience. They were not merely court observers; they were registered voters who enjoyed this circus. And Judge Gates wanted to turn this deputy district attorney into his court jester. Stein envisioned him in a colorful uniform with a pointy hat and bells. "Why is it that any time an attorney precedes his statement with 'all due respect,' it usually means the opposite? He really means 'with all undue respect,' don't you?"

"No, sir. With the utmost respect to this court, we can still try Mr. King in absentia. There is certainly precedence for this, and there is a principle involved, and the prosecution feels—"

Judge Gates had heard enough. He rolled his eyes and waved his right hand dismissively to the prosecutor, kindly directing him to shut up. "Let's go in chambers, counsel, and I need Sheriff Johnson in here immediately."

The five bailiffs in court bobbed their heads in unison to the court. "Yes, sir, will do…"

An hour later, Judge Gates was in his chambers along with Stein, Speck, and Sheriff Johnson. "Well, Bob, what happened to my defendant?"

Big Bob appeared nervous and always felt uncomfortable with Judge Gates. Big Bob had been extracted from the safe confines of his comfortable world and forced into this hostile environment. Surrounded by three lawyers, he felt claustrophobic. Fuckin' lawyers, he thought. Even a wild bear is intimidated if he's out of the wild. Big Bob rose and addressed the court with unusual deference. "Judge, Mr. King was on suicide watch. Sometime this morning, he apparently got hold of a razor and slashed his wrist. He must have bled out within ten minutes, from the looks of it. Pretty bad…

"There's absolutely nothing our deputies could have done. If someone really wants to kill himself, like this gentleman, then they will always find a way." Big Bob rested his case and thought there was nothing else to explain. He slowly sat down, satisfied that his compelling argument would mollify the concerns of all.

Stein sat back, crossed his legs comfortably on the leather couch, and said, "Looks like you guys messed up, Sheriff. Who was guarding him? Barney Fife and Otis? Shit."

"You little Jew bastard." Big Bob's mind could not quickly think of any clever riposte except the standard anti-Semitic epithets. He thought that was better than the classic "fuck you." But his limited repertoire of insults couldn't go further. Sheriff Johnson's hatred of Stein was not just based on anti-Semitism. It ran deeper, deep in the core of the sheriff's heart, and was almost primal.

Stein didn't react, nor did he even make eye contact with Big Bob, which made the sheriff feel even more disrespected.

The judge interceded to regain control. "Now, now, gentlemen. Bob, I don't appreciate the anti-Semitism, and it doesn't add anything to the conversation. Damn, Bob, didn't your dad fight the Nazis?"

Big Bob lowered his head slightly and muttered with half-assed sincerity, "Sorry, counsel."

Stein said nothing and nodded his head.

Speck said, "Your Honor, getting back to my previous comment. We can still try Mr. King in absentia. It is the principle of law we are trying to uphold, and I think the law enforcement community will support this." He peeked at Big Bob, who looked befuddled.

"In absentia?" asked the sheriff to no one in particular.

"Sheriff, that means they want to spend our precious court time and resources to convict a dead guy."

"Oh really? Can they do that? A dead guy…what's the point?" Sheriff

Johnson failed to understand the strange vagaries of the law the more he dealt with lawyers and judges. Fuckin' lawyers. The good sheriff despised lawyers. They spoke in their own code and thought themselves above it all with their own language, their own sense of humor, and their own codes of behavior, all of which were anathema to Big Bob. They spoke in acronyms and numbers.

"The 187 with the tail enhancement is what we're looking at."

"The defendant is not NGI, and the GBI is still solid with this 245."

"The writ on the habeas is frivolous."

Fucking lawyers. They all think they are above it all.

Stein broke in. "This is absurd. We have three dead people. Let the thing rest. Your Honor, if you let this case proceed in absentia, I can assure you that it will be appealed until the end of time. And I don't think you want the name Judge Gates next to the word 'reversed' in an appellate opinion."

Big Bob thought, What the Sam Hill is in absentia?

Judge Gates slightly nodded in tacit agreement. "Listen, Mr. Speck. I have no doubt your intentions are rather noble. And frankly, I wouldn't be surprised if your boss is pandering for some cheap publicity. I've been known to pander here and there. Election time is coming. We have several major news outlets covering this thing.

"What I do know is that I doubt this case will even get past a preliminary hearing. Mr. Stein here is just itching to try a goofy case like this that might actually get the attention of our Supreme Court because he wants to return to his precious San Francisco, and this might be the case that's his springboard out of this backwater court. I don't see Stein disagreeing with me, as offensive as I might sound. Right now, he can just smell the San Francisco Bay, and he actually hears the fucking cable cars. This case is his ticket back to the real courts of San Francisco and his goddamn radical buddies up there.

"However, if your office proceeds with this case against a dead guy, the only thing IN ABSENTIA might be your boss's name next to the title

Allen County District Attorney after the next election, which, incidentally, is in two years. Metaphorically speaking, the voters might see your boss committing necrophilia—screwing with a dead guy. By the time this case is barely at the initial appellate stage, the voters will understand the monetary cost of this frivolous venture."

"Sir, I respect your comments and the candid nature of your position. I do take offense to your vulgar comments, for the record. I will certainly convey this message, in no uncertain terms, to the district attorney, and I will get back to you. I think he will see it your way."

"Good. Now I want you three to go outside the court once the case is dismissed and make a joint message to the news. Perhaps Mr. Stein could craft a prepared statement that you can all live with. Good day, gentlemen.

"And, Sheriff Johnson, you can leave unless there's anything more. Thank you."

Fuckin' lawyers…necrophilia?

Part Six

IN THE BEGINNING

Allen County was created in the nineteenth century by the sheer will, sweat, and blood of the farmers, ranchers, and working families who settled the area. Okies, Mexicans, Filipinos, Chinese, Italians, Portuguese, Swiss, southern Blacks, hustlers, and cattle thieves all created this area in the southern end of California, changing it from a bleak wasteland to one of the richest farmlands in the world. Anything and everything grows in Allen County twelve months out of the year because of the mild winters. Centuries ago, the valley was a sea, and when it dried over the ages, it left a rich deposit of silt perfect for farming.

Those who settled the county must have been either geniuses or lunatics, but they converted a large wasteland of desert into a rich farmland once they were able to tap into the Colorado River, which bordered the east end of the valley. Once the river was controlled through the massive construction projects dam building, it was meekly tamed by the early 1900s. But the miracle that was the Allen Valley came at a high cost. Many workers perished due to sweltering heat, diseases, construction accidents, and just plain foolishness and negligence.

When I was about five, my nana took me to an area in the south end of the valley near the Mexican border. At first, I thought it was a vacant lot with nothing more than dry shrubs and desert rocks. As I approached the land, I realized I was looking at gravestones with names such as Bill Jones, Casey Holliday—and Pedro Mendoza, my grandpa.

My grandmother was mesmerized by my grandpa's gravestone and told me, "This is where they would bury most of the workers who died building the canals. There are so many here, but this is where they belong." The cemetery was surrounded by fresh-picked fields of tomato and sugar beets; the fresh soil was still thirsty for the next crop. I stood there alongside my grandmother that warm spring day as she quietly spoke to my grandpa.

"Here lies Pedro Mendoza. Devoted father and husband. He will never be forgotten. RIP.

"Born: May 28, 1896, Pecos, TEX.

"Died: July 12, 1947, Allen County California."

The valley was named after James Allen, who settled here in 1890 and developed it. Legend has it that when James Allen traveled from the California coast, crossed the Guadalupe Mountains, and first saw Allen Valley—an untamed low desert with wildflowers blooming forever to the eastern horizon—he said to his wife, "this is the warm side of paradise, and this is where we'll live." He failed to see a bleak wilderness and envisioned a thriving paradise where he could build an empire. Where others saw an arid chimera, Allen saw a thriving bounty.

Originally from Italy, the Allen family name was actually Alliso, but it was Americanized to Allen when the family landed in New York City. His family is iconic in this county. My father always said good things about the Allen family since they "were from the earth and not afraid to build with their hands." He eventually purchased twenty thousand acres of what became the best farmland in this county and, in the early 1900s, expanded his empire to include ranching, radio, banking, and several other business ventures that always made a profit—the Midas touch. Considered an engineering genius, James Allen diverted water into the valley through a complicated maze of rivers, dams, and man-made canals. He was considered one of the richest men in the country by the 1930s and even made money during the Depression through some shady business dealings in San Francisco and the pueblo of Los Angeles. Most of the farmland he acquired ran parallel to the complicated canal system that siphoned precious water from the vast Colorado River. Thus, the Allen land owned the water rights to the land—water that was shared with other states of the west.

Eventually, Allen Farms cultivated over five hundred thousand acres of the nation's richest farmland. And the county became one of the major suppliers of sugar beets, tomatoes, broccoli, lettuce, carrots, and okra in the US. As the West Coast became more populated in the early twentieth century, the demand for the valley's crops was exceeded by the demand for the water itself. Los Angeles had already begun to tap into Owens Valley water early in the century, but it was not enough to quench the selfish thirst of the major cities along the coast. And James Allen owned the rights to hundreds of thousands of acre-feet of water—clear liquid gold. He controlled the spigots. Those spigots gave farmers 90 percent of the Colorado water plus 10 percent for the municipalities. Thus, Allen could squeeze the farming community, and he carried a great deal of weight in local government. James Allen had the best land, the best water rights, and the best lawyers.

The Allens clashed with other farmers in the valley who had played an important role in its development. Mobsters clashed over territory and the grafts within. Gangs clashed over neighborhoods. But with no less ferocity, the six original farming families clashed over farmland, crop prices, land boundaries, and contracts that were often sealed with a handshake. There were lawsuits, shootings, arson, vandalism, petty personal vendettas. But they all prospered together. The five other families were part of the original six who toiled for decades to bring agriculture to the valley. But James Allen was by far the smartest, the most tenacious, and the most successful. And for that he was resented by the other five families, resentment that passed to other generations. James Allen often felt surrounded, but the arrows flung his way never found the target. He was just too smart.

Allen was also generous. The water he sold to farmers was priced reasonably. He recognized the delicate symbiosis that was created between the six families, and he always tried to collaborate with other farming families when they shared mutual interests. Allen money funded scholarships for the local high schools. He was instrumental in building football stadiums for the high school as well as gymnasiums. He was generous at the yearly agricultural fair. He supported most charitable groups in the valley. It was hard to dislike James Allen. But some did.

Even though he could have lived anywhere in the country, he remained in this county his entire life, with homes in Monterey and La Jolla, California. He married a local girl, a quiet Swiss named Gabriela Andersmith who died after bearing his only child, James Jr.—Jimmy—in 1928. The elder Allen later remarried, but he often said later in his life that there was no human being on this earth better than "my Gabriela."

Little Jimmy grew up in this county, and his father made sure that the family riches didn't spoil him. Even though the schools in the valley were partially segregated, Jimmy went for a few years to the Mexican and Negro elementary schools and developed an affinity with the poor families of the valley—many who had also developed the valley without the benefit of its spoils and largesse. Jimmy was required to work in the fields picking tomatoes, lettuce, okra, and melons alongside the Mexicans, Filipinos, Okies, and Blacks. He ate with them, laughed with them, and sometimes cried with them.

He eventually went to Stanford to study business. Even though he could have gone into any business anywhere within his father's empire, he chose to return to the valley and learn the family business, much to the delight of the elder Allen.

With his sterling education, he could also speak Latin, Italian, French, and the Spanish variation unique to the Allen Valley. He took over the family business after his father suddenly died. Jimmy remained on the family farm on the west end of the valley, along the foothills of the Guadalupe Mountains. This was near where the elder Allen first laid eyes on the valley and its stark beauty.

Their farm was comfortable but lacked the overt pretensions of a nouveau riche family. It was about four thousand square feet, two story, hacienda style, and constructed of the rich orange flagstone found nearby in the Guadalupes and strong mountain oak. From a distance, the home blended into the brown landscape, as if it had been there since the millennium—an old remnant of an earlier time before the land faced the inexorable conquest of man. The elder Allen personally supervised its construction and even had some local masons prepare the rich Saltillo tile that flowed throughout the interior floor. Italian artisans created the intricate woodwork in the interior: rich ceiling beams, aged oak trim throughout, and interior doors. My father would occasionally brag about how my grandfather helped attach the huge oak frames and stucco walls in the home. Mexican artists finished the project sometime in 1920 with vibrant wall frescos throughout the interior walls. Slightly looking eastward, the farm, which sat on a small bluff, offered panoramic and dramatic views of the beautiful desert vistas, the same view that had enamored the elder Allen.

The histories of the Allen and Mendoza families ran along parallel roads. Those roads would eventually meet at a violent intersection.

■ ■ ■

From the *Sonora Desert Review*, July 13, 1966:
In a stunning development yesterday, the district attorney dismissed the homicide case against Thomas King. Mr. King was charged with vehicular felony homicide in an incident that took the lives of a local family last year. While awaiting trial,

he apparently committed suicide in the Allen County Jail.

Deputy District Attorney Dennis Speck made the surprising announcement today before Judge Gates at the courthouse. Speck added that "the district attorney's office, after due consideration, feels that this is the only viable option for us to pursue. Our thoughts and prayers are with the Lewis family."

When asked to comment about the suicide in his jail, Sheriff Johnson said the following to this newspaper: "This is just the end of another sad chapter to this case. I guess Mr. King just could not stand the stress of spending all those years in prison. He was just scared. Like John Wayne said, 'All battles are fought by scared men who'd rather be someplace else.' And I guess he is now someplace else."

■ ■ ■

"Let's get back to LA!"

Kenny Roberts and his girlfriend, Debbie, were exhausted. But after their harrowing experience, they were also relieved. After crossing the US-Mexico border, they wanted to get on their knees and kiss the sanctified land of America. Their trip was a success. They had scored three kilos of high-grade, seedless marijuana ("Sinaloa's best!"), now safely tucked away under Debbie's tight jeans, and were headed back to USC where a growing number of student customers eagerly awaited them in the fraternities and dorms.

Their Mexican connection assured them that it "was good stuff" from Sinaloa, and they were getting a good deal after some haggling. They had taken $1,000, not knowing the exact price, and the final deal was $650. Crossing the international port of entry was smooth since the customs officer kept his eyes on Debbie and spent most of his time flirting with her, oblivious to the large bulge of leafy contraband pressed against her buttocks. He waved them through with a wry smile. After the pot was broken up into smaller amounts, the yield would give them a nice profit, although coming from upper-crust families, they didn't need the money as much as the adventure.

Cruising along Highway 10, parallel to the US-Mexico border, in Ken's 1965 Mustang convertible, they both felt a lonely sensation on that desolate road. They had passed few cars once they left the small border town of Rockwood, fifteen miles back. Debbie rolled one of the joints, and both took deep hits.

"This is good shit," said Kenny with a smirk.

Debbie giggled and nodded, agreeing. The Rolling Stones blasted from the radio as the pot kicked in, and they relaxed. With hungry eyes, Ken looked at his girlfriend next to him, falling asleep. Her simple attire increased his desire: tight jeans that revealed all her body's contours, a tight tank top with flowers and a peace sign, and Mexican sandals she had just bought. Soon they would be back at their apartment near USC, and he would devour her.

Debbie dozed off after she placed the marijuana under the seat. Leaving Allen County, they would shortly arrive in LA, back to civilization, Hollywood, glamour, college, football games, and frat beer keggers. Maybe a few cold beers at Santa Monica beach with Debbie's sorority sisters.

Ken began dozing but was blinded by the fast-approaching vehicle in his rearview mirror. He thought it was a sedan and thought he could discern something on the roof of the car. Without any moonlight, the highway was swallowed up in thick blackness, and the dark road merged with the black horizon. The twinkling stars offered no light.

The car tailed them for about a mile, then its red lights flashed like an alarm.

"Oh shit," he mumbled to Debbie. "Get up and hide the pot. Cops."

Debbie lethargically grabbed the three kilos and pushed it deeper under her bucket seat. She instinctively put the joint in the ashtray, forgetting to snuff it. With the top down, the cop probably wouldn't smell it.

Ken slowly pulled to the side of the dark road and felt a growing knot in his stomach. His mouth dried up, and his throat tightened. Uh-oh, we're busted, he thought. As he turned off his headlights, he realized just how dark it was out there in the middle of the desert. A hungry coyote howled somewhere in the dark, answered by a nervous owl hooting far in the distance. The cop car behind him blinded him with a large spotlight. As the sedan slowly parked behind him, Ken's eyes adjusted, and he could make out the words "Allen County Sheriff" on the side along with the motto To serve and protect the public.

For what seemed a long minute, no one emerged from the cop car, as Ken looked anxiously in his rearview mirror. Shit, maybe I was going a little fast—maybe sixty-five miles per hour. But he began to relax as he thought, I'll just talk to this hick cop and, at worst, pay the fine and send it back to this crappy place. It can't be that much.

A silhouette slowly emerged from the cop car, and Ken could see he was smoking a plump cigar. It was odd that this sheriff was not wearing normal cop clothes but wore all black: a large, black Stetson, tight black jeans, an open-collar shirt, and black boots of some unknown reptile. The revolver dangling from his holster looked disproportionately large compared to the rest of him. Finally, as the Barney Fife-ish cop approached, Ken could read "Big Bob" on his silver belt buckle.

Debbie, feeling the effects of the pot, whispered to him, and giggled. "He kind of looks like Yosemite Sam."

Ken slapped her knee.

"Son, you were driving pretty fast in this bitchin' car, don't ya think?"

The word "son" had no paternal overtones as far as Kenny was concerned. "Son" sounded more primal, mean, and angry. That was what this cop meant. He wanted to let Ken know who was in control out there in the desert.

"Yes, officer, possibly, but we saw no other vehicles on the road, so I thought it might be safe to drive at that speed."

As the sheriff poked his head into the car, he glanced around as if looking for something—even ignoring Ken's good-looking girlfriend. "Let me see your license, son, and where you two coming from?" The cop made Kenny nervous because he seemed in no rush to go anywhere, as if he had all the time in the world, and they were out here in the middle of fucking nowhere just shootin' the bull.

Debbie lazily smiled at "Big Bob" as she adjusted her tight shirt and pulled her jeans up past her hips. Big Bob noticed her more, and Kenny thought that was a good sign.

Big Bob also noticed the half joint in the ashtray and grabbed it, never taking his eyes off the young girl. In one smooth motion, he lit the joint from his Cuban cigar and took a deep hit with his right thumb and index finger. He inched closer to Ken and exhaled the marijuana in his face. "That's mighty good shit, son." Big Bob lightly stroked Kenny's thick sideburns and shoulder-length hair. Ken nervously stroked the love beads around his neck as if he didn't know what to do with his hands. The young couple exchanged frightened glances.

As Big Bob looked at them, he asked, "You two aren't Commie college students, are you? Those fucking kids burning the flag, rioting, and shit. It's disgraceful to our way of life. My dad didn't fight in North Africa for this shit. Son, you should have gotten a haircut while you were in Mexico, and a nice shave too. Those Mexican barbers are the best. I got this large buck knife in my holster here—it might do just the trick." He took another deep hit.

"We just went across to Mexico to check it out. We've never been there, and we thought it would be fun. By the way, officer, what was the probable cause for this stop?"

"'Probable cause.' One of those lawyer words I always hear. 'Probable cause.'"

"I took a prelaw class at USC."

"Son, probable cause is what I say it is. Maybe excessive speed. Maybe you were weaving. Hell, maybe I saw you grabbing your girlfriend's titties—must be some violation I can find in that penal code. 'Grabbing a girl's titties while driving.' That's under California Penal Code I-don't-give-a-fuck. You see, son, the California Penal Code is like the Bible—you can cherry-pick anything in there to justify my conduct. I'll figure out probable cause eventually.

"I don't see any souvenirs. You know what I like, son? I like those ceramic Mexican mariachis they sell; I even have one in my office. You know the set of seven fat Mexicans having a good old time singing, along with that one fat Mexican bitch?"

Kenny could feel perspiration under his armpits, and the dryness inside his mouth was now warm and raw. His stomach turned into a tighter knot and felt warm.

"Yeah, I saw those. They looked cool, officer. But we didn't buy any souvenirs. We just wanted to look. We ate a few tacos and had some cold beers, nothing more officer. We can't afford much."

"By the looks of this nice '65, I doubt it. Wow, I like those bitchin' racing stripes on this baby. How much horsepower ya got under the hood? Son, please exit the vehicle, and young lady, please get out also." The commands were stern. Big Bob was in absolute control out there, and all three knew it. This fox was just playing with the chickens before dinner.

Ken and Debbie meekly exited the car and stood along the passenger's side. Kenny checked his watch: 3:30 a.m. Big Bob conducted a cursory pat down of Kenny and slowed down with Debbie, sliding his experienced palms along her inner thighs, hips, and breasts. Kenny said nothing; Debbie began to quietly sniffle. Big Bob did not even look them in the eye.

"Officer, can't you just write me a ticket or something? Maybe we can make an arrangement."

Big Bob slowly looked him up and down and quickly slapped him hard. Ken began to fall against the car before Big Bob grabbed him.

"'Out here a man settles his own problems.'" *The Man Who Shot Liberty*

Valance. "Boy, shut the fuck up. I didn't ask you anything. Now, where's the stuff you picked up in Mexico? Should I strip this damn car? Or maybe strip your bitch over there. She looks sweet."

"What stuff? We have nothing…we told those guys at the port of entry. They checked us out already—" Before he could complete his futile responses, Big Bob punched him deep in his gut, knocking the breath out of him. Ken keeled over in front of Debbie.

"Listen, asshole. Tell me: WHERE IS THE STUFF YOU BROUGHT FROM MEXICO? I don't have all night. Do you want me to take this little slut out in the desert right now? She looks mighty fresh to me. Or I could take her back to the holding cell and let some fat Mexican have his way with her. You little shit." Big Bob then kicked him with the pointed cowboy boot like a field goal. Ken felt his left eye swollen shut and had flashes of fear in his imagination: rape, assault, or even being murdered out there in the middle of nowhere, buried until the coyotes devoured his skimpy remains. "Around here I live in the shadows of the sun. My world is in these shadows…my world. Out in these shadows, I do whatever the hell I want. Give me the stuff, son."

"Ken, just give him the stuff, man." Debbie was resigned to the inevitable. "The worst that can happen is probation and a hefty fine. Daddy will take care of it."

"Hey, Kenny, you might wanna listen to her."

Ken reached under the seat, retrieved the three kilos, and handed it to Big Bob. He held the package like a ticking time bomb. Fresh weed, sinsemilla from Sinaloa. "Can't we make a deal out here? There's just you and us, and no one will ever know."

"You're not trying to bribe me, are you?"

Rubbing his eye, Ken said, "No, sir. But there must be some room for negotiation. We've never been in trouble, believe me. And we promise never to come down here again. Trust me."

"Well, son. I'm not interested in that. I don't usually smoke that crap—

only fine Cubans. But I'm guessing that you two haggled your way into buying this contraband and probably had some excess. I would guess at least one thousand. That might make this thing go away. You keep the pot, and you can make up the difference with those fucking rich college friends of yours, anyway. Capice?"

Big Bob's eyes were slowly diverted as he saw Debbie drop her jeans below just above her ankles, revealing long tanned legs. Big Bob could feel his excitement growing under his jeans. She slowly pulled out the wad of money inside her panties below her navel and quickly offered Big Bob all of it.

"Please let us keep some for gas and food," she said demurely.

Ken finally had the courage to chime in: "Sorry, Officer. You can rest assured this won't happen again."

Big Bob said, "'Sorry won't get it done, dude'" *Rio Bravo.*

"Take as much as you want, sir. Consider it a political donation."

"Well, now that you put it that way. I guess I can't refuse your generous offer." Big Bob grabbed the money and placed it inside his reptilian boots after counting two hundred. Returning the balance to the girl, he gave her a lecherous smirk. He bowed to them and said, "It's been a pleasure. Make sure you all don't come back to these parts, cause ol' Big Bob will be waiting for you here in the shadows of the sun. And every time you turn around, expect to see me. 'Cause one time you'll turn around and I'll be there, and I'll kill you, Ken.'" *Red River.* With an effeminate gesture, Big Bob blew them a soft kiss, stuck the Cuban into his mouth, entered his vehicle, and peeled off onto Highway 10, swallowed into the blackness of the cool desert.

"Kenny, your pants are soaked with piss. Was that asshole quoting John Wayne?"

▪ ▪ ▪

From the *Sonora Desert Review*, September 30, 1966:
Rockwood Theater will be showing a double feature matinee next Saturday with *The Blue Max* and *Fantastic Voyage*. Discounts of twenty-five cents will be offered when you show a valid Rockwood High School student ID card. In addition, if you bring ten bottle caps or Pepsi or 7-Up, you will receive free entry for the afternoon matinee only.
- Surveyor 2 crashes on the moon. America's hopes of landing a man on the moon years away.
- Dodgers close to clinching National League title.

PART SEVEN

THE ORIGINAL SIX

"Do you mean to tell me that if someone dies…what's that word? 'intestate'?…with no heirs, the state of California gets dibs on that person's estate if there's no will?" Walter McCoy was dumbfounded. He was sitting in the trim panel–lined law office of Travis Robinson, Allen County's best probate attorney. Like most locals, Travis was a single practitioner who generally was ethical and hardworking, trying to scrape together enough money to pay the never-ending bills of a law practice. Originally from New York, Queens, he had moved to Allen County ten years before, after buying a law practice from one of the retiring locals. His original plan had been to sell the business for a profit and move back to the big city of Los Angeles, San Francisco, or back home. After two years, he began to love it, except for the brutal summers. He married a local girl, raised a large family, and never doubted his decision. He was as good as any lawyer in any city.

"Yup. That's right. The term is 'escheat.' The state gets all unclaimed property." Robinson spoke with animation; he loved the esoteric subject of probate law, something he wanted to practice halfway through law school.

It was a rather lonely area of practice with lots of "paper pushing," in the provincial vernacular of other probate attorneys.

In common law, a person who died without any will gave that property to the king. Today, they give it to the government. Why the sudden interest in probate, Walt? No one in your family has died."

"Well, you know, I just wanna be prepared for the future. Mildred and I are preparing our estate. Let me ask you another question, and I'll make it quick because I know how busy you are." Walt knew that wasn't true.

"OK, what is it you want to know?"

"If someone dies and does leave more than one will, how do they know which one is going to go through probate? Let's use, for example, the will and trust of Jim Allen Sr."

"That's an easy one. The last in time supersedes all others. That is, a person can make a will and then subsequently modify it through a codicil. Assuming the codicil is valid, the last codicil would be the one recognized. Sometimes the second codicil can simply supplement the first, or it can replace it en toto."

"What happens when there's a will, but it's lost?"

"In the vernacular of our business, those are referred to as 'lost will' cases. In some situations, a copy is admissible if you can authenticate its validity in terms of the parties' signatures and witnesses.

"Here's the chain of scenarios in a nutshell: (a) if there's a will, it is probated; (b) if there are no wills at all, the guy is deemed to die 'intestate,' and it goes to next of kin, whoever is closer to the deceased; (c) if there is no kin, then to the state it will escheat."

"So, hypothetically, if no will and no kin, then the state gets it?"

"Yup. Now, hypothetically, if Jimmy Allen Jr. had a codicil, a second will, and it was not found, then the law presumes he intended to destroy it. If someone can produce a copy, it might be valid if the person can prove that the testator, Allen, had no intent to destroy it. One of the caveats is that the person who wants to claim the copy is good must produce the copy or, of course, the original within one year after death. If not, then the original will, Allen Sr.'s, would be the controlling will or trust. I heard that Jimmy Allen Jr. retained the right to modify the terms of the first trust that his father prepared—just rumors. What's this, Walt? A bar exam?"

"I see...how much do you know about Jim Allen's estate?"

"What do you mean?" asked Robinson, curious, sitting up in his soft leather chair.

"Well...does he have a will, or are all his holdings in trust or something?"

"That's a good question. As you know, his family's legal affairs are handled by a prestigious law firm in San Francisco, one of the best. I assume they prepared his estate, as they did for Mr. Allen's father.

"These are only rumors, but I hear that in the Allen Trust II, Jimmy Jr. will bequeath all his holdings and estate to charity in the form of a philanthropic foundation. I'm sure it's all taken care of. So it boils down to this: Allen Trust I, the five families get half of a multimillion-dollar estate, and the rest goes to charity. Allen Trust II, if it's legally valid, the five families don't get shit. Nada."

"Nada of a million dollars is a lot. Well, thank you, Travis. I'll see you next week at our Elks meeting." McCoy rose from the chair, stretched, and walked to the door.

"Wait...since you are so interested in the Allen estate, there's one other interesting thing about his holdings. When the elder Allen prepared all these complicated water agreements with both the state of California and the federal government, he inserted a provision that, before the estate goes to a philanthropic trust, all the original five farming families would be given priority to bid on the estate, including any water rights, mineral rights, etc. The five families could bid on half of the Allen estate, and the rest would be distributed to philanthropy. The elder Allen wanted his local brethren to get the first crack at the lucrative holdings before the government intervened. The old man was old school and never trusted the federal or state government.

"Ya gotta understand that when these agreements were made with the federal and state governments, there weren't too many people living on the coast like today. The government thought the elder Allen was a crackpot anyway, and they did not believe that these agreements amounted to anything.

"Unlike Mr. Allen, the government could not envision what water rights would mean in the context of the future development of California." Robinson was animated.

"OK, I'm not too quick with all this legal stuff. But if (a) Allen Jr. dies with no heirs, and (b) there's no second trust, then (c) the original remaining five get first dibs on half the estate from the original trust?"

"Yeah, in theory. But the odds of that happening are almost nil. There has to be a harmonic convergence in the stars for that to happen, and everything has to be aligned in such a way as to make that scenario come true. Jimmy Allen Jr., despite his outward appearance, is one of the most astute businessmen you will ever meet. He got that from his father. You know that. You and the other farming families have clashed with him, as you did with his father. And I'm sure he has his codicil ironclad will under lock and key with his expensive lawyers up in the penthouse office in San Francisco."

"Any idea what that estate is worth?"

"Can't count that high."

■ ■ ■

Despite Curt's absence, 1966 was a happy year. I had all my parents' attention, played baseball, found my first love, went to the public pool, and saw the Beatles on TV. I was only casually aware of Vietnam, although my parents would always tune into the TV for any news.

I heard portions of Walter Cronkite and the evening news, but I was honestly not too interested. My dad would often change the channel when I was watching *Leave It to Beaver* or *Sky King*. The names of Vietnam and its provinces slowly entered the American lexicon: Dien Bien Phu, Saigon, Mekong Delta, and Vietcong. These names are embedded in my generation's collective memory. Westmorland. LBJ. Nixon. McNamara. Kennedy. My parents spent a great deal of time—my time—watching news about the war. Whenever there was brief footage of Vietnam, my mom would get closer to the TV to see if she could spot Curt.

One day the news covered a large battle near a place called the DMZ, and all my family silently and somberly watched the news.

"Elements of NVA engaged today with US and South Vietnamese marines along the Mekong Delta. Initial reports indicate that casualties were heavy on both sides as B-52 bombers saturated NVA positions. This is a highly contested area since it is a staging point for VC forces to engage along the Laos border. The enemies' forces concentrated their effort to dislodge American base camps offering support to elements of South Vietnamese forces. American Special Forces repelled several prolonged attacks after suffering moderate casualties…"

My nana whispered, "I know he's there. I can feel him. I can see him. Let's pray for him to come back to us…" Growing up in the sixties, I vividly remember the body counts. Every week, the news reported the number of Americans dead vis-à-vis the number of Vietnamese dead. Not unlike the baseball scores: Yankees 4, Red Sox 0. American killed 68, Vietnamese killed 590. It appeared we were winning as much as the Yankees were.

■ ■ ■

From the *Sonora Desert Review*, Nov. 11, 1966:
Letter to the editor:
I fought for this country in the big war. I want to know why we can't win this one quickly. Kennedy and Johnson said we would since we are the most powerful nation on earth, and we are only fighting a backward race of people—the so-called

Viet Cong—who are fighting with inferior weapons, training, and experience. These kids over there don't know how to fight a war. Let's end this thing and get these boys home. Semper Fei! Signed, an impatient marine from Clarktown.

■ ■ ■

Ironically, Curt wrote to us from Vietnam more often than Hank, who was busy with his legal career. His letters were filled with vague generalities, as if he were bored. "Everything is OK here. I am safe. The food is interesting, and the country is beautiful…"In early 1967, he sent a tape, and my parents played it in front of the family and some neighbors.

"Hey, guys…I hope to see you all soon. I can't tell you where I am, but I am fine."

("Yo, tell them your bud, the Redeemer, is here. Ha-ha.")

"That was one of my buddies, Willis, who is always looking out for me…"

Shouting and soft thuds were heard in the background, and the tape went silent.

Curt's voice then returned. "Sorry, guys, I dropped the tape. Sorry for all that noise. Everything is good. Anyway, I hope to see you soon, Ma. I miss your food like crazy. You keep sending me fresh tortillas, and by the time I get them, they're hard. But you know what? I still eat them and share them with my buddies. They are sooo good, Ma. Dad, I miss you. We will have a beer soon. Hey, little buddy, I can't wait to play catch with you. How is your batting average? Are you pitching? How big are you? Send me more pictures."

More noise, grunts, then silence.

"Sorry again, guys. This damn tape is hard to manage, and it keeps falling. Tell Nana if she's there that I love her, and I always think of you guys. Nana, when I get back, you and I will smoke some of your rolled cigarettes, OK?"

Muffled laughter in the background.

My mom played the tape two more times. After, she cried to herself. My father quietly retreated to his room and closed the door. I heard the familiar sound of his private bottle of nectar pouring into a glass behind the bedroom door.

My nana only said, "Damn Chinos…"

■ ■ ■

Curt gently placed his tape recorder down. He was inside a bunker on a mountain base, and they had been receiving sporadic bursts of sniper fire and mortar rounds all morning. It usually stopped around 1100 hours. But US Special Forces, as always, held their own. The shelling and gunfire abated. After Curt emerged from his bunker, he turned to his buddy, Tony Franco, a young Chicano from south San Francisco, and asked him, "Where the hell you going?"

Franco asked him to help load some fifty-five-gallon containers in a storage area that was hit during the barrage. Curt always wanted to keep active and did not like being hunkered down in a bunker—like a sitting duck. As they approached the storage area, Curt noticed some orange-striped, fifty-five-gallon drums of liquid. Some had been hit by the mortars.

"What the hell are these?" he asked Franco.

"This is the stuff they spray around the base-camp perimeter to defoliate all the brush. After spraying this, Charlie can't hide, and Charlie can't eat. They call it Agent Orange. Give me a hand to clean up this mess, and then we can help load this crap on the choppers so they can spray. You need to protect yourself; put on some gloves.

"This stuff is all over, man. One time out in the bush, we got sprayed with the crap when the C-130s flew near Charlie's position on the perimeter."

Curt looked at the drums with curiosity.

"The Ranch Handers that spray this shit have a saying: 'Only you can prevent a forest.'"

"Yeah, that's funny," Curt said sarcastically. He looked at the liquid in the broken containers, and he thought that it looked harmless enough, kind of like the large tanks of fertilizer and pesticides he used to see back in Allen County.

Curt looked puzzled and asked, "This shit smells strong. Isn't it, like, a pesticide or something?"

"Command told us it's safe to handle, so don't worry if the shit gets on you."

Curt continued in this work detail for a few hours, loading and cleaning the Agent Orange.

"According to the military, it's safe, man; after all, if you can't trust the United States military, then who the fuck can you trust, eh?"

■ ■ ■

From the *Sonora Desert Review*, February 16, 1967:
The War Department announced that PFC Victor Gomez of Blakewood, California, Allen County, was killed while on patrol near the DMZ in South Vietnam. He leaves behind two brothers, a sister, and his parents, Hector and Delia Gomez. He was nineteen years old, in the class of 1965 at Blakewood High School. He was a member of the marching band, lettered in track and football, and vice president of the photography club. Services are pending at the Hart Mortuary.

The senior class of Westside High School has announced a bake sale this Saturday, February 20. According to Shelley Barton, senior class president, all proceeds will go to the senior prom this spring. It will be from 9 to 4 at the corner of Fourth and Peach, in front of Randy's restaurant. The theme of this year's prom is Springtime in Paris. Go Lions! And go class of '67!

■ ■ ■

Dear God:

I know I don't talk to you too much, but my nana thought I should tonight. I don't know how much you can help.

I love my brother, and I don't know if he will come back alive from the war. I know my mom and dad and nana worry about him, but they don't talk too much to me about him. I miss being around him. He's so cool and is the best big brother anyone could have. I have another brother, and he's cool too. But I think he is safe in Boston, and I don't worry about him. I just want you to protect Curt and bring him home here so he can be a part of our family again. I know that would make my mom, dad, and nana happy. I don't want him to die. Please, God, take good care of him. My parents cry about Curt when they think I can't hear. I know they always worry about him getting hurt in the war. Please talk to them also.

Also, please make sure I have a good season this year in baseball. We have a good team, and our coach always tells us to pray to you before each game, and sometimes I haven't. I promise that I will.

Well, I think that's all for now. I promise to say ten Hail Marys and ten Our Fathers before bed. And I promise to go to church more often.

Thank you, God.

■ ■ ■

A few months after Curt left for Vietnam, our family was visited by one of my father's war buddies. He arrived at our house in a light 1949 Buick Roadmaster convertible with a white top and red interior. When they spotted the gorgeous car cruising through the neighborhood, some of the neighborhood pachucos probably thought their wet dreams had come true.

Curtis Field Wellens proudly hailed from Iowa and joined the marines at seventeen after he faked his birth certificate. He saw action in the Pacific, where he met my father. They were in two campaigns together in the same squad: Tarawa and Leyte.

He sort of scared me. Mr. Wellens was short but husky, with broad forearms full of tattoos. He had a flattop haircut full of white specks. Bloated bags circled his wild-looking, bloodshot eyes like an old hound dog, but he appeared full of restless energy that he needed to burn. When he saw my father, they embraced like brothers, and my dad became misty. Since the war, they had not seen each other and had written to each other a few times. My parents were invited to his first wedding in 1947 in Iowa but could not attend.

My mom and nana cooked him a huge Mexican meal "'cause they don't make good Mexican food in fuckin' Iowa," according to Mr. Wellens. He devoured multiple helpings of enchiladas, *elotes*, beans, tortillas, rice, and flan until he could no longer eat. All this was watered down with scotch, and the scotch was watered down with beer and rum—Curtis's favorite.

Curtis was crawling through his third shaky marriage, but he maintained an excellent job selling cars at the Des Moines Buick dealership. He had refined the art of bullshit and could sell cars easily whether he was "drunk or sober, and I probably sold more drunk." As he laughed with my dad, he told him it was ironic that he was the dealership's best salesman when he didn't have a driver's license. After his fourth DUI, it was gone for a year. Suspended. But he had to work hard selling Buicks to pay off multiple alimonies "that keep coming after me like those fuckin' Japanese banzai attacks."

The sentencing judge lectured him, saying, "If you weren't a World War II vet, you'd be in jail for a whole year..."

HOORAH!

He was the source of my brother's name: my parents named him after Curtis Fields Wellens, my father's most loyal friend from the war, my brother's namesake. He was just passing through and wanted to go down to Baja California "to get away from wives three and four...and maybe look for number five..."

Later, I could see them from my bedroom window as they spent that night in the backyard under our mesquite tree laughing, crying, talking, farting, and joking. But mostly, I think they felt relieved to be together away from the Pacific. After my father finally dozed off on the patio chair around two o'clock, I went outside to pick up the empty bottles so Nana wouldn't get mad at me. Mr. Wellens was still clutching a cold beer like he was in a state of rigor mortis, seated by himself, staring out into nowhere, and I didn't want to disturb him.

"Hey, kid, come here," he told me with a shaky voice. He wiped the dry spittle with the back of his left hand. "Your dad...that man". He pointed to my father asleep next to him with spittle drooling down his chin— "that man was the best goddamn marine I ever saw...and I saw a lot...both dead and alive.

"He saved my ass out there on the islands many times, and all the guys in the squad looked up to him. Always cool when the shit went down. He... we killed a lot of Japs. Man, there were a lot. They never touched me...a lot because of your dad. I love that man." He leaned over to his side, and I thought for a moment he was slowly passing out.

Mr. Wellens slowly removed his wallet from his back pocket. "Look... here we are in Leyte. That's the only photo of us back there. I think some news photographer took it, and I got this from a war buddy of mine a few years ago."

He handed it to me. I could make out a grainy black-and-white picture of a squad of five exhausted marines. In the background were blasted palm trees, a tank, and ocean waves. Their M1s were quietly resting near them. They looked like a crew of construction workers on a lunch break. Upon a closer look, I saw the body of a dead Japanese soldier in front of the group. His contorted body looked discolored and bloated, with a gaping mouth full of rotten teeth in the center of a lifeless face looking upward. His left eye was blown out. One of the marines had his foot on the dead soldier's chest and was casually smoking a cigarette, staring right through the camera lens with a slight smirk at the corner of his mouth. He looked like he was staring directly at me.

"Kid, that's me on the far right. Damn, I was only seventeen years old then. And that's your dad standing on the dead Jap's chest…his trophy…"

■ ■ ■

Two klicks south of Phan Nem, somewhere in the Li Trang Mountains, South Vietnam, Special Forces, Fifth Special Forces Group (Recon)

Military Assistance Command, Studies and Observations Group (MACV-SOG)

0230 hours:

Curt looked up at the clear night. Through the canopy of the thick jungle, he could see the millions of stars glowing. It was nearly 0300 hours, and he was briefly resting near his base camp. He was part of a team of Special Forces conducting recon near their base camp, and their orders were not to engage but to observe. Intelligence indicated that elements of North Vietnamese regulars and Viet Cong were staging a massive attack on US Marines on Hill 521, and Curt was assigned to assess their strength.

As he looked up at the sky, he wondered if his family in Allen County could see the same stars, and his mind briefly wandered home—Mom's food, Nana's cigarettes, Pops, his buddies. He heard her sensuous whispers in the dark: "Hey, Curt. Hi, baby…You OK?" Sally's voice was unique, and she used to ask him that question when they were together. It made him feel wanted and secure. "You OK?" He would hear her in the jungle, in his dreams, in the lonely dark. A soft voice that spoke only to him, and he sought refuge and comfort in her lovely voice.

She's there in the dreams,

100

An apparition in daytime shadows,
At nights an ephemeral ghost prances…beguiling…inviting,
Wafts of her sweet hair,
In the soft winds of the mangrove forest,
Never far from his dreams,
In the limelight of the lazy afternoon,
Crying for her,
In fleeting moments of serenity,
In endless moments of despair,
He speaks to her,
Near the corner of time and space,
On the edge of sanity,
Missing her,
More than life itself,
And cannot wait for that day,
He returns to her,
Near the corner of time and space,
In the gray shadows of a cool mountain,
Together
On a soft bed of desert wildflowers.

PART EIGHT

4-F

After playing basketball all morning, we all plopped down on the bleachers.

"I'm already tired of the Beatles. The Stones—that's where it's at, man. They're so hip and groovy, nothing like Jagger and the Stones. The Young Rascals are also right on!"

"Hey, Stinky, you still an Elvis fan? He's washed up, man, and no one will ever remember him once he's dead. His songs are garbage, from the ice age…along with that chick Nancy Sinatra. Skip It over there still likes that Mexican garbage music his parents are always playing." Laughter.

"Moe, you're full of crap. You just like that shitty Black music. Aretha gives you R-E-S-P-E-C-T? Shit. Have you guys heard The Dave Clark Five or the Seekers? They're bitchin'." A few nods.

It was the end of the baseball season, my last. And 1967 was almost over, but I waited impatiently for year's end. My brothers were coming home in a few weeks, and I was hanging around playing basketball with my four best friends and Little League teammates:

Maurice "Moe" Smith: one of the few Black kids in my school who had more Mexican in him than most Mexicans.

Perry "Stinky" Coughlin: a kid who moved here from the good side of town a few years before 1967 and a heck of a baseball player. I had my first crush on his sister, but I kept it to myself.

Alonzo "Skip It" Garcia: got his nickname at an early age when he began to stutter, and he sounded like a record player playing a scratched LP that would skip. Our coach told him not to chatter in the infield because it distracted his teammates who were attempting to understand what the hell he was trying to say.

Finally, Jimmy Flores managed to avoid any nickname mainly because he was the largest kid—almost six feet and 175 pounds—in Little League and would punch anyone's lights out if they uttered any disparaging remarks about him or his friends on or off the field. He was a good friend to have. I was also afraid of him because he was one of those kids who would do unpredictable things, and I was always on edge around him. He would look through you, almost sideways with no focus, as if he were in a different place. Although he was only twelve years old, he could hit the ball as far as any high school player. We didn't lose a game that year.

We always argued about the best rock bands. I still liked the Beatles, and I thought they were the standard against which all the other bands should be measured. The Stones were on the "edge and rougher," but the Beatles' songs made us feel good.

"All those English bands are soo cool, man," Stinky interrupted. He was growing his blond hair in a mop-top style and began wearing black Beatle boots and black pants. He had seen *A Hard Day's Night* at least ten times and screamed louder than his sisters. We all thought it was a bitchin' movie. After he completed his crappy rendition of the entire *A Hard Day's Night* album, I hit him in the head with a basketball. Enough.

I asked, "Hey, Skip It, what's wrong? Are you pissed or something?"

Alonzo remained diffident throughout our elevated music conversation, looked serious, and finally blurted: "My brother fffffinally is going to...

to…to Viet…Viiiiii…iiiiieeeeetttttt…"

"Nam!" someone impatiently interjected. "V-I-E-T-N-A-M!" Laughter. Our singing stopped.

Alonzo's brother, Steve, graduated from Rockwood High the year before, in 1966, and exhausted his strenuous efforts trying to avoid the military draft, a brutal and inexorable rite of passage for young American men in the mid-1960s, at least for those who lacked the resources to avoid the process legally. Sixty days after graduation, Steve turned eighteen, and the Selective Service System called for his ticket to Vietnam. The US supply chains delivering young human fodder were ramping up. They called Steve 4-F, the classification in the draft that makes one ineligible for various reasons such as physical or mental impairment. Coincidentally, the nickname acquired a dual meaning; it also reflected his dismal academic record dating back to the third grade—both years. He usually brought home at least four Fs to parents who were resigned to the notion that their son would either go to Vietnam or would be an auto mechanic at Bob's Filling Station on Fifth Street. Changing oil, replacing batteries, and filling gas for thirty years was his future. But he was in perfect health. The supply chain had a seat reserved for him.

Avoiding the draft made him feel unpatriotic, but he wasn't deep down. He didn't understand what the war was about. The who, what, and why of Vietnam were not apparent in his mind. Like many other young boys thought, Canada might be the only option, but Steve felt Canada was the last resort. Moreover, as he eloquently put it, the "fuckin' weather is too cold. I'm a desert rat *por vida!*"

4-F became a legend in this town for his incessant and creative attempts to legally avoid the draft. He didn't want to get the college deferment since he thought he was too "dumb" to survive college and barely survived his fifth year in high school. An absence of mental acuity was one of his few observations about himself universally shared by all who knew him—parents, friends, guidance counselors, and strangers who met him for five minutes. He abandoned the college deferment idea after discovering that woodshop or auto shop were not course offerings at the local college and that he would need to take more than one class.

Steve ignored the growing crescendo of the chorus of friends, family, and neighbors who repeatedly advised him just to enlist and avoid the inevitable and questioned his patriotism. He discovered a group of antiwar doctors in LA who were treating and advising kids on how to get their medical 4-F status in order to circumvent the Vietnam fiasco. If you had high blood pressure or were obese, you could get out. A verifiable mental illness might be a way out. Patriotism and death vs. draft evasion and life. Even Steven Garcia could do that math. After confiding in his English teacher, his favorite, about his conflicting dilemma, the teacher suggested he read the classic *Catch 22*. Steve declined to do so and wondered "why the fucking teacher would recommend a fishing book to me." So, at 130 pounds, Steve was prescribed water retention pills that presumably would trigger high blood pressure, elevated pulse, and weight gain.

After two months, his stubborn weigh scale remained the same, and his blood pressure was perfect: 120/75. He could eat all day and not gain a pound, although his mom loudly wondered why he urinated too much and soaked the bed. His antiwar doctor was amazed and attributed it to 4-F's high metabolism. "There's always Canada, kid…"

Flat feet! Flat feet would get you out of the draft! After several painful attempts at jumping off his roof, his beautiful arches remained intact. A podiatrist commented later, "Those are a pair of the most beautiful feet I ever saw. Exquisite arches. Not even bone spurs!"

Utilizing the limited arsenal of options within the small confines of his cerebrum, he finally decided on one last desperate plan. The following month he went to the desert with a revolver borrowed from his father, a cold six-pack of beer, an old bottle of cheap whiskey pilfered from his parents' kitchen, and a first-aid kit with plenty of gauze. The last option was implemented: an idea simple in its design, flawed in its execution, and ultimately, tragic in its consequences.

On a cool day in the fall of 1966, 4-F began his final venture on this quixotic quest to dodge the draft. He reached the desert on the outskirts of town, and he took his girlfriend to make sure she was ready to deliver him to the hospital once he completed the task. He found a large boulder under the cool shadows of an ocotillo among desert lilies, sat down, chugged some whiskey and the six-pack, and tried to calm himself.

"Hey, 4-F—I mean, sweetheart—I don't think this is a wise idea. There has to be another way," she said with a terrified expression.

"Listen, Gloria, you don't want me coming home in a black body bag, do you? I don't look good in black. I don't even know where the hell Vietnam is. You know I didn't get a good grade in geometry."

"Geography, sweetheart…"

"I flunked that too. Shit, don't you listen? Now let's do it!" Steve pulled out the heavy revolver and carefully pointed it down at his foot. He did not want to blow off the entire foot, only enough of it to get the coveted 4-F.

His well-endowed girlfriend, Gloria, thought she could distract him and persuade 4-F not to go through with it, so she had worn her tight white miniskirt that showed enough cleavage and leg to make even a blind man squint. She could not offer many other options for him. Her logic was sound: distract the simpleton with her natural endowments, and he might abort his ingenious plan to focus on her physical attributes and his manly yearnings. Newly hatched mosquitos had longer attention spans than this dolt.

As Steve carefully aimed at his foot, he took a quick glance at her phenomenal torso and gawked. "Damn, you have nice tits…" The momentary distraction of her remarkable pair of lodestones caused the pistol to move an inch off target, and, instead of a shot to the center of his foot, the revolver completely blew off his left pinky toe.

After administering the only first aid she had learned from being a proud two-year member and vice president of the Rockwood High Future

Nurses Association, Gloria dutifully rushed 4-F to the hospital.

Two hours later, the doctor approached her in the waiting room.

"How is he?"

"Oh, I'm sure he's in a lot of pain, and the little toe is gone, vaporized. But he'll be able to walk. Hell, we don't need the small toe anyway. It's like the appendix, a useless appendage of the human body that evolution neglected to jettison."

As the evolutionary reference whizzed by her, she asked: "But will he be able to march?" The doctor quickly caught the dual meaning of her question.

"Oh, yeah…this won't fall under the ambit of '4-F,' if that's what you're asking, young lady. He can march just fine out there in Vietnam. Yup, he'll do a LOT of marching out there in Vietnam. Marching in the monsoons, marching in the hills, marching in the villages. He has beautiful high arches—and no bone spurs!" The doctor proceeded to a physicians' break room, where she could hear laughter behind the door.

Two months later, after recovering from his self-inflicted wound, 4-F enlisted in the US Army. He muttered, "Fuck it; I guess they'll get me no matter what." As he resigned from civilian life, he wondered how and when he would die in Nam. He just knew he wouldn't survive.

On February 12, 1967, while on patrol in the Qua Trang Valley near the Laotian border, 4-F, against the stern admonishments of his boot camp drill instructors, gulped two liters of mosquito-infested river water. He also did little to discourage the mosquitos from biting him. The after-action report submitted by the army failed to surmise whether 4-F's acts were simply accidents committed by a green soldier or intentional acts by a young private seeking an easy way out. Five months later, he returned to the States after being hospitalized in Hawaii for complications from malaria and was honorably discharged from the US Army. In his defense, 4-F claimed he didn't actually drink any water but "was attacked by a giant, vicious malaria-infested mosquito that drew blood."

After many frantic heavenly calls from 4-F, providence had finally answered his pleas and returned him to the world after only ten days in country. The legendary Steve "4-F" Garcia eventually returned to Allen County a Vietnam vet, married Gloria, and moved to Victoria, British Columbia, Canada, in 1970. He returned to Rockwood periodically to march in the veteran's parade, accentuating the limp on his left foot with a cane.

When asked about his missing toe, he usually brooded for a moment, then quietly responded, intentionally cryptically, "I lost it during Nam, but I don't wanna talk about it..."

His right pinky toe remained MIA, and his quest for a Purple Heart from the mosquito bite, which did—for the record—draw blood, remains pending further review by the US military.

■ ■ ■

Every Sunday after mass, I used to wait for Jimmy. As an altar boy, he usually helped the father put things away. I think Jimmy, who was naturally reticent, found solace in the church. He felt safe in church and told me he often confided in Father Fernando Roman—Father Fernie. He was popular in the congregation and was involved in helping the community. My grandmother often invited him to the house to join her in praying the rosary. He blessed Curt before he left for Vietnam.

Father Fernie oversaw the altar boys, all thirty of them. They were ten to sixteen years old, and he was their mentor, confidant, and friend. I was never interested in being an altar boy, even though some of my buddies were.

On this day, Jimmy took over an hour before he exited the rear door of the church. We had plans to play some football at the school. He had a strange look—a mixture of confusion and depression as he departed. He said nothing.

"You OK, Jim?" I asked. Maybe he was worried about his mother, who often doted on him and depended on him for many things. He usually was sullen, and I was used to that. But this was different.

"He gave me some wine…" Jimmy confided.

"Who? Father Fernie?"

Jimmy nodded yes, saying nothing. His nose began to run as if he were about to cry, but he held it in.

"He…He also ddddddidddd stuff…"

"What the hell are you talking about?"

"He did things to me…hell with it."

"Should I tell someone? Maybe we should go tell your mom."

"Nah, she won't do nothing. Besides, I got back at him. I pissed in the holy water, and I spit in the wine he uses for mass. He makes me drink that stuff after mass when we're alone, and I don't like it. I don't like him."

■ ■ ■

"Hey, are you alone? Can you talk?"

"Yeah. Any new developments?"

"I heard through my source that Allen intends to piss it all away to charity just like we thought. Probably within a few months. This is our only chance, and we need to act fast. Like we discussed before, there's so much money here, more than we ever dreamed, right in front of us, and he's gonna just squander it. Shit."

"That's what I thought he would do. He's going to piss it away…what a damn waste of money as far as I'm concerned."

"Legally, there might not be anything any one of us can do. It's in Mr. Allen's hands, and after all, it is his family's money."

"Don't be so negative. I'm sure I—uh, we—can figure something out."

"Well, our window of opportunity is closing. His last meeting with his attorneys in San Francisco tells me that he is close to sealing the deal and the trust—a trust that none of us will ever touch."

"I think we need to get the others and have a meeting to see what we can do. I will call you within the week. We'll meet at the usual place. We cannot avoid this chance and run away from it. 'There are some things a man just can't run away from.'" *Stagecoach*. He hung up and slowly removed the chubby black cigar, a Cohiba, sniffed it, cut it, then lit it. He was lost in his deep thoughts as he enjoyed the mild smoke. "That's a goddamn lot of money," he whispered out loud to himself. He noticed his cigar and hand trembling as he quietly puffed the Cohiba.

■ ■ ■

From the *Sonora Desert Review*, August 14, 1967:
Police dispatches indicate that Rockwood Police were dispatched to the 1200 block of Magnolia Street at approximately 3:00 a.m. after multiple reports of a disturbance. The husband had returned home drunk, and his wife threw his belongings on their lawn. Both were given stern warnings, and the wife refused to press charges.

Police dispatches indicated that Rockwood Police responded to the 300 block of East Third Street at approximately 5:21 p.m. A young child at the residence advised police that her dog had been missing since the prior evening. Despite a two-hour canvass of the neighborhood, the police department's search proved unsuccessful. Sparky, a cute brown poodle, remains missing.

■ ■ ■

At the end of my 1967 baseball season, I had a lot to look forward to. My brothers were coming home—Hank for a visit and Curt for good from the war. They were both expected on September 2, and my family had never been happier awaiting their return. The house was spotless, and the kitchen was stocked with more food than I had ever seen. Nana hovered over a hot stove with three large ollas cooking as she was stirring. At sixty-eight and only 4'10," she was strong and nimble as she took command of the family kitchen.

"Come over here, son. Keep an eye on the beans, and don't let them dry out." Her wrinkled hands looked like beef jerky. Tough. She had more arm strength than I. A thick mane of white hair cascaded around her small shoulders, and her deeply wrinkled face reflected a long, tough life. Every other word she uttered was a swear word, but when she cussed, it never seemed malicious—only teasing. She was proud to be from Texas, and her inner strength and wisdom never waned in my lifetime.

"Nana, how was my dad when he returned from the war?"

As she was kneading the tortilla masa, she looked at me with a puzzled smile and said, "Well, it was hard for all of us. There was little work here, but we always had food. Your dad came back and had to get used to his life like before. Get me those bunches of cilantro and onion…"

"What do you mean 'like before'?"

"He left for war, leaving behind a wife and a young child, Enrique. We thought he might not come back. A lot of those guys didn't. Your grandpa and I lost two good friends in 1943 and 1944, kids we knew in the neighborhood. And another kid, Mark Berry, came back without any legs. He and your dad used to play marbles all the time, I remember. He hung himself a year after he got back.

"Your mom ran this household and worked as many jobs as possible: picking crops, sewing, caring for children. What little money your dad made in the military he would send home.

"I think your mom worked so hard so she wouldn't have to think about the unthinkable. We only knew he was in the Pacific, and his letters never said much.

"I liked Roosevelt, and I trusted him that we would win. But I had to prepare myself for the possibility that your dad might not. I'll never forget when he got back about four months after they dropped the bomb. You never saw so much music, dancing, food, and drinking for three days.

"We were picking fruit up in a place called Planada in Northern California. Several other boys returned among the families in the labor camp. I think we all spent every dollar we had on that *pachanga*, but it was worth it, I tell you."

She paused, working on the tortillas and, with a blank smile, peered out the kitchen window as if she'd returned to 1945 and continued. "Your father changed so much in a lot of small ways. He did not smile and laugh as much as before and was absentminded, as if he were someplace else. I probably should not tell you, but he also drank more." The kitchen was well lit with candles that the local priest had blessed.

"But after a few hard years, he got back on his feet, found a good job at the school, and raised a good family. I never asked about the war, and I don't think he ever mentioned it to your mother or me, so I never ask. He will keep those memories locked up inside until he dies...I pray those things don't get out too often."

I didn't ask her more, and I thought I was picking the scab of an old wound of hers.

■ ■ ■

Curt arrived one lazy afternoon at the bus station on the west end of town and took a taxi home. My mom was the first to greet him as he approached the porch. She bent down on her knees, hugged his waist, and cried, saying nothing. Curt looked at her and smiled. My father hugged him hard and didn't let go for what seemed a minute. Nana gave him a blessing on his forehead and nodded her head as if she always knew he would return safely.

He looked a bit haggard and gaunt. His Green Beret uniform fit him loosely and hung languidly on his thin frame. He had left for Vietnam built like a muscular bull but had lost at least twenty pounds. His eyes looked like deflated brown balloons, dry old skin hanging under his eyes.

Sadness. He had begun to resemble my father more, as if his face had been contorted into a sad older man.

But the most disturbing part of his change was his eyes. His eyes said nothing, and he never focused on anyone, as if he was staring past people, looking toward the horizon. His eyes had always had a warm spark, and he was always engaged with those around him. It now seemed like a cold flicker was in his eyes. His light returned eventually.

After he settled in that evening, my parents and Nana fell asleep to save their energy for the next day's festivities. Curt and I were alone in our bedroom, and I had not said much to him. Frankly, I did not know what to say except that this was one of the happiest days of my life because one of my big brothers had returned for good and was safe. We could now play catch together and hang out like before.

He had a puzzled look on his worn face, as if he were in a dream. He slowly glanced around the room, looking at every detail, which was unchanged since he left overseas: baseball pennants on the wall, simple twin beds, record player with a Rolling Stones LP on it, all the sports trophies we had won throughout the years, old drawers my father built out of scrap wood from the school, posters of John, Paul, Ringo, and George. He looked at each item, locked his glance at it, then scanned another item. He looked at me with a puzzled smile. He was not sure whether he was dreaming. All he said before going to sleep was "home." And he fell asleep in his uniform, clutching his green beret.

■ ■ ■

On Pink Avenue...

In a drunken stupor, he emerged from Juana's Cuban Bar late one evening, unzipped his pants, and pissed on the side of the bar, a wooden wall. The urine left a round mark on the old wood.

First came the elderly Mexican ladies dressed in black, with shawls enshrouding somber faces, rosaries clasped in hands. They were the first to hear about it through the vast network of neighborhood gossip that passed from house to house. A finely tuned communications network in Allen County was now in full throttle. Some knelt; others only whispered to one another, looking at the southern wall of the cantina, "J.U.A.N.'S B.A.R." The bar had a wooden siding that was aged and rough, and the sun had shown it no mercy.

In the first week, only a few dozen appeared at the wall, but they numbered over one hundred by the second week, including some skeptical news reporters and a local Catholic priest.

Some approached the image on the wall, and the courageous ones held out their hands to touch it. If you stood about fifty feet away during certain late-afternoon times, you could barely discern the Virgin Mary looking downward demurely. The image, to most people, would lose focus and seem only like irregular wood-grain patterns. Some thought they could see a spider or a plant. Or a mark where someone pissed. Some saw nothing, trying to find something in the wooden image like taking a Rorschach test.

But to the believers, they saw the clear image of the Virgin Mary. Small pieces of the wall were pilfered as mementos and taken to Father Roberto for a blessing. Others snapped photos. My nana even went and left flowers and yellow roses at the base of the image.

"Mijo, pray with me to the Virgin Mary."

Reluctantly, I knelt and felt awkward in front of a seedy bar in the late afternoon. A drunk had taken a piss near me at the base of the wall, unaware of the surrounding religious fervor. The Virgin Mary—or an old piece of wooden siding, depending on your version of the religious Rorschach test—looked down on him.

The crowds were swelling, and now the sighting evolved from a respectful religious occasion to a mob of people. The proprietress of the bar was now encouraging the crowd to drink a few cold beers and listen to Cuban music inside the cantina. A few enterprising individuals sold chips, candy, and Cokes.

■ ■ ■

"Listen, *mijo*. You know I love you very much, and I think when you get older, I will answer all your questions. But now is not the time."

"Is it that big white man that comes over? Is he the one? My father?"

She paused to gather her thoughts because she wanted to handle the question with delicacy and discretion. "Son, I cannot tell you now, but I will, promise. I have to respect my promise to this man, and I promised I could not tell anyone, even you, until we both felt the time was right."

"I'm twelve years old, and I feel I need to know. I know my father is not dead. You would have told me, and all you ever tell me is 'soon.' Well, Ma, when is 'soon'?"

"Please, mijo. You are my only son, and you are my life. You have to trust me, and I cannot just tell you."

"It's not fair." Jimmy Flores ran crying out the front door and down the street with all his speed. He didn't know where he was going, but he knew he wanted to be far from home, and many conflicting feelings swirled in his mind. As he reached the north end of town, he slowed down to catch his breath and spotted a dog, a mutt, squatting in the middle of an empty street. He thought he could take this one home. She was about medium size with mixed colors, gray and brown. As he approached the dog, he knelt to pet it and pick it up like a child.

The animal slowly turned his head, looked at Jimmy with vacuous eyes, and Jimmy tossed the dog back onto the street. It had saliva drooling from the left side of its face, with an empty, sick look. Lifeless eyes stared at the sky. As he dropped it, it turned to him and growled, and it sounded more like a low hiss from a rattlesnake.

I was four blocks away at home helping my mom and grandma get the meal ready for the party when I heard our neighbor, Imelda, yelling frantically to no one in particular: "Rabies! That dog has rabies. Call the police! Someone!" She was pointing toward the north end of town.

My mom and I went out to look, and we could see in the far distance a dog near a large boy. It looked like a mangy street dog, part Lab, part terrier, but all mean. I focused and realized Jimmy Torres was near the dog, backing away. Instinctively I began to run toward Jimmy because I knew he would do the same for me. He always had my back on the baseball field and at school with the bullies. I felt a strong hand grab me by my left shoulder and lift me off the ground. It was my dad. "Stay here, son. I'll take care of it."

"But I need to go and help him, Pops. Look!"

My father held my shoulder tight, and I knew he would not let go.

From the corner of my eye, I also noticed he had a bolt-action rifle, .22 caliber, in his right hand. "Pops, be careful. That's Jimmy near the thing."

"Son, don't go near the dog or near Jimmy. DO YOU UNDERSTAND WHAT I'M TELLING YOU?" His eyes were serious, and his tone was clear. I meekly nodded yes. My father sprinted as I had never seen him before, kinda like Curt. He carefully approached Jimmy and spoke a few words to him. Jimmy nodded and backed away as my father shot the dog twice; then the ambulance arrived.

My father returned and later explained to me that Jimmy had touched the rabid dog and he would have to get painful shots in his stomach for the next few weeks. All I could do as his friend was offer support. He patted me on the head, coolly entered the house, and placed the rifle back in its hiding place. Damn, that was my pops.

■ ■ ■

Big Bob was the last to arrive and strolled in about thirty past the prearranged time of 3:00. He sat at the end of the room. They were in the living room of the Rossi ranch, ten miles north of town. Besides Walter Rossi and Big Bob, there were four others present. Together, they represented some of the wealthiest farmers and ranchers in the county, if not the country. Five of the Original Six.

All were smoking cigars or cigarettes, and some had drinks in their hands. The slanted shades only allowed warm rays of sunlight into the room, illuminating the paneled walls lined with photos, certificates, and books.

Rossi looked around and spoke first. "OK, no one except us is here. First, I'm glad you're all here.

"It appears that the Allen kid will be leaving his entire estate, along with all the water easements and mineral rights, to charity in a complicated trust fund that is contained within the second trust. The actual document is in his lawyer's office, according to our sources, and the trust has not been signed by him.

"As I indicated before, if he dies without signing that second trust, there is no trust, and his estate will be processed in accordance with the agreement his father made about thirty years ago with the state and federal government. This means we may have a chance to purchase portions of his estate if there is no change."

"It sounds too complicated to me, and the odds of all these conditions materializing are against us," said Victor Pressley.

"But, Vic, it has a chance of succeeding. Besides, we have also invested our entire lives in this county, like our parents and grandparents. We're no different than the Allens." Rossi was animated, and the others quietly nodded.

"How do we get rid of the second trust? Won't Jim know about it once it's missing from his safe at home? Also, the first trust becomes effective only upon Jim's death." Pressley now expressed noticeable anxiety at where the discussion was heading.

"In the simplest scenario, the bottom line is that if the second trust is not found at the time of Jim's death and cannot be located within one year from his death, the estate will be distributed in accordance with the original trust. You all know that would mean we all get a big cut of millions of dollars in land rights. My estate attorney spelled it out for me."

"Then what should we do? Just wait until Jim is dead, then hope and pray the second trust gets lost?"

Big Bob interjected with some cryptic remarks: "Well, you know, the future has a funny way of being guided by the divine or other forces at work. We can't just wait for some date on the calendar in the future for these things to happen. 'I don't guess people's hearts got anything to do with a calendar.'" *Hondo*.

"We've got to make things happen so that these events align in our favor. I have some ideas that would be indiscreet to share with you now, but trust me, I can make it happen. Big Bob always makes it happen."

"You're not going to do anything illegal, are you, Bob?" Nervous laughter.

"Of course not. But if and when we can cash in on the estate, I also want you to acknowledge my role for whatever it may be worth, money-wise. And I think it might be worth five percent of your collective cut."

"You have always been a trusted public servant, Bob. And that's why we asked you a long time ago to join in this situation, in this battle to get what our families should be entitled to."

Big Bob stood up, adjusted his jeans and boots, and said: "'All battles are fought by scared men who'd rather be someplace else'" *In Harm's Way*. "We will have to make some tough decisions, but there is enough opportunity in this venture to make money for all of us, more money than any one of us thought possible."

Rossi unfolded a large rectangular map of Allen County with some colored blocks. "If you look at the county in terms of the ownership of the farms, I have put all those holdings of farms with more than one thousand acres on the map, the magic cutoff through the Allen agreement. Then I have put marks on the Allen estate.

"When you look at how the elder Allen—damn, he was smart—put his lands holdings in connection with the water agreement he made with the state and federal government decades ago, you can appreciate the lucrative power of his holdings beyond simply farmland. In effect, the Allens control the water for the entire region, including the coast, which will only increase in population.

"The Allens have land at the end of all major canals and at the beginning. Whenever water is diverted elsewhere, the water easements mean that Jim Allen gets a fee. It's kind of having ownership of a water hose both at the source and at the end. Every time that water is turned on, and every time the hose is diverted, Allen gets a fee.

"If you have ownership of the water easements, you have control, period. The demand from the coast for water will only continue to increase as the population increases. From San Diego to San Luis Obispo, those communities lack primary resources for water, so they will be buying rights to have water diverted from the Colorado River west to their communities. And Allen County, with its canals, is right in the middle between the Colorado River and the coast.

"Mr. Allen the elder was a visionary who could see the demand for water in this part of the state. One day countries will fight wars over water, and one day cities in this country will fight legal wars over water. Don't forget: Why is gold so precious? Do you think it is because it's nice and shiny and looks good in a chain or watch? I know I'm saying the obvious, but the real reason gold is a precious commodity is because it is not too abundant.

"In the future, when the coastal cities grow, people will need the water to keep their precious lawns green, to keep the golf course green, to drink and play. But the amount of water, like gold, will still be the same. And when you think about it, water will be more in demand than gold because we need water to live. If you guys were trapped on a fucking island and had a choice between a pound of pure gold or a gallon of fresh water, what would you choose?"

"My wife would probably prefer the damn gold and die happy and thirsty." Laughter.

"OK, Walt, I get all this legal mumbo jumbo. But what does that have to do with us?" This was the question that all these powerful men had come to ask.

Rossi quickly responded with a canned answer: "We have an opportunity to be a part of this if conditions are ripe. Now, I personally like Jim Allen. But we all know that his father was not all that ethical and was known to twist people—and the law—to get his way. Shit, he probably stole some of this land and bought out the small farmers to accumulate his vast estate. So the Allen family does not come with clean hands, as the lawyers like to say.

"Again, the bottom line is that all of us can bid for parts of the estate and its water rights if Jim dies with no second trust. We get the first bid, not the government. He has no heirs as far as I know, and his deceased wife had no heirs, and he's the last in the Allen line."

Big Bob chimed in. "There's more: I think that his property near the Guadalupes has some natural gas deposits that might also have potential for drilling in the future, and those future rights are also possibly worth millions." Big Bob was smug, as if he had insider information.

"You know, I've always heard those rumors about the gas. I heard there have been engineers snooping around that area."

"Boys, leave it up to me to make this happen. You've all been kind enough to front me the funds to buy my one thousand acres, but I hope you realize that I will get us to this property because I'm the only one who knows how."

"Big Bob, what're you going to do, kill him?"

All laughed except for the sheriff. "Don't worry about what I do. I will make it happen because Big Bob has always kept his word. You'll see." Big Bob could feel the cool ocean breeze of the Mexican ocean that he dreamed about.

"We hope that codicil never sees the light of day." Big Bob nodded in agreement with a smile.

PART NINE

"IT WAS ALL ABOUT THE DOVES"

Our coming-home party for Curt lasted two days. Our families drank, they ate, they fought, they made up, they laughed, they cried. Curt was home for good. Two days later, he was gone.

When he returned two weeks later, he brought a young girl with him. She was about nineteen and plain-looking with heavy dark makeup, a thick beehive hairdo, and a tight mini skirt that had been worn for a few long days and nights. Light stains were splattered on her dress like an abstract painting by a drunken artist.

"Hey, Ma, this is Trini. She's my wife. We got married yesterday in Mexico, and she's beautiful. What do you think?"

My mom said nothing and looked at my father, who didn't realize his mouth was partially open. He did not or could not say anything except "Son, that's nice. It's a pleasure meeting you, young lady, and welcome to the Mendoza family." My grandma took one look at her, looked at Curt, and lightly tapped him on the head in disgust as she turned away, mumbling something about the Virgin Mary.

The new Mrs. Mendoza nodded her head. Her bloodshot eyes were sad and indifferent, and she smelled of stale beer—not the kind that's left in a can overnight but the kind you smell in a toilet after someone has puked. She was not shy about displaying her ample cleavage, and my mother kept staring at her. The beehive bouffant collapsed and cascaded languidly around her shoulders, and I don't think she noticed.

They stayed in the house for three days, primarily in the guest bedroom at the back of the garage. It wasn't really a bedroom. My father converted a small storage room and added a small sink, bed, and closet to accommodate guests who occasionally spent the night. Nana christened it as a "pinche honeymoon suite." I could hear them in the late hours when they were partying, arguing, or having sex.

Finally, on the third day, I heard a scream from their pinche honeymoon suite. We all ran to find out what was going on.

"Get the hell out, you slut!"

"Go to hell, puto!" Trini was noticeably drunk or high and could barely walk. She looked mean, tired, and old, wearing a black eye, a swollen upper lip, and multiple purple bruises on her arms. Curt didn't fare much better with deep scratches crisscrossed on both cheeks. Trini finally composed herself, bowed to us with feigned respect, and staggered down the block into the darkness, carrying her broken high heels and dirty coat.

"Son, don't you think we should at least give her a ride?" my father asked with a concerned look.

"Nah, Pops. She wants to hit the bars before closing. She'll be all right."

I didn't notice my grandma in the back of the commotion. She shook her head, slapped Curt on the head, and told him, "Looks like the honeymoon's over, *menso*. Now get on with your life."

Curt gave her a mean stare. I had never seen his facial muscles contort like that. I had always known him to be the nicest person in the world. And now he was giving my nana a menacing glance as though he were possessed by some asshole I had never met.

"Nana, I love you. But I'm going to tell you this once: don't hit me like that."

She then pushed him by his shoulders.

"Go ahead, menso. You're tough, huh? Hitting your wife like that. Now you wanna hit your grandmother? You bring shame to this family, mijo. Get on with your life, tough guy. If your tata were here, he'd teach you a lesson."

"C'mon, Nana, I was just kidding. I know you love me…"

Nana said nothing, looked at Curt, puzzled, and returned inside. Two days later, Curt and my father went across the border to Mexico for a "quickie divorce" that took only two hours and twenty American dollars to process, and Curt returned to the US a single man.

Curt returned home before sunrise, drunk and bloody. He staggered into our house, went to the room in the garage, and fell asleep. About 4:00 a.m., I woke up to pee and found Curt crawling in the darkness of our living room.

"Curt, hey, you OK?" I asked.

"Yeah, I think they're here. Be quiet and stay low." He pulled me down next to him. "Fuck, it's so dark here, man. I just wanna stay here awhile, and don't turn on the lights. I wanna wait till the sun comes up. I like the sun."

As my eyes adjusted to the dark, I could see he was in a trance.

"Sally, baby, I can't hear you."

My father entered the room and, without turning on the lights, grabbed Curt by the shoulders, lifted him, and led him back to bed. I slept in the living room and never repeated that incident to anyone. For the next three months, Curt was nowhere and everywhere. Local rumors followed him: he was using drugs, fighting in local bars, involved with criminal characters. We even heard he was smuggling stuff from Mexico. My father would drive around the valley looking for him late at night—at bars and drug hotels on Alamo Street, at friends' homes, and at the local morgue.

A few weeks before Christmas, the Clarktown police pulled up at our house in the early evening. They opened the door and escorted Curt from the police unit. My father and I scampered outside. Curt looked terrible: thin, unshaven, unbathed, and angry. He was practically being held up by the police officers. He made no eye contact with either my father or me and only quietly glared at the young police officers. I overheard the police officer speaking with my dad.

He was escorted into the home and staggered to his bedroom, mumbling, "Fuck it…fuck it." His demons were his only friends, his nightmares his only solace.

"Officer James, what happened?" my father asked, but he knew the answer.

"Mr. Mendoza, you need to take care of him and get him some help. He's been raising hell all over the valley. We think he's using heroin. Check out his arms. And there are suspicions he's crossing drugs into the county from Mexico, up by the Allen farm. You know, those mountains and foothills are old smuggling routes. He's already been arrested once, disturbing the peace and assault. No formal charges were filed, and we let him sleep it off.

"A few weeks ago, he took on three hunters from out of town and beat them to a pulp. Damn, three against one, and he put all of them down. Hell, they were big, tough-looking guys just passing through going up to Las Vegas, and they did some dove hunting for a few days. According to the bartender, one of them said something to your son, nothing too offensive, just a joke about the military, I heard.

"Curt approached them and asked them why they shot small, defenseless creatures like doves. 'They never harmed you guys, and they can't fight back, assholes!' One of these guys told him, 'Fuck you, Mexican, so—' Poor guy never finished the sentence. Your son then tore into them like a…like a…"

"Like a beast?" my father added. "That's how they trained him."

"My officers told me that one of them had a broken nose, another a broken arm. All their faces were mashed to a pulp, and Curt had to be restrained by three other guys in the bar. Damn. They didn't want to press charges, said they 'all fell.' They couldn't tell their buddies a little crazy

Mexican did this to them.

"Damn, those poor guys are probably way past Vegas by now. You won't see them down in these parts again for a while." Officer James tried to contain his laughter under his breath. "All about the doves…"

My father nodded quietly and asked, "What should we do?"

"I brought him here to you 'cause I know your family. You folks have always been good people, and I know Curt's working through some tough times. Shit, I used to watch him play football. Great player. I've seen enough of these guys coming back from Vietnam, and I know some of them need some space. But if he ever gets arrested by Big Bob…well, Big Bob handles things differently, you know? Get him cleaned up and on the straight road. Right now, Curt's a danger to himself. Maybe some of the veterans' groups can help him. The next time, I'll take him in if he messes up, OK?"

"Officer, thank you so much. We'll take care of it."

Curt slept for two days and woke up to eat homemade albondigas, meatball soup my grandmother prepared. She also gave him some tea made from herbs, *yerba santa*, planted in our backyard garden to "calm his nerves," as she said.

We all pretended to ignore the two injection sites on his left arm. He told my nana they were only *granos*—pimples. After two days, he was gone again.

■ ■ ■

I went with Jimmy to the local doctor for his first weekly rabies shot the following week. He would only admit to me that he was scared to go alone since his mom had to work.

Ironically, the only thing Jimmy loved next to baseball was his dogs. The only time he showed human emotion was around those mutts. He would take in any stray, nourish it, and adopt it as a pet. He had a real knack for relating to dogs, and they instinctively trusted him. He now had seven at home, and his mother never objected since she thought, in the long run, the dogs were good companions for him. They were mutts of all sizes, breeds, and colors. The only thing they shared in common was their undivided loyalty to Jimmy. His mutt family was his only company as an only child, and they all loved him without conditions. He told me they all had their individual personalities: stubborn, taciturn, aggressive, moody, affectionate, timid—almost like people. "But I don't like most people," Jimmy once told me, a somewhat cryptic remark I attributed only to the ramblings of a complicated guy like Jimmy.

Dr. Evans was about fifty with thin gray hair, bushy eyebrows, and a slightly hunched back. He spoke with a funny accent as if he were from New York or somewhere far away from here.

At that moment, I thought of my nana's comments to me. She had this profound intuition about things, and she could tell you your thoughts before you even uttered a word. She even had nightmares about Curt in Vietnam, about him being in danger, running in the jungle, being chased by unknown and unseen devils. She once told me, "Mijo, listen. That friend of yours, Jimmy, be careful with him. He is cursed. Bad things follow him. He does not go looking for bad things; bad things chase him. And they will catch him. Down inside, he's not too good. I know he is your friend, but always be careful around him." She turned away from me and made the sign of the cross.

"Jimmy, you doing OK today?" We were now alone in the private doctor's office, a sterile room with a white metal bed, a table, some metal instruments on a counter, and some sterile pads. On the wall were some old diagrams with posters.

Jimmy said nothing and nodded his head. Dr. Ellis pulled out a needle that was the longest and most menacing needle I had and have ever seen. It looked about six inches long. He casually had Jimmy pull up his shirt front, and he placed the needle into his stomach. I thought it looked like he stabbed him, as if he were torturing him from a time in the Dark Ages.

Jimmy closed his eyes and said nothing, but he was quietly sniffling to himself. I felt light-headed, and my stomach jumped upward to my throat. Jimmy had thirteen more shots left.

A few weeks later, I went to his house to see how he was doing after his shot. As I approached his front porch, it seemed unusually quiet. Most of his dogs knew my scent and sound, and they would commence barking when I was nearly a block away. But now it was quiet. No dogs. Jimmy's mom greeted me on the porch and hugged me like she always did.

"Why so quiet? Did Jimmy take the dogs somewhere?" I asked.

Her face was serious, and she grabbed my hand and escorted me to their backyard where the dogs were usually kept. A powerful stench punched my nostrils and went into the far reaches of my throat, and I felt like I wanted to vomit again. I wasn't sure if the smell was burned rubber or some kind of meat. My grandmother liked to cook *tripas* (not my favorite), and the smell was terrible.

A smoldering fire in the corner of the yard looked like burned trash or leaves. Jimmy's mother pointed to the pile and said, "Look, all his dogs. He beat them all to death, and then he burned them together this morning. I honestly don't know what's wrong with him. I need some help for him."

"Why would he do that? He loved those dogs. I think he loved them more than most people." I felt repulsed at the look of the smoldering carcasses and even more repulsed at the thought of Jimmy beating them to death and then lighting a fire like they were pieces of meat. Feeling dizzy, I could feel warm bile slowly crawling up my throat, and I fought to suppress it. They were beautiful living creatures who had never harmed anyone and gave Jimmy only unconditional love and attention.

His mom led me inside, away from the smell. "After being bitten by that rabid dog, he got real quiet. He's mostly in his room all the time and hardly speaks to me. It wasn't just the shots. He felt sorry for that dog because it looked so tired and sick. All he wanted to do was bring it home like all the others and care for it. And the dog bit him…with rabies. You know he had a real skill, a real knack for helping those creatures."

I listened quietly. "I know Jimmy was good to all his dogs, and that's why it's a shock to see that mess back there.

"When the dog was killed and Jimmy realized it had rabies, he began to mistreat his dogs, especially after his shots. He started to kick them and not feed them. He lost his love for them. He probably thought this was probably the only way, so he put them out of their misery. I don't think he wanted them to suffer too much. He loved them, but he blamed that rabid dog for his misery with the shots. And he no longer trusted dogs after that rabid dog bit him."

"Where is he now?"

"I don't know. He sometimes wanders off by himself. But he'll return. You're his best friend. Talk to him and be a friend to him. He needs someone to listen to him." She looked dull and sad. I remembered Nana's observations: "That Jimmy is bad. Bad things always come looking for him…"

■ ■ ■

Matt Bradley felt relaxed. He enjoyed the solitude of the desert and found himself uncomfortable with others—especially when he received mindless stares at the scar. He overheard some young kids refer to his scar as "the blob," from the movie with Steve McQueen. As the scar aged, it looked purple and menacing. The embarrassment would make him blush slightly, and he could feel the heat as the blood rushed into the blood vessels in his face through his scar.

The solitude of the work was comforting: patrolling the border, tracking smugglers, and even helping those stranded out in the desert. Bodies were commonplace out there. Mexicans who crossed into the US didn't respect the inherent dangers of the desert—strikingly vast, intensely barren, and often deadly. He had few thoughts about why they crossed, but he only knew he had to catch them and sometimes save them. He was proud of his work, and the work made him avoid thoughts of Nam and the buddies he had left behind. Maybe he could save people.

He searched his memory for his last conversation with Mr. Lewis, his boss. "Matt, there aren't many men I trust in this job. Between the dopers, the smugglers, and the bad guys, this job will wear on you. But I think I did well by hiring you. Many in this line of work don't like being around Mexicans, but they're human beings, some good and some bad; they're people like you and me. Treat them with respect when they've earned it."

Bradley found a niche in his job: tracking. He was good at it. In Vietnam, he often tracked Vietcong, and conversely, he knew how to evade being tracked by the enemy. As a civilian, he often tracked smugglers entering Allen County from Mexico. He apprehended many aliens through his efforts, and he knew the backcountry well, the slight permutations of the landscape that would give him clues: the direction of travel, the size of the individuals, and their purpose, whether it was to bring in aliens or drugs or both. The steep hills, the rocky ravines, and the bleak desert silently spoke to one who was trained to listen. And the landscape gave signs. The wind gave hints. The weather gave him a direction of travel. Occasionally, the trails led to grim discoveries of individuals who didn't make it. They didn't listen to the desert. In the summer, daytime temperatures reached 125 degrees, and in the winter, they plummeted to well below freezing. Finding bodies, including remains of entire families, was not something he had the stomach for. He could not understand the gravitational forces that led these people to sacrifice everything—including their families—so they could cross the most foreboding area in the world.

What particularly bothered him was an elusive smuggler who evaded him for a few months. He first noticed the tracks recently. He knew a few things about him: the guy was familiar with the terrain, and he was probably a heroin addict, judging by the drug indicia casually jettisoned along the trails in the foggy bottoms of the western foothills—certain identifiable wrappings and occasional syringes, empty with brown residue. Matt concluded that this particular smuggler was tough as nails because of the territory he covered.

What bothered Matt the most was that he surmised that the smuggler had a military background. His tracks indicated he was about 160 pounds, and he used army-issued boots, size ten. He could travel long without much food, which Matt gathered from the trash discarded along the trails. He traveled in much the same way Matt would have if he were a smuggler, as if he were evading Vietcong. Matt also understood that he had to catch the smuggler, and he knew it was only a matter of time. The trails from that particular smuggler often went cold, especially along the rocky hills in the western portion of the Allen Valley, along the western perimeter of Allen Farms.

He parked his new pickup, a '68 Ford, off the road in the desert. He had an ice chest full of cold beers, twelve of them. This became his ritual after a long working day. He also brought his service revolver and placed it on his lap as he downed the beers. He found it impossible to push out the memories of Vietnam that crept to the surface of his thoughts. Sleeping only four hours every night, he couldn't push out glimpses of the forbidding jungle, its heat, its dangers, bloated bodies, firefights, shelling, torched villages, exhaustion, lost friends, guilt, and boredom. And Willie, his best and only friend in any world.

He wanted to go back. Sinister internal forces pulled his thoughts back to Nam. They tugged at him, teasing him. Maybe he would reenlist for another tour. He felt he had some unfinished business over there but could not pinpoint exactly what it was. What was normal to him was turned upside down. In Vietnam, the norm was hell. He wanted to go back because he found that this world in Allen County no longer felt normal, or maybe it felt too normal.

The juxtaposition of lush fields of crops—freshly planted lettuce and okra—near the outer reaches of an arid desert reminded him of the beauty of nature. The stark colors of the desert browns next to the sharp colors of acres and acres of lush green crops provided a kaleidoscope of beauty. How could a place as dry as Allen County yield so much food?

He often thought of the stark beauty of Vietnam. Nature blessed Southeast Asia with conflations of astonishing beauty: waterfalls, lush jungles, gorgeous green valleys, rivers and lakes, clear nights full of stars—all a stage and backdrop for the brutality and killing that was the Vietnam War. Only the human species could produce abundant fields out of a desert, and only the human species could produce a profoundly terrible war in a Shangri-La. He found only solace out there in the desert. His beer, his gun, his protector. Matt liked to target shoot in the desert, usually empty beer cans, and it relaxed him.

He carefully stroked the revolver, placed it up to his mouth, closed his eyes, and then placed it back onto his lap. The only thing that kept him from blowing out his brains was the thought that Willie would find shame and cowardice in the act of suicide. He would be home in bed in a few hours, clutching a warm pillow, the revolver nearby.

■ ■ ■

"Bless me, Father, for I have sinned. My last confession was too long ago to remember."

"Son, that's all right. What do you wish to confess, my son?"

"Father, I have done many bad things, terrible things. And I don't know how to fix it."

"Son, we all are human beings, and we go through life making mistakes. You can only trust in the Lord to offer solace, guidance, and, most importantly, love."

"I saw too many bad things, hellish things. I killed people, and I saw others get killed…"

"I'm listening…"

"These people were also human beings, and I saw them slaughtered like animals. I saw my best friends slaughtered. Women, children, old men, suffering, hatred. How can this happen? Why did God allow this to happen? There's no reason for it, and I need answers for this, Father. Please help me."

"Son, the Lord works in ways only He knows, and he must have a reason to allow this on earth. We are all not without sin, and suffering is part of human existence, and God knows we're imperfect human beings. Your experience will make you a better person and make you appreciate your own life. You can take that experience and turn it into something positive for you and others."

"But I don't feel I am a better person. I killed people…I murdered them. I don't understand. Why did God allow this to happen?"

"There is a reason for all this. He must have a reason, and you need to explore why he allows this misery on earth."

"Father, I need answers from you. Why did God allow this? Why couldn't he stop this? Why couldn't he stop me? All this suffering. For what?"

"I offer you solace in the Bible. Your answers lie in there."

"Father, goddamn you. There's no answer in the damn Bible! Tell me what I need to know. Why? You're not telling me a damn thing except empty crap!"

"Son…calm down…please. This must be a test for you before everlasting salvation. You need to find the answers for yourself."

"Why would He let this shit happen? All this suffering. Why? Give me some answers, Father."

"Son, I don't know. Maybe you should recite ten Hail Marys and Our Fathers and get some help."

"Thank you, Father, for your help and guidance. I apologize for the cussing."

Part Ten

JUANA LA CUBANA

Juana Gomez was born in Cuba in 1948. In 1961, at the age of thirteen, she fled the island along with her brother in what was known as the flight of the "Castro orphans." Thousands of children were allowed to escape the island without their parents after the revolution, and many were adopted by American families. Her brother, Rafael, was one year younger and depended on her for protection and guidance as they entered the vastness of America.

The Gómezes were considered aristocracy before the revolution. They owned thousands of hectares of arable land, radio monopolies, hotels, European villas. The dictator Bautista would often visit their house for dinner before he and her father "talked business" privately. Juana clearly remembered sitting on his lap, and he would stroke her hair, commenting to her parents about her stark beauty. "She's old-world beauty—European. My Juana!"

Juana and her brother Rafael lived in a gilded world of servants, expensive European vacations, mansions, French lessons, polo, and exclusive schools far removed from the poverty and violence just below on the Havana streets.

Their gilded existence and their enduring fairy tale crashed abruptly on January 1, 1959, when Fidel Castro assumed power and Bautista escaped into exile. Juana and Rafael remember that date as if a giant clock had been smashed and time stopped.

No more servants. No more piano or French lessons. No more mansions. No more vacations. No more Cuba.

She remembered menacing men with beards and rifles coming to their home outside Havana and destroying everything: the expensive cars, the priceless jewelry, the European furniture. Along with all her worldly accruements, her past was also destroyed.

Her parents disappeared that day. Like an old photo, her last and lasting image was her mom and dad being herded out of the home with rifles at their backs by the smelly, dirty, bearded ones. She saw some of the rebels pissing in their pool, and she found human feces in and around their rose garden. Their fleet of expensive cars disappeared. She and Rafael hid in the hills for three weeks, eating only bananas and sugar cane before they reentered Havana. They quickly accepted the fact that their parents would never be seen again.

After fleeing the island on a plane with only the clothes on their dirty backs, they landed in Miami in early 1960 with the help of relatives. All Juana and Rafael brought with them was a photo of their parents taken in Havana Harbor, circa 1942. Their parents looked happy and successful, with thoughts of a prosperous future.

Juana and Rafael were put into a foster home in Miami for two years. After partially assimilating into American culture, Juana and her brother rebelled—missing school, taking drugs, and spending more time in the streets than in the safe confines of their foster home. Consequently, they were separated and sent to more secure facilities.

They loved what America had to offer: endless potential and boundless opportunities to do anything they wanted unconstrained by the tiny Cuban island and the strict parameters of upper-class existence. They wandered from different foster homes in the Midwest to juvenile detention facilities and the streets. Juana eventually ran away from an abusive foster home and hitchhiked to California in 1966 at the age of eighteen, where she desperately sought success in Hollywood with her good looks. She was tall like a model with exotic, classic looks: green inviting eyes that were like beacons to starving men on a lonely ship; an olive complexion with flawless skin, high cheekbones, and a tiny nose, making her face look like it was carved from ancient gods; and long, sensuous legs not unlike a seasoned dancer's. When she spoke to men, they didn't hear a thing she said, always bewitched by her stark beauty.

She never succeeded in mainstream movies but did in the porn industry, which was beginning to thrive in West Hollowood. Juana grew up quickly and avoided the normal failings of young prostitutes by utilizing her intelligence, business acumen, and brutal tenacity. She managed to save her money from prostitution, dirty movies, and selling anything and anyone she could on Hollywood Boulevard. She trusted no one and hoarded her savings like a cheap banker.

Her only viable plan was to save money and look for her little brother, whom she had not heard from since their brutal separation.

One day she received a letter and quickly recognized Rafael's exquisite penmanship. Their Cuban tutor had taught them well. He had read the literary classics and practiced nothing but his penmanship for endless hours—a dying art among the Cuban bourgeoisie.

It was addressed from a place called Allen County, the Allen County Jail. Apparently, he was serving one year in the county jail for possession of drugs—heroin. He begged her to help him because he thought the jail was too violent—a "breeding ground for every vice imaginable," he wrote. What was worse, once he completed his sentence, the US government was going to deport him back to Cuba and certain death—as "an undesirable alien." Juana gathered all her earthly belongings with alacrity—clothes and cash (small bills)—hopped a bus and arrived in Allen County on July 12,

1966. She thought, "For the first time, I miss Cuba. This damn place is hell on earth, 110 degrees by midmorning."

Juana kept her relationship with her brother a secret and needed to establish a local front while she figured out how to help him. All the lawyers she spoke to gave her the same answer—Rafael would languish in jail until the US authorities could figure out what to do with him. On the one hand, the US had severed diplomatic ties with Cuba, and thus it did not recognize Cuba as a government. Rafael could not be returned to a country that was not recognized. Nor could he remain in the US indefinitely since he had committed a deportable felony. He might have to be deported to a neutral country. He had few viable options as far as Juana was concerned.

Paying in cash and circumventing local red tape, she opened a bar on the north side of Rockwood, on Pink Avenue, which was littered with cheap motels (five-dollar hourly rates), vacant buildings, seedy bars, taquerias, and prostitutes—mostly young Mexican girls from the interior of Mexico seeking a better life. The cuisine was good, mostly Mexican and American food, with a sprinkling of Cuban fare—black beans and sweet bananas.

Juana wanted something classy and poured most of her savings into the bar, Juana's Cuban Bar, as reflected in a gaudy neon sign in front of her establishment. The lighted sign was victim to young vandals who broke the "a" so that it read "Juan 's Cuban Bar"—a continuing source of vexation for Juana, who took pride in her establishment. It was her bar. Juana's. There was no Juan. She had live music, a well-stocked (diluted) bar, and working girls hand selected by her to ensure discretion. Soon she gained what no other bar in Allen County had—respect. She catered to only those with money: local businessmen, politicians, and cops. This pool of local glitterati would undoubtedly serve her ultimate interest in seeking Rafael's release.

One of her best customers and friends was Sheriff Bob Johnson, who would come into the bar on a weekly basis and order a few beers, on the house, of course—"donations." Despite his open suggestions and flirtations directed at her, she never capitulated to his veiled sexual demands.

138

Unbeknownst to Big Bob, Juana was not exactly virgin territory; that land had been trampled repeatedly. Few bodily apertures had seen more traffic than hers. She just wanted to save the sex for the right moment, for a price—monetary or political. Big Bob would be needed to get her brother out of jail and away from this godforsaken place. She didn't know exactly how or when, but the sheriff would be the only one who could reunite her with her brother.

On a slow Thursday evening before closing time, Big Bob entered the bar. There wasn't much action inside until the end of the month when most patrons received their paychecks—farmworkers, laborers, teachers, attorneys, etc. And she would do her best to make sure they cashed their checks in the bar. She was smart enough to understand that not too many places in town cashed checks; it was understood that she would collect if the check was not good. She had enough physical and political clout at her disposal to deal with any problems that might arise.

Sheriff Johnson was alone, and Juana was tending bar, counting the sales from the register. He was already drunk and slurring his words. Drool was slowly dripping from the side of his lips onto his shirt. The star on his lapel was now wet with spit.

"Hey, Juana, how come you and I don't get together? You know what I mean? I like you. You're one of the most beautiful women around here. With my help, I could make Juan's Cuban Bar the most popular in the state!"

"That's Juanassss Cuban Bar, *puto*. Juan-a."

Juana said nothing more, knowing the less she spoke, the more he would talk.

"I could make you happy, and you don't have to worry about money running this fucking dive. We could go away and live. I mean really live…"

Under normal circumstances, Juana would have taken offense to this idiot since she had put a great deal of her savings and labor into this cantina. However, she was looking for his power and connections to help her brother out of his legal predicament. One thing about the US court system: you can't just buy your way out of a problem like in Cuba or even Mexico—unless, of course, you know the right paths and persons. And Big Bob might be that person. Her ears also perked up like a Labrador when he mentioned the word "money."

Now he began to whisper, even though they were the only two left, except for the bouncer sitting at the far end of the bar beyond hearing distance.

"Hey, Ruben, you can go home now. It's been a long night, and I know you're tired. Get out and go home, all right?"

Ruben was about thirty years old, well over six feet, and squarely built. He was dedicated to Juana since she posted bail for him in the local jail and spoke to the local deputy district attorney about his case. He had assaulted his girlfriend and put her in the hospital with a broken nose. Juana promised the prosecutor she would keep him out of trouble and persuaded Judge Gates, an occasional patron of the bar, to let Ruben work there at the bar as a form of community service instead of serving additional jail time. Judge Gates and the prosecutor acquiesced to her proposal. Juana's skills of persuasion were unmatched even for seasoned attorneys. Her flirtations aimed directly at the judge sealed the deal.

After Ruben left, Big Bob continued: "I have a big deal brewing, and I know I can retire on it and leave this shit hole. Soon, Juana…soon."

"Let's go to my place, have a few more drinks, and tell me about these deals." She touched his hand softly and, with the other, stroked his privates firmly. Like his father with the killer bees, Big Bob was defenseless.

In the morning, Juana and the exhausted sheriff had a quiet breakfast at her house, eating eggs, refried black beans, and strong black coffee— "like in Cuba," Juana said. Bob then proceeded to tell her that he was working on a big deal involving Mr. Allen and that he would make enough money for a lifetime.

"And where exactly is all his money?" she asked, as if she were a naive schoolgirl.

"He has cash and some gold at his ranch, but that's not what I'm after.

That's only a small part of his riches. I can't give you the details, but I want you to be a part of the deal."

Juana said nothing, only listening intently, trying to feign indifference. Bob told her how rich they could become but offered only hints and no details.

Juana slowly unbuckled his "Big Bob" buckle, unzipped his pants, and went to work on him for the next ten minutes. Bob thought that John Wayne probably never felt better.

■ ■ ■

The Allen County Jail facility greeted Juana with the inviting glow of a Cuban prison: dull, dirty walls, no windows, barbed wire hanging languidly along the fence perimeter like dead vines. Thirsty Indian laurel and pepper trees surrounded the building, choking for moisture. The stench of urine, rotting vegetables, and putrid sweat greeted a visitor at the entrance.

Housing four hundred of the region's finest inmates, Allen County Jail was a two-story architectural monstrosity made of cement blocks and faded white stucco. Aged wooden beams were exposed at intervals, with a few broken tiles remaining on the roof, cracked by forty years of sun, earthquakes, and general neglect. A few shattered pieces of Mexican Talavera tile greeted visitors at the entry along the walls. Discolored Saltillo tile paved the walkway into the jail. Broken sections of a wrought-iron fence surrounded the entrance. Evidently, the jail architects in 1930 were going for the hacienda look for their aesthetic masterpiece, an old-world vibe, but then halfway into the project, they abandoned their artistic flair, discarded their design specs, and decided "hell with it. It's a jail for crooks and degenerates, not a Spanish hacienda for lords and noblemen."

Local trustees kept a small rose garden in the front entrance, as visitors passed the Welcome sign. Someone had scribbled "to hell" on the sign after "Welcome." No one bothered to remove it.

Surrounded by dry alfalfa ready for cutting, the facility looked peaceful amid its pastoral location—a languid ocean of green farmland extending in four directions to the mountains, forming the four walls of Allen Valley. Between plantings, the farmers would burn the fields to replenish the soil, and the jail was forced to close the few windows in the facility because of the choking smoke that enveloped it. The inside temperatures often surpassed 120 degrees under normal circumstances in the summer. (Air conditioning was about two years and five deaths away, when the local politicians were threatened with a major lawsuit from the ACLU that sprinkled the term "cruel and unusual" throughout the pleadings submitted in the federal court.)

With Big Bob's help, Juana was able to secure a private visitation room with her brother.

A jail trustee escorted her inside. "Hey, don't you work at Juan's Cuban Bar? You look familiar."

"That's Juana's Cuban Bar. I am the owner, thank you."

Rafael entered the room slowly, like a tired old man. He was almost six feet tall, thin, but strong with jet-black and oily hair. His skin was light brown, clean with no blemishes, and he lacked facial hair, except for a thin mustache that looked like someone had drawn it with a pencil. A tiny nose with effeminate brown eyes completed the fawn-like picture.

These outward features created a facade that hid an unmitigated, violent soul that festered near the surface. Rafael had spent five months in this jail and already was the target of numerous assaults, all of which resulted in other inmates receiving punishing and sadistic reprisals from him. Big Bob removed him from the rest of the inmate population but lacked the room to place him in his own cell. The jailers had to keep a constant vigilance over him, for his protection and the protection of other inmates.

When he first entered the facility, he kept his tormentors at bay by teasing them. He was offered boxes of cornflakes and cigarettes. In return, during showers Rafael would show them his butt and caress himself. Some would just watch him, and others would pleasure themselves in the shower as they viewed him. Fortunately, their advances never progressed further, but he knew it was just a matter of time. He didn't smoke cigarettes and was tired of cornflakes.

He embraced his sister, and they said nothing for a while, only looking at each other with tears.

"You found me." He slowly wiped his tears, looking affectionately at his older sister. She said nothing for a few moments, as if trying to absorb his image.

"You are too skinny, Rafael. You need food—good food—not this vomit they feed you. I hate Mexican food, peasant food. I can explain later, but now we focus on getting you out of this rat hole. Have you been safe in here?"

"It has been pretty bad, but I do what I need to do to survive in here. These people are vulgar savages. These Mexicans have no culture, no up-bringing, and no sense of class. I miss Cuba. They smell." He caressed her soft hands in his. "Did you find out anything about mother and father?"

Juana nodded slowly even before he completed his question. "Only rumors. When the bearded ones came that day, I accepted the fact that we would probably never see them again. Those bastards. Kennedy should've had more balls when he tried to get it back. I'm glad he's dead. He never helped get our country back."

Rafael said nothing and quietly nodded, looking away. He took a deep breath and scratched his cheek, covered with fresh stubble.

"I don't think I'll last here longer." Rafael looked away. "This place is where I'll die. I think I've accepted that. The government cannot send me back to Cuba. They will probably keep me here for a few years, then send me to Mexico. Can you find me a good lawyer?"

"Brother, I don't think we'll need one. I have other plans for you to get you out. Just trust me."

"Who else can I trust?"

"Be patient."

■ ■ ■

From the *Allen Chronicle*, December 1, 1967:
Rockwood Middle School will hold its Christmas dance on December 23, in the high school gym. The theme is "Winter Wonderland in a Desert," and all participants are asked to dress in white. The dress code will be strictly enforced. No miniskirts, and boys must wear ties.

Casualties for November were low in Vietnam. Only 220 Americans were slain in combat, and military authorities expect a lull in the fighting for the next few months as Vietnam will be celebrating the Tet holidays.

■ ■ ■

I dressed with breathless alacrity for the Rockwood Christmas dance: crisp, white short-sleeved shirt, black cotton tie, black slacks, and polished shoes. My mom splashed my face with Dad's Aqua Velva—probably too much based on the strange glances from my nana and our dachshund, Brownie. My hair was slathered with half a bottle of Vitalis. Only my mom, God, and I knew that I had new *calzones* to mark this special occasion. (And if, by chance, I peed in my pants, my new underwear would be christened like a new battleship.) I was awkward with girls and quiet in groups, so a dance was the last thing I wanted to attend. But all my buddies were going.

And she would be there.

We were all to meet at my house, then walk to the dance as a group. Safety in numbers: this principle applied in the jungle, in war, and in the most treacherous theater of social conflict and intrigue—a middle school dance. This field of battle often resulted in heartbroken casualties. But I was prepared with my armor of cheap cologne, a keen wit, and a tenacious drive to accomplish my goal...with her.

Her name was Adela. We had been in the same class since kinder. She was barely five feet tall, with thick black hair that was always shiny and fresh. She was smart—especially in math. A tiny nose centered her face and had four freckles at its tip—I took my time counting them when she wasn't looking. They were kind of arranged in a circle. Her eyes were dark brown and expressive, almost like a friendly beacon. Her dimpled smiles were never forced but emerged naturally, almost shyly. But that beautiful smile made things around her brighter—kind of the feeling when the sun rises on a cold morning. I never saw a frown on her face, and she had no enemies, which was difficult among all the hostile factions prowling the halls of Rockwood Middle School. I already knew her before I even met her.

We were good friends, good platonic friends. We often studied together, and throughout the years I tried to sit near her in class, close enough but far enough so she wouldn't feel my presence. She played flute in the band, and fortunately I played trumpet with the brass section positioned two rows behind her. I could filter out the entire band to hear only her playing like it was a beautiful solo for my ears only. I knew she liked to play hopscotch and jacks during recess, she had Mickey Mouse pajamas, and she was allergic to cats. I also knew her favorite singer: Aretha Franklin. She ran track with her long legs and only liked one flavor of ice cream: rocky road. These were all intimate details that few people knew. Adela was my goddess, and after worshipping at her altar from afar for years, that night I would share my true feelings that had been bottled up tightly in my lower gut. My suppressed love and adoration for her would burst open like a broken dam. And the dance was the night.

So, Moe, Stinky, Skip It, and I sauntered into the gym for the dance like hungry bears entering a feast. Our sartorial choices were carefully crafted for the occasion:

Me: I looked like Beaver Cleaver going to church. The only people I could attract with this outfit were Catholic nuns (and maybe Catholic priests).

Moe: He looked like Linc from *The Mod Squad.* He slopped a two-month supply of Afro Sheen on his puffed afro, and a metal spiked comb was embedded in it to provide street cred. He wore a dashiki with bright red floral patterns, white bell-bottoms with matching shoes, and a fake gold chain that was already turning hues of oxidized green from his sweaty neck.

Stinky: He wore a Hawaiian shirt with puka shells, dark John Lennon glasses, extra-large denim bell-bottoms that dragged on the floor collecting random floor shit like a push broom, black Beatle boots, and a mod haircut "like Ringo."

Skip It: He put together an amalgam of these three styles like someone had stuck random clothes onto Mr. Potato Head. Moe said, "Hey, Skip It, did your blind mother dress you, man?" He wore a tie-dye shirt, jeans, Converse sneakers, a Bobby Sherman haircut, and a fur hat like the one John Phillips wore from The Mamas and the Papas that looked like a marsupial rodent clinging to his small skull.

Collectively, we looked like the dysfunctional offspring of the Mod Squad. We didn't want to make fools of ourselves on the dance floor, so we prepared by watching endless hours of *American Bandstand* and *Shindig!* I rehearsed Chubby Checker's "The Twist" with my nana, until she pulled an oblique muscle and rested on our couch clutching a frosty, medicinal beer.

Mrs. Myers greeted us at the entrance with a twelve-inch wooden ruler like a Roman sentry.

"You boys aren't bringing in anything you shouldn't?" Mrs. Myers had a way of making a statement sound like a question. She held the ruler in both hands like a cop on the beat, slowly looking us over like suspects, slapping the ruler into her open palm like a dominatrix.

"Hi, Mrs. Myers!" We almost spoke in unison like a bunch of Eddie Haskells. On our best manners, we just wanted to breach this final obstacle before entering the dance. She was the last line of defense, and after her, the coast was clear. She stood between us and dozens of nice-smelling girls waiting to dance. Mrs. Myers was in her fifties and had been teaching since the Depression. Plump and small, she had faded brown hair with white streaks and placed it in a bun with a gold pin. She taught English and often volunteered her time for sports, dances, and student government. We never fully appreciated her impact on us until much later in life.

Stinky was curious. "What's with the ruler?"

"Mr. Coughlin, I'm delighted you even recognize this twelve-inch tool. I guess you did learn something in math class. The girls know they can't have dresses more than two inches above the knees. Dress code, you know, strictly enforced."

"Have you busted anyone tonight?" Stinky was curious.

"A...a...yeah, yeah, any...anyone, Mrs. M...M...Myers?" Skip It joined in.

She patiently waited until Skip It was finished. "No, gentlemen, the young ladies are all appropriately attired tonight." We all must have seemed disappointed after hearing that. "Although I think Mary's skirt is too tight." She was referring to "Scary Mary," the school tomboy who could throw a football farther than most boys. She never wore a dress, just jeans and sweatshirts. All the boys were a little afraid of her since she would always challenge boys to anything: running, throwing baseballs or footballs, shooting baskets, arm wrestling, or even competitive marbles. No sane middle school boy would take the challenge and risk the ultimate embarrassment: losing to a girl in sports. Seeing Scary Mary in a tight dress was probably worth the price of admission.

Mrs. Myers's passing remarks as she allowed us entry were "Mr. Coughlin, have a good time. And boys, next time don't put on too much cologne—my allergies, you know."

They all turned to me.

We entered the gym like Roman gladiators, ready to feast upon these innocent cubs. Once inside, however, we felt like eunuchs.

I honestly didn't recognize the old basketball gym. All the walls were covered in white crepe paper with small glittering stars the art class had cut out. Tables and chairs were set up across the floor, all covered in white—the result of Mrs. Anderson's home economics class. The centerpieces on the tables were small Christmas trees donated by the local stores. The lights were dimmed for a soft effect.

On the stage was Pythagorean, the best garage band in the valley according to most local pundits. With two guitarists, two saxophones, one trumpet, and a badass drummer, they could belch out anything—the Beatles, the Stones, the Dave Clark Five, Motown favorites. Already warmed up, they began with a soft medley to get the kids dancing. At the other end of the floor were about one hundred young girls, looking awkwardly at us. All were dressed in their finest, with their hair and faces made up. I could not recognize most because of the dim lights and the heavy makeup. Like animals in the wild, we joined the herd of boys on the other end, adhering to the aphorism "safety in numbers."

I saw her. I heard my heart pounding and felt my hairs standing up—among other things. The micro apertures of my facial pores slowly opened like flowers.

She was in the middle of the group. Among all one hundred, I saw only her. Wearing a soft, short dress that probably barely passed Mrs. Myers's inspection, she looked radiant. Her hair was in soft curls, and she had a small white daisy in her hair with a gold pin. Her eyes caught mine, and she smiled. My confidence boosted, I now began to execute my plan.

First, I had previously asked the band leader to play "Will You Still Love Me Tomorrow" by the Shirelles. (He owed me a favor since I tutored him in math and taught him the Pythagorean theory—hence the band's name, which he thought was "cool, obscure, and refined.") Their first song was a warm-up, something from the Monkees. The girls on the other side began to bobble their heads and swivel their hips to the beat of "I'm a Believer."

That was my cue to initiate my brilliant plan. For Adela. And me. I would grab her in my arms, take her to the dance floor, and, at the right moment, ask her to "be mine"—to go steady. I had saved enough money from my newspaper route and my mom's green stamps to buy a small silver bracelet as a symbol of our commitment, to ward off any potential suitors so they would know she was taken. The plan was meticulous and flawless in design, but like most brilliant plans, its execution failed to consider unexpected forces of nature.

As the sound of the Shirelles softly began…

I crossed the basketball court to the area where all the girls were standing. This was a "no-man's-land" where you either came back onto the dance floor with a pretty dance partner, or…you came back empty, a victim of a humiliating repudiation. A casualty of war.

I don't know how I gathered the guts to even cross the floor, but there I was crossing the Rubicon. Once you're in no-man's-land, you have to keep going and not return. I boldly went straight to her, gently held out my clammy hand, and escorted her to the dance floor. She smiled up at me and nodded approvingly as if she was expecting me. I held her gently, then I tightened. It not only felt like we were the only two souls on the dance floor; it felt like we were the only two on earth.

The Shirelles continued playing to us…

A breezy waft from her soft hair smelled like vanilla and coconut. I could see she had a thin layer of lipstick, but not too much. Her skin had a thin patina of makeup; but even without the lipstick and makeup, she was the same: beautiful, radiant, and warm. She was now in my arms, and I was not going to let go. Soon she would be mine.

"You look…uh, beau…nice, Adela. You guys did a great job decorating."

"The social committee worked all night and this morning fixing the place up. Looks pretty…"

Although the Shirelles continued, their song began to fade away as I focused on Adela and me.

"Adela, I wanted to ask you something…something important…"

"Me too. I'm glad you came. Can I also ask you something?"

Cool—I think we were on the same page. She probably wants to express her feelings to me also.

"Perry's a good friend of yours, right?" She bit her lower lip nervously.

"Perry? You mean Stinky? Yeah, we're good friends. He's cool…"

"Does he have a girlfriend?"

"What…huh? No, not that I know of. Why are you asking?" I was confused, but the obvious was slowly sinking in. My head started to spin, and things moved in slow motion. I swear I could hear the fucking robot from *Lost in Space* blurting out to me: "Danger! Danger! Danger! Mr. Mendoza! Abort the plan. Abort the plan! Danger! Danger!"

"Well…I haven't told anyone…but I like him. He seems so nice and handsome. I was waiting for him to ask me to this dance, but he never did, so I assumed he had a girlfriend or something…"

"I don't know if he is interested in any girl. But I also wanted to ask you something."

She interrupted dismissively, not listening to me. "Can you still tell him hi from me? And it's OK if you tell him I like him…a lot. I mean, I like-like him. Maybe he might wanna dance with me. What were you going to ask me?"

"Nuthin'…" Damn those Shirelles.

Like a true gentleman, I escorted her back and bolted straight to the exit. On the way out, I heard Stinky yell something about how "hot" Scary Mary looked. I ignored him and retreated home to nurse my wounds—the casualty of a brutal war.

Part Eleven

THE POWER OF APPOINTMENT

"Mr. Allen, we are almost finished with these documents for your signature, and we need to amend a few things. We have the final version of your power of appointment. This trust is the most consequential document this firm has handled. We had to double-check every aspect with accountants, law professors, and outside counsel specializing in this field. Frankly, as your attorney, I don't think you should rush into this thing and should really think about it. You are this firm's most important client, and I hope I may speak honestly with you. Your father was one of my father's first clients when he began the firm here in San Francisco after the big quake."

Jimmy Allen leaned back on the soft leather sofa on the thirtieth floor at 40 Market Street. The entire building was owned by the firm Smith, Shelton & James. At fifty dollars an hour, he did not need to hear what he already knew, but he trusted these lawyers as his father had.

"Well, Ira, I'm only doing what was in my dad's heart, and I think he would have been proud of what I am about to do." Jim leaned forward and scanned the oak-paneled room. Three other partners were in the shadows listening.

"Once you modify your father's trust, it will be one of the most significant philanthropic endeavors in the country. Let me play devil's advocate for a moment: some might argue that you are throwing away your father's legacy. And for what? Scholarships for poor Mexicans, libraries, research for third-world diseases, donations to museums, creation of a philharmonic, etc.?"

Jim Allen paused for a moment. He usually refrained from engaging in banter when he had his mind made up. He looked out to catch a glimpse of the Golden Gate Bridge, which was being enveloped by the blanket of thick fog. It reminded him of the Steve McQueen movie *The Blob*. Yes, the blob was swallowing the Golden Gate Bridge.

"Ira, the more I think about what I am about to do, the more I know it is the right thing to do. I'm forty years old, and I have all the money I will ever need in a hundred lifetimes. I have no children, and I don't plan to marry…never found the right one."

"But are you comfortable leaving the legacy to a board of trustees mainly from this firm?" Ira asked almost rhetorically.

"Listen. My father entrusted your firm all his life. You stuck with him when he first started. All the business investments and advice you provided over the past fifty years have always been sound, and most importantly, he trusted you as I have learned to trust you. You and some of your partners will be the trustees, and you have also locked in mechanisms to make sure there are checks and balances and oversight."

Smith said, "Wow. Once this is completed, it will make headlines at the *Wall Street Journal*. We have already had a reporter sniffing around."

James looked distracted and said, "Gentleman, I will hear from you soon to complete the deal. I have a lunch date with some college friends. They want some Chinese food down in Little Italy. Chinese food in Little Italy, huh? That's why we love San Francisco. Then we'll spend some time at the family vineyard in Sonoma. I heard the harvest this year will be great for the merlot, and I might buy another vineyard. It's been a pleasure."

All the attorneys, accountants, and assistants rose respectfully as Jim Allen quickly exited the spacious boardroom.

Ira escorted him out the front door. They inhaled the brisk San Francisco air outside on Market Street, held it, and slowly exhaled as cable cars and Muni buses sped by along Market and Pine.

"Jim, I again want to admonish you in no uncertain terms. I want to make sure that this trust amendment is protected. We have plenty of copies that are of little value without your signature. The power of appointment has to be clear and in writing with your signature. You decided not to let us store it for you, knowing we have the best protection for documents in the country. I hope you're not keeping it at your house."

"Don't worry. It's safe where it's at, Ira. You always remind me how important it is to maintain its safety. I will keep it temporarily at the house, and I will review it; then I will sign it just when it feels right."

"What?" Smith asked with a frightened look.

"As you know, when my father built the family home, he built an underground cell under the bedroom floor where he could put his Mosler Safe, one of the best. That thing weighs 1,500 pounds, and no human being will be able to remove it."

"That instrument, the original, is your only protection, if you die, that will allows us to proceed with this foundation. If, God forbid, something happens to you without the will, your wishes for the foundation will not come to fruition."

"Only you and I know the combination. I will move it once we complete the paperwork for the foundation. I want to keep it close to me; it's my dad's legacy."

"What else is in there?"

"My mom's wedding ring, some old gold coins, and a family heirloom. I just want those things near me. Don't worry, Ira; the trust amendment is safe, and I'll protect it with my life," Allen said with a hint of sarcasm.

Jim Allen stored away a mental note that he would remove the written document "EXERCISE OF THE POWER OF APPOINTMENT OF JAMES ALLEN II" from his home safe to a trusted bank. Anyway, once the foundation was created, the will would not mean that much. He was satisfied that soon the Allen family legacy would be fulfilled.

■ ■ ■

Ira Smith Jr. returned upstairs and waited a few moments until all but the partners remained in the boardroom, the ten partners of one of the oldest established law firms on the West Coast, founded by the legendary Ira Smith Sr. in 1908. The firm had made its millions and its priceless reputation on insurance litigation after the San Francisco quake. Most San Franciscans lacked earthquake insurance, but many had fire insurance. Interestingly, many fires erupted after the earthquake, causing most of the damage, and the claims against the insurance companies were battles fought in the courts for years to come. Ira Smith Sr. was at the forefront of these claims, relentlessly pursuing these claims for hundreds of San Franciscans, becoming a legal icon in a city full of icons.

"Gentlemen, this firm will be the primary trustee of one of the largest philanthropic trusts in this country. It will change our lives and elevate this firm into the stratosphere. My father would have been proud of this firm's efforts. The Allen trust fund will reach worldwide and improve the lives of thousands of people who most need it.

"The water rights that the Allen family has in the Allen Valley will continue through the current seventy-five-year lease arrangement created in 1910 until the Allen Trust II becomes vested. We estimate that the lease alone, aside from all the other income-producing assets of the Allen portfolio, will yield $20 to $25 million per year until the end of the lease, funneled into the Allen Foundation Trust fund. In addition, we are exploring the feasibility of accessing the natural gas and other minerals our geologists think lie under the Allen farmland. The mineral rights alone would make its owner a wealthy individual. The mineral deposits that might be under the land in the form of natural gas might be tapped in the future when the price and demand are higher and the processing is cheaper and more sophisticated.

"It is estimated that Jim Allen will become this country's—the world's—first billionaire. I don't think I have ever uttered the word 'billionaire' audibly. Jesus. And he's giving most of it away to charity. I don't know about you, gentlemen, but I am in awe of this man. He's an absolute saint."

"Or a nut." Someone whispered in the back. Muted laughter.

"Now, let's compose ourselves. Never let this man fool you. He doesn't drive a new car, and as you can see, he looks uncomfortable in a suit. When I was down at his house, we drove around in a fifty-eight pickup. He usually wears overalls down in the Allen Valley. Unlike all of us in this room, his hands are weather-beaten with thick calluses. However, he is undoubtedly one of the brightest, savviest, and most honorable men I have had the pleasure of being associated with. The only person who might have been smarter was his father. We are lucky that he decided to maintain his business connections with this firm after his father died. It's a bond forged in trust and honor.

"This firm has always lived up to the highest principles of ethics and hard work, and we will continue doing so as we become the functional component of the Allen II Trust Fund in the years to come. When Mr. Allen executes the new trust, it will take this firm to a whole higher level, gentlemen; welcome to the ride."

■ ■ ■

In his white twin-engine, Jim Allen was cruising at about two thousand feet above the Allen Valley. Outside of his ranch, he felt most comfortable floating in the heavenly solitude. His 1966 twin-engine Piper Comanche was his only toy, and he loved to service it and wash it personally. He even painted the decals on the side with the inscription "Allen Family Enterprises."

The valley below was emerald green juxtaposed with soft brown patches of desert. Noticeable grids marked the hundreds of fields like a vast checkerboard. It was near sunset, and the shadows of the Guadalupe Mountains began to spread like long, dark fingers over the desert and fields of the valley. A kaleidoscope of green, blue, and brown merged as the sun disappeared in the west. He never failed to marvel at how one of the most arid places on earth could produce all this food and always felt pride that his father had indeed been a true genius. Flying in his beloved Piper, Jim Allen saw what his father envisioned on that bluff many years ago. He wished he were there with him on the verge of fulfilling their destiny: offering charity in the purest tradition of the Mennonites to those who could least afford education and art through the Allen Trust Foundation.

■ ■ ■

1931

Over the years, I began to know my grandpa through snippets of family anecdotes and faded photos. I filled in the gaps and felt like I really knew him even though he passed fifteen years before I was born. Elias Mendoza's family had lived in west Texas since the early nineteenth century and owned a humble farm just east of Pecos. He met and married my nana in 1916 when she was only fifteen, a typical age in those days. The heavens were kind to him. On November 10, 1918, he boarded a train heading for boot camp—one day before the armistice was signed that ended World War I.

He avoided the killing fields of Europe, but the Spanish influenza spread to west Texas in early 1919. Nothing could stop its wrath. My nana claims that she and my grandpa were protected from the flu by her mother-in-law, my great nana. As the story goes, no one knew of any vaccine or other type of medicine that would offer protection from the deadly bacterial pneumonia that killed millions. Subject to the usual embellishments tacked on throughout the years, my great grandma was convinced that totally immersing someone in a bath of cheap alcohol would ward off the flu. So, she got hold of twenty gallons of Tex-Mex moonshine and (forcibly) placed my grandparents, and their siblings, one after another, in a tub of that crappy beer. As she dunked them in, one after another, she turned her Bible to Proverbs 31.6 and repeatedly cited, "Give strong drink unto him that is ready to perish…"

She was not sure if this biblical passage applied to this particular situation, but not one Mendoza died from Spanish influenza.

The Depression hit them hard, and my grandparents packed up their worldly belongings and three young children in a Ford Model T—including my father—and headed west in 1931. After a year on the road, primarily in farm labor camps, they made it to Allen County and scrounged for work. They traveled no farther and wanted a home in which to settle. Allen County was that home.

My grandpa found steady work as an irrigator working for James Allen Sr. throughout his vast ranch. Mr. Allen was good to the Mendoza family and allowed our family to live in a small house with modest rent near the Allen hacienda. And my grandpa was also close to his work, maintaining the irrigation systems, which demanded long hours. The elder Allen trusted my grandpa and paid him a living wage. My nana helped with the domestic work on the hacienda. My dad and his siblings never lacked food, clothing, or a strong roof over their heads.

The year 1937 was a volatile one in the county. Allen farms were constantly skirmishing with other farming families, primarily with others from the Original Six. Lawsuits, sabotage, and bitter personal bickering over land rights, water rights, farm wages, boundaries, easements, and crop prices flared up. Some disputes were petty, personal disputes between the younger members of the families. The original six families all helped develop the county, but mostly not in unison. Their relationships rested on a tense and fragile symbiosis that periodically snapped violently. In the early summer of that year, someone tinkered with a major floodgate from one of the major canals on the Allen farm. Presumably, over time, the gate would come loose and flood thousands of acres of lettuce and tomato crops ready for picking. The sabotage was not intended to kill anyone. But my grandpa attempted to repair the damaged gate, and the water burst, drowning him. His body was found in the middle of a rotten tomato field. That tragedy temporarily quelled the internecine fighting among the feuding families but at a devastating loss to the Mendozas. James Allen was honestly distraught by the tragedy, and he felt partial blame for my grandpa's death. But his generosity and compassion for our family remained, and he was always close to our hearts.

Part Twelve

"AND MAY 1968 GREET US WITH JOY, PEACE, AND PROSPERITY"

Curt Mendoza felt as good now as he did during his Special Forces training. The forty-pound load of marijuana in his backpack felt light, almost nonexistent.

Reaching the crest of the Western Mountains—five thousand feet—he could sense the downward slope heading into Allen Valley. The valley heat rose through the mountains, whipping through the hilly labyrinths and slowly melting the fresh powder of snow. That part of the trek was the easy part. Snow was a little early that soon after Christmas. Behind him were three hikers closely following him. Between the ages of sixteen and twenty, they were frightened after crossing from Mexico the night before. But they gained confidence in Curt's hiking skills, and they simply took his cues and orders without saying much. Curt's Spanish was limited, but they understood his commands and made sure not to leave clear footprints.

After this job, he would quickly clear $300 for two days' work. He had already made peace with his conscience and rationalized his criminal behavior: the drugs, the alcohol, fights, all he could attribute to, or blame on, Vietnam. Easy to accept. Vietnam made me do this shit. And if I didn't die there, I'll die here—in country. Feeling more secure as he approached the valley, he removed the small pill from his breast pocket and quickly swallowed it. It was only the second time he had taken LSD, and the experience wasn't too bad—crazy images, a little paranoia. He thought he could handle another as he ended this trip and would be well compensated for it.

Hiking at a brisk pace, they all felt energized by the warmth from the valley below in their descent. At two thousand feet now, the desert and farmlands opened to them. The lush green fields of lettuce, broccoli, and green onions were plump and ready for market on the desert floor.

One of the Mexicans asked Curt, "Que es eso?" Below, among all the green, a large hacienda perched on a small hill became visible like a fleeting mirage in the desert.

In his broken Spanish, Curt replied, "That's the Allen ranch. I know it well. We can get water down there and probably some food. I don't think there's anyone there a few days after Christmas." Curt wiped the spittle from his lower lip and could feel the low thunder in his stomach. Damn, I could eat a fucking ten-pound hamburger right now. "Follow me, and we'll take a look…"

■ ■ ■

Matt was near the end of his shift as the western horizon slowly swallowed the setting sun. He didn't mind working during the Christmas holidays… someone had to. There were no friends to share the holidays, and the overtime would help pay the bills. Following four pairs of tracks toward the Allen ranch, the lead tracker of the group was the same guy he had tracked before. The fresh powder of snow offered new opportunities to follow paths more quickly into the valley.

He sketched a mental image of the lead tracker based on all the essen-

160

tial variables up to this point. From the shoe size, depth of impressions, gait, and manner of hiking, Matt guessed the smuggler was about 5'8" and weighed between 140 and 160 pounds. Probably stocky and clever at hiding the tracks—always hiking on rocky trails, along streams, and not disturbing the brush. He must have been in fairly good condition since there were few signs he stopped to rest, probably averaging fifteen miles a day in rugged terrain. The VC couldn't hump these hills much better. Matt thought, This guy had to have some army training 'cause he tracks like one of ours. This thought had never left his mind since he started tracking him. With the new snow blanketing the mountains, the tracks were harder to hide. Seeing the Allen hacienda below as a beacon, he began to hike on a downward slope into the warm valley awaiting him.

■ ■ ■

Jim Allen sat alone in his bedroom, reviewing the codicil. Taking a deep breath, he slowly reviewed it for the tenth time. It was signed, witnessed, and properly dated. Only the formalities remained: making copies, having it stored in his lawyers' offices, and waiting for its contents to emerge like a rare flower about to open. The full impact of this Allen Trust II would not be felt until long after he was gone from this earth: scholarships for needy children, research for deadly diseases, donations to universities, new schools in Allen County. His father was looking down and would feel only pride that his only son would seal the Allen legacy for years to come.

He placed it carefully in his father's old leather Indian pouch and returned it to the safe. He would fly it to San Francisco for storage at his attorneys' law office. An early flight would get him in San Francisco before noon. He looked forward to getting this business out of the way so he could enjoy some fresh lobster and wine at Fisherman's Wharf. As this momentous event sank in, he lay down on the bed, exhausted, for an afternoon nap. The long shadows of the mesquite trees covered his western windows, and the dry desert air slowly drifted inside the home. He quickly dove into a deep slumber, unresponsive to the cautious footsteps outside.

■ ■ ■

The Mendoza New Year's Eve tradition consisted of all family, neighbors, friends, and strangers bringing as much food as a human could consume and waiting for midnight. A feast awaited: sweetbread, pozole, menudo, tortillas, tamales (cheese, beef, and pork), beans and chiles of every kind, vegetables, and cold beer. At our house there were over fifty people who came and went that evening as we waited for 1968 to arrive.

After regaining my appetite from the Christmas dance debacle, I ate all I could but somehow made room for my nana's flan—that sweet custard that had to be slowly savored.

I knew my mom was depressed since Curt was not there. His absence felt heavy among us. He had called a few days before to let us know he was OK, but he was not OK.

The guests, exhausted from the festivities, left a little before midnight, and my dad and uncles were all who remained in the backyard, sitting in lawn chairs, taking in the night. The last few minutes of 1967 were in the rearview mirror of our memories. Strewn about the backyard were half-empty beer bottles, paper plates with discarded food, and a torn poster that said "1968." The moonless desert sky was clear and black. The soft breeze from the east was heavy and misty—but sweet. The Mendoza New Year's tradition was simple: bring out the family guns and blast them into the black space. I don't know the provenance of this dumb tradition, maybe in the old west. But my uncles always paid homage to the gods of tradition and were brandishing their respective weapons of choice:

My dad: a small black revolver.

My uncle Ray: a large bolt-action deer rifle.

My uncle Diego: A heavy-looking Arisaka carbine he bragged came from a dead North Korean during the war. (My dad later told me it came from Freddie's Pawn Shop on Third Street.)

My nana: A twelve-gauge shotgun, pump action.

I was allowed to light a small string of crappy firecrackers concurrently with the guns, like a rite of passage into the world of drunk relatives. I began to respect those gods of tradition.

"OK, ready, set, GOOO!"

The thunderous rapture of this Mendoza custom was stupendous as twenty rounds were blasted into the air, softly punctuated with my small string of crappy firecrackers. We all breathed a sigh of relief as the blasts dissipated into the cool winter air, the aftershocks still ringing in our ears.

Someone blurted sluggishly, "Here's to 1968. Let us…hope that 1968 will bring…us all joy, prosperity…and peace to all. 1968 will be a good year…"

■ ■ ■

From the *Sonora Desert Review*, January 2, 1968:
JIM ALLEN MURDERED!
The body of Jim Allen Jr. was found yesterday in his home. He was the apparent victim of a robbery. Details are sketchy, and investigators converged on the scene of his ranch in the western portion of the county.

Sheriff Bob Johnson discovered the body after a local farm-worker called to inform the sheriff that Mr. Allen had not responded to his doorbell. The Allen bedroom was ransacked, and all items stolen have not been accounted for. Robbery may have been the motive since investigators revealed that some rare gold coins were stolen from a safe, and no other items were found. Sources close to the investigation indicated he sustained blunt force trauma to his head.

While awaiting pathology reports, Sheriff Johnson reported that Mr. Allen was possibly beaten to death sometime on December 29 or 30. More than one person is suspected of having entered the house, a large hacienda that majestically sits on a small bluff on the property. Forced entry may have come from a rear door, and the individuals also apparently drank water and ate food from the refrigerator. Sheriff Johnson also indicated that "wetbacks were spotted on the property, and we are following all leads."

More reporting will follow. Sheriff Johnson finally indicated that "we will find these animals who did this, and justice will be served. I think John Wayne said it best: 'Tomorrow hopes we have learned something from yesterday…'"

■ ■ ■

My father quietly sat in our small, cluttered living room, reading the local paper. After he finished reading the article about the murder, he paused, swallowed some air, and read the article again, slower than the first time. My mother relayed all the neighborhood gossip to my nana in the kitchen. As Nana rolled out a few flour tortillas, a pot of beans was brewing on the stove. I waited with a glop of butter for the first one.

"It was a Mexican gang that did this."

"Maybe it was the mafia, and Mr. Allen was involved in bad stuff."

"El diablo."

"It could be anybody. We should buy guns for protection. They might come into town."

There were rumors of "hippies" passing through the valley.

"I know for a fact that a few were seen doing drugs near the park on the east side. They looked filthy and probably could have killed him for money or for fun."

"I heard from good sources that Sheriff Johnson is looking for two Negros that might have some information."

My grandmother just nodded and said, "He was a good man. Good to our family. How could anyone do this?" She blew her nose. "Sorry, mijo, I got some *mocos* on the tortillas."

"S'all right, Nana. I'll wait for the next one," I said as my saliva glands bubbled.

My father then brusquely interrupted. "Has anyone heard from Curt?"

My mom and nana pretended not to hear.

■ ■ ■

Sheriff Johnson sat alone in his office at county jail, reviewing the autopsy reports and glossy black-and-white photos of the Allen crime scene with a magnifying glass. All the photos were fanned out on his desk in a sem-icircle, along with the initial police reports. A soft fan droned overhead, and he instructed his secretary to hold all calls. He gently stroked his chin, now sprouting brown and gray whiskers. A bright industrial desk lamp illuminated the top of the desk. He was the only one so far who was aware of the missing codicil and leather pouch. No doubt Allen's lawyers would soon know and would come sniffing around asking questions.

Fuckin' lawyers…

According to Dr. Glen Humphrey, the victim succumbed to one or two blows to the head and sustained about six injuries to his upper torso. The head blows might have come from a blunt cylindrical instrument, probably like a pipe. The blows to the torso were very likely from punches, including one to the throat that crushed the Adam's apple. The blows might have been from violent kicks to the body as a *coup de grâce* to the mortally wounded victim. There were no defensive wounds on the victim, indicating Allen did not offer much defense and was probably subdued after the initial blow to the head. Maybe he knew or recognized the assailant before the volley of deadly blows rained down on him.

Sheriff Johnson closely examined the photos of the crime scene: Allen on his back, staring vacantly at the ceiling, soiled pants from his bowel's evacuation. The safe was not forcibly opened, and its contents spilled on the floor around the decedent, almost framing the body. The victim's hands, in rigor, appeared to be gesturing like he was making a conversational point to the attacker. Sheriff Johnson surmised that the attacker had fortuitously entered when Allen opened the safe, or he might have done so to mollify an enraged interloper. The photo also clearly showed at least twenty gold coins on the floor near his body. Fingerprints were being processed.

Johnson knew Allen was an amateur numismatic with a gold coin collection passed down from his father. But no one knew of an accounting of all the coins he collected. Thus, it was difficult to tell if any were missing. Maybe we can find someone who might give us insight into coin collecting and who might know a list of all the coins in the safe. Johnson smirked to himself, thinking this hobby was only for rich pricks like Allen. He thought there might have been more than one killer since the strange border patrolman, the one called *Mapa*, concluded more than one individual entered the house near the attack.

He remembered the initial contact with Matt Bradshaw. Strange guy. And that ugly purple blob on his face. "Sheriff, I tracked four individuals down to the Allen ranch but lost the trail at a small stream. The bedrock around the stream was too hard for foot impressions, but I know they were headed in the direction of the Allen ranch."

"Why the fuck didn't you continue?"

"I was called to an emergency in another part of the county, sir. Once I heard about the murder, I thought to call your department the next day."

"Anything else?"

"Well, the lead guide knew what he was doing. He deployed many tactical maneuvers to avoid detection, and—this is just a guess—I think he might have a military background. He used some of the stuff I learned in my training."

"Who did you hunt?"

"VC, sir."

"Did you kill any of those gooks you hunted?"

"It was war, sir. Yes, sir, I did. Anything else, sir? I will prepare a report."

"No, I know where to find you if I need anything more," Johnson said dismissively. What an oddball, he thought. This guy saw too much combat, and I think his brain got rattled a little. And that fuckin' mark on his face…probably doesn't get too many dates. Big Bob snickered to himself.

Johnson didn't know what to make of that information. The footprints leading from the house were useless after the responding officers—and the local press—made shambles of any forensic evidence around the property as they stampeded like a herd of frightened cattle.

Johnson parsed the questions down to their basics.

Who would kill the old man and why? Robbery? A pissed-off employee? Was there anything missing besides the leather pouch and the codicil?" Why not take the cash in the safe and the gold coins on the floor?"

AND WHY WOULD THE PERSON EVEN TAKE THE LEATHER POUCH AND CODICIL?

He turned off the light and sat in the dark, wandering into his thoughts. Blackness soothed him.

. . .

Curt clutched the cold beer with both hands. He thought about that moment as soon as he completed the trek down from the mountains. Three hundred dollars is not a bad payday for a one-week crossing and hiking; he had done ten times as much in half the time in Nam.

He thought Juan's Cuban Bar would be a quiet haven where he could relax. A bowl of Cuban black beans and cold beer would give him a mental ballast to stabilize his thinking. LSD spun the inside of his head over and over. Lounging in a dark corner of the bar, Curt realized he was the only patron, and no one had entered for the past hour. He didn't expect anyone at the end of the holidays; most folks were still at home recovering from presents, travel, alcohol, food, and church. A calendar on the wall above the bar depicted a large-breasted woman with the inscription "Mando's Garage." It was January 4, 1968.

The bar felt like a sanctuary. Curt tried to dig into his memory and recreate the past few days. His memory was like a jigsaw puzzle broken into pieces scattered throughout his head, many of which would be lost forever. LSD does that to a person, creates a false memory of things that might or might not have happened—more frustrating than trying to remember a dream. Ruben, the bartender, was keeping himself busy, wiping glasses, straightening liquor bottles, and checking the cash register. Curt also got an uneasy feeling that was creeping into his mind that the bartender kept eyeing him from afar—the same feeling you get when you pass a painting, and the eyes follow you.

Ruben's nickname that no one called him to his face was *Masca Fierro*—the iron chewer. Ruben grew up near the Cobre Mine in Cuba. The mine's minerals leached into the local water sources and produced a vitamin deficiency that caused his teeth to turn dark brown, almost reddish, like rusted iron. He never smiled, except when he beat or stabbed someone. His lips parted horizontally sideways when he wanted to laugh or smirk, never revealing his rusty teeth.

Under the bar counter, Ruben kept two folding buck knives and a sawed-off shotgun. He was better than most surgeons with a knife—quick, clean, and surgically accurate. Curt had heard the rumors around the county that said he had killed at least four men with knives, but tales are often embellished with time. Ruben's loyalty to Juana was total, almost fanatical. He was the one she called on to "handle business things": collect money from petty debtors, remove unruly patrons, discipline the whores, and look out for any business opportunities that might arise.

Juana Gomez sat alone in her office, counting wads of money. A small revolver rested under her desk nearby. The office was strategically located next to the bar, with a small viewing window.

Curt vaguely remembered coming down from the Western Mountains into the valley. A bit of his memory popped up, and he could recall entering the Allen hacienda with the three Mexicans looking for food and drinks. LSD really messed with your memory and created illusions, past and present. He remembered slithering into a bedroom and seeing a monster lying on the floor looking up. He wasn't sure if it was dead, but it was bloody. Lots of blood. The monster appeared to look at him with a vacant expression. He remembered small, shiny objects dancing on the floor like gold insects. That confusing scene was the clearest thing he could remember before the image, and the rest of the dream, vanished like a chimera in the blazing desert—shit, no more acid trips for me.

"Hey, Masca…er, bartender, another beer, please," Curt was now more conscious of his surroundings. He came in from the clouds and could now see clearly as the LSD wore off.

Ruben glared at him as he pounded a cold bottle on the counter. "That's a dollar twenty-five."

"A dollar twenty-five?" Curt asked. "Shit, that's higher than usual, man."

"Holidays, you know. Boss lady says a dollar twenty-five for beer during holidays…and it's a dollar twenty-five for holidays, and it's a dollar twenty-five."

"I thought some guy named Juan owned the place," said Curt inquisitively.

"Her name is JUANA…JUANA. She's the owner." Ruben's teeth now grimaced like a dog about to strike.

Curt reached into his pockets, avoiding a display of $300 in bills. He reached into his back pockets, looking for loose change, and grabbed a handful. With his digital dexterity still impacted by LSD, he clumsily spilled all the coins on the bar floor—including two gold coins. Ruben caught a glimpse of the shiny gold coins bouncing on the bar floor, and his eyes lit up. His lips widened into a rusty smile.

"That's a dollar twenty-five," Ruben ordered as Curt picked up all the coins, hoping Ruben hadn't seen the gold ones.

After Curt paid and returned to his table, Ruben entered the office and whispered something to Juana. She patted him on the shoulder, made a phone call, and nodded her head several times as if following instructions from the other end of the phone line. Curt did not pay much attention to them and thought nothing of it—just a crazy bartender and Juana talking business. *None of my business.*

She hung up the phone, locked her eyes on him, quickly slithered to his table, and pulled a chair close to him. Ruben stood behind her, glaring his rusty teeth. Months later, Curt would look at this moment in detail and regret ever sitting in that bar.

"My name is Juana, the owner of this place." She spoke slowly, making sure he could hear every syllable. Curt nodded and thought of a rattlesnake about to strike. Calmly clutching the beer bottle as a potential weapon, he tried to digest his surroundings. Time in the jungle created a sixth sense about when danger was about to approach, and he could sense it now. Every hair follicle popped up.

Curt slowly lessened the grip on his beer and sat up. "Hey, I paid for the beer. I don't like being hassled."

Masca Fierro was now positioned behind the bar, with both arms under the bar counter. His eyes locked on Curt.

"I know you were there," she said. "The Allen house when he was killed."

"What the hell you talking about?" Curt now remembered the bloody monster and the gold insects from his LSD trip.

"Those gold coins, mijo, are from Mr. Allen, aren't they? May God rest his soul."

"What the fuck does that have to do with me even if I was there? Why are you giving me all this shit? I come here a lot and never hassle anyone.

Juan's Cuban Bar is my favorite."

"That's Juana's Cuban Bar. Juana…na. You haven't heard, have you, *pendejo*? Allen was murdered a few days ago. Haven't you read the papers?"

Curt showed no visceral response to the information slowly bleeding into his brain. "This is the first time I heard. Again, what the hell does this have to do with me?"

"Those coins were taken from the crime scene." Juana kept looking at Ruben and the front door. She nodded to him, and Ruben then approached the table.

"You think I killed him? You, lady, are crazy."

"The other thing missing besides gold coins, which you have, was a leather pouch…and old Indian leather pouch and those papers inside. I don't give a fuck if you killed the old man. I need to know what you did with the leather pouch."

Curt just looked at her with a blank expression.

"Listen, *puto,* in a few minutes, dozens of cops are coming through that front door with all their guns pointed at you. One of those dumb hillbillies might have an excited trigger finger and accidentally fire at you. I wouldn't want that to happen 'cause you seem like a nice-looking kid. Ruben over there doesn't like to clean floors.

"If you just tell me where you put it, I can tell Sheriff Johnson, and they would probably go easy on you. The jail can be a bad place for someone on the wrong side of Big Bob. And I also have connections with the judges and the prosecutors and will use all my weight to make things better for you…and your family. Just tell me what the fuck you did with the Indian bag, OK?"

Curt thought for a few seconds, then said, "I don't think I can help you, 'cause I don't know shit, lady." At that point, Ruben cracked a beer bottle over Curt's head, and Curt staggered off the chair, looking up at Juana glassy-eyed and confused. As if on cue, Sheriff Johnson and ten deputies stormed the bar and grabbed a limp Curt like a wounded animal. Juana glanced furtively at Big Bob and nodded to him to make sure he understood she could not get the information he wanted.

"Shit, shit, shit…" Sheriff Johnson muttered to himself. "Look at those hands. They look swollen like he punched someone to death. Right boys?" Several of the deputies nodded in unison. While the deputies propped up Curt against the wall, Big Bob swung his leg and kicked Curt in the right knee. "Shit…I think he'll talk to me."

Ruben's impish smile spread his thin lips, and his corroded teeth saw the light of day. He folded his knives and returned them to the counter.

■ ■ ■

Robert Stein rented a small second-floor apartment on West Fifth Street in Clarktown. It was a two-story brick edifice, and his apartment faced the west, away from the blazing summer suns at day's end. It offered some solitude, was conveniently located near grocery stores, and was relatively quiet. He could walk to court only ten blocks from the courthouse and worked out of his apartment. He would typically see clients at court or the restaurant—"as long as they don't bring trouble," he was kindly told by La Senora. The summer days were empty, but the streets below came to life after sunset. The tall Indian laurels along the boulevard provided cool shade. He enjoyed observing all the lively activity: young mothers strolling with crying children, older Mexican couples walking hand in hand, kids playing street football, and young lovers on the park benches whispering sweet nothings. In the summer, street vendors would push their carts along the street hawking *raspados* of all flavors, elotes, candies, cold Mexican juices—lemon, vanilla, strawberry, hibiscus. During the tortuous summer, the bright Tacoma bushes would explode in yellow, and in the winter, the night jasmine would spring to life with its redolent scent that blew open the nostrils. To someone who grew up in a working-class Jewish neighborhood in New York City, living there was like looking into a fishbowl of life that was foreign, alluring, and beautiful. He was uncomfortable with the feeling deep in his gut that the longer he stayed there, the longer he would remain.

His apartment was spartan—books scattered throughout, a typewriter, a small stove, a wooden bench, a mattress he called a bed, posters of Jimi Hendrix and Gandhi, and a giant peace sign. His wooden desk was used for eating, studying, and writing. LPs were scattered near a wooden record player—the Rolling Stones, Miles Davis, Jefferson Airplane with Grace Slick and her sizzling eyes. An ashtray with the blunt end of a joint dangled at the edge. The marijuana smoke was camouflaged when it mingled with the smells of the Mexican restaurant below. There was nothing like the smell of refried beans, machaca, and pot.

He rented this space from the Aguilar family, who operated a Mexican restaurant on the first floor:

Karina's Mexican American Food

Best in the county for over thirty years

The family matriarch, Magdalena Aguilar—La Senora to most—was kind to him. Her family had adopted this young bachelor and treated him like he was part of their family. He learned about Mexican and Catholic culture, and the Aguilar family learned a bit of Jewish culture. He had been in this town for nearly two years, and this was where he found himself on January 3, 1968. Although the Aguilars recognized that Beto did not celebrate Christmas like Mexicans, he was invited to their restaurant on Christmas Eve to partake in all the festivities. He hoped to return to Berkeley in a few months since his caseload there was dwindling—it was barely enough to pay the bills and the pot.

During the Hanukah holidays, the Aguilars had modified their menu for Stein and added "Combination Plate No. 7, The Stein Plate": a dish with "some heavy Old Testament vibes that is damn fucking good," to quote Stein directly—kosher carne asada with hot sauce in a split challah bread sandwich, latkes with jalapeños and nopales, deep-fried doughnuts, and pan dulce.

He had the takeout plate No. 7 before him as he read the local paper. The morning sun was still low on the eastern horizon, and the air was crisp, clean, and smelled like cinnamon. A strong waft of beans and tortillas from the restaurant below filled the small apartment. The entire paper featured known details of the murder and implied that an arrest "was imminent," quoting sources within law enforcement circles.

Stein leaned back, lit a joint, and dozed into a deep slumber. Miles Davis and his cool melodic rift greeted him in his dream…strolling through San Francisco and its chilly fog enveloped him deep down.

Part Thirteen

QUINN'S MEANDERING PATH
TO REDEMPTION

Court Clerk: "Calling People of the State of California v. Pedro Ramos. Case No. F-4529."

Hon. Tim Gates: "Counsel, are you ready to proceed with sentencing?"

Deputy DA Berry: "Yes, Your Honor, the People are ready."

Hon. Tim Gates: "Mr. Quinn? Ready?"

Defense attorney Tobias Quinn III thought Judge Gates was like a carnivorous dinosaur with poor peripheral vision. Such a prehistoric creature looks for any furtive movement in their narrow field of vision, and then they quickly strike a nervous prey. Like those small jungle animals long ago, Quinn tried to camouflage himself in court and tried not to move too much in Gates's courtroom, or the judge might strike. Courtroom survival. Quinn moved. The judge struck. "Uh, what? Yes, Judge, I think so?" He nervously fumbled through his file as if he had lost something.

Hon. Gates: "You THINK SO?"

Tobias Quinn III, Esquire, arrived in Allen County sometime in 1959.

He married his college sweetheart just after law school, and they moved to Allen County after their physician told them the air here was better suited for Quinn's severe asthma. Los Angeles was growing too fast, and its dust and auto pollution would likely strip years from his life. His young bride reluctantly agreed.

Attorney Quinn was only thirty-two years old but looked much older: a soft gut cascading over his belt, a quickly receding hairline, thin brown hair, medium height, and a hunched jumbo-shrimp back added twenty years to his physical persona. Normally with a serious countenance, he rarely smiled. Hobbies were nonexistent, and the lawyer spent most of his time dedicated to his law practice—weekends, holidays, and birthdays, including his wife's. He reluctantly took up golf only to cater to his growing clientele.

He handled business law—bankruptcies, corporations, and estate planning. His acute probity, keen intellect, and warm professionalism attracted new clients without much effort. The business community flocked to him, and business was good. As a young college Republican, he looked beyond his law practice and was interested in politics. Photos with VP Nixon and Goldwater adorned his office. The local business community—farmers, bankers, and merchants—pushed him to consider running for California's vacant Forty-Eighth Congressional District in the 1962 elections. As a leader of the local Nixon for President in 1960 committee, his conservative bona fides were firmly established. His spouse encouraged him to run (so they could "get the hell out of this backwoods hellhole"). Washington, DC, was now in her view, with Allen County slowly disappearing in her rearview mirror.

On the tragic evening of February 6, 1962, Quinn and his wife were driving home after a political fundraiser. Quinn, who rarely drank, felt compelled to join a toast in his honor for the upcoming political race and quickly chugged three martinis.

Here's to the next US Representative of Allen County!

Tobias Quinn—you're the one!

A great church-going family man with good values, a great attorney, a great Republican, and a GREAT FUTURE US CONGRESSMAN! HEAR! HEAR!

Quinn left with a light head full of visions of his bright future. As he drove home, he turned to his sweet wife, snoring softly in the passenger's seat (probably dreaming of a two-story brick townhouse in Alexandria, white picket fence, two maids, and a shining black four-door Cadi in the driveway). He turned to her and gently stroked her hair. At a later inquest, he testified that he "never saw the coyote until the last second." Trying to evade the terrified animal, Quinn swerved into a ditch, and their 1961 Mercedes sedan rolled over a few times into an alfalfa field. Quinn escaped unscathed. His wife was thrown clear and slammed her skull against a concrete ditch. She died instantly, along with her vision of the Alexandria brick townhouse.

After being convicted of vehicular manslaughter, Quinn served one year in Allen County Jail. Despite pleas from his narrowing circle of friends and family, Quinn was not allowed a twenty-four-hour release to attend his wife's funeral. Suspended from the state bar for one year, his inchoate political career was prematurely aborted.

After an arduous process of community service and AA, he regained his bar ticket and retained his law license, but he struggled to find paying clients. His previous circle of friends and potential clients shunned him. He took on only small criminal and divorce cases that barely paid the rent for a small studio that also served as a law office. Copious amounts of cheap rum served as a personal anodyne to soothe his growing depression. Local attorneys gave him their leftover cases as if he were a starving dog: petty thieves, small drug dealers, hookers—and Samuel Williams.

Early in 1964, a Black couple entered his office and retained him for a murder case. Sammy Williams, their young son, was accused of a shotgun killing. They could not afford his $5,000 retainer, but he agreed to take the case with payments. Quinn quoted this high fee knowing they probably could not afford it and honestly was not interested in the case. Defending a young Black kid would not get him back into the good graces of the Allen County Republican glitterati.

The Williams family explained to Quinn that they had tried to hire some Black attorneys from the Los Angeles NAACP, but they "weren't interested in such a low-profile case out in the middle of nowhere." No other qualified attorneys were interested, assuming they would not get paid, and a homicide involving a drug dealer simply couldn't attract a seasoned attorney. Tobias Quinn was a bottom feeder who swam deep down in the dark, murky depths of the legal ecosystem, and the Williams family accepted this. They knew they had hit rock bottom when they sought his services.

To his surprise, after a brief interview, the defendant's parents shook hands with Mr. Quinn and assured him the retainer would be paid "because local Black folks want justice for this young boy." Church bazaars, home barbecues, car washes, and anonymous donations collected most of the retainer within a month—almost half of Quinn's yearly income. The rent would be paid on time, and Quinn's sophisticated palate could finally enjoy something other than frozen TV dinners, tuna, and cheap rum.

Sammy Williams was just out of high school in 1962, and his family lived on the east side of Rockwood City in the south end of the valley. He was just a normal kid, trying to figure out his way in life, and hoped to join the army "to make my parents proud." Unfortunately, he crossed paths with Jimmy Wells. Mr. Wells preferred the moniker the Vulture and was a local hoodlum. The local scuttlebutt was that he was Sheriff Johnson's paid informant, and thus he had a thick veil of protection around him. Mr. Wells could act with impunity in all his nefarious endeavors—drug sales, thefts, and assaults. Because of Big Bob's thick umbrella of protection, he was never convicted of any offense. Witnesses to his crimes often had fading memories or never appeared in court.

One late, lazy afternoon in the winter of 1963, the Vulture entered Garcia's Groceries on Eighth Street for ice cream. He encountered Alton

Williams, Sammy's father, who had just purchased a cup of chocolate mocha ice cream and groceries after working twelve grueling hours in the cotton fields. Chocolate mocha was the Vulture's favorite. The Vulture said he wanted it; Alton said no. After working all day in the fields, the elder William refused, but his refusal was not the result of defiance. He was just too exhausted to think of the ramifications of defying the Vulture. The Vulture forcibly grabbed the mocha cup from Williams and proceeded to punch the elder Mr. Williams, who sustained a broken nose. Mr. Williams never fought back.

After his son saw his father's bloody, swollen face, Sammy retrieved a twelve-gauge, two-barrel shotgun from the closet and racked in two shells of birdshot the elder used for dove hunting. Sammy found the Vulture three blocks away, eating his father's chocolate mocha in his car under a shaded Indian laurel tree. Next to him was a sixteen-year-old runaway from Alabama whom the Vulture was trying to groom for his inchoate prostitution trade. The day was gorgeous—no wind but a whiff of rain from the east, clear blue skies with a few lazy clouds drifting to the west.

With the shotgun in tow, Sammy approached the car from the rear. In front of at least ten witnesses, Sammy, almost politely, gently tapped on the driver's window; the Vulture turned and rolled down the window, visibly annoyed. Sammy gently nestled the twin barrels two inches from the Vulture's face and fired. Like a powerful sandblaster, the force vaporized the left side of the Vulture's face. His nose, teeth, and left eyeball were later recovered twenty feet away among some rose bushes. Brains and a part of his face were scattered over the front of the car and partly on the aspiring prostitute's new dress—a bright-pink skirt with yellow sunflowers. The car radio still played Ray Charles's "I Can't Stop Loving You." The Vulture died painlessly, and to quote the inscription on his grave, "This precious child went sweetly up to the good Lord."

Irony can be fucked up.

The Vulture's sweet tooth was never recovered.

The young runaway, Loretta, responded, "Shit, my new dress!" Dramatically, she then fainted. In a bit of irony, the cup of ice cream emerged from the incident undisturbed on the front seat. Sammy grabbed the cup, calmly returned home to wait for the police, and lovingly slurped all the chocolate mocha, still cold.

Local folks raised money for Loretta, the aspiring hooker, and dumped her on a Greyhound bus with a one-way ticket to her backwoods home near Mobile, Alabama. Little Loretta kept the sunflower dress with blood and brain stains "'cause I wanna keep this bloody dress just like Jackie Kennedy." As a footnote to this story, the dress was mysteriously incinerated during one of the fundraising barbecues, and Loretta returned home.

So, the young Mr. Williams was represented by Tobias Quinn III, who had never actually tried a criminal case through a jury trial. He would simply "plead out" his clients to the "best deal they're offering." The legal funds were raised after an astonishing outpouring of community support in the Black and Mexican neighborhoods. The only person outraged by this homicide was Sheriff Johnson, who lost his best snitch and persuaded the district attorney to pursue the murder case "with the utmost vigor." Reluctantly, the DA charged the case knowing the odds of trial success were unlikely. But the criminal complaint was filed not in the noble search of justice or in the practical pursuit of public safety, but only in the interests of mollifying Big Bob. When the victim was such an odious human being devoid of any redeeming qualities, even the most skillful prosecutor might have difficulty mitigating the victim's persona. The complaint should have read People of Rockwood v. The Vulture.

At the preliminary hearing, the following series of colloquies ensued:

Deputy DA to Witness No. 1, a sixty-year-old grandmother: "Did you get a good look at the shooter, ma'am?"

Witness No. 1: "Oh, yes, sir. He was about sixty years old, with white hair, and I think he walked with a limp. The Vulture—I mean, Mr. Wells—didn't know what hit him. I heard the Vulture and the shooter had a beef…"

The court: "The record will reflect the witness appears to be giggling."

Deputy DA, pointing to the defendant in court: "Was this the assailant you saw that day?"

Witness No. 1: "Why you call that young boy an ass?"

Deputy DA: "I said assailant, ma'am."

Witness No. 1: "No, he wasn't the one. That boy's a child, and the killer was an old gentleman. I know young Sammy would never hurt anyone— even if the Vulture deserved it."

Deputy DA: "Thank you, ma'am. Nothing further."

Judge Gates to Quinn: "Counsel, any cross-examination?"

Attorney Quinn, sweating like a malaria patient and doodling nervously with his notepad: "No, Your Honor." Not blinking or moving, he was still in camouflage mode in that courtroom jungle.

Deputy DA to Witness No. 2: "Now, miss, I understand you clearly saw this killing. Is that correct?"

Witness No. 2, an elderly African American woman, nods in the affirmative, with a wry smile at the right corner of her mouth.

Deputy DA: "Can you tell this court what the assailant...the shooter... looked like?"

Witness No. 2: "He kinda look like that guy from *Rawhide*—you know, that tall cowboy. You watch *Rawhide*, young man? He kinda cute, you know?" She squinted her eyes and adjusted her thick bifocals. "I usually watch *Bonanza*, but *Rawhide*'s OK. But he sure looked like that tall cowboy in *Rawhide*, though. I'm sure of it."

The exasperated Deputy DA: "You sure, ma'am? Maybe he looked like Hoss Cartwright..."

Witness No. 2 nods with feigned alacrity. "Naw, Hoss, he too fat. That cute cowboy from Rawhide is much thinner. Not Hoss, no sir."

The DA's sarcasm spread to Judge Gates, who asked: "Ma'am, you sure you're not mistaking the shooter for Hoss Cartwright? Or maybe Adam...or Little Joe? Don't answer that. You are excused. I don't think the prosecutor has any more questions for this witness. Is that correct, counsel?"

The deputy DA shrugged. "No, Your Honor."

Judge Gates: "Mr. Quinn, do you have any questions?"

Attorney Quinn, not moving: "No sir, no questions."

Deputy DA: "Your Honor, these were the only two witnesses subpoenaed by our office. They were our best witnesses. The other ten percipient witnesses were somewhat problematic, and after careful review, our office decided to pursue this case with only these two. The forensics arguably yielded nothing significant. We could not find the shotgun or the passenger, a runaway juvenile from Alabama. No prints…someone at the sheriff's decided to wash the car. Sonny's car wash scrubbed it clean."

Judge Gates: "A nice hand job from Sonny's, huh?"

Deputy DA: "What? Well, anyway, no further witnesses, Your Honor."

Judge Gates turned to Tobias Quinn, who was discreetly camouflaged behind counsel table, not making any furtive gestures: "Mr. Quinn, do you have a motion?"

Attorney Quinn: "A motion, sir?"

Judge Gates: "Yeah, a motion. It's one of those legal thingamajigs attorneys might ask for from a judge…like if the attorney wants the judge to rule on something."

Attorney Quinn: "Uh yes, sir." (Clearing his throat, wiping sweat droplets from his forehead and spittle from his parched lip.) "The defense moves to dis—"

Judge Gates: "GRANTED. Mr. Williams, you are discharged from this case and free to go. This case is hereby dismissed."

The local newspaper ran a dramatic photo of Sammy Williams crying in the arms of his attorney with the headline "LOCAL YOUNG NEGRO FREED IN MURDER CASE." The news story further detailed the sheer legal bravura displayed in court by Tobias Quinn III in front of a packed courtroom (half of whom were probably eyewitnesses to the Vulture's premature demise).

The dismissal triggered a hyperbolic frenzy of news accounts in the spirit of old-fashioned journalistic sensationalism:

"a legal titan…an avatar of justice…"

"Brilliant!"

"Quinn's subtle yet aggressive style carried the day with few questions— like a courtroom magician!"

"Atticus Finch LIVES in Allen County!"

The courtroom magician, Tobias Quinn III, Esq., prevailed in the Williams case and regained his dignity. So as he continued traveling along his meandering road to partial redemption, four years later he was swerving toward an off-ramp before the honorable Tim Gates…

Judge Gates: "You think so? Mr. Quinn, are you ready for sentencing? Your client, Mr. Ramos, has been convicted of robbery and bringing heroin into the county jail. Do you have anything you want to add in mitigation?"

Defendant Pedro Ramos was a fourth generation of devout *cholos* and criminals. His proud pedigree dated back to the early century with a grandfather who ran stolen cattle across three counties and two countries. Despite being shot to death during a card game, Pedro's great-grandfather passed his tainted genes to several generations of thugs, rapists, and thieves. Those tainted genes were Pedro's familial inheritance. Unfortunately, the tainted DNA failed to skip Pedro's generation.

Pedro, a.k.a. Little Monster, a.k.a. Little Peaty, appeared to be on his last stop before his entry into the California Department of Corrections. Folsom prison had a cell waiting for him after this latest conviction, and probation was not something on his travel itinerary. This was not Pedro's maiden voyage to the land of stupid—he had visited that land many times. Just a rite of passage that four generations of Ramos men and women inevitably expected in life. Birth. Death. And in between, prison. He was thirty years old, just a hair under six feet tall, and thin, about 140 pounds (Pedro's unmitigated heroin habit kept his weight down). His light facial complexion was framed with thick, oily black hair. A sharp nose that centered two small eyes made him appear as though he was always squinting—especially when he spoke. He often exhibited what psychologists labeled "inappropriate laughter." That is, he laughed during occasions when most human beings wouldn't and didn't when most others would.

Interestingly, his lengthy record showed nothing of a violent nature, and he naturally had a calm disposition. What set him apart from most criminal elements in Allen County—and what garnered respect, fear, and curiosity—were two tiny teardrop marks below his left eye. Each teardrop presumably indicated one killing. And the Little Monster had two. Since he was light skinned, the marks were visually highlighted and stood out like two warning signs to anyone who thought about crossing him.

After a short and uneventful trial, Mr. Ramos was convicted of robbery and smuggling a small bundle of Mexican black-tar heroin into the county jail. The jury was entertained with detailed testimony from correctional officers of a search deep into the dark shadows of the Little Monster's gluteus crevasse. A rookie correctional officer, Mitch Adams, three days from the academy, volunteered for the search with enthusiasm. Equipped with a small light tied to his forehead like an Appalachian coal miner, he searched Little Monster's butt for contraband; the treasure trove of heroin was eventually located deep in the defendant's aperture. (During the trial, Ramos whispered to Quinn that if they had looked further, "the pendejos would have found a six-pack of cold beer and chips. Right there, eh, it's real clear, eh." Little Monster giggled at his own joke. Quinn jabbed him in his ribs, giggling.) With a lengthy record dating back to 1955, he was statutorily ineligible for probation unless the court found "unusual and compelling circumstances," which means anything a judge can articulate that won't get him reversed on appeal. He accepted his fate like a proud Ramos man—unflinching and without remorse. Folsom Prison wouldn't be so bad. He had heard Johnny Cash might play there soon and hoped for front-row seats. He'd be away from the wife, from his six kids, from all the mundane responsibilities that pestered him daily—throwing away the trash, paying bills and rent, dealing with difficult in-laws, listening to his old lady's incessant bitching and his kids' incessant crying. He'd trade that for Johnny Cash and Folsom.

And the teardrops would offer a veil of protection against unruly elements at the California Department of Corrections.

"What a badass!"

"Two kills…this *vato's* serious!"

"I wouldn't mess with him!"

Little Monster did little to quell the fear from his two teardrops.

The judge even encouraged Little Monster to give a statement. "Well, Judge, it's real clear, eh. I never killed nobody, eh. Do what you want, eh."

Judge Gates rendered his sentence after the usual perfunctory arguments by both attorneys. "I have thoroughly reviewed the moving papers of both counsel and listened carefully during the trial. The defendant's long record speaks for itself. However, counsel, after reviewing the factors in mitigation and aggravation, I do find unusual and compelling circumstances in this case. No violent record, plus a loving and supportive family and a clear expression of remorse. Therefore, defendant Pedro Ramos, a.k.a. Little Monster…a.k.a. Little Vato Loco…a.k.a. Little Petey…will be placed on probation and serve six months in county jail. I will suspend his five-year sentence."

Deputy DA, horrified: "What the…Judge? We strongly object for the record! We suspect he's killed twice! Look at his record! What the…"

Attorney Quinn, puzzled, whispered to his client: "What the hell?"

Little Monster, smiling: "What the fuck? I'm not going to Folsom? Damn! I'm gonna miss Johnny Cash, ese. Real clear, eh."

Completing the quartet of bewilderment, the court stenographer's face also reflected a "what the fuck?" countenance. She just shook her head, looked at the ceiling, and continued with her shorthand.

Judge Gates then abruptly commanded both counsel to his chambers. "Gentlemen, I want to discuss another case with both of you. Mr. Quinn, the court needs your services, and I want you to represent another young man in an unrelated homicide case—now that you have one murder case under your belt."

Quinn nodded demurely, and the district attorney smirked, still fuming at the judge.

"I just learned that an arrest has been made in the Allen murder case—a young local boy named Curtis Mendoza—and I need someone with homicide experience to represent him. Mr. Quinn, can you?"

Quinn was still puzzled by Little Monster's sentence. "Can I what, Judge?"

"Mr. Quinn, dammit, can you represent the defendant? He'll be arraigned tomorrow, and I need to ensure he has an attorney with your experience. There aren't too many locals who have handled a murder case. And your record is 1 and 0. You have a winning homicide record. Undefeated."

Quinn resisted, knowing he could not handle the Allen murder case. He was smart enough to understand the Williams murder case was an aberration. "Uh, sir, I don't think my calendar would permit me to take on another lengthy case, and I am trying to take cases other than criminal and build up my civil base of clients."

"You can't do it. Just say it…" Judge Gates understood Quinn would quickly be in over his head in a high-profile murder case and didn't want to force it on him. He called his court clerk. "Hon, get me Mr. Stein ASAP, please. Shit, we're scraping the bottom of the attorney barrel."

"Uh, yes, Mr. Stein, I'm glad you can accept the appointment. He will be arraigned tomorrow in my court at nine o'clock sharp. You might want to get here early because of the crowds, you know." Judge Gates was keenly aware of how obsequious he sounded speaking to an attorney—especially this attorney—but he knew sweet talk would be more effective. Soothing Mr. Stein's ego wouldn't hurt too much. "I have a deputy district attorney with me here in chambers, and I would like you to come here ASAP—within twenty minutes."

Quinn and the trial DA were still in the judge's chambers overhearing the discussion. They could see Gates nod his head as he listened on the phone. "Mr. Stein, you want what? That's a bit unorthodox…but wait, I think I can arrange that as long you're here within twenty minutes so we can discuss tomorrow's arraignment here informally. Mr. Stein, I'm going to appoint you only 'cause I know there aren't too many lawyers in these parts who can handle a case like this. Mr. Quinn has indicated he's unable to represent the defendant." He giggled. "Yeah, I know…OK, see you soon. Hon, get me the sheriff, please."

■ ■ ■

Robert Stein put down the phone, quickly gulped a cold cup of macho Mexican coffee, strapped on his only dark three-piece suit recently purchased at the Salvation Army, picked up his briefcase, and took one last glance at himself in the mirror. Damn, I need a joint, he thought, but the coffee felt good. He hoped the bloodshot eyes would clear once he arrived at His Honor's chambers.

He sprinted out the door, jumped into his pastel-blue VW beetle, and waited. In the rearview mirror, he saw them—two Allen County patrol cars headed his way with sirens. His only condition for accepting the Mendoza case was delightfully simple—a police escort to the courthouse one mile away. He turned the ignition, cranked in an eight-track tape of the Rolling Stones' *Out of Our Heads*, and floored it to the courthouse through the streets of Clarktown with two patrol cars in tow, sirens blaring and lights flashing. To the casual observer, it appeared the police escorts were in hot pursuit of a pastel VW bug, and most pedestrians stopped to stare at the procession.

On the corner of Fifth and Pecan streets, a skinny Black teenager, recognizing Stein, raised his bony right arm in a Black power salute as the VW passed with the angry officers losing ground. Stein turned to him

with a peace sign.
MEEP! MEEP!

Part Fourteen

JUSTICE

After my brother's arrest, our house, family, and future became chaotic, confusing, and plain scary. An endless stream of neighbors, relatives, and some strangers would visit or pass by the house to get a glimpse of the Mendoza household, as if they could gain new insight into the murder charges pending against Curt. My father's hushed discussions with my mother and grandmother were out of my presence, but I heard snippets of their conversations about Curt.

"What do you think?"

"Maybe we should ask Hank to help him…I don't know much about this guy Stein."

"No, Hank can't help him in this kind of case."

"This is a nightmare…*dios mio*."

"I can't understand this…we need to talk to his lawyer soon."

"His life's ruined…I know he was doing bad things…but this…"

After my return to school from the Christmas holidays, I felt a change in the ambiance. Some kids gave me prolonged stares, some averted eye contact with me, friends avoided me, and some teachers treated me differently; some were overtly condescending, some awkwardly distant, and some extra nice. Even my Adela was acting odd with me, as though we were now strangers. I was over her, but I still treasured her friendship—and I didn't even know if that could be salvaged. Once your family's reputation is stained, the reality of who your friends are or aren't comes into focus. And it wasn't my imagination. The acute discomfort was palpable.

When I returned from school one day, I entered the house, and my father was on a long-distance phone call to my brother Hank in Boston.

"Enrique, he has this criminal attorney, Stein. We don't know much about him, but they say he's pretty good. I heard he's kind of a radical, but I have not met him yet." My father stroked his whiskers on his chin, waiting for a response on the other line.

"Well, father. In this situation, it's imperative that he receive the best representation, especially when the stakes are high. I've never practiced criminal defense, but our firm does handle some cases pro bono. How's Curt doing?"

I could see my father gripping the phone tighter. "'How's he doing?' They're talking about the death penalty, son. How do you think he's doing?"

"Well, father, if he committed a special circumstances offense, this would fall within the ambit of the potential death penalty."

My father was quickly growing impatient. My mom and nana also listened to the conversation in our living room. "Enrique, this is your father. Talk to me like a son, not like an attorney. OK?"

There was an awkward pause on the other end. "Pops, sorry. I'm in the middle of some important projects here, and the firm has put me under a lot of pressure. But what can I do? Curt might have to pay the price if he violated the law."

My father gulped some air and tried to formulate his next response. "YOUR BROTHER IS IN THE FIGHT OF HIS LIFE. WITH ALL YOUR EXPENSIVE LEGAL EDUCATION, NOT TO MENTION

THIS IS YOUR BROTHER, ISN'T THERE A GODDAM THING YOU CAN DO? If not, tell me now, and we won't bother you again, but we'll make sure to invite you to the gas chamber when it's goddamn time."

"Sorry, Pops. What can I do?"

"Get your butt down here. Visit your brother—he'll be happy to see you, like your mom and nana. Is that too much to ask for? And I want you to help Curt with his case in any way you can."

"I'll look for a flight out there, Pops. I'm sorry…this can wait. Family first."

My father's face was a mixture of fear, anxiety, anger, and depression as he slammed the phone. He looked at my mom and sadly shook his head.

■ ■ ■

Curt slowly emerged from a deep slumber. His first sensation was metallic, cold, and unwavering. He was lying on a metal bench—his bones and muscles, tight and sore; his brain, slow and heavy; his fear, acute and intense. The bench reminded him of the metal slabs in morgues where they pile the corpses. Considering all the dead he had seen in Vietnam, he never remembered slabs over in Nam. Calling them "mass graves" was a vile embellishment. Most dead VC and Vietnamese were dumped in holes sprinkled with lime. No matter where he was, Vietnam followed.

He was in the bunker.

In 1962, the Allen County Sheriff's Office decided that it might be prudent to build this bomb-proof bunker twenty feet below the ground in case the Russians lobbed nuclear missiles from Cuba during the missile crisis. After the Russian-Cuban scare abated and it looked like Allen County was not on Nikita Khrushchev's list of prime targets, Allen County was stuck with this fortified hole in the ground. For all his faults, Sheriff Johnson was a resourceful and pragmatic administrator. He displayed his acumen in all his glory when he converted the Russian bunker into a "forensic interview lounge" bereft of windows, microphones, noise, and, most importantly, witnesses who might inadvertently observe questionable custodial techniques. Curt was about to enjoy the pleasures of the "interview lounge." Johnson would proudly train new officers in "enhanced interrogation techniques" in this room.

As the nerve fibers in his brain slowly sparked to life, his other senses awoke from an alcohol-heroin-LSD slumber. His lips were parched, his body aching. Heroin's downside was creeping into his body, deep down to a place he never knew. The details of the interview lounge came into focus. It was windowless, about fifty-by-fifty feet, and made of thick concrete blocks. In the center was a rectangular metal table strapped with two long, heavy benches on the side. This is where he sat. The only colors were soft hues of gray. His right hand was tightly handcuffed to a medieval iron bracket under the hard table. As his swollen eyes adjusted, he saw a small toilet and sink. The concrete floor was splattered with dry stains—vomit, blood, piss, and shit, he thought. This was what he imagined a North Vietnamese prison might look like.

He had no idea of the time, place, or even day. This directionless sensation triggered an acute flood of fear to fill his mind and body. He had a vague memory—a dream, maybe, of being arrested at Juan's Bar—but was trying to piece together the scattered pieces of the puzzle in his brain. The throbbing pulse on his nose and jaw reminded him of being roughed up by faceless cops in the bar. And Sheriff Johnson's smirk came into view. Sheriff Johnson was the common denominator in his memory.

Curt had to rely on every one of his six senses for jungle survival in Vietnam. His smell, sight, and hearing were never more acute in those times than in the festering jungles. Now in the interrogation room, those senses slowly awakened. He was in survival mode. His nostrils flared to the odor of urine, feces, and sweat—his own. He was trying to force scattered images into his memory to piece together the recent surreal events. Those pieces of the puzzle were floating untethered in his scrambled head.

What the hell had happened? He vaguely remembered crossing the mountains from Mexico and approaching the Allen ranch. Where did the three Mexicans go? The amorphous image of a body, blood, coins, and legal papers came into focus. But what did all this mean? He grabbed his head with his free hand in dire frustration. His facial throbbing pounded louder, and he could hear only one sound in this metallic box—his heartbeat banging onto his chest. Why was I arrested? What was Juana trying to tell me before the sheriffs arrived?

The weighted metal door slowly opened, and Curt held his breath, trying to suck in the heavy air.

"My name is Sheriff Robert Johnson—sheriff of Allen County." Big Bob's empty eyes locked onto Curt's as he sat down across the table. He clasped his hands together like he was about to start a friendly poker game. "I thought we could talk a little before, you know, it gets complicated… lawyers, courts, and whatnot might complicate things a little."

Johnson looked at Curt from head to toe as if he were inspecting a prize stallion. "Hope my boys didn't hit you too hard. They can get a little overzealous… 'zealous'…I like that word. One of them lawyer words. You know how they like to use big words. Anyway, is it Mr. Mendoza? How do I call you?"

"My name's Curt." Glancing at the badge and the face stoically, Curt then slurred heavily. "What the hell am I doing here? What did I do?"

Big Bob had reviewed a general sketch of his prize suspect: twenty-three years old; Green fucking Beret; two tours in Vietnam with a Silver Star and two Purple Hearts; local hoodlum since returning to the States, including bar fights, domestic violence, and drugs. This kid in front of him didn't fit the image squarely. To Bob, he looked like a frightened prep-school kid after a bad night in a fraternity. Big Bob felt a tiny pang of warmth for his prize inmate.

Big Bob leaned back a little, relaxing. "Looks like you might be in something deep, Mr. Mendoza—Curt—with a murdered man. Shit, not any old man but probably the most beloved human being this county has ever known. And this is not—what's that fuckin' lawyer word—hyperbole. This is not hyperbole; it's a solid fact. You are in deep, deep shit, son."

"So? Who killed him? And again, why the hell am I here?" Curt's senses slowly returned out of the lifting fog.

"Well, I'll get into the ugly details in a moment." Big Bob then pulled out a clear evidence bag and pulled out three gold coins, placing them on the table. "I'm not gonna grill you to ask you if you recognize these, 'cause I fuckin' know your answer. We pulled these from your pocket, and we have an eyewitness who saw you with them. I want you to do all the talking, 'cause some brilliant lawyer might misinterpret this conversation—which, by the way, never happened.

"The dead Mr. Allen and his dad used to collect rare coins, and our thorough investigation found only two things not accounted for—one was these coins. There is no dispute. They were found on you when we arrested you, and I know you weren't stupid enough to display them—they probably just accidentally fell out of your pockets. But the point is, they were on you."

Big Bob turned to spit a large wad of brown phlegm onto the floor. "Coming down with a cold. You must excuse me. Anyway, here's another lawyer word—*nexus*. These rare coins are the nexus between you, Mr. Mendoza, and the Allen homicide. Nexus—the connection. You're connected, Curt, to some very bad shit."

Curt said nothing, looked away from the coins, and focused on his interrogator.

"Now, there's only one other thing that we couldn't find, and you won't find this item in any of the official police reports. The only other item we could not find—and, Curt, this is what I'm most interested in…" Big Bob's fatherly voice was now soft as he edged closer to Curt.

"Listen, son, a leather pouch—an old Indian pouch—with documents is also missing, but this was never mentioned in my reports because it's a point not too many are privy to.

"I've got a pretty good idea that either you grabbed it or know where it's at. Maybe those greasy wetbacks with you thought it was valuable and took it. But that makes no sense to me. I know a lot of dumb Mexicans, and with all due respect, I don't consider you dumb, son. If they were with you inside the Allen ranch, they would only have taken other stuff like food, water, and anything of value. Am I right?" The sheriff rose, pulled up his belt, swallowed some air, and began pacing the room like an expectant father in a maternity room.

"You know those rich assholes that collect these coins…nu…miasmatic, yeah numismatics? The elder Allen was one, bless his rich heart, and he gave his now-dead son these three coins. As far as I know, they were always kept in a safe in Mr. Allen's bedroom—along with a small handgun, a .38, legal papers, and, of course, an Indian leather pouch." Big Bob gathered more phlegm in his throat and planted another wad onto the floor, admiring the distance and trajectory sideways like a golfer on a long fairway.

Curt remained frozen except for his heavy eyes following the sheriff closely—survival mode.

"By the way, one of my friends—an amateur nu…mis…matic—told me these coins are 1908 Indian Gold halves…whatever that means. But they might be, 'cause of the markings, see? But I'm not here about the coins. These Indian golds are only of forensic value to me because they're the nexus, a nexus, between a brutal murder in my jurisdiction and a fucked-up Vietnam vet—a Green fucking Beret. Son, you're in deep shit.

"Now, the Allen County DA is not the best in the state, but any dumb prosecutor would have no trouble convicting you. Heck, Jim Allen is not only a pillar of this county, as they say; he's the whole damn building—pillar, walls, roof, floor. I bet most of those dumb jurors they select probably owe something to the great Allen family. I heard even your own family worked for him out in the fields. Although he never gave me a dime for my political campaigns, and believe me, I asked, he was generous with many of the folks around here—even spics, coloreds, and chinks. We now even have some of them on the juries. Can you believe that?

"Now, back to the Indian pouch. If you know where it's at, that knowledge, between you and me, is worth a thousand of those Indian coins…'cause it just might be worth your life.

"If you tell me where it's at, I can make most of this case go away. Evidence can disappear in the evidence locker because of some incompetent cop. Witnesses can be made to forget. These coins—the nexus—might get lost or end up in the hands of some greedy asshole. Poof—there goes the nexus and the DA's case. There's only one person who can make that happen. I am your only way out of this holy hell."

Johnson then peered at Curt's left arm. "What kind of tat is that? Wow looks like a skull in a green beret. Bet you're proud of that, huh? A fucking Green Beret in this holy mess. Murder. What do ya think your war buddies would think of you now?"

A metallic thump on the door interrupted Sheriff Johnson. "Yeah, what is it? I'm busy…it better be good!"

A voice on the other side responded demurely, "Mr. Mendoza's attorney is demanding to see him now, sir."

"What asshole attorney wants to see him?"

"It's Mr. Stein, sir."

"Stein…shit…your attorney is here, Mr. Mendoza. We'll finish this conversation later. But all this crap we talked about…it never happened. And I suppose you know what's good for you while you're enjoying your accommodations in my facility. In that case, you won't repeat this conversation even, and especially, with your attorney, the great Mr. Stein.

"Cool tattoo, Mr. Green Beret. Fuckin' lawyers. Cool tattoo…"

Curt was quickly escorted from the enhanced interrogation lounge upstairs to the general room reserved for attorney-client interviews. The escort treated their star inmate carefully and respectfully per Sheriff Johnson's order.

Curt was shoved onto a wooden bench, still handcuffed although looser. He observed a disheveled young man, thin and unshaven with shoulder-length hair, slightly brown. Forsaking a tie and coat, he wore only a wrinkled T-shirt with a peace sign emblazoned on the front. He looked hungover…just the way Curt felt. His pale-green bloodshot eyes began to focus. "My name is Robert Stein—you call me Bob. I'm pretty laid back except in court. I have been assigned to represent you in what I expect to be a murder charge. What can I call you?"

"Curt."

"Cool…right on. Looks like they roughed you up a bit. You OK?"

"I'll survive. Who hired you? What the hell is this all about?"

"We'll get to the details soon, but for now, I just wanted to introduce myself and lay out some basic rules you need to follow. If you can't follow these simple rules, then I probably cannot represent you 'cause I cannot protect my clients from their stupidity." Stein paused briefly and wet his parched lips. Swallowing the stale air, he continued. "The sheriff's office has not completed their initial reports, including the autopsy results. I'll return when I have more information to share." When he heard the word "autopsy," Curt sat up, and his ears flinched.

"First, don't do anything stupid in here. You're on your own best behavior, nothing that might be used against you later in court. What little I know about you tells me you're intelligent—but that Special Forces training can be a curse. Use that discipline, and only use physical force in here if you…absolutely…need…to. It will always be your last resort. I heard rumors they recently installed hidden cameras in this decrepit hole. Always have your guard up.

"Second, don't trust anyone—"

"Why should I trust you? I don't even know you, man."

"Third, you quickly need to accept one thing: except for your family, I am your best and only friend that you will need to trust. If we can't form a reciprocal trust, I will cease representing you, period. We don't need to like each other. I will not pamper you, and I will not feed you a bunch of empty platitudes. Only the real deal. You might even get to like me." Stein

197

offered a twisted smile to his new client.

"Finally, do not talk to anyone or show any reaction when the alleged homicide is brought up directly or indirectly. And did I mention, DO NOT TRUST ANYONE? PERIOD. Whether it comes from inmates, staff, or especially from Sheriff Johnson. What did you guys talk about in the forensic interview lounge?"

"Nothing…nothing at all."

Stein looked skeptical. "All right. We're on the same page. I will return shortly. Any questions?"

"Yeah. That peace sign on your T-shirt. Next time we talk, don't wear it."

Stein shrugged. "Cool…"

■ ■ ■

It took Stein two days to receive the initial discovery from the investigators and a preliminary report from the autopsy. Stein knew Sheriff Johnson was one of the first at the murder scene, yet he had not memorialized a report of his findings. As a defense attorney, Stein knew intuitively that what was omitted in a police report was more important than what was included. Glaring omissions had to be filled in.

Preparing for a murder trial, Stein needed more elbow room to work, so he cleared out a corner of his tiny studio / law office, discarding trash he had accumulated: plastic frozen dinners, empty wine bottles, newspapers, magazines, ashtrays with the pot ashes still clinging, roach clips, a half-eaten, two-day-old burrito that was either chorizo with papas or carnitas—he couldn't tell. Like most trials, Stein began first to craft the general parameters of his defense. He knew he won over juries with credibility but lost them with empty histrionics and dull platitudes. He knew he won over judges with legal preparation but lost them with vacuous arguments and specious legal positions. His concentration almost caused him to ignore the clarion blare from his phone.

"Law office. This is Robert Stein…Who? What law firm? Ugh, huh? OK, I can meet you nearby. There's a Mexican restaurant—Karina's—and I'll be in the back booth in one hour. We should have privacy. What was the name of your firm? There were too many names; all I heard was Smith from San Francisco. OK, thanks."

■ ■ ■

From the *Sonora Desert Review*, January 7, 1968:
In national news, the Democratic primary is set for June 4 in Los Angeles. No challenger has emerged against President Johnson. However, Senator Eugene McCarthy of Minnesota and Hubert Humphrey are considering runs. Robert Kennedy has discounted rumors that he may be interested in running. The Republican Party's favorite is Richard Nixon.

The crosstown rivalry between Rockwood High and Westside High will continue on January 20 as they battle in the Westside Gym. Both are expected to be at the top of the Desert Conference, as they have both made strong showings in preseason. Tickets can be purchased through the ASB offices at each school. Pep rallies are also planned.

Murder suspect Curtis Mendoza was attacked by other inmates recently and suffered several superficial wounds. Neither the cause of the attack nor the suspect has been identified, according to Sheriff Johnson, who is personally conducting an internal investigation.

■ ■ ■

Stein slithered onto a small booth in the back of Karina's, where he normally sat preparing for court or nursing a hangover. The restaurant staff knew him well enough to give him some privacy. Mr. Mendoza's arraignment was scheduled for the following day, and he needed rest. The macho Mexican coffee and pan dulce would be soothing and filling for an empty stomach. It was nearly ten o'clock, before the lunch crowd began to filter in. A few patrons were quietly eating nearby—three farm workers who had probably finished picking lettuce and a young couple with a sniffling newborn.

Feeling restless, Stein looked at his watch again. *Who the hell is this lawyer that called, and why would he want to speak with me?* Before arriving at Karina's, he quickly called one of his lawyer friends in the Bay Area and asked about this law firm.

"Holy shit, these guys are one of the oldest corporate firms on the West Coast. Old-money attorneys. Ira fuckin' Smith. He wrote the hornbook on trusts and estates. Have you already forgotten your real property class? He died a few years ago, but I think his son is one of the partners."

"Nah. I slept through my property class. But I think I vaguely remember that hornbook. Damn, I hated real property. I was probably stoned during most of the lectures."

"Why would they want to talk to you? You think it might have to do with this murder case you're involved in?"

"Don't know. Maybe they wanna hire me…" Stein chuckled.

"Shit, you think those establishment pricks need a token Jewish radical for window dressing? They might lose some of their waspish clients, and it would trigger an exodus from the firm of biblical dimensions." Another chuckle on the other end of the line.

"Your guess is as good as mine."

"Robert Stein, you're not thinking of selling out to the establishment, are you?"

"I hope you're joking, but no. I should be back in Berkeley in a few months, resuming the good fight. We gotta end this fucking war, man. See ya. I'll let you know. Peace, brother."

"Right on."

The young waiter carefully placed the pan dulce and coffee on the table in front of Stein. "Careful, Mr. Stein; it's hot. Is the light good enough? I know you like to read here, and sometimes Mama Karina keeps the light low. Too expensive, you know."

"Mr. Stein? Excuse me, young man." The young waiter looked back demurely with an odd look and probably thought this guy was overdressed. "The waitress at the entrance pointed me to you. Looks like you're well known here." Ira Smith II formally extended his hand to shake across the table. "May I sit down? Thank you so much." Trying to get his buoyancy in unfamiliar surroundings, Smith grabbed a napkin and wiped the bench before sitting carefully as if he were on a rickety boat in rough water.

"Have a seat."

"Mr. Stein, thank you for seeing me on short notice. I realize you have no idea what I would want or, for that matter, who I am."

Stein's success in a courtroom was quickly sizing up individuals: lawyers, jurors, witnesses, cops, judges, and even court clerks. A witness on the stand might make a subtle gesture that Stein could interpret, or the tone or inflection of their voice might send silent clues about what they were really trying to say at the subconscious level of human interaction. He could pick up nuanced terms in their speaking style and quickly decipher them. Under the full weight and pressure of a court proceeding, laypersons often reveal silent clues like poor poker players. During voir dire, he would carefully look for any discernible unspoken gestures from jurors that might give him hints about their general attitudes, and that might flush out defense-prone jurors.

He was quickly assessing Mr. Ira Smith II in front of him in that dimly lit Mexican restaurant. A little over six feet tall. Thin but strong. Appeared to be a bit foppish. Probably exercises daily. Stein guessed Marin County or Nob Hill, several generations back. His thin hair was beginning to recede, and he was probably in his midforties, but he was probably comfortable with his looks. His subtle discomfort suggested he probably rarely ate in

Mexican restaurants, and what was even rarer, he was probably not around Chicanos much except from a distance when he waved to his gardeners and maids, all Pedros and Marias. He sported a crisp white shirt open at the collar with a tailored blue sports coat. His loafers looked so soft, comfortable, and expensive. Probably Italian. Stein took a quick glance at his own shoes—Mexican leather huaraches that had the thick rubber Michelin tire pieces at the bottom. His pedicure-starved toes stuck out. An earnest countenance suggested an intense formality. His soft blue eyes were inviting in a friendly sort of way, but behind them, Stein could not figure. The eyes always told him something, but not this guy's—somewhere between Norman Bates and Ozzie Nelson. His general aura was somewhere between self-confidence and arrogance, between friendliness and snideness.

But Stein thought the most intriguing feature of Ira Smith's physical makeup was his skin. Flawless. Smooth. No marks or bumps. As if his face had never been exposed to the elements of heat, cold, or wind. His tan was not a tan. It was a soft, glowing patina that humans develop only in Aspen on the slopes or in the South of France. Guys like him have difficulty hiding their wealth; it lurks not too far beneath the glowing skin. This guy came from old San Francisco money. His DNA probably looks like intertwined dollar bills, Stein thought.

"Mr. Smith, I actually have no idea what you want. Don't you want to order something? You're probably hungry."

"I…I'm not too sure. I am hungry and I haven't had a bite since I left the city. What are you having?"

Stein slurped his coffee as he shoved his pan dulce into his mouth as if he were in a hot dog eating contest, oblivious to the crumbs and coffee stains splotched on his shirt. "I like the menudo here, red menudo, not too chile. The broth is fantastic and comforting. Mexicans swear by it for helping with hangovers. I can personally attest to that." Both giggled.

"Let's order two. I'll try it. And I think you order it with tortillas?"

"Yeah…Miguel. Get us two bowls of menudo, and *tortillas de arina.*

And more coffee, please. How's La Senora?"

"Bien, Mr. Stein. A little gout, but Mama's doing good. I will get your nonkosher menudo."

Smith looked puzzled. "Nonkosher?"

"*Orale*! You doing better in school, Miguel?"

"Yeah, I got a B in math. Calculus is hard! I will get you that menudo right away. Our cook was late—too much drinking last night, I think. Oy vey!"

After Miguel returned to the kitchen, Smith asked, "When that Mexican waiter referred to the menudo as nonkosher, was he being anti-Semitic?"

"First, Miguel is not Mexican. He's as red-blooded American as you are. He likes the Rolling Stones, the Dave Clark Five, and he watches *Leave It to Beaver* and *Bonanza* religiously. He has a collection of comic books. I think my bumbling Spanish might be better than his in a year if I use it more. I don't think he's even been to Mexico, and it's only a few miles from here.

"Second, this family has treated me well here. It was quite an adjustment for a guy from the Bay Area. Aren't too many Jews here. My mom doesn't know, but the nearest synagogue is ninety miles from here. I rent a small room above, and I eat here daily. Although I don't practice as much as my parents would like, I am a Jew, and these people respect that. They even prepared a kosher burrito plate in my honor during Hanukkah. It's got eight ingredients. It's on the menu as *El Plato de Kosherrr*." He emphasized the rrrr. "So, I help Miguel with his math, and he helps me with my border Spanish. He's learned some Yiddish, and I've learned some Spanish—a mixture: Spanyid.

"He wants to go to college, the first in his family if he does. I think his parents want him to inherit this business. I hope he does go to college. In my family, college was a nonnegotiable expectation. In Miguel's family, it's a faraway dream. You know how things are. Anyway, they are good people."

Smith nervously glanced at Stein's greasy Che Guevara T-shirt, dirty bell-bottom denims, and puka-shell choker. Stein's sartorial splendor was completed with Mexican sandals—the cheap ones with parts of a Goodyear tire tacked to the bottom, offering an "airy and comfortable sensation," according to the Mexican vendor at the port of entry. His unclipped toenails were disgusting. Smith thought, you probably would need a power chisel and shovel to extract the brown stuff embedded in the deep cracks of his toes. Smith thought the stains probably came from thick coffee, beer, Mexican food, or drool. His eyes and sense of comfort were slowly adjusting to this foreign environment. "Well, Mr. Stein, I am fully aware that you have just begun a serious homicide case involving the death of Mr. Jim Allen. I do not want to broach any attorney-client areas or work product. In our business, we fully understand those areas are sacrosanct. Please do not think I am overly presumptuous to think you might give me any information. However, I would like some information on matters that might only be collateral to your case but are critically important to my law firm."

Stein ate another large piece of sweet bread and quickly swallowed it with one bite, listening to the person sitting in front of him, who had pristine manners and a glowing complexion.

"I'm listening."

"Your client, Mr. Mendoza, was found with some gold coins that allegedly belonged to Mr. Allen and arguably might form a nexus to his involvement in this tragedy."

"*Allegedly* is the operative word here, counsel." Stein could feel a growing sense of unease in his gut.

"Mr. Allen is—or was—a client of our law firm, although we now represent his estate. Our firm has been associated with the Allen family since before the war—World War II, not the current one. Jim was in our office just a few weeks ago in San Francisco. I've known him since he was literally in diapers, when his father was my father's client.

"Anyway, we are looking for an important document that Jim should have had in his possession at the time of his death. It was an amendment to a trust, and we think it was kept in an old Indian pouch that is a family heirloom. A very distinctive leather pouch with Indian marks—Navaho—and the initial 'A' on it.

"We were unable to glean any information from Sheriff Johnson about the property recovered. His response to me directly was, and I quote"—he cleared his throat— "'Fuck you and all the lawyers'; end quote."

Stein broke in, saying, "That might be the most articulate sentence he's uttered in a long time."

Sarcasm didn't register with Ira Smith II. Just a passing blip on his cerebral radar.

Smith continued. "Needless to say, it was a distressful conversation that yielded nothing significant from our perspective. In an abundance of discretion, I did not mention the missing document to Sheriff Johnson."

"Listen, I wish I could help you, but I have more pressing concerns at the moment—like keeping a young soldier from the San Quinten gas chamber. This county has never seen the likes of this kind of murder, and only once in this county's illustrious legal history has the local DA sought the death penalty. Back in 1952, a young farmworker got into a scrape with an off-duty sheriff and killed him. Since it was in the 'line of duty,' the death penalty was triggered."

"The line of duty?"

"Oh, yeah, the officer was ostensibly 'investigating' some robbery on his own time at this bar. Well, despite several mitigating factors—the officer overtly fondling the farmworker's wife in front of him, spouting the usual racial epithets, and pistol-whipping the poor schmuck—the officer was eventually killed with his own weapon after a brief struggle.

"In some cases, juries here are a slight notch above those in Mississippi. The jury took two hours to convict, and the poor guy was on death row for three years."

"Was?"

"He thought he might save the state the expense of his execution and hung himself."

Smith slumped down slightly in his seat. Somewhere near the busy kitchen, the rich baritone of Vicente Fernandez sprang from a jukebox bellowing lyrical tales of fleeting romance, untimely death, and the cruel caprices of life. Families began to trickle into the restaurant. A beautiful amalgam of familial sounds all mixed—children, old ladies, parents barking at their children, quiet laughter. It now felt crowded.

"Mama, can I have a paleta?"

"Mijo, be quiet in here!"

"Tata, get me some pancakes!"

"Sir…sir, are you ready? Be careful, 'cause the bowls are very hot, freshly made this morning." Miguel carefully placed two bowls of red chile menudo, corn tortillas, rice, beans, cilantro, and white onions in front of them. "Anything else?"

"Just a couple of those *pinche* hot jalapeños for me and Mr. Smith. I think he might like them. Miguel, it looks good. I want to see your math homework this week, OK? You'll be taking calculus next year."

"Yeah, Mr. Stein, but the calculus teacher is no good. He's also the football coach, and they got him to teach 'cause no one else would. What a schmuck!"

"Don't worry about that, *vato*. Just do the work. *Orale!*"

"Mr. Stein, your RRRRRSSS sound much better! You talk like a Chicano cholo! Haha!"

Stein turned as Smith was now diving into the bowl of menudo, along with tortillas slathered in butter. "I have some preliminary reports but no mention of this document—or the Indian pouch. You wouldn't travel all this way to Allen County unless you and your firm thought it important. What's its significance, and what's more important for me and my client, how does it help my case?"

"Honestly, I don't think it does, but I don't have all the relevant information you do or your experience in these matters. This menudo broth… is fabulous."

"Let us assume at some point in the discovery process I come across this pouch…what does it mean?"

"Just some historical context. In 1920 the elder Allen—a genius, in my opinion—created a trust that was to change, on its own terms, in fifty years—January 1, 1970. Half of his holdings—millions of acres of the best farmland in the world—would be divided among the original five other families that settled this county: Johnson, Rossi, McCoy, Romano, and Pressley. Mr. Allen was loyal to these pioneering families that created this oasis in the desert and wanted to repay their families. They struggled with him in the early days with pests, floods, heat, bankruptcies, family tragedies, with sporadic episodes of violence primarily directed at Allen's workers. Despite the animosity, Allen felt he owed them something. And the other half would be placed in a charitable trust 'for the benefit of Allen County's citizens.'

"You must be aware both parents passed away in 1957. Allen, the elder, named his only surviving child as the alternate trustee in the event his wife could not or would be able to manage the trust. Although Beth Allen was undoubtedly capable of this duty—she received an accounting degree from USC and handled some of her husband's business affairs—she had no interest after the elder Allen's death. She was in a deep state of depression for years until she committed suicide in 1957.

"Our firm just completed the final draft, or amendment, of a second trust—it will be known as the Allen Trust II, or actually, technically, it's a written exercise of a power of appointment given to Jimmy Jr. from the initial trust signed in the 1920s.

"I don't know how much of estate law you are familiar with"—Stein was looking cross-eyed—"James Sr. wanted two things: one, a charitable trust for Allen County, and two, the other half for the original five families to be divided equally among them."

Smith continued. "Here's the problem now. The terms of the original trust are locked in, and the only legal mechanism to modify it lies in the hands of Jimmy Allen II—the deceased. As the only surviving Allen, only he can modify the trust with the power of appointment given to him by his father. In fact, he did change it so that the five families are excluded as beneficiaries. For the past two years, our firm has been diligently working with Jimmy so that he can exercise this crucial option. The new trust, once the original five beneficiaries are excised from the original trust, will award 100 percent to charity for medical research, hospitals, academic and athletic scholarships, and museums. It's not hyperbole, Mr. Stein, to say the Allen II Trust will rival, if not exceed, the most extensive philanthropic endeavors in the world.

"Even though the Allen family squabbled quite a bit with the other five families, Allen Sr. still felt he owed them something since they all struggled together in the early years of this county's development. Although they all fought one another in one way or another, the relationship between the five families and the Allens was symbiotic. So, in essence, half of the Allen trust would go to charity and the other half to the five families.

"Now, here is the catch. Allen Sr. gave his son, as a beneficiary, a power of appointment integrated with the original trust. I know it by heart, and the salient portion is: 'Upon the death of James Allen II and Beth Allen, if such event occurs before January 1, 1970, the surviving or alternate trustee may distribute the remaining balance of the Allen Trust I to said beneficiaries in said trust or may modify the noncharitable beneficiaries with a change in circumstances subsequent to the death of James Allen Sr. and Beth Allen.'

"The bottom line is, Jimmy Allen Jr. is given the power to completely omit the five families from the original trust. With this important caveat"— Smith gulped another spoon of menudo—"Jimmy must exercise that power in writing, showing his clear intent to do so. This broth is tasty! Anyway, last month, our firm prepared the final version of that document. You see, Mr. Stein, Jimmy Jr. felt that the other five families mistreated the Allens, and while his father put that aside, Jimmy Jr. did not. He has...or had... harbored a deep-seated animosity toward the other five families. He cut them out from the trust completely, which, under the terms of the original trust, was clearly his prerogative.

"That document is now missing. Jimmy took it with him a few weeks ago against our stern admonishments to preserve its integrity. He had stored it in an old leather Indian pouch that had a great deal of sentimental value to the family. As wealthy as they are, this was their most valuable heirloom.

"In the next twenty years, we anticipate the fund may be valued in excess of a billion dollars…potentially larger than the Carnegie foundation."

Stein gulped an entire mouthful of menudo and tortillas. He moved up in his seat and looked at Smith with a growing interest. "I thought I heard you say a billion dollars."

"Yes, Mr. Stein, you heard right. I rarely speak in hyperbolic terms." Stein believed him. "I had never uttered the word 'billion' in my life, but our firm is quite familiar with the Allen family holdings and its future potential. After the elder Allen's death, the five families created hell for the Allen family. Lawsuits, land disputes, personal antagonisms, some petty, some serious. The five families used every legal and illegal manner to destroy the Allen businesses, and Jimmy, of course, bore the brunt of those personal and professional battles.

"The five families were unaware of the terms of the original trust until much later during one of the endless court proceedings through routine discovery in court. And of course, they changed their attitude with respect to Jimmy. He was now holding the purse strings of the trust—a billion-dollar trust.

"Now, there's some irony here. Those same five families were always at odds with the elder Allen once they realized he had put himself in a better position with the land. He was simply a better businessman who understood the long game, and the long game often prevails over the short term—especially where avarice is concerned. Over the past five decades, some of the original five sued him for one thing or another, but we always prevailed in court. The Allen leases and holdings are ironclad, but the original trust remains, notwithstanding the lawsuits and growing animosity that developed. Our firm has the best water rights attorneys in the world. Our lawyers wrote the hornbooks on water rights. You were at Boalt Law, right? Spencer Hayden teaches water rights there."

Now Stein's ears perked up like a Boston terrier. "You mean these millions of acres of farmland are worth that much?"

"It's more complicated than just the farmland, per se. It includes the mineral and gas rights under the farmland. Preliminary tests indicate a fast potential from liquid gas and oil. But the clincher is this: the water rights. If you look at a map of the Allen properties, there's a pattern that's not discernible to the naked eye. When these pioneers settled this land, it was desert and scrubland—worthless on its face. But by exploiting and taming the Colorado River, its water was diverted into the valley through a series of interlocking canals that operated on gravity. The county is actually below sea level and is an ancient seabed. Allen's farmland parallels most of the interlocking canals.

"Runoff from snowpacks provides the water for the Colorado River. An interstate compact in 1922 among the upper basin western states—Colorado, Utah, Wyoming, and New Mexico—required that they deliver 8.25 million acre-feet to the lower basin states, including California. That's a lot of water since one-acre foot can cover an acre of farmland—325,000 gallons. As the west grew, the water demand grew exponentially, not just for farming but for golf courses, green lawns, parks, etc. California and Arizona have few water resources except the Colorado River.

"But—this is his genius—he owns most of the land and the rights where the Colorado River forms a T-bone connection to the canals. Imagine the Colorado as a large pipe full of water, and the canals interlock with it to divert some of the water. That's what the Allens own—those water rights. They own the spigot into the Allen Valley, and like everything in this wonderful country, there's a price for this water. It is liquid gold, clear, cool liquid gold. And millions on the coast are thirsty for it. Allen ensured that the major canals, the smaller arteries west of the Colorado River into Allen County, were primarily contiguous to Allen farmland. Brilliant in simplicity. The Allens can control where that water goes and how much it goes for. Those rich coastal cities are getting thirstier each day. And he controls the price within some legally defined parameters.

"The Colorado River basin and the contiguous states have a finite water supply. Allen foresaw a growing need for water as the cities on the coast grew and will continue to grow. He knew there would be droughts and possibly climate change. Those golf courses and homes all need water—the Allen water. His family has the spigot to turn it on, turn it off, and divert it wherever and whenever the Allens want, for a price. Yes, the Allen holdings will easily be worth billions within a few years. Billions."

Stein whispered audibly, "Billions…"

Swatting away the comment, Smith continued. "The final draft was prepared and was ready for signature in our office last week. We even planned a public announcement that would be national news. But for some reason, Jimmy wanted to bring the trust document with him to review; he promised to care for it in his safe, then return it to us next month. Against our advice, he did so. We attributed his desire to an eccentricity probably inherited from this father." Smith quietly giggled to himself.

Stein: "Damn! A billion dollars…"

"So, there you have it. If anything of value to us comes across you during the course of this trial, please contact us. You will be compensated for your time, of course."

Stein's thoughts then returned to Curtis Mendoza. "So, the bottom line is those original five families will become enormously wealthy if the new trust never sees daylight."

Smith: "Because of probate law, that amendment needs to be located. Otherwise, the original trust—Allen I—will prevail."

Stein: "Speaking hypothetically, if someone murdered Allen then took or destroyed the written amendment, there would be five families in this county that might have a reason to rejoice—or maybe a billion reasons. Now we might have a TODDI defense."

Smith: "TODDI defense?"

Stein: "THE OTHER DUDE, or FIVE DUDES DID IT—TODDI. Mr. Smith, I once represented a guy who killed someone over a two-dollar heroin dispute. You think someone might kill for a billion dollars? Mr. Smith, in spite of evolution, humans are avaricious beasts, and money feeds those beasts. We're still evolving slowly, maybe too slowly."

. . .

From the *Sonora Desert Review*, January 14, 1968:

The Westside High Future Nurses Association proudly announces a gift drive for all the soldiers in Vietnam. Sharon Lighter, president, reminded donors to send mostly socks, undershirts, canned food, and letters of support so they can all return back home safely.

A youth is recovering from multiple stab wounds received during a New Year's altercation on the east side of Rockwood. Police are still looking for suspects. The assailant was described as a young Hispanic male, medium built, slick, black hair with a tattoo of the Virgin Mary somewhere on his body. If anyone has information fitting this description, they are asked to call the Rockwood Police Department.

The arraignment in the Allen murder case is scheduled for January 30 in front of the Honorable Tim Gates, with the preliminary hearing very likely set at the end of next month, according to the district attorney. His court-appointed counsel, Robert Stein, could not be reached for comment.

Residents on the east side of Clarktown were alarmed when they reported multiple gunshots in the early morning of January

1. Police investigations yielded no suspects and attributed the shots to overly zealous patriotic revelers.

The US military has announced an increase in enemy activity throughout South Vietnam but does not view it as a coordinated effort, especially during the Tet holidays. A lull in combat activity is expected during this holiday—the lunar new year.

The opening of *Bandolero!* will be shown starting this Friday at 6:00 p.m., with two showings Saturday and Sunday at the Crestview outdoor drive-in. The movie is a thrilling western starring James Stewart, Dean Martin, and Raquel Welch. Admission is $2 per person, and students can get a 50-cent discount with their current student ID. Every Friday, individuals will get a free entry with ten bottle caps of 7-Up. Vehicles are subject to search for stowaways and alcoholic beverages, and the law will be strictly enforced.

PART FIFTEEN

A JAIL VISITOR

Sheriff Johnson visited Curt a day after the first visit and had to initiate plan B. It was obvious Mr. Curtis Mendoza…Mr. Green fuckin' Beret…was not interested in playing ball with Big Bob and could offer nothing about the Indian pouch—except to claim he "didn't know shit." Johnson had a good guess that he must have taken it, hoping it might contain something of value—more coins—and taken the pouch with him and hid it somewhere. They all only know how to steal, he thought. Steal, procreate, and avoid work. Damn Mexicans…like roaches.

So now Big Bob might have to exert a bit more pressure on the young inmate so he would clearly appreciate his limited options in the predicament. First, he arranged for Ruben to be taken into custody on the pretext of some nebulous charge— "disorderly conduct." Ruben was now in a cell adjacent to Mr. Mendoza's so he could pay a neighborly visit and send Mr. Mendoza a message. Ruben was skilled in this kind of endeavor, and Sheriff Johnson had confidence Mr. Mendoza could be persuaded to cooperate. Ruben's unique skills would soon be demonstrated. His only order from the sheriff: "Just don't kill him…"

Curt's crucible awaited.

■ ■ ■

When an invasive species enters a relatively stable environment, its presence is felt quickly. It can alter other species, contaminate their milieu, and infect its inhabitants with its unique traits.

Ruben Masca Fierro's entry into the Allen County Jail had an immediate impact on the other inmates. Ruben quickly infected that human ecosystem. They knew who he was, and he quickly established his presence. One inmate, ignorant of Ruben's reputation, tried to steal bar soap and suffered the consequences—broken jaw, part of the left ear lobe removed by Ruben's rusty incisors, and part of his nose surgically sliced off. He cut it with such panache and skill, he could have been whittling wood during a lazy afternoon. By any civilized standards and measurements, Ruben was plain crazy. He was the product of survival in the Cuban "penal system." This psychotic human virus quickly controlled the Allen County Jail.

After three years in a Cuban jail, Ruben, like a true sociopath, missed being in a violent environment. By Cuban standards, he was bad, by American standards, a monster. Surviving a Cuban jail was no small accomplishment. While a guest of the Cuban penal institutions, he was stabbed, beaten unconscious, gang-raped, electrically shocked, whipped, kicked, and cattle prodded, but he survived. No human being could have survived three years of this unmitigated brutality. But he did because he wasn't human. The lines of human evolution had taken a slight detour with him and entered the beasts' realm. And Ruben, the sociopath, entered Allen County Jail with one assignment, and he acted quickly. He knew Curt Mendoza was going through severe heroin withdrawals and was also in a cell alone. Ruben promptly recruited a team to pay Curt Mendoza a visit with specific details about how to approach. Big Bob gave Ruben any liberty to complete the task.

■ ■ ■

Ephemeral flashes of hot lights. Anger. Medleys of wailing screams in the distance. Abject horror. Shadows of soldiers walking in the gray jungle, zombie-like. Beastly grunts, far away—yet close. Flickering gray images—old Asian men, tiny children, laughing and crying. Pounding staccato blasts nearby. Acrid smells of jungles, humans, soil, dampness…of death…Sally…

Curt sat up in his bunk; the heavy fog of his nightmare lifted slowly to reality. He sensed it was late at night. The jail was eerily quiet. His armpits were soaked, and he could hear his soft heartbeats. Time for inmates to think, to cry, to hurt. Curt was hurting like never before. Cramping in his lonely cot and vomiting for ten straight hours, he hoped to ride it out, hoped it would pass soon. He had seen death up close in all its human forms, and when he saw himself in the mirror that morning, he recognized it.

The jail bunk felt comfortable, and the only sound came from the lazy drone of an overhead fan. He had lost twenty pounds in the last three months. Heroin gave him no appetite except for more heroin. Sick from withdrawals, he only wanted to stay in bed forever. He joked to himself, Shit, I wish I were Dorothy in *The Wizard of Oz*, and I could click my shoes together and get out of this. His joke, surprisingly, made him laugh by himself.

As he was waking, a myriad of thoughts crisscrossed in his mind like floating pieces of a crossword puzzle—his family, Vietnam, the Allen ranch, Sheriff Johnson. And Sally. He had been in jail for only two days—two days of vomiting, cramps, and shivering sweats. All he needed was more time, more food, more strength, and more luck.

As he finally began to doze, he squinted his eyes in the darkness of his cell and could see shadows near his cell. He recognized the bartender.

■ ■ ■

School returned to normal after Christmas and New Year's vacation. Adela and I resumed our previous light platonic relationship, sharing lunch, talking about math class, homework, mean teachers, movies, and TV. But I saw and felt her differently. Her scent no longer aroused something inside like it used to. I no longer smelled vanilla and cinnamon on her—just Dial soap and cheap talcum powder. I noticed pink pimples on her cheek instead of pretty freckles, and her halitosis—garlic and milk—hit my nostrils with a blast. The tingling around her ceased inside me. But Curt's court case lingered heavily in the air wherever I went, and I couldn't avoid it; it was like trying to outrun a storm behind me. Teachers stared at me differently, some slightly curious, some overtly repulsed, but a few sincerely sympathetic.

"You think he did it?"

"The gas chamber? Really?"

"Poor family…what will happen to them?"

"He used to be such a great football player."

A big murder case. Honestly, part of me felt like a celebrity with a brother currently charged with killing one of the most famous people in our county. I think some of my older schoolmates felt more respect for me. The school pachucos acknowledged me in the hallways; the big jocks talked to me, and the pretty girls smiled at me more. It was uncomfortable. And what made it worse, my parents did not allow me to visit Curt.

"You're too little."

"It would be too hard for you."

"Curt might have a hard time seeing you while he's in jail."

I missed my brother dearly. My absence from his life left me in despair, and I had no idea how his murder case would end. I felt he was my only brother, since I hardly knew Hank. Hank was an empty ghost to me, only vague memories from my childhood before he abandoned our family for law school. He left when I was still in diapers. Curt was my hero.

Adela never brought it up, but I knew she was interested in Curt's case. The local papers covered it weekly, but she treated me the same…

albeit more distant and reticent. After the Christmas dance, I was more realistic and relinquished any further notion that we would be anything more than friends.

I could live with that.

■ ■ ■

From the *Sonora Desert Review*, January 28, 1968:
Hilda and Walter McBride announced the engagement of their daughter, Frances, to Jim Higgins of Clarkstown. Both are 1967 graduates of Westside High, and no specific wedding date has been announced. The McBride's hosted an engagement party on December 27, with dozens of families and friends in attendance. A sumptuous dinner of prime rib, roasted potatoes, and farm-fresh vegetables was served and was finished with Mrs. McBride's chocolate mousse dessert. Jim studies business in college and will work in his father's insurance company. Frances says she hopes to be "the best housewife she can be and have lots of babies."

The family of Paul and Ester Campos of Clarkstown was notified that their son, Bill, was wounded in early December while on patrol near the DMZ in Vietnam. While the specifics of the injury are unknown, the Campos family was informed that their son, a US Marine, would recover from his wounds. He is expected to return stateside and should be home within two months. Bill is a 1967 graduate of Rockwood High and was active in football, marching band, and Key Club.

■ ■ ■

Stinky called me early one morning, a month after Christmas. "Hey, Mendoza, get to my house right now…I got it." For some reason, Perry "Stinky" Coughlin always called me by my last name. I told him I still needed to do my household chores or incur the wrath of the Mendoza women. (My mom: stern admonishments with a veiled threat of a belt spanking. My nana: no veiled threat, just the *mata mosca* that I would never see coming.) "And bring the guys. Moe and Skip It are gonna flip, man! Hurry! IT'S BITCHIN', MAN…"

I welcomed the distraction from Curt's troubles. "How about Jimmy? He's cool, man."

"Nah. He makes me nervous. Plus, I don't think he enjoys anything except those dogs and baseball." I couldn't argue with his last point but still made a futile effort to include Jimmy.

"All right, I'll call the guys. We'll be there in a few."

"Right on," Stinky replied.

I rounded up Moe and Skip It, and we made it to the Coughlin household in an hour. Stinky lived on the good side of town, the west side, but all his friends were from my neighborhood.

A panoramic view of the Coughlin home was the paradigm of 1960s middle-class nirvana. A Norman Rockwell painting come to life in three dimensions. Upon arrival, a visitor was greeted with a golf course–like, emerald-green lawn that looked like it was manicured with tweezers. A small army of nameless/faceless Mexicans and Filipinos delicately trimmed the bright-yellow rose bushes, lantanas, marigolds, and petunias. Two mature Indian laurels framed the home like protective sentinels. An American flag hung proudly near the porch entrance. A freshly waxed 1967 Chevy sedan was parked in the driveway, and a faded bumper sticker that read "America: Love It or Leave It" clung patriotically to the rear bumper. The house was a stately four-thousand-square-foot, two-story brick manor. Upon entry into the living room, you were greeted with the soft sounds of Perry Como, spotless pastel sofas, coffee tables, and deep shag carpets. An amalgam of subtle fragrances filled the house. Prince Albert pipe tobacco and coffee intermingled with a slight waft of American conservatism and its unflinch-ing support of the Vietnam War, Nixon, Bing Crosby, and law and order.

I often had daydreams of their cocktail parties in that living room with men smoking fat cigars while clinging to crystal glasses of martinis and scotch and pompously bullshitting about politics, sports, and their secretar-ies' tits—with the wives invariably separated nearby, gossiping about other wives who weren't there, church bazaars, and exchanging recipes—and also gossiping about their husbands' secretaries' tits.

Upon our loud arrival, Stinky's mom answered the door and let us in as if she was expecting us. "He's up in his room. Go up, boys. I'll get you some refreshments and cookies in a bit." She smiled as we stampeded up the stairs to Stinky's bedroom. A Frank Sinatra ballad was blaring somewhere in the background, and I could still smell a fresh Christmas tree.

Stinky was their only child, and his family had more money than most folks around there. His dad owned an insurance business and always wore a gray suit, polished wingtips, and a red tie with polished hair—very Ward Cleaver-ish. He always smiled at our group, but that smile hid something that I could never figure out. Kind of an angled smile that never seemed straight. But that's where the comparison ended: Stinky was not Theodore "Beaver" Cleaver. He was Eddie Haskell, with a cool side of Maynard G. Krebs. His mom was always at home and seemed to always be in the kitchen cooking something or cleaning something. The Coughlins were, as they say, "good people" who treated us well. And Stinky always shared his stuff with us—new baseball bats, footballs, marbles, anything that was his was ours. Whatever the source of his *noblesse oblige*, we honestly took advantage of him. But he knew it, and I think he thought of us as distant brothers.

Perry "Stinky" Coughlin did not grow up in my neighborhood. Living on the west side of town, he went to Lincoln Elementary School, one of the good schools in town. On my side of town—at Roosevelt Elementa-ry—we got their hand-me-down books, their hand-me-down playground equipment, and their hand-me-down teachers. But Stinky, an only child, was also a loner who was constantly in trouble from failing in school, playground fights, and a dozen more subtle forms of youthful defiance—placing chewing gum under the school desks, teasing girls, lobbing M-80 firecrackers into the toilets. He was an angry kid who was headed, as his principal often said, "on a highway straight to perdition."

Stinky's parents then initiated one final draconian plan, which they thought would be a temporary off-ramp from the proverbial highway straight to perdition. As punishment, he was transferred to the other side of town to finish sixth grade—to Roosevelt Elementary. As his father bluntly put it, "See what it's like going to school with all those coloreds and Mexicans. Then you might be more appreciative of all the things we provide. You'll straighten up."

That was when I met him, and he naturally melted into our group of friends. To his surprise and the shock of his previous teachers, neighbors, friends, and especially his parents, Stinky morphed into a disciplined above-average student who was respectful to teachers, popular with students, and active in school activities. The girls especially liked the "cute Guero" with the soft blue eyes and easy manner. The good kid inside that was suppressed simply oozed out. He told his parents he wanted to stay on the east side "with his buddies." His parents obliged, and I think they had a subtle appreciation that their son was a happier kid with us. And so, Mr. and Mrs. Coughlin treated us well.

And that was what brought us to their house that day. Moe, Skip It, and I slowly entered Stinky's bedroom and stopped in our tracks like a six-legged centipede. There it was, in the center of Stinky's bedroom.

We quickly surrounded it with ardent fervor, gasping breathlessly at its simple beauty. Our collective enthusiasm increased as we were able to touch it and feel it. I felt like one of the monkeys around the monolith in *2001: A Space Odyssey*. Moe and I glanced wide-eyed at each other.

"Cool, man. This is outta sight, man!" Moe couldn't contain himself.

But this wasn't just a simple black monolith on the moon. It was a

Crosley stereo. At that wondrous moment in the late morning, the sun pierced through the bedroom window, and the rays splashed it with light as if the heavens were pleased. This work of art was ensconced in beautiful wood grain with a mesh chrome grill fresh out of the box.

"I got it for Christmas, but it didn't get here till today—special delivery. It's even cooler than I thought. It's bitchin'." Stinky looked at us with pride.

"Who wants to be the first, like a virgin? Mendoza, you're the only virgin here, so go ahead." (I don't know why Adela's image popped up in my head when Stinky mentioned "virgin.")

Ignoring the joke, I carefully investigated Stinky's bin of albums and pulled out Younger than Yesterday by the Byrds. My hands trembled as I slowly unwrapped the LP and gingerly placed it on the Crosley turntable like a priceless artifact. Like a nervous surgeon, I carefully placed the needle on the album, turned on the machine, and it powered to life. The sound was unreal, as if the Byrds were actually in the room with us. Skip It was just quiet, his eyes wide. Stinky pulled out his old guitar, strumming the only two chords he knew, and we all lip-synced to "So You Want to Be a Rock 'n' Roll Star" and played to the whole album three times.

A heavy knock preceded the entrance of Stinky's dad. Without saying a word, he opened the door, briskly walked in, and handed me an album— *Sinatra at the Sands*. He only had one simple demand: "When you play this, crank it up so I can hear Frank and Count Basie downstairs. I want the walls to shake!"

In unison, we all said, "Cool."

For the next four hours, we stormed into Stinky's LP collection like ravenous wolves devouring the Doors, Jimi Hendrix, Motown, Bob Dylan—and Frank Sinatra. To complete that perfect day, Mrs. Coughlin drove us to the new McDonald's restaurant on Olive Street, and I got my first taste of the new Big Mac. As I write this fifty years later, I still remember that time like it was yesterday. Wonderful memories are never fleeting. My three friends are still with me fifty years later, and I'll never lose them.

■ ■ ■

My brother Hank arrived home on a quiet, cold evening on January 30. My dad brought him from the bus station in town after a fifteen-hour flight from Boston to Houston to Los Angeles. I honestly didn't know if he came to help with Curt's case or just to visit Curt and our family. I don't think anyone had a specific plan. The initial shock from the arrest had not receded. We were still reeling from the abject pain, part familial humiliation, part fear of the unknown—the courts.

I waited up for him as he entered the front door just after 3:00 a.m. My mother and nana made empanadas—pumpkin, his favorite—along with a fresh pot of beans, tortillas, and *chile colorado.* When he saw me, I don't think he recognized me, examining me from head to toe like someone examining a prize stallion at auction.

"Darn, you've grown! You're almost bigger than I. How are you?" I thought he would extend his arm to shake my hand as if I were at some board meeting, but he thought again and warmly embraced me, picking me up. He felt warm and soothing. My big brother. My nana and mom kept telling him how skinny he looked, "*bien flaco.*" They conspired to fatten him up while he was home, like a hog for slaughter.

"In Boston, there's no decent Mexican food like here. This is great, Ma. The closest I could find is a small Cuban restaurant, but it's not the same." Hank slumped down in the soft leather recliner my dad usually sat on. He looked tired. Bags under his eyes were drooping like dead weight. The outlines of a beard were popping out, and his clothes looked like they needed a good washing. He kinda looked like one of those poor men I saw on Pink Street—no home to return to, no family to wait for, and no hope to pray for. A ten-hour flight and eight-hour bus ride had taken their toll. It was also the brutal work regimen he had practicing law in a demanding firm. But he was my big brother, and I loved him and missed him dearly.

Our family spent most of the night catching up on our lives: My dad's boring janitorial work fixing broken pipes, repairing desks, helping teachers at the school. But he took pride in even the most mundane tasks. Next came Nana's vast myriad of physical ailments, some of which we suspected she imagined. Neighbors. Deaths. Marriages. Divorces. Births. My school. Family gossip. Baseball. I bragged to Hank that I won the marble championship and hit six home runs the past summer. But I was proudest when I told him I received all As in school all year. Mom only had a doleful look and didn't say much.

Any semblance of a normal family reunion slowly evaporated when the subject of Curt's dilemma came up. That large elephant in the room could not be ignored. My father hoped Hank could help Curt. "What do you know about his lawyer, Pops?"

"Mijo, I really can't tell you. Your mom and I have spoken with him, and he is very informative. I heard he's a really good criminal attorney with a lot of experience."

"What law school did he go to? Do you know?"

"I think up at Berkeley."

Hank stroked his stubble on his soft chin as though he was impressed that his brother's lawyer went to Berkeley. "Great school. Some of our associates at the firm went there."

"Son, maybe you can go to bed so we can discuss this without you." My father looked at me somberly. I told him I was old enough to listen, and I wanted to do all I could. I had not even seen Curt since his arrest.

"Get your butt to bed!" My nana's words were sharp and to the point. I could argue with my dad and sweet talk my mom. But Nana—she says, I do, no questions. I sensed the mata mosca lurked nearby within her arms' reach. But I saw a smile on her as she barked at me. I marched to my room but left the door slightly ajar. My hearing was good. All I could hear were snippets of their conversation.

"jury trial…murder…life…defense…hope…fear…and death…"

I learned the following day that my brother was planning to meet Curt's attorney before visiting Curt at the county jail. Hank always acted with a clear methodology—first, get vital information on the case, then analyze and process that information, then visit Curt. I guess that's how lawyers work. Thinking clearly somehow defused the emotional impact of Hank's visit with Curt. Hank was just not an emotional human being. Even with our family, he shook hands and rarely hugged. He smiled with a frozen face and rarely laughed out loud. Whether he lacked emotion or just hid it, I never knew. I doubt if he ever cried in his life.

I look back at that time in my childhood with lingering memories filled with abject despair, profound confusion, and impending disaster.

■ ■ ■

The early spring of 1968 was the most beautiful I ever knew. The Western Mountains glistened in the distance with a light powder of snow sprinkled from our heavens. Even Mount Sentinel was covered with white at its peak. The normally barren desert to the west was terra incognita as heavy rains altered the landscape into a temporary paradise. The desert air was clean and crisp as the light west winds blew in from the ocean through the mountains and cooled the desert floor like a refreshing wave of spring water. The parched sandy desert gulped the heavy rains from late fall like a thirsty sponge. Sharp red flowers popped from the ocotillos across the cracked desert. Desert poppies, wild sunflowers, yellow brittlebush, and rare daisies exploded onto the desert floor, producing a wild kaleidoscope of color. Our heavens had created a new world.

Usually around that time, I would start thinking about the upcoming baseball season and would round up some of the neighborhood buddies to toss a ball around and hit a few. I lost interest. Baseball was not something I thought about too much. And my father showed no interest in anything related to sports, whether it was boxing on TV or any news of the Dodgers' upcoming season.

Hank met with Curt's lawyer, and I think he only wanted a brief outline of the case against Curt. My parents hoped desperately that somehow Hank might help on the case. "Two lawyers are better than one, and Hank is smart," my father told me.

I could only hear snippets of the adults' whispered conversations, but I heard enough to get an idea of Curt's situation. Hank and Mr. Stein were going to meet with Curt, then try to sketch a legal strategy and try to salvage his life.

■ ■ ■

"How yeah feeling, son? Better?" The jailhouse nurse had a kind, motherly air about her. About forty-five years old, short and stocky with fading blond hair in a bun, she had been one of the nurses in the jail for ten years. And she had seen it all—stabbings, sodomy victims, drug overdoses, mental breakdowns. Nothing fazed her, but when she saw Curt, a lump formed in her throat. The patient in front of her with a swollen eye, cracked nose, and dozens of body bruises looked like a frightened child who might not survive much longer in that awful place. "My name's Bess," she said as she carefully removed gauze from his broken nose. She examined him from head to toe as he lay languidly on the gurney and sighed heavily. She felt tired of seeing the daily mayhem that humans inflicted upon one another with casual banality and indifference.

"Can you tell me the extent of my injuries?" Curt instinctively knew but wanted to hear from her. His body ached, but the pain was not centralized; his entire body throbbed like one giant organ.

"Well, nothing's broken except your nose. You now look like Rocky Marciano kind of." She smiled and gave a soft wink, which soothed him. "Curt, you have some pretty bad bruising all over. They also cut your right shoulder, but I don't think it looked like a normal stab wound. I've seen many. But this cut on your shoulder looked like the assailant meant to gouge out a piece of your skin…kind of like a butcher would remove unwanted parts of a good rib roast. Odd. But that will heal with a scar. They went pretty far into your shoulder—almost to the bone. But no tendons or—thank God—nerves were damaged. It's almost like they wanted that specific part of your arm. Go figure. You'll heal just fine, son, with a pretty good story to tell your grandkids one day." She gently placed fresh bandages on her patient's nose and ointment on some of the bruises. Curt said nothing and just stared at her like a helpless puppy.

"Get me back to my cell, and I'll be OK." He tried to rise from the bed, but Nurse Bess forcibly pushed him back down.

She bent toward him and whispered, "Some bad guys are after you. I don't know why. Maybe it has to do with your charges. I don't care, and I don't get involved in prisoners' personal issues. I only do what's best for my patients, and I will protect my patients as best I can. You, son, need some protection right now. In this medical ward, I will do that. But you need to get strong, not only for your health but also for your survival. Now get some sleep, and work on getting your strength back. Just in case."

Curt took her advice to heart and quickly fell into a deep slumber, praying he wouldn't dream.

For the next two weeks, Curt put on as much weight as he could—hard protein, not the crappy jail food. Nurse Bess made sure he ate well. He was up to two hundred push-ups daily and felt like he was back in Fort Bragg. He could feel his strength returning and his mind clearing, preparing for anything coming his way. Ten pounds were added to his heroin-savaged body, and he felt good.

PART SIXTEEN

1955

James Allen Jr. graduated from Stanford University shortly after the war. The guilt of avoiding military service haunted him throughout college as he thought of the empty seats of classmates who were overseas and never returned. He also imagined Keiko Yamamoto, a childhood friend and, without a doubt, the best student he ever knew. She was destined to be a physician and was expected to join him at Stanford upon graduation from high school. Although shy and reserved, she warmed up to him with the Allen charm and humor. They often studied together and spent many great days on the Allen farm eating lunch, riding horses, and fishing. He even took her up on the family plane after learning to fly solo. Their relationship developed but never evolved beyond the platonic, like close siblings.

Her family owned a small dairy with a growing herd of two hundred cows. In 1942, the Yamamotos, third-generation patriotic Americans, were herded to the domestic internment camps after Pearl Harbor. All their possessions, land, generators, tanks, pasteurizing equipment, trucks, cows, were sold for pennies on the dollar primarily to local businesses and competitors. His 1942 yearbook mentioned her name—along with the other five Japanese students—but had no photos. Ghosts. Jim would often think about her while daydreaming in class. What was she doing in the camps? Could she read like he knew she loved to do? Was she playing kickball—her favorite sport? Was she happy? Could she be happy? The last time he saw her was when she was quickly packing family suitcases for Manzanar. "Don't worry; this will be over in no time. I'll save you a seat at Stanford," he told her with a hint of fear. She glanced at him with a hardened look, and they both knew it might be a long time before they reunited. He never saw her again despite a few letters he wrote that were returned "undeliverable." It was also apparent the letters had been opened and resealed.

Although his father secretly did all he could to keep him out of military service, Jim Jr. would never serve: scoliosis. It hit him early as a child and continued into young adulthood, with a curvature of the spine measured at 13 percent and increasing. At the age of eleven, a medieval back brace was strapped onto him, and thus, he would never be able to serve, even if there had been a desk job carved out for his talents and education—business and accounting. The recruiters, although desperate for manpower for the war effort, could not find a place for him. He finally gave up trying to enlist, so he spent the war years listening to professors droning on about philosophy, macroeconomics, French history, taxes, and accounting principles while kids his age were going through hell overseas.

After graduation, shortly after World War II, he wandered throughout Europe to view firsthand the abject devastation that was left of Western Europe. Paris was great and dynamic, but the rest of the European cities were reduced to horrifying rubble. Cities, generations of families, and whole societies were left in shambles and chaos. He also spent time in South America to learn Spanish. He saw Africa's utter poverty and its sheer beauty, learning much more than he ever did at Stanford. This wanderlust had a profound impact on him, and oddly, it made him yearn to return home to Allen Valley. Simple. Protected. Home. After two years of wandering through a profoundly changed world, he returned to his family ranch and told himself that the noble thing to do in his life was to dedicate himself to the family business, with a deeper appreciation of those not as fortunate as he was. The prodigal son returned with a new zest and desire to groom himself for a bright future in the land as if by preordained design.

Quickly learning the breathless scope of his parents' empire, he immersed himself in the world of riparian rights, farm leases, contracts, accounting, the esoteric area of water rights, agronomy, and climatology. By 1950 he felt he would be ready to assume the business if his parents, at some point, could not.

The Allen farm was usually a hub of activity. The Spanish hacienda's main house stood on a small bluff with a 360-degree view of the valley. By modern standards, it was not a mansion—five thousand square feet and two stories tall. In constructing this residence, Allen Sr. sought to create his architectural statement of hard work, comfort, and humility over pretension, sloth, and avarice. Wooden balconies surrounded the upper floor with ardent views of the mountains to the west. White stucco walls, old timber protruding from the walls, faded roof tiles handmade by Mexican laborers, and purple bougainvilleas accented the front. The thick windows minimized the summer heat and primarily faced the north. Upon entry, guests were greeted by Saltillo floor tile with bright Mexican Talavera tile accenting the interior kitchen. The ceilings were replete with exposed dark timber, giving the interior a sense of strength, dignity, and comfort. Mrs. Allen had commissioned a local artist to paint a mural on the living room wall depicting a purple and orange sunset among ocotillos accompanied by a myriad of desert flowers and wild bush. Like the hacienda, the mural's beauty grew as the years passed. The central feature of the kitchen was a huge wood-burning stove that still functioned even after the introduction of electricity and gas in the 1920s. The open interior invited fresh breezes throughout winter and spring while keeping the interior cool during the hostile summers. The elder Allen could certainly afford a mansion, but he took pride in maintaining this household, which was the original family residence that he had built in the early century. The Guadalupe Mountains, a few miles to the west, formed a picturesque backdrop, adding to its remote beauty among the green agriculture fields juxtaposed against the stark loveliness of the arid desert.

On any given day, countless workers milled about the Allen house and adjoining land—farm labor contractors, majordomos, canal workers, engineers, lawyers. A crew of domestic workers helped clean and cook for the Allen household. That was where he met her. She began working as a domestic in 1954, probably just out of high school. For the first few months, they just consciously glanced at each other as they went about their regular daily business. She helped clean laundry, mopped the Saltillo tile, washed bedroom sheets, and cleaned outside. She consciously and awkwardly never looked at him squarely.

One afternoon, Jim Jr. entered the home for a quick lunch that the domestic crew had prepared for him. Fresh corned beef sandwich, fresh orange juice, and empanadas. Jimmy had already tasted several variations of empanadas in Mexico and South America. He locked his eyes on a new worker in the kitchen. Feigning ignorance and trying to draw her into a pretextual conversation, he turned to her and asked, "What are these?"

"Empanadas. My mother made them just this morning." She made no eye contact, and Jimmy could not figure if she was shy, intimidated, or wanted to just avoid conversation. He had little experience with women and failed to detect any of their nonaudible cues. He had dated at Stanford, but nothing serious. But there, in the kitchen, he was trying to know her. After all, his family was her employer. When they remained alone in the kitchen, he extended his hand to introduce himself, and she politely reciprocated. The warmth of her small palm rushed into him like a burst of oxygen, and he didn't want to let go. He finally caught a passing glance of her whole face: smooth olive skin, small nose, thick lashes, eyes as dark as ebony. Her high cheekbones suggested a strong presence of Native American lineage with a hint of European influence. A certain haughtiness lay hidden in her shyness. She didn't smile but parted her lips slightly as they shook hands.

She quickly resumed her work in the kitchen and nervously left to complete her other domestic work outside. Before she left, she turned and told him, "By the way, I know you've eaten empanadas before. My mom told me that's why she made them."

He did not see her for another week, but the glowing image of her beautiful face was emblazoned in his memory and was never far from his daily thoughts. Although he could not sense it, something deep inside was growing like a light wind before a summer storm.

Although he was normally busy addressing the myriad of Allen business demands throughout the county, he purposely went out of his way to return to the family ranch for lunch at least twice a week, hoping to get a glimpse of her. They would often talk about superficial subjects—weather, rock bands (which he knew little of), his business (which she cared little of). She, however, remained somewhat reticent, and he could not breach her thick wall of shyness. After a few months, she became more comfortable with him but intentionally avoided developing anything more than an employer-employee relationship. It was not proper, and she assumed he never sought anything more. The other three domestic workers never noticed their growing relationship, although she was admonished "not to speak too much to him, and focus on your work."

Over the next six months, they slowly became more comfortable with each other. Jimmy built up the courage to invite her to the movie theater. She said she could not go with him, knowing her parents would disapprove. ("No dating until you're twenty!") But she did tell him she was going the following Saturday with her two girlfriends. Jimmy and his best friend, Rick Vail, decided to attend the same movie.

Rebel without a Cause came to town in November 1955, and the Mayview Theater on East Third Street had no empty seats. Jimmy spent the entire movie looking for her but could not find her. He slowly made three pretextual trips to the concession stand and finally spotted her on the upper balcony. The flickering light of the projector high above the balcony seats illuminated those in its path like a giant flashlight, and he knew it was her. Her profile, her hair in a ponytail, her demure smile. She was the only one not looking at the screen during the climactic car scene with James Dean. She was looking directly at him.

After the movie, Jimmy and Rick conveniently bumped into the three young girls outside and invited them for a milkshake and hamburger at Oden's Drive-in two blocks away. Rick whispered to him on their way to the burger joint, "How do you know these…these Mexican girls?"

"They work for my parents."

"OK…" replied Rick, a bit confused.

After introductions, all enjoyed slurping milkshakes and gulping greasy fries and fat hamburgers. Jimmy didn't want the night to end but had to avoid the obvious—he and the girl could not keep their eyes off each other.

As he dropped Rick at his house, Rick told him, "Man, I've never dated a Mexican girl before. They were pretty…and fun."

Jimmy said, "I know."

Over the next few months, Jimmy lost focus of the increasing work thrust on him. He took every chance to see and talk to her—during lunch, outside when he reviewed the stables of horses. Although he knew discretion was crucial in avoiding others' prying eyes and ears, he always thought someone would notice their burgeoning attraction to each other.

On a warm summer morning, he finally kissed her under the shade of a mulberry tree near the entrance to the Allen home. The shadows of the giant tree offered protection and privacy—an opportunity they both sought. Jimmy wasn't sure how long the kiss lasted—could've been a second, a minute, or maybe longer. Time passed. His other senses, however, were more acute. He could smell her fresh hair. Vanilla, he thought. He could feel the coolness of her soft lips against his. He could feel her waist and her heartbeat racing. He released her and she raced into the house to commence her daily chores. He was never the same. A light head. Yearnings he had never felt before. Her image floated inside him at most times of the day and night. He knew she felt the same.

Although keeping their incipient relationship private was challenging, they managed to see each other on and off the ranch. They pretended to run into each other at a market, the post office, or the local parks. Although Jimmy Allen had never intellectually processed the word or the idea of "love," he knew he wanted nothing more than to be with her now, tomorrow, and before, if he could. He was finally honest with himself and admitted this is what love is.

They managed to spend a weekend in San Francisco. As a pretext, he went ostensibly on "family business." She had to concoct a more elaborate ruse to get away. She told her parents she wanted to go to her cousin's wedding in San Mateo. Her parents reluctantly acquiesced, and she and Jimmy spent their time together absorbing the beautiful city by the bay, picnicking in Dolores Park, strolling through the bookstores in North Beach, and eating fresh oysters at the wharf. For the first time in their relationship, they also spoke in terms of the future, their future together. Upon returning to Allen County, they resumed their secret relationship, although friends and family and friends began to suspect. Jimmy and Raquel's lives were profoundly changed after San Francisco. Both shared their dreams of their futures together; their love and adoration would only grow. They pledged to keep their romance a secret "until the right time," then they would let their families know. For the first time in his life, Jimmy Allen envisioned a future shared with another human being. In their naivety, both assumed their respective families would warmly embrace and gladly nurture their relationship. However, their tunnel vision failed to anticipate the peripheral factors that came into view later.

Then she was gone.

About three months after their return, Jimmy quickly noticed she was not working. He assumed she was ill, and he did not want to draw unwarranted attention by asking about her. The domestics just went about their business like before. He was still reticent to probe about her absence for fear of revealing their secret relationship. When he began asking some of his trusted workers, he could not get any information about her. The workers' stoicism could not hide the fact that they knew more than they let on. After another month, Jimmy went to her house to ask if she was all right and to express his concern about her absence. He had difficulty focusing on work and sleep and had lost weight.

Was she ill?

Was she hurt?

Had she gone to another place of employment?

Jimmy made a pretextual visit to her house to "make sure she had received all her back pay." Her mother, a stout, dark-skinned woman of forty, answered the door.

"My name is Jimmy Allen—"

"I know who you are, Mr. Allen. She's not here. She moved to Mexico with my cousins, and she probably won't return. How can I help you?" The response seemed rehearsed to Jimmy, as if she had been expecting him.

"But I simply wanted to—"

"She is not coming back here. Please, Mr. Allen, don't ask me again. Good day, sir." She then politely closed the front door. He heard the lock behind him like an exclamation point.

After a few months of asking, searching, and thinking, Jimmy simply gave up and accepted the harsh fact that she was the one who had left Allen County and him. How could I have misjudged our relationship? he thought. It was more than a brief fling, and it was more than a teenage summer romance. He wasn't a teenager. He thought it was something solid and beautiful. He wanted it to grow. He knew their love was bottomless in its depth and fervent in its intensity.

But she had left his life, and he finally accepted that. He had felt real love, and he never found it again. The empty spot deep in his gut was never filled. Her warmth, smile, smell, and touch were never too far from his memory as the years passed. He would think about their magical time in San Francisco, and it felt as if he had opened an old photo album to reminisce.

He immersed himself in work as his parents began to give him more responsibility in the business. His mother seemed to have no idea of his private suffering and depression after Jimmy's heart was shattered.

Jimmy's parents were grooming him to take over the business one day. That moment came too soon, on December 2, 1957, when his father, a humble genius and pioneer, died from influenza, which spread its ugly tentacles from an unknown origin. His stepmother was profoundly devastated and succumbed to a lingering and debilitating depression that culminated in her suicide six months later in the master bedroom. She clutched an empty bottle of antidepressants and a family photo of the three. At thirty-two, Jim Allen Jr. was an orphan.

PART SEVENTEEN

GOODBYE

Early in February 1968, the cover of the *New York Times* displayed a shocking photo of a Vietnamese police captain splattering the brains of a captured Viet Cong fighter in the streets of Saigon, South Vietnam, during the Tet Offensive, an uprising in South Vietnam that took the US command and the entire world by surprise. That same week, the cover of the *Sonora Desert Review* covered stories of local weddings, high school projects, the Allen murder, and the upcoming local baseball season. The stories of Vietnam and the Vietcong soldier on the receiving end of a small revolver were briefly mentioned on the back-page blurb—between the classified ads, local beef sales, and high school basketball.

■ ■ ■

Matt Bradley gulped the last beer of a six-pack as he headed north on Interstate 5, ninety miles from San Francisco. Taking care of unfinished business.

The cold beer soothed his throbbing face, a reminder of that last day in the helicopter. Vietnam. He could still smell it: the monsoons, jungles, beauty, death. But the facial scar and the pulsating pain would remind him of it even in the moments he pushed Vietnam out of his memory. A part of his face melted away from the hydraulic oil. Something inside also melted that day. Something he couldn't quite grasp. But he hoped to mend that inner wound as he raced to San Francisco on the spur of the moment. Going to visit Willie's family and visit Willie's grave.

During the past few weeks, he had become a bit perplexed. He told the Allen County sheriff that there might have been multiple individuals on, and possibly in, the Allen property besides the young Mendoza boy. Bradley was confident in his tracking skills. He specifically told Sheriff Johnson that he tracked three people down from the western slopes and onto the Allen property. He concluded that the three individuals entered the home and then left all in different directions. The person with the military boots went toward town, and the other two headed south along the western slopes—very likely to Mexico. The most critical point, he stressed to the sheriff, was that he observed another set of footprints entering the main entrance that was not part of the group. Because of the overlapping foot impressions, it appeared that this individual entered before the group, and factoring in the wind conditions, Matt thought this fourth person was there at least one day earlier.

He even gave the sheriff the guy's approximate size based on the impressions and the distance between the prints. All ambulatory mammals have different manners of natural gaits, and the distancing might give a tracker a general idea of the weight and size of what they're tracking, whether it's a lion or a human in a jungle. Matt was confident, given his training and experience, that he could visualize the persons through their foot impressions.

The size of the fourth person was as follows:

Shoe size: 10

Weight: Between 160 and 180 pounds

Height: 5'9"–5'11"

He even remembered joking to Sheriff Johnson that the fourth person was his size. Johnson didn't get the joke or ignored it. This evidence might be important to the murder investigation. Another piece of corroborating information was his conclusion that the guide had military training. What is more important than tracking is evading trackers and giving trackers false hints or signs. The hunter and the hunted both employ technics in a cat 'n' mouse game. And often, mistakes in the game can have deadly consequences. If you want to avoid detection, it's important to toss in as many red herrings as possible to draw the fox hounds off the scent, metaphorically speaking.

The fact that the prime murder suspect was a Green Beret confirmed Matt's belief that this Green Beret was the guide and possibly the killer. But others who might have entered the house might also have had something to do with Mr. Allen's murder. Either way, it was information that should be considered; however, Sheriff Johnson seemed dismissive of that information. He wondered if he should also let the defense attorney know that information, which might exonerate an innocent young man like Mr. Mendoza. The more he thought about it, the more he realized he should let someone know of his observations.

Before long, he was in San Francisco. With a map on his lap, he meandered through the Hunter's Point neighborhood and parked in front of 3419 Magnolia Street. Willie's home was located in the middle of a sleepy, shady block.

It was Sunday morning, and he saw many folks dressed for church, hopping into waiting cars or walking in unison. The fog from the bay was lifting, and the sun slowly emerged low on the eastern horizon, splashing heat onto his face. The facial scar came to life and began throbbing like a beating heart. The neighborhood was also springing to life. Small girls in shiny, bright dresses with white shoes. Hair neatly combed. Young boys with dark suits, tugging at the tight collars. Old ladies in their Sunday best clutching purses with one hand and a squirmy grandchild in the other. A few children were playing jump rope to a rhyming song. Mothers were leading the pack, marching to receive their blessings from the pulpit.

He arrived: 3419 Magnolia. Willie's home, a simple two-story home that was blue pastel with white clapboards around the windows. A neat lawn with a brick walkway leading up to the front door and red rose bushes along the path greeted visitors. A simple porch surrounded and embraced the house like a warm blanket. A "Harris Family" sign hung on the front door near an American flag on the wall that quietly flapped in the soft ocean breeze from the bay.

Matt gingerly approached the door and lightly tapped it.

A small Black woman dressed for church in a bright pastel dress carefully opened the door. She had thick glasses perched on a small nose, and she squinted, looking out at the glare of the warm morning sun. She was a little heavy but strong looking, and her thick arms were the result of someone who had worked hard all her life. She appeared annoyed and impatient. She inspected Matt up and down, pausing for a second to focus on his facial scar. "May I help you?" Her lips were slightly parted as she squinted nervously at Matt.

"Good morning, ma'am. Is this the Harris family residence?"

She slowly glanced and swiveled her head at the "Harris Family" sign on the porch five feet away.

"Oh yeah, I saw that."

"Please, sir, whatever you're selling, we're not interested. I'm on my way to church services."

"Is this where the family of Willie Harris lives?"

She took a small step back, crossed her arms, and focused her eyes on this stranger. "And who, may I ask, wants to know?" She felt growing anxiety at this random stranger on her front porch, but she also sensed this stranger perched on her front porch meant no harm.

"My name is Matthew Bradley, ma'am. I was a good friend of your son, Willie…in the service…we were in boot camp…and overseas together."

After an awkward pause, she looked curiously at him. "You're Matt

Bradley, my son's…my Willie's friend?"

"Yes. We were best friends."

"You're Matt Bradley?"

"Yes, ma'am."

She exhaled as her facial tension relaxed, and a small smile cracked at the edge of her lip. She started to sniffle, and her eyes began to water. "All this time, I thought you was Black. Sorry for seeming so rude."

"No, ma'am. Last time I checked this morning, I was white."

Both giggled. Like ice melting on a parched afternoon, their tension quickly thawed.

"When Willie wrote to me, he often mentioned you, and I know you were pretty close…looked after each other. And I felt he would make it back 'cause, you know, he had a good friend looking after him. When he finally went over there, to Vietnam, he mentioned he and you were in the same outfit. Of course, he couldn't say much in his letters about what was going on over there with him. Most of the stuff he wrote sounded like he was on vacation—you know, like 'It's so pretty here, Mom.'

"'Everything is good. Miss your food.'

"I'm not stupid, and I knew he put sugar on everything so his letters wouldn't taste harsh. I know you boys had it rough over there. But I knew he didn't want me to worry. And as long as his best friend, Matt, was with him, I knew he'd be safe." She tried hard to avoid looking at the purple facial scar on his left cheek.

"We tried, but—"

"He's my only child—couldn't have any more—but he was a blessing. He told me you were like a brother to him, a brother he never had. So naturally, I thought you were Black. Are you sure you don't have Black blood in you, son? Maybe a few generations back?" she said with a sly grin. She stepped back and opened her arms to embrace him. She squeezed him, and he could feel her heavy breath on his shoulder, then tears. "Welcome home, Matt. Come in and have something to eat. Or coffee. It's still warm from this morning."

Matt spent the morning having a lazy breakfast—biscuits, pancakes, bacon, and fresh orange juice. He met Willie's father, confined to a wheelchair from the ravages of multiple sclerosis. He and Willie's parents went through a photo album of Willie.

Willie in diapers.

Willie riding a bike at five years old. Matt recognized the toothy smile like his mom's.

Little League photos. High school football. No. 83. Probably a lineman.

Willie's prom pictures. Class of '65. Prom theme "Going to Tahiti!"

Willie's boot camp photos showing a proud, stoic marine with only his future ahead of him. You could see it in his eyes captured by the still photo.

Mr. and Mrs. Harris shared stories of Willie as a young boy. He had many friends in the neighborhood and was gentle. He stayed out of trouble in high school despite the tempting distractions in the area. He wanted to go to college and had been looking at some of the local junior colleges. But a marine recruiter visiting his high school persuaded him to enlist and postpone college. "You'll have steady pay, and the government will pay for your education when you're out!"

Much to the dismay of his parents, Willie enlisted, was in Camp Pendleton in a week, and they never saw him again.

"Willie and I had some good times before we shipped out. Mr. and Mrs. Harris, one time we got some time off at Camp Pendleton. Well, you know Willie. He wanted some of the guys to go to this place near the beach in Oceanside for a cold beer. He heard the food was pretty good there.

"So off we go about six of us."

Chomping down another pancake, he continued. "Well, we get to this place about a block from the beach. I think it was called The Seaside Shack or something. It looked cool, and we could smell the fish and crab cooking."

"Oh, my Willie loved all sorts of seafood," Mrs. Harris said quietly.

Matt continued. "So we go in, and the place was packed, mostly locals, surfer types, and college kids. I know we stood out 'cause, you know, we had those marine haircuts. And Willie stood out mostly—"

"'Cause he was colored?"

"Yeah, but also 'cause he was loud with that deep voice. And always laughing."

Mrs. Harris wiped her thick glasses and sipped coffee. "That's my Willie."

"I taught Willie some Spanish, and he learned the word *gabacho*—White boy. The bartender made it clear that Willie would not receive the best hospitality in there…if you know what I mean. So he breaks into this strange accent and tells the bartender he's a tourist from Spain, from the region of Gabacho. I think he tried to sound like Sidney Portier—you know, kind of sophisticated and refined, from the land of Gabacho in northern Spain.

"My guess is if the redneck bartender thinks he's not Black, he might treat him better, thinking he's European. AND IT WORKED!

"He makes up a country with the only Spanish word he knew—Gabacho, the country of Gabacho. Willie told him he was a proud Gabachoan, and, like all Gabachoans, he loved America! Telling him he just met these marines, and he just wanted to buy them a drink.

"Well, after convincing the bartender he was not Black but was a Gabachoan, the bartender gave him, and the rest of us, a free drink. Before you know it, Willie, the Gabachoan, was making friends with everyone in the bar.

"Someone paid for his crab sandwich and beer, and I don't think he paid one cent for anything in there. All night long, he shared made-up stories of the country of Gabacho—its nonexistent history— 'Once a part of France'; its nonexistent culture— 'We're known for our horse culture and breeding of refined mules'; its nonexistent music— 'It's where the mandolin art of twenty-string guitars was cultivated'; and its nonexistent national sport— 'A combination of mule polo and field hockey.' According to Willie, they hoped to get the sport introduced at the 1968 Olympics in Mexico City.

"Excuse my French, Mrs. Harris, but your son had the biggest line of bullshit I ever heard. He was probably praying that no one had a world atlas handy."

Matt and Willie's parents enjoyed a loud laugh together in the comfort of their living room.

After an awkward silence when they closed the album, Matt felt compelled to tell them about Willie's last day in the helicopter. He spared most details of that day—details that he wished he could forget. The hardened anguish of that day was replayed in his mind almost daily like a movie reel that keeps on spinning. Neither his dreams nor his beer allowed him to escape it.

"He was always telling the guys about coming home to you, to your cooking, to your wonderful home. Getting his life back. See Willie Mays and the Giants. Getting a good job. Maybe going to college. Maybe finding the right girl. Maybe…" Matt began to drift to another place. Mrs. Harris gently reached out and held his hand.

"Mrs. Harris. I'm here because of Willie. He saved my life and probably the lives of other marines that day. I can never repay him, and I came here to tell you that. I wish I could have done something else that day to protect him. I wish he were here. I wish I could go with him to Candlestick. Have a cold beer. Maybe even go to his wedding. He was also my brother." Like a dam cracked, they both had difficulty holding back the flood of tears inside.

Later that afternoon, Matt visited Willie at his last resting place on top of a slight green bluff with a panoramic view of the bay, now placid in the late-afternoon sun. A tranquil ocean breeze refreshed him, and it helped dry the tears. A giant redwood tree shaded Willie's place of rest like a protective sentry. Out to the south, he could see the light fixtures of Candlestick Park, where the Giants would be enjoying the start of another season in a few months.

Goodbye, my brother. Willie would have liked the view.

∎ ∎ ∎

I learned from my nana that Hank visited Curt's attorney just to get information about the case. I don't know if he was going to help him professionally or just offer support as a brother. For some odd reason, he was going to meet Mr. Stein in Karina's Mexican Restaurant. Before the meeting, all he told Stein on the phone was that he was Curt's brother and nothing more. When Hank was directed to Stein in the back of the restaurant at his usual table, Stein looked at Hank and saw only a light-skinned, gray-eyed, slightly blond man, and he looked past him. He assumed this Anglo was looking for the bathroom.

Somewhere in the crowded restaurant, a TV set was playing, and the newscaster was lazily reading a list of US casualties from the growing Tet Offensive throughout South Vietnam. To add to the banality of the news, the newscaster's monotonic voice sounded lifeless and somnolent: "The US military confirmed heavy US casualties in heavy fighting around major cities and airbases. But the situation is nearly under control according to President Johnson's administration—"

Someone changed the channel to an episode of *Laugh-In*.

"Hello." Hank stood in front of Stein's table and said nothing.

"Sorry, I'm waiting for someone. Can I help you?"

"Mr. Stein, I called you earlier. My name is Hank Mendoza, Curt's brother."

"You are my client's brother? You're a...a...Mendoza?" He thought, was this guy adopted? Babies switched at birth?

Later, after they spoke, Stein said, "You're a lawyer?"

Hank failed to see Stein's mild surprise that (a) he was a Mendoza—or any other Spanish surname, for that matter, and (b) that his client's brother was a lawyer educated at Stanford. Stein bit his lip and was tempted to compliment Hank on how well he spoke English. But on further thought, that oblique compliment might be misunderstood.

Hank carefully sat down and got the waiter's attention. "*Solamente, un cafecito, por favor.*"

Stein carefully observed the juxtaposition of this light-skinned person with a law degree and the last name of Mendoza. He couldn't figure why it seemed odd. It just did.

"The *nopales* plate here is outstanding. Our family used to come here every Sunday after church, and it's Curt's favorite too."

"You know, Mr. Mendoza, when I spoke to your brother, he never mentioned he had a brother who was an attorney."

"Well, Curt and I were not too close growing up. I left for college when I was sixteen and rarely visit back here. I even went to a different high school, so Curt and I have not been close for several years.

"I wrote to him a few times when he was in Vietnam, but he never wrote back. I never took that personally, and I attributed it to the fact that he was in a war. My parents gave me a general idea of some of his difficulties once he returned—the drinking and the drugs and so forth, which I'm sure you are aware of. And now this…"

"Mr. Mendoza, he's looking at the death penalty. The gas chamber. The last client I had who was facing the gas chamber almost got me disbarred."

"Why?"

"'Cause the fucking prosecutor kept throwing farts when the judge called the case in court. He told me he farted so my client would get used to the smell of gas. I told him 'Let's go outside' because I wanted to kick the shit out of him. So, he told the court about my threat."

"What did the judge do?" Hank's question was more clinical than emotional.

"Well, Judge Gates—you will see him pretty soon—he told the prosecutor that if he ever smells any fecal gas in his courtroom, he knows where it came from. As only Judge Gates could so eloquently put it, and I quote, 'Keep the sphincter valve shut tight, Mr. Prosecutor or I'll shut it for you.' End quote."

Stein gave Hank a dry synopsis of the case and the general parameters of legal strategies. It was clear to Hank that Curt was in deep trouble.

Hank remained stoic, said nothing, looked almost distracted, and rarely maintained eye contact with Stein. "Mr. Mendoza, your brother is in deep shit. You don't seem to understand." Stein curiously observed Hank rearrange the table condiments in order of size. Bottled chile, then salt and pepper, then sugar. All in perfect order—at least in the mind of this oddball sitting across from him. A Mendoza. A lawyer. An oddball. Stein stroked his unshaven chin, trying to figure this guy out.

"I do, Mr. Stein. I do care. He's my brother. If my outward appearance suggests my indifference, nothing could be further from the truth. I...I just don't react with much outward emotion. My therapist in Boston says it's something called Asperger syndrome, but he's not too sure. It's not even in the DSM. Mr. Stein, all my family is profoundly terrified about these events and Curt's dire situation."

Stein looked perplexed and thought the guy in front of him was a bit off center. "Asperger...never heard of it."

"Mr. Stein, I have heard you are an excellent criminal attorney and have postponed your return to Berkeley to help Curt. And we appreciate that. My parents assume I came here to volunteer my legal services to help you, but they don't understand I cannot.

"First, I have to return to Boston since I have a great deal of work to attend to with deadlines approaching and a great deal of money at stake. I have a responsibility to my firm and my clients to complete the work.

"Second, I do not practice criminal law. Our firm does have a small and dedicated white-collar criminal unit and handles a few cases pro bono—like draft-dodging cases. But my specialty is mergers, corporate mergers. It's an area I am especially suited for since I prepare a lot of paperwork and rarely have to deal directly with clients. It's solitary work, but I love it. I haven't studied crim law since the bar exam, and frankly, it was not one of my favorite subjects in law school.

"If I did help you—and I know you didn't ask—I would be an albatross around your neck since I could inadvertently imperil my brother's case with a legal mistake. And I could not live with myself if I did.

"Finally, my condition—whether it's Asperger syndrome or something else—might undermine your efforts in court. I rarely appear in court and have never argued in front of a jury. After a few years of therapy, I have finally recognized I have this social disorder and have tried to mitigate any negative effects on me. But it's too risky for you and this case. I'm not what they call a 'people person.'"

"OK. Well, I respect that. I could use help with legal research, preparing motions, etc. I don't have too much of a budget. I get only one investigator. I use Bud Lemon. He's good, thorough, and resourceful. He may have already hunted down a few interesting leads that might help. But the state of California wants to legally kill your brother Curt."

Hank said nothing and only nodded, looking away. "My brother never intended to go to Vietnam. Tragic circumstances in his life were an impetus to go, I think."

Stein looked curious.

Hank then recounted the tragic death of Sally and Curt's reaction. "I think Vietnam was his escape, which is something neither you nor I can ever understand."

"Well, maybe that can be used in the trial's penalty phase. Any tragedies that can humanize a defendant in front of a jury."

"I don't follow."

"Well, a death penalty trial—the one where our government trained and sent your brother to Vietnam to kill—now, our government wants to kill your brother. Kind of a circle of death. A trial of this nature has two phases: the guilt phase; that is, the jury decides if he's guilty. Then there's the penalty phase, where the same jury that just decided that your brother bludgeoned an icon of this county like a wild animal, that same jury will then decide whether he should die or spend all his life in jail. A bifurcated trial. If we can humanize Curt, then there's a chance they won't kill him."

Hank said nothing, sipped his coffee, and looked away.

"Mr. Stein, I hope to visit my brother sometime tomorrow. I was told he got into a bit of an altercation in the jail, and I'd like to see him. I lost my appetite. I would, only as a matter of curiosity, like to review the discovery you've received thus far."

Stein then showed him his thick manila envelope with crime scene photos, police reports, and autopsy reports.

"Thank you for the coffee."

"OK. I can arrange a visit tomorrow. I can go with you. My investigator will be visiting your family for background information. By the way, I need to find out from him about a piece of evidence that appears to be missing—an old leather pouch. Maybe he might be more forthcoming about it with you. It might be important."

When Hank returned home, he told my parents and nana about his conversation with Mr. Stein. The sobering reality was soaking in.

"And you think this Mr. Stein is any good? Can he help Curt?"

Hank simply offered a no-nonsense appraisal of Curt's dire situation— the raw evidence pointing in only one direction: to Curt.

"Son, can you help him?"

"I really don't know, Pops."

■ ■ ■

Juana slowly rose from her bed and poured herself some coffee. She missed the Cuban coffee and could not adjust to the American brands. Too toxic. Too mild. Too soft. Just like most Americans she knew.

The odious cretin beside her was still in bed, snoring like a fat bear. She found him repulsive, but she needed him to get her brother out of jail and out of the reaches of the US Immigration Service. Her patience was waning, and Sheriff Johnson only told her cryptically, "I have my plans, and your brother will be out with you in no time." As long as her brother was protected in jail, she did anything Sheriff Johnson asked. Anything.

He kept dropping hints to her that he was going to come into "some real money soon" and that they could have a future together. Juana knew she would have no future with him, but she needed to string him along until the right moment. As soon as her brother was released with no legal troubles, they were out of there.

■ ■ ■

The Allen County Courthouse was imposing. It was built that way. At the western edge of Clarktown, its two-story facade dominated the surrounding business center, which included dress shops, cafés, garages, movie theaters, and department stores. Built in 1931 at the height of the Depression, it replaced Allen County's first courthouse built down the block between a whorehouse and a blacksmith shop, both of which included local lawyers and judges as their best customers. The land and most materials were donated by the original six families, and it took three years to build, providing locals much-needed labor during the Great Depression.

Texas flagstone formed the exterior facade, and its soft brown, yellow, and white hues glistened in the afternoon sun like a Greek temple. Its exterior colors only grew richer and deeper over the years. As you approached the steps to the main entrance, you were greeted by gigantic iconic columns. Above those majestic columns was inscribed in stone "REGNANT POPULI—THE PEOPLE SHALL RULE."

Stone carvings above depicted Allen County's pioneers: a scene of fearless cowboys, proud farmers, dedicated women, and children toiling under a punishing sun. In the background were faceless workers tending to the fields. The main ten-foot double doors of oak, brass, and stained glass welcomed all. The exterior was built to intimidate all who entered so they would revere the power of the law and the (mostly) men who ran the local legal system. Marble floors and walls, oak wainscoting, and large oak benches dominated the interior. Arizona Native American artists painted soft brown frescos on some of the interior walls, depicting more scenes from the early days of Allen County—Native American families drinking from the local rivers, faceless brown farmworkers picking fruit, children playing, carts of vegetables filled to the brim, snow-capped mountains hovering over a lush green valley. These quaint Norman Rockwellian scenes surrounding the courtrooms belied the brutal business of criminal law.

The first floor was normally a beehive of activity. All five criminal departments were nestled on the main floor, with Judge Robert Gates the presiding in the criminal department, Department 15. Among the courtrooms were administrative offices, clerks' offices, information and payment windows, and waiting rooms. Clerks with heavy files scurried between offices. Lawyers talked with their clients and their families. Children cried. Bailiffs were positioned along the walls like granite statues. Along the marble walls were long, heavy oak benches that resembled church pews, many with small carvings etched in. ("Mary and Emil, forever." "Fuck the War." "Adrian, Class of '65." "Puto.")

Morose prisoners were herded down the hallways into holding cells behind the walls, escorted by stern deputies from the Allen County Sheriff's Department before their court appearances. As they were shepherded into the courthouse single file, they were instructed to only look down at their shackled feet. They looked somber, with faces that had any semblance of life sucked out. Signs admonished the public not to converse with inmates. As you climbed the marble and wrought-iron stairs to the second floor, you immediately noticed the stark difference in ambiance and tone. It was almost as if you had climbed a mountain to a higher elevation where the air was clearer, the movement was slower, and the noisy traffic below was muted.

The second floor hosted five other civil, juvenile, and traffic departments. At the end of the western hallway was Department 2B, the probate department. It was referred to as "the second-floor mortuary" in local parlance. Judge Earnest Giles had presided over this department for seven terms, and at the age of seventy-four, he would probably retire or die there. Efficient, no-nonsense, and somber, he was well respected throughout the local legal community. With a strong ethical compass, Judge Giles performed his daily tasks "by the book," as most would say. Judge Giles's two books were the Holy Bible and the California Probate Code. Normally, Department 2B was quiet, somber, and reverential, with attorneys submitting paperwork on estates of the deceased—small homes, farms, and equipment, or humble money accounts to disburse among survivors. Rarely were there any disputes, as long as all the *i*'s were dotted and the *t*'s properly crossed per the California Probate Code.

February 5, 1968, was an exception. First on Judge Giles's morning calendar was "Motion for Injunctive Relief" filed by Walter Rossi et al. Judge Giles had spent the previous weekend reading the pleadings and the responsive pleadings filed by the Ira Smith Law Firm.

Judge Giles was aware of the moving party's background, and he knew they were known as five of the Original Six, the powerful farming families that had settled Allen County.

They were seeking the following:

1. Approval of administering the Allen Trust I; appointment of a trustee to "administer the estate in an equitable manner consistent with the spirit of said trust"; and
2. An order recusing the Ira Smith Law Firm from representing "any other known interested parties in this proceeding."

The Ira Smith Law Firm responded with a ninety-page document arguing that they represented the estate of the late James Allen and James Allen II, seeking leave of the court to submit the written amendment to the trust—the Allen Trust II—within a "reasonable time as the court permits."

As the case was called, Judge Giles approached his bench and was noticeably taken aback by the packed courtroom. He had never seen his courtroom filled like that. Reporters from as far away as Los Angeles and San Francisco sat with notebooks ready. Curious lawyers had come to observe what they thought might be something important. Sheriff Johnson stood up against the back wall of the courtroom, scanning the audience like a hungry coyote. Walter Rossi, one of the leading plaintiffs, sat in the front row behind his attorney. Rossi, aged seventy, wore simple, old denims and a blue work shirt that revealed a working man's sunburned arms, and his family took up the entire first row, along with some of the other Original Six. Rossi's stoic demeanor and humble exterior were deceiving. He was a wealthy businessman with multiple beachfront homes and millions of dollars in the bank. His lawyer, Elliot Rhodes, turned to him and nodded confidently.

On the other side of the attorney's table, Ira Smith II sat flanked by two junior associates from the estate section of the law firm. A pile of thick worn law books was placed on counsel table.

Judge Giles had a gift for skillfully worming through a morass of legalistic mumbo jumbo and filtering out the essence of an issue. Judge Giles: "Counsel, good morning. I hope your weekend was well spent. I know mine was, reading through your respective pleadings. First, I will deny the plaintiff's request to recuse the Smith law firm."

Plaintiff's attorney, Elliot Rhodes: "Your Honor, with all due respect, I don't think this court fully appreciates our concern with the Smith law firm as counsel for the Allen Trust I. They have an ethical conflict since they might arguably be the trustees of this trust and possibly the mythical Allen Trust II—if the latter even exists."

The Court: "Mr. Rhodes, I appreciate you schooling me on what I should or should not 'appreciate'"—the Court raising bunny ears—"but I read the pleadings thoroughly. I even missed my granddaughter's, Emery's, birthday party Saturday as I was sorting through the moving papers. They left me a tiny piece of stale chocolate cake. Unless you have anything—anything—to add that was not expressed in your moving documents, allow me to make my findings and rulings. As I was saying, there is no basis to recuse the Smith law firm from this case."

Turning to Ira Smith, he said, "Now, with respect to the main issue here, one involving a vast estate, Mr. Smith, there is no dispute that James Sr. gave the power of appointment to his son, the recently deceased. But there is nothing of evidentiary value that establishes James Jr. even signed a written instrument reflecting his intent to exercise that appointment and modify the terms of the Allen Trust I."

Ira Smith rose and formally adjusted his coat. "Your Honor, the written instrument was prepared by our firm in San Francisco. It was given to James Jr. for final review and signature. All he had to do was sign it, file it with the state, and the changes to the original trust should be legally established. We have reason to believe that the document was with him at the time of his demise, and someone took it from the premises for reasons unknown. We cannot assume those reasons were nefarious or inadvertent."

Mr. Rhodes: "Your Honor, they are just buying time. The only legal document this court should, and can, consider is the original trust. My clients have a vested interest that this court approve the trust, appoint a temporary elisor, or approve someone to act as trustee for the Allen trust I."

Mr. Smith: "Your Honor, all we are asking is for some precious time to locate the addendum." Smith placed his written briefs on the counsel table, took a deep breath, and dramatically lowered his tone. "Judge, with stakes this high, it is not asking too much for more time. I can assure you we will exercise our due diligence in locating this document."

Judge Giles: "It boils down to this. The Allen Trust I is administered with half of the trust going to five of the Original Six, or the Allen Trust II is administered if the lost document is located with a 100 percent charitable trust and nothing to the other five families. That's as crudely as I can put it, gentlemen. Mr. Smith, you got six months to produce a valid document. If not, I will appoint an elisor to temporarily administer the Allen I Trust. Good day, counsel."

Sheriff Johnson stormed out. "Fuckin' lawyers…"

Part Eighteen

"IT'S REAL CLEAR, EH!"

Third grade in Principal Howard's office.

In his mind, Curt was transported across time to Principal Howard's inner office in third grade, intentionally windowless, utterly drab, and honestly scary. As a kid, you never felt so alone and isolated as when you were in Mr. Potter's office, like a tiny animal trapped in a lion's cage. A paddle hung like a menacing trophy on the back wall in full view to any kid who entered. It was heavy oak, two feet long, four inches wide, and an inch thick. It looked worn out from its use on the butts of elementary children. Principal Potter had previously taught wood shop and inserted holes in the paddle to "enhance the stink upon these hoodlums." The sadistic educator was proud of his custom-made instrument of pain from the Dark Ages. This was what Curt was thinking when Sheriff Johnson entered the medical ward to pay him another "visit."

What brought Curt to Principal Potter's office years ago was gum. He had committed a major elementary school faux pas—chewing gum in math class. In elementary school, this transgression was ranked somewhere

257

between fighting and grabbing a girl's butt. In a burst of epiphany, Curt finally understood why his parents were very strict about his school comportment—clean, pressed clothes; combed, short hair; good manners to all; respect to all teachers; completed homework; and no gum. Any violations of these Mendoza family rules would be met with Nana's *mata mosca*.

During a heated game of four-square at recess, Temo Martinez, the highest-ranking school hoodlum with the well-deserved moniker Madness, dared Curt to chew gum loudly in math class. Mrs. Jamison, the math teacher, was his favorite teacher. She abhorred noisy pupils and, worse, noisy pupils chewing gum.

While quickly contemplating the provenance of the Madness moniker, Curt succumbed to pressure on two fronts: because of the nine-year-old sociopath who dared him and because of the peer pressure from his playground buddies. Refusing the former might result in fleeting pain, but the latter would be more permanent. As Madness looked on, Curt stuffed a whole pack of peppermint gum, loudly interrupted Mrs. Jamison's primer on fractions, and was quickly escorted by his left ear to Principal Howard's office and his ugly wooden paddle.

Now in the medical ward, Curt felt the same as he did that day in Principal Potter's office—guilty and defiant but scared. When Sheriff Johnson entered the infirmary, he was Principal Potter reincarnated.

He knew Sheriff Johnson was coming even before he entered because of the nurse's reaction. She stopped attending to him, looked up like a Labrador sensing danger, and walked away from his bed demurely. The hairs on the back of his neck sprang up.

"Hi, Curt!" Johnson casually pulled up a chair near the bed. He nodded to Nurse Bess, and she quietly left the room. She gave Curt a prolonged look before exiting. Johnson looked at Curt from head to toe like he was a prize specimen. "Hope you're doing better.

"Curt, these inmates in here...some are just animals. No sense of human decency. I heard they roughed you up a little. Probably 'cause you're a new guy in here. Shit, guys in here get killed for any reason. Someone looks at someone else the wrong way. Someone steals another's food. Personal beefs are brought in from the outside. Hell, sometimes a guy shanks another guy 'cause he's just crazy…fucked up…and has no reason."

Curt said nothing but grunted softly, adjusting himself on the bed, thinking defensively. He licked his upper lip, still swollen. It began to dawn on him that both his arms were shackled to the metal bed.

Johnson noticed. "It's a precaution, you know…for security. The medical folks here insist on it. You can never be too careful in this place." Johnson's eyes locked on Curt's.

Curt was dismissive. "Sheriff, I don't know what you think I did. Should I even be talking to you without my attorney?"

"Nah, between us boys, we can have a private discussion. Fuckin' attorneys just complicate these matters.

"You know, Curt, I know you're a warrior. A Vietnam badass. Military guys like you have been through a lot, and I respect that. My dad fought in North Africa. Helped fight Rommel. He saw a lot of action. Probably killed his share of Germans and Italians. So I admire what you've gone through. What brings me here again is a follow-up to our last discussion that we never had."

"What's so fuckin' important about those papers in the pouch, anyway?" Curt pulled on the shackles, but the metal tethers were tight.

"This item is worth a lot to me, and I just wanna know if you can help me find them. That's all. Curt, this is your ticket out of here. Your tragic predicament can end if you just play ball with me." Big Bob's eyes grew large as he emphasized the word "predicament."

"If I got this stuff for you, what would it be worth for me? If I knew where it was."

Sensing Mendoza's sarcasm, the sheriff ran out of patience. "Listen, you little fucking spic. I'm not gonna negotiate with you. You need to get me that pouch, or I think you might not make it outta this place in one piece. You'll be lucky to make it to San Quentin. Now, where's that pouch?"

Curt turned his head up slightly. "Can't help you, Sheriff. Go fuck off and leave me alone. I can take care of myself."

"Well, now, I guess that's it, soldier boy, Mr. Green Beret. You'll change your mind…and I think you will. If you need me for a further conversation, I'll be here.

"By the way, lemme explain what's in store for you at the gas chamber in San Quinten. The good folks up there are gonna strap you into a chair in this small chamber that's airtight. There's a window around so folks can observe you in the chair—you know, families of the victims, cops. I know I'd like to be there to see you. Even your mom and pop and your nana can see if they want. You think they might wanna see their war hero all fucked up? Maybe. Then—this is the best part—the executioner drops these little pellets—they look like rabbit shit—into this kinda bath. The pellets are potassium cyanide, and the bath is sulfuric acid. You know, I was never interested in chemistry, being a bad student and all, but this is interesting stuff. So, when the pellets combine with the sulfuric acid…voilà! You get hydrogen cyanide. Hence, the 'gas' in gas chamber. This is nasty stuff when you inhale it.

"Your wrinkled old nana will see you take a whiff of this shit, and she'll see you drool, shit, piss, vomit, and probably cry like a little punk. That's the last thing they'll see of their big, badass Green Beret before you leave this earth. I need to know where that pouch is, Mr. Curt Mendoza."

Johnson slammed his fist onto Curt's left shoulder with the bloody bandage. Curt flinched not so much from the pain but from the surprise. Johnson reared back and punched him again. "You know why your arm's bandaged, Mr. Mendoza? This is why." Johnson opened the palm of his hand and revealed a small item that looked like dry leather.

"This, Mr. Mendoza, this is your Green Beret tattoo that one of your unknown attackers sliced out of your shoulder, asshole. Pretty good job… should've been a surgeon. Your proud Green Beret tattoo. I'll leave it here for you as a gift." Johnson thrust it onto the table and left.

■ ■ ■

Pursuant to Sheriff Johnson's direct order, inmate # F39784, Curtis Mendoza, was moved from the jail infirmary to the general jail population in module D1, where one hundred inmates were housed in two-man bunks arranged alphabetically.

Curt was assigned to bunk 35A, the upper bunk. Newly convicted inmate Pedro Ramos, a.k.a. "Little Monster," was assigned to the lower bunk, 35B. Curt's strength was returning, and he felt better than he had in a long time. His mind was clear and his body rested. But he sensed a certain tension in the air. No one talked directly to him, and he got the feeling that many of the inmates—and staff—were talking about him.

It was 10:00 p.m., and the lights were turned off. The inmates were recounting the betting from the basketball game that afternoon on the TV set. UCLA had been upset by Elvin Hayes and the University of Houston. The adjacent exercise yard splashed a dull light into the module, outlining gray hues of bunks and inmates' heads, and the noise diminished into whispers. While most jails were painfully loud, that night was eerily quiet, as if all the inmates were holding their collective breath, waiting to exhale. The stillness was heavy.

"Hey, ese!" a faint voice whispered from the bunk below. His assigned bunk partner poked his head up to the upper bunk. "Hey, ese, what's going on, man?"

Curt was guarded and in no mood to talk. His attorney was adamant and advised him not to talk much with anyone. Too many snitches. "Hey, man, let me get some sleep."

"Hey, who's Sally?"

"Sally? Why the fuck did you ask?"

"You were dreaming or something, man. And you talked a lot of shit.

But I could hear the name Sally. Someone you know?"

"None of your business, man. Shut up, all right?"

"Hey, ese." The Little Monster pulled up to the side of Curt's upper bunk. "Hey, ese...*Los Pelones* are coming. It's real clear, eh..."

"What the hell you talking about, *Los Pelones*?"

Pedro cleared his throat and carefully whispered, "I saw some of these guys shaving their heads this morning."

"Hey, Ramos. Listen, man, I need sleep. Shut the hell up. I don't want any trouble, OK?"

"Trouble's coming here, *ese. Los Pelones*. The bald guys. It's real clear, eh."

Curt sat up, now curious. "Who? Why do I care about bald guys?"

"It's real clear, eh. When something's going down, some *vatos* shave their heads 'cause these Anglo officers all think we look alike—and we probably do. And later, when they try to pick out inmates who might have done some shit or that shit, they say, 'It was a Hispanic male with a shaved head—*pelon*—who did this or that.' With all these Chicano *pelones*, it's like trying to find one brown Chicano sheep in the brown flock, ese...No way, *ese*...No ID, man...real clear, eh.

"Something's going down, *trucha*..."

■ ■ ■

Hank Mendoza and Robert Stein were waiting impatiently in the jail lobby to see their client.

"Hello, my name is Captain Jim Garza. Sheriff Johnson asked me to take you to his office. There's been an incident involving Curt Mendoza, and I think you should see the sheriff before you see your client. He should be released shortly from the infirmary anyway."

"Infirmary? Now what happened to him?" Stein stood up and clenched his fists.

Hank only nodded passively.

"Calm down, sir. First, he's all right. But we can give you the details. Please come."

They entered Johnson's office, and Garza left. Both attorneys sat down on the edge of their seats. Big Bob gave Hank a look over and asked, "Who the hell are you?"

"Sheriff, this is Hank Mendoza, attorney at law."

"You're a Mexican? And a lawyer? Shit, you look whiter than me."

Hank said nothing, as if he were ignoring him.

"Mendoza…related to Mr. Green Beret?"

Hank nodded.

"Well, goddamn. Now we have Chicano lawyers. lordy, lordy…"

Sheriff Johnson then recounted the recent altercation involving Curt and some inmates. "That fucking brother of yours killed one guy and seriously wounded another. If I don't get him for the Allen murder, this one will get him to San Quinten!"

"Sheriff, first, I don't appreciate you talking about my brother in that tone. Second, I would like to talk to him, along with his counsel, Mr. Stein. Third, my understanding is that you monitor all inmate movements—especially a high-profile inmate like my brother—which leads me to my question: Did you authorize his movement to the general population after his release from the medical ward knowing he was injured and going through drug withdrawals? You have a legal obligation to preserve the safety of those confined."

Johnson looked a bit perplexed at the impudence directed at him. "Listen, you little fuck. Who do you think you are coming into my jail speaking to me like that? Lawyer or no lawyer, I should just kick the shit out of you right now, and you can join your fuckin' brother in here. Probably have a lot to catch up on."

"Mr. Johnson—"

"That's Sheriff Robert Johnson—"

"Mr. Johnson. Please don't threaten me. I can assure you of three things.

One, I will see my brother. Two, you will move him to a safer cell. And finally, if you touch me or Mr. Stein or are responsible for any harm to Curt, my law firm will paper you and tie this jail up in litigation until you're way past retirement or your early removal. Your state attorney general is a good friend of our firm in Boston. He and one of our law partners were room-mates at Yale. And the US attorney would probably find something amiss here in your facility—body part sales to the black market; indiscriminate beatings; planted evidence; missing funds from inmate property; embez-zlement of facility moneys; not to mention your activities in the enhanced interrogation lounge. So, Sheriff, let's dispense with this pointless banter and let us see my brother."

Stein said nothing with a slight smile and looked for Johnson's next move.

Johnson sat down as if winded. "Fuckin' lawyers."

Captain Garza then entered the office holding a projector and tripod with another item, a movie screen.

Johnson's temper was percolating. "Garza, what in the hell are you doing interrupting? You know better. And what is all this?"

"Sir, you remember a few months ago? We got some funds for better security around here. I mentioned to you I purchased some high-tech se-curity cameras—Super 8 millimeter—to install around the jail. You know, sometimes things happen around here, and we…you…need to know what might have happened if there's some kind of incident. I made several copies in case the attorneys needed them." Garza continued setting up the screen along the back wall of the office.

"So, again, Garza…why are you barging in now?"

"Well, sir, what you'll see is connected to the Mendoza case. Not the Allen murder, but the incident last night, and I think you and his attorneys should see this."

Stein and Hank said nothing, curious.

"I will set up the film so we can see it. Our electrician modified the circuits to activate the cameras when a light switch went on. As you can figure out from the angle, the three cameras are about twelve feet above the floor, hidden in a loudspeaker. I don't think any inmates would have known about its presence."

Johnson tensed up and adjusted his chair.

Garza dimmed the lights and turned on the projector. "Let me narrate. So, we have three cameras positioned in the main barracks where this incident occurred, and you'll see three different images that show this incident. At around 11:15 p.m., someone, for reasons unknown, turned on the lights, and that's when the cameras were activated.

"The bunk on the far right is bunk 35, occupied by Curt Mendoza on the upper and Pedro Ramos on the lower. Ramos, for some reason, is not in his bunk. You can see that Mr. Mendoza has now jumped from the bunk onto the floor, presumably because the three individuals who are twenty feet away quickly approach him. They appear to be walking side by side in unison."

Garza stopped the film to add narration.

"The three individuals—all bald headed—were identified. The first is Ruben Fierro, a.k.a. Masca Fierro, the iron chewer, 'cause he has corroded teeth. Mr. Fierro is a bartender at Juan's Bar and came into our jail last week on a vagrancy charge. He was arrested and booked by you, Sheriff. To his left in the middle is Rafael Gomez, who is currently serving a one-year jail term for drug trafficking. By the way, he also happens to be the brother of the owner of Juan's Bar, and we know her as Juana La Cubana. The third individual is Carlos Pena, a local thug awaiting trial next month, a.k.a. Whimpy. Now, I'm gonna play this in slow motion so we can clearly see what happens."

Someone quietly asked, "Why Whimpy?"

"'Cause all he likes to eat are hamburgers. From the Popeye cartoons. Mr. Fierro apparently promised him all the hamburgers he could eat. Whimpy is an amateur boxer, and as other fighters say, he's 'punch goofy'—too many blows to the head. But he liked to fight, which is why he was probably recruited to join this crew. Anyway…

"As the three assailants approach Mr. Mendoza, they each produce a sharpened inmate-manufactured shank…you can see them there on the screen. Now they're approaching Mr. Mendoza five feet away. Mr. Gomez takes the lead and starts to thrust his knife at Mr. Mendoza's upper torso. Then you see Mr. Mendoza grab Gomez's right wrist and snap it, break it, and dislodge the shank, making it fall onto the ground. I'll stop the image so you can actually see Gomez's wrist snap at almost a ninety-degree angle. Snap. Crackle. Pop.

"Mendoza then grabs Gomez by the neck and slams his head onto the metal rail of the bunk bed twice. All that stuff you see splashing on the screen is Gomez's teeth and his left eye popping out. His skull cracked with several fissures…you know, kinda like when you crack a hard-boiled egg before you peel it. I make a lot of egg salad at home. Gomez falls to the ground. Apparently, he sustained major brain damage and is being fed out of a tube in the infirmary. The eye that fell was squashed during the altercation. Whatever brain he had is now useless.

"Then, Mr. Fierro pauses for a split second, gets into an offensive position, and tries to thrust his knife into Mendoza's stomach. Mendoza avoids the thrust, grabs Fierro and the knife, and pushes it into Fierro's right eye. The knife had a four-inch blade, which pulverized his eye socket and entered the brain's frontal lobe. You can see him drop to the floor, and he's still clutched to his knife as he's quivering. The doctor told me he probably died before he hit the floor. Gentlemen, if I can add some levity to this incident, one of the inmates quipped that it looked like Mr. Fierro committed suicide holding his own knife as he lay prone and lifeless on the floor."

Stein said, "That's funny, man."

"Finally, the last of the trio, Mr. Pena, Whimpy, dropped the knife and ran. He later told us everything Fierro recruited him to do, and he was promised that he would be released early by Sheriff Johnson. I personally felt bad for Whimpy and promised him hamburgers if he gave us a truthful statement. He got two giant monster cheeseburgers from Oden's with extra onions and jalapeños."

Stein glared at Big Bob. "Looks like this was a hit. Mr. Mendoza was just defending himself. Damn, I've never seen anything like this."

Garza slowly turned off the projector and turned the lights back on.

All were silent for a few seconds, trying to soak in what they had just witnessed on the screen.

Hank finally spoke. "Sheriff, the person who killed Mr. Allen was a butcher. Your reports and the autopsy showed at least twenty blows on the decedent's body, likely a combination of fists and a blunt instrument. That killer was a butcher—an angry, sloppy butcher. My brother Curt, in this recent jail fracas, acted like a surgeon. He deftly eradicated a deadly threat from three armed assailants with only five flawless moves. A surgeon. That's his military training on display. Sheriff, my brother didn't murder Mr. Allen. A butcher did. Now, I would like to see my brother, please."

Big Bob motioned Garza to open the door, and the tired sheriff left. "Fuckin' lawyers."

■ ■ ■

"Help wanted. Bartender. No experience required. Contact Juana Gomez within."

Juana Gomez slumped despondently in her bar. The place was quiet and had been closed for a few hours. The lights were turned low, and the air felt cool but stale. Tito Puente's timbales were blasting on the jukebox. Her brother Rafael was seated in a wheelchair with two tubes tethered to him—one to his mouth for feeding and one to piss into a bag on his left side. Juana was making a few signs to post. With the untimely demise of Ruben "Masca" Fierro, she needed an extra hand to run her establishment.

Rafael had been released from the county jail earlier that day with early parole granted by Sheriff Bob Johnson. Moreover, the US Immigration Service declined to initiate deportation proceedings. Rafael would simply be required to report monthly and would remain floating in a political/judicial state of limbo until immigration could figure out what to do with him. The immigration officer admonished him: "The US Immigration Service will monitor you, Mr. Gomez." Rafa quietly grunted in response. For the US Immigration Service, the math equation worked in favor of the US government: one sociopathic Cuban was dead, and another brain dead. They could go easy on Rafael.

The damage to Rafael's brain was apparent partial loss of speech, major cognitive impairment, and loss of control of his bladder functions, and his mouth and left side of his face were frozen like he was about to say something but forgot. Juana gently wiped the spittle from his cheek as she finished serving him warm broth. Rafael's mental acuity was somewhere between a dim-witted two-year-old child and a lab-tested chimpanzee, but he did understand some things. "Rafa, I will take care of you, and we'll get out of here to go someplace nice. Promise." She had learned that Rafael had been lured into the Mendoza hit by Big Bob, who promised him an early release. He also promised Juana that Rafa would not be involved. Sheriff Johnson had to atone for this, and she actually bore no wrath toward Curt Mendoza. The dumb kid had always been respectful and quiet in her bar.

"I will take care of the one responsible for this. That fucking *jamonero* Johnson will pay. That gringo will pay."

Rafael grunted and nodded his damaged head. "Wh…what…whatta…you…gonna do with Juan's Bar?"

"That's Juana's Bar, baboso…my bar…Juana…there is no Juan. I'll sell it after I take care of some business."

Rafa's final coda to his protective sister: "OK." And a wet fart.

Part Nineteen

PEOPLE OF THE STATE OF CALIFORNIA VS. CURTIS MENDOZA

Case No. F-68-2410

This is KTWN Radio serving all of Allen County and beyond! Here's a recap of all the news of the day.

Former Alabama governor George Wallace formally announced his third-party campaign for president today. His third party is known as the American Independent Party. According to some, this is a far-right party that endorses Wallace's segregationist views. The candidate has clearly stated his platform will revolve around law and order, states' rights, and continuing and expanding racial segregation. He will run against Richard Nixon, the presumptive Republican candidate, and the Democratic nominee, likely incumbent Lyndon Johnson.

Military authorities are concerned about the increased military activity in broad portions of South Vietnam, now labeled the Tet Offensive. What appeared to be a small uprising has now spread to many parts of the country. US casualties are mounting. However, the US military is confident that the situation is firmly under control.

In sports, the 1968 Winter Olympics is underway in Grenoble, France. The US Olympic ice-skating team is led by medal hopeful Peggy Fleming. The US team is still recovering from the devastating 1961 plane crash tragedy that killed the entire figure-skating team, including Fleming's coach.

In local news, Curtis Mendoza will be arraigned on February 15 at 9:00 a.m. in the superior court of the Allen County Courthouse. District Attorney Ron Phillips will formally submit one count of first-degree murder in James Allen Jr.'s death in early January. In a press release, Phillips stated, "The evidence is strong against Mr. Mendoza, and our office will vigorously pursue this case for a conviction—and possibly the death penalty." Mr. Mendoza's defense counsel, Robert Stein, could not be reached for comment. The defendant was arrested on January 2 in Clarktown at Juan's Cuban Bar with evidence allegedly connected to the homicide. He remains in Allen County Jail without bail.

Finally, the Allen County Fair will be underway next Friday. Take your family for the warm festivities of good food, animal exhibits, auctions, games, rides for the kiddies, and much more. The Allen County Fair is celebrating its fiftieth anniversary, and tickets can be purchased at your local food markets.

And now, let's enjoy the groovy sounds of Jefferson Airplane and Grace Slick with "Somebody to Love," here, as always, at your number one station KTWN with your favorite DJ, Rick "The Master" Lewis!

■ ■ ■

As they entered the holding cell to visit Curt, Stein thought Hank should visit privately with Curt for a few moments. They had not seen each other in three years—since Sally's funeral.

"Hey, bro...damn, you look old man. Hank, are those gray hairs?" Curt smiled and sat down on a metallic chair. Hank said nothing and just stared at his younger brother. Curt's shoulder was still bandaged, and he had noticeable bruises on his face and neck. They first talked about old times when they grew up together before Hank left for college in 1957. "Hank, the one thing I will always remember like yesterday was the marble tournament. 'Member? I was too young, but Mom and Dad always talked about it, and you were probably in eighth grade. Nana told me you would practice flicking those marbles for hours in the backyard, over and over, until you could hit one from twenty feet away. Man, you won the valley marble tournament; Mom and Dad still have that trophy in our bedroom."

Hank said nothing and just nodded passively.

They shared warm memories. Shooting their BB guns out in the desert. Swimming the local canals in the summer. Hank remembered teaching Curt how to multiply when Curt was in second grade. But those memories now seemed remote, as if they belonged to others. Curt recounted the events in the jail but left out most details. The pending murder case was awkwardly avoided. Vietnam was also avoided. Two elephants in the room. Both instinctively knew these subjects would eventually enter their discussions, but not now. They just stared at each other like lost souls who were meeting again in the shadows.

"So, you gonna help Stein represent me...show off all that hotshot legal stuff in court?"

"He didn't ask, and I don't handle criminal cases."

Curt looked away and swallowed a lot of air. "I been through a lot all these years. Sally, Nam, screwing up in front of Mom and Dad. I hurt people without meaning to, you know? I don't think they're proud of what I've turned into. Not proud of myself. I figured I could always take care of myself." He clenched his fists, bent down, and cried like never before. "Sorry, Hank."

Hank tried but could not look away from his helpless kid brother, and he sensed something strange—a hard lump in his throat. He saw his younger brother like a child. Lonely, unprotected, and confused. "I'm with you, brother. Whatever I can do in your case, I will. Promise." They both remained quiet for a few minutes and stared at each other. Hank thought much more separated them than plexiglass.

"Let's get Stein in here. He probably is wondering what's taking us so long."

■ ■ ■

After visiting Curt, Hank and Mr. Stein came to our house to fill us in on the case and answer any questions. Mr. Stein seemed nice, smart, and kinda funny. We all sat in our living room listening to Stein's updates.

It was serious.

They left nothing out "so we understand the magnitude of this dire situation." After they described the latest attack on my brother, my mother started crying quietly. My nana was taking a nap, and when she heard about the attack, she simply muttered, "Pinche animals." Reporters called, but both attorneys vigorously instructed us not to make any statements to any reporters without consulting them first. Stein had already hired an investigator by the name of Bud Lemons, who Stein said was "hardworking, loyal, and discreet." He would interview all of us for background information that might be helpful to Curt's case.

They carefully walked us through the criminal court process and what to expect from the prosecutor. No case like this had ever been heard in the county, and the district attorney would expend all its resources to get Curt convicted.

The most dramatic moment of the visit was when they told us Hank would also help with the case, "mostly preparing motions and prepping any potential witnesses." It seemed like Hank was going to "work behind the scenes" in the trial, and I think that made Mom and Dad feel better. Hank would be there until the trial was over, and we all could get to know him again. Hank had to make arrangements with his law firm in Boston to take time off, and he didn't think it would be a problem. Since Hank was not licensed in California, Stein explained that he could seek the court's approval to allow Hank formal entrance into the case *pro hac vice.*

As he was chomping down my nana's enchiladas, Stein joked that Hank and he would work well together—like Captain Kirk and Spock. I laughed, and my parents looked puzzled. I had watched *Star Trek* with my nana since it came on our TV a few years before. (She had a secret crush on Sulu.) They explained what was going to happen at the preliminary hearing, then the trial. After Stein left, my father gave Hank a tight hug and said nothing.

■ ■ ■

"Hey, Mendoza, you awake?"

It was early morning, with the sunrise about an hour away. The barracks were quiet except for the sound of the Beach Boys on someone's transistor radio. The ambiance felt eerie and tense. Curt had been restless all night, going over the attack the previous night. Lying back on the bunk, he could smell rotting onions that had recently been picked in a nearby field. He remembered picking onions one summer in high school. He wished he were back there.

"Hey, Mendoza, who's Sally, eh? Your woman?"

"Why the hell you asking?"

"'Cause you was saying her name all night long. Kinda like someone's looking for someone, you know? But you were looking for her, maybe in your dreams…real clear, eh. So, who is she?"

"No one. Did I say anything else?"

"Nah, just Sally. Other shit I couldn't understand."

"Hey, Mendoza…you fucked up those dudes, man. Really fucked 'em up. All the *vatos* in here are scared of you, man. Some even wanna know if they can give you their dessert at tonight's chow…chocolate cake…and they put those fuckin' sprinkles in them, you know? A few said you can have theirs."

Curt said nothing and lay in his upper bunk, looking up at the ceiling. An air conditioner droned quietly. A rooster's crowing echoed in the distance.

"Ramos, who were those guys? Do you know? I think I recognized one from before."

"The main guy was Fierro…'Masca Fierro'…pretty messed-up Cuban. I heard he spent a lot of time in prison in Cuba. He came in here a few days ago and right away acted like some fuckin' shot caller…bossing people around. One time he grabbed my dessert at chow—strawberries, my favorite. I couldn't do shit, man. He showed me his shank, and I know he knows how to use it. Fuckin' puto. Those strawberries looked good. I used to see him over on Pink Avenue at Juan's Cuban Bar. He was a bartender… and probably something else."

"I think that's Juana's Cuban Bar."

"What?"

"Juana's Cuban Bar."

"OK…anyway, I never liked that prick. You fucked him real good. I saw him with his own shank in his own eye, and it looked like he still held onto it! Fuckin' knife probably had some sentimental value for him." Ramos yawned and caught his breath. "And the other guy was also a Cuban…Rafa something. You know, I heard his sister is the owner of that bar, Juana's. He's also pretty messed up, I heard. The last guy, don't know him. He ran like a pussy, dropped his knife. Goes by Whimpy."

Curt said nothing, absorbing the information. "Hey, Ramos…you turned on the lights, didn't you?" Ramos giggled quietly and said nothing. "How come you helped me and told me they were coming?"

"Dunno…just didn't wanna see shit happen to you, I guess. Don't think I'm attracted to you, see…fuck no…just wanted to help is all. I also think somehow Sheriff Johnson was involved. I heard he personally brought in Fierro, and he also has something on Rafa…not too sure what. That sheriff is a motherfucker. I stay away from him…here and in the streets."

Curt nodded quietly, still in thought.

"I heard you killed two people. Is that right? You got those two teardrop tats below your eye."

"Shit…how many guys you kill over there in Vietnam? Probably a lot."

Curt pressed his lips together and said nothing.

"Sorry, man…I know you guys don't talk too much shit about what you did over there. Real clear, eh.

"Hey, Mendoza"—Ramos inched closer to Curt—"let me tell you a secret, man." Ramos pulled out a photo from his pocket. "I never let go of this. Check it out, eh."

Curt squinted like Mr. Magoo and closely examined the photo of a small child on a horse. Probably at an amusement park, Curt thought. "OK…what the hell am I looking at? Some kid on a horse? What about it?"

"See that cute *chavalio*? That's me when my dad took me to the zoo, and I got to ride a fuckin' pony. I was about five. Only time I remember my dad doing something fun with me. Damn, that was cool. I rode that little pony for at least an hour. But I wanted to show it to you for something else. Look closer at that cute little kid—me—on that pony. Look at the face. You can see my birthmarks right below my left eye. Two dots. As I grew, the dots stretched down and began to look like teardrops. These aren't tats, man…they're birthmarks. I think God put them on me to protect me. Everyone thinks the teardrops mean I killed two people, and everyone around me is scared when they see those marks. Even the pinche cops treat me differently, sometimes in a good way, with respect. Never killed anyone in my life, except probably my future. I don't like violence. Ask my old lady. She kicks my ass all the time, and I have never hit her back. She and my kids think I'm a pussy. These are birthmarks. Everyone is scared of fuck…ing…birth…marks. I'm a thief, doper, and a lot of other things—but no killer, man…real clear, eh."

"Holy shit. Birthmarks. Damn."

Both Pedro and Curt belted a laugh and woke up a few inmates. No one complained.

■ ■ ■

"You sure you wanna be co-counsel with me? Many around here think I'm an asshole."

Stein and Hank Mendoza were seated at the usual rear table at Karina's Restaurant. It was early, 8:45, before the late-morning crowd arrived that Saturday, February 17. The morning was misty and the air heavy. Angry-looking purple stratus clouds quickly floated into the valley from the east, blocking the rising sun, along with muted thunder. It might rain.

Stein was slurping some black coffee, and a macho plate of huevos rancheros awaited him on the table. Hank only had coffee and a warm, buttered tortilla. Stein was still reading the *LA Metro Tribune*. The headlines included the expansion of the military draft to Vietnam to grad students. "Shit, my cousin might have to go," Stein muttered. Page four also contained a brief blurb about the Allen homicide.

Hank sipped his coffee and said, "But there's some good news: I read they're going to renew *Star Trek*." After another gulp of coffee, Hank looked away. "Oh, with reference to your initial question, one, yes, I would be honored to work alongside you, and two, yes, I also am aware that you are indeed an asshole, which I believe is a universal assessment. Your reputation precedes you, Mr. Stein."

"You know, Mr. Mendoza…you're one strange dude."

Hank's law firm had sent him volumes of research on criminal law and procedure, and Stein had also shared his research material with him. Hank had spent three entire days at home going through the material and felt he was on terra firma in the harsh land of California criminal procedure. Curt's arraignment hearing was scheduled for the following Tuesday.

Stein carefully gathered his thoughts and said, "Look, I want to outline the parameters of our work in this case. Our investigator will be joining us later this morning. First, it is imperative that you not ask your brother if he did it…if he killed Mr. Allen. Doing that at the onset could ethically compromise you and might limit our defenses."

"I don't follow."

"Well, if a client told me at the beginning of my representation that he entered a house and raped a girl in there, then he testifies under oath that he did neither and was actually in Puerto Vallarta drinking beer, you know he's committing perjury. And if you pursue that line of questioning, then you are part of the perjury. Knowing that information at the inception will ethically handcuff you. And if you elicited that bogus information in front of the jury, you would be suborning that perjury. Understand? You would be a party to your client's perjury. And suppose you don't want any part of your client's perjury. In that scenario, he would be denied his right to the effective assistance of counsel as guaranteed in every fuckin' constitution in this country—federal, state, administrative, city. At that point, you've reached an ethical Rubicon because your guy is already on the witness stand in front of the jury and judge lying about the rape and burglary, and there's no way for you to back out. And if you ever thought to convey your dilemma to the court or the jury—that your client is lying through his teeth—you would have some major problems with the California State Bar.

"Let's get all the discovery in front of us, and then we can delicately ask him about his role in this case within the context of those alleged facts within the reports. And let's force the prosecutors to prove the case. Even though Curt might want to get something off his chest, don't ask him if he did it."

Hank said nothing, slowly exhaled, and drank more of Karina's thick Mexican coffee.

"I will handle the voir dire and the guilt phase of the trial. In that first phase, you will assist me with any pretrial and trial motions. There might be an issue regarding the search of Curt, so you might wanna research a 1538.5 motion. If we can suppress the admission of the coins before the jury, we stand a good chance. That's all I need, a chance to win. Just a chance. You might want to explore a motion to change the venue. This case has generated so much publicity, and the Allen family is venerated here. I don't see how we can get a fair trial here in Allen County. You might look for an expert to analyze all the blood found in the house and any that might have been found or not found on Curt. The victim was beaten, and the crime scene was a mess. There had to be some traces of the blood on Curt's clothes if he was the assailant.

"Another thing that's always bothered me is the general makeup of the jury panels. The population of this county is about three hundred thousand, and as I understand it, about 70 percent are Mexican American. Yet most juries are overwhelmingly Anglo. Maybe we can look into that angle.

"If we don't prevail in the guilt phase, then we throw ourselves at the mercy of the same jury, who will decide whether Curt should live. And I think you should play a more active role since you're his brother and the jury might sympathize with you. You can personalize the presentation much more than I can.

"There's another item that may or may not be important in this case… just a little odd. Apparently, there was another item taken during the incident, an Indian pouch with some probate material. I can fill you in later. But Sheriff Johnson thinks your brother took these documents for some reason. I don't know if it's part of this case, but keep your eyes and ears open for any mention of this item. My gut tells me it's the key that might unlock the mystery to this whole murder."

"That's a good general plan. I think we'll collaborate well together. Like you told my parents—you are Captain Kirk, and I am Spock."

"Hank, you do have a sense of humor!"

"That's from my human side. Vulcans lack a sense of humor, Mr. Stein…"

■ ■ ■

On Sunday the eighteenth, Sheriff Johnson issued informal (that is, verbal commands that could not be memorialized, proven, or traced) edicts as follows:

1. All investigators connected with the Allen case should not speak or cooperate with the defense team of inmate Mendoza;

2. Any informants currently incarcerated would be considered for extra jail credits if they come across any information from inmate Mendoza;

3. Inmate Mendoza will not have shower privileges until further notice (ostensibly for his safety);

4. No one has access to the evidence locker where physical evidence from the Allen crime scene is stored without the sheriff's permission;

5. Inmate Mendoza will not be allowed any change of his jail-issued clothing until after his preliminary hearing; and

6. Assistant Sheriff Garza is not, under any circumstances, given any notice of the aforementioned directives.

Johnson was still not sure if Mendoza knew anything about the Indian pouch. Did he take it? Did he bury it? Maybe he never even touched it. But Mendoza would not budge despite Big Bob's efforts to extract information from him. He knew in his gut that Mendoza knew more about the Indian pouch than he let on. No one else could have taken it from the Allen estate.

■ ■ ■

The arraignment calendar on the morning of February 15 appeared, on the face of it, routine. Twenty cases were on Judge Gates' calendar—a mundane amalgam of drugs, assaults, car thefts, probation violations, and one murder: People v. Curtis Mendoza. Prosecutors, defense attorneys, investigators, and clerical personnel all formed a confusing beehive of nervous activity. Stein and Hank quietly sat behind the main counsel table, waiting for their case to be called. Both had briefly spoken to Curt to prep him for the hearing:

look straight ahead, show no emotion, and be overly respectful of the court.

They learned that morning that the district attorney had assigned the case exclusively to Travis J. Johnson, a twenty-year veteran of the office. Stein hardly knew him and had never tried a case with him. In a trial, the personal quirks of opposing counsel are almost as important as the facts of the case. While you might build your defense around specific themes within the realm of the given facts—real or manufactured—the opposing counsel's strengths and weaknesses can also be exploited. Stein had no qualms about taking advantage of an unprepared prosecutor. Does the prosecutor relate well to the jury? To the judge? Is he lazy? Does he have a temper? Can you goad him into losing his temper in front of the jury? Is he quick on his feet? Does he prepare his witnesses well? Johnson was smart and always exhibited professionalism in court. Stein liked him since he was always fair to defense counsel and always willing to listen to any proposed settlements. And he had prosecuted at least five murder cases in his career—all convictions.

Because of the Allen murder case, the courtroom was filled to capacity. Local reporters, nosy attorneys, a few sheriffs, and interested members of the public were all anxiously waiting for Curt's case to be called—like hungry spectators at a wrestling match.

When Curt was hauled into court before Judge Gates, Stein and Hank were a bit shocked—shocked by Curt's slovenly appearance. They were not aware of Sheriff Johnson's unwritten directives. Without bathing, shaving, or having fresh clothes for three days, Curt looked like a decrepit vagrant in shackles being led into the courtroom with five deputy sheriffs. His hair was matted, his dark stubble formed a light beard, and his angry red eyes had bloated bags under both. And the bandages from his recent attack were visible along with stains of dry blood—presumably from the late Mr. Fierro. Stein had been assured by Undersheriff Garza the night before that Curt would be allowed to bathe and dress in clean orange prison garb. Judge Gates could smell the stench from the bench, but he guessed that Big Bob had something to do with it. He directed all three counsel to approach his bench and quietly excoriated Johnson for the defendant's appearance. Johnson indicated he would "look into it." Stein took him at his word.

"And who are you?" Gates pointed to Hank.

"Your Honor, this is my co-counsel, Hank Mendoza. We've already arranged through the state bar so he can be my co-counsel pro hac vice since he's licensed in Massachusetts."

Gates looked at Hank like an inspector. "Your last name is Mendoza? You don't look like a Mendoza. You're not related to this defendant, are you?"

"Yes, Your Honor. He's my brother, and we're prepared to elicit any waivers if his honor wishes."

"Nah. That's not necessary. He's your bother, eh? Were you adopted?"

"No, Your Honor. My natural parents raised me."

"No offense, son, but you don't look like a Mendoza, that's all. I haven't come across too many attorneys with your last name. No offense. Welcome to my courtroom." Looking at DDA Johnson, the jurist added, "I expect your office will ensure this defendant will be properly dressed next time he comes into my courtroom. Have a talk with the good sheriff."

All nodded respectfully as they returned to the counsel tables. Curt slowly shuffled up to the table between his two attorneys as the charge of murder was read by the clerk. Stein waived a further reading of his constitutional rights, and Curt Mendoza formally entered a plea of not guilty to the sole count of murder, a violation of California Penal Code, section 187. The preliminary examination was then scheduled for March 15.

As Stein and Hank left the courtroom, Garza whispered to them, "Sorry, this won't happen again."

■ ■ ■

A brief winter storm brought light showers and a cold westerly wind that sliced across the valley like a sharp blade. Curt returned from the courthouse to the cold barracks and his warm bunk. The crisp air splashed him like a cold shower, and the jail seemed cleaner as the rain washed away the surface grime and stench from the facility. He was greeted warmly by Pedro Ramos, munching on a giant hamburger. "The chow line's closed…want mine? They surprised us with hamburgers for lunch. Man, I can't eat any more." Curt took his offer and devoured the hamburger with two gulps. A full stomach felt good as he was beginning to feel normal. Maybe this is a good sign, he hoped.

"Whimpy told me to tell you he's sorry, man. He's the one who gave me these extra burgers. You cool with that?"

Curt nodded. "Tell Whimpy we're cool. Any more hamburgers?"

■ ■ ■

Stein's preparation for jury trials began with a broad sketch of the case—the outlines of issues, defenses, motions, questions, and arguments. Then he began to fill in the intimate details, trying to get a focused legal portrait. Usually, the picture did not come into view until the trial had already started, given the vagarious nature of most judicial proceedings. Like a rudderless ship, trials often go where the current takes them, and attorneys are usually along for the ride, trying to steer the ship in their direction.

He was in his apartment with only a legal pad and pencil. Among empty wine bottles and half-eaten burritos were half a dozen law books strewn around his small dining table and chairs. His apartment looked ransacked. *California Reporter, Cal Jur, Criminal Procedure* by Jerome Hall. He began to jot down some of the salient elements of the complicated trial with high stakes—the life of a good kid, a soldier, a brother, a son.
His legal pad showed the following:

> *P V Mendoza Outline*
> *INVESTIGATION*
> *-subs for officers' notes*

-court order for testing vic's/def clothes-blood? Hair?

-interview wits: M. Bradley? Officers? Character wits? Military record/ friends?

-get forensic experts; need to ask for $$

-explore Indian pouch. Research Allen estate and trust. Research estate law. Who benefits?

MOTIONS

-venue change ?

-PC 1538.5 re: coins seized from def

-racial makeup of jury

-gag order?

-1118 motion?

-chain of custody of ev if tampered

GUILT PHASE

-other suspects/other motives to kill Allen

-mitigate to manslaughter, diminished cap? drugs/alcohol research P v. Moore, Wells cases

PENALTY PHASE

-Should Hank do it? Can he?

-military background, display? Ask jury?

APPEAL ISSUES

It was early evening, and he wanted to get fresh air, so he decided to walk to the Mendoza household to give Hank a copy of his brief outline and discuss the case. As he approached their home, he saw an elderly lady, perhaps seventy, sitting on a rocker smoking a hand-rolled cigarette. For some odd reason, a flyswatter lay on her lap. As Stein approached, she carefully inspected him and yelled, "Sorry, don't come no further. I got no problems with you hippies, but if you need money or food, you can go to the Catholic church so they can help you." She sat up, puffing away, and looked like she was daring him to take one more step toward the house. The flyswatter was firmly clutched to her hand like a baton.

"Ma'am, my name is Robert Stein, attorney at law. I represent Curtis Mendoza. I'm here to see Hank."

She pointed her crooked index finger at him, "You're my Curt's lawyer? *Dios mio*. I didn't meet you before when you came the other day. *Mijo*, you look like you could use some food…and other stuff. Come in, and I'll get Hank…and some food for you. *Dios mio…*"

As Stein passed the front threshold into the house, he told Nana, "I heard you make *chignon pozole*. Do you have some?"

Nana nodded yes.

"*Orale, Nana!*"

"*Dios mio.*"

Over Mendoza *pozole*, tortillas, refried beans, and a few beers, Stein and Hank spent the next four hours planning the initial phases of the preliminary hearing, pretrial, and trial. For the first time since the bar exam, Stein felt fear.

Hank asked Stein how to approach the jurors during voir dire, jury selection.

"Approaching the jurors during selection might be a bit delicate. We must get honest answers about their attitude toward the war. And we might wanna think about asking jurors these questions individually in private, so their answers won't influence and infect the other potential members of the jury panel."

"Mr. Stein, I honestly haven't given much thought to the Vietnam War in terms of my politics. Obviously, I was worried for my brother when he went. But still, I haven't fully processed it. By nature, I think I'm a pacifist. And I can see the myriad of reasons why we entered the war and as many reasons why we shouldn't be there."

"It's fucked, man. It's irresponsible. It's immoral. A catastrophe on a grand scale. But we must focus on getting the best jurors in Curt's trial. Some might see him in a good light. Green Beret. Volunteer. All the medals. Jurors might like shiny objects. Others might see him on the opposite side of the spectrum. Vets from World War II might think he's brought dishonor to the uniform. And many can't get around the fact that a beloved man who treated the poor around here well was viciously murdered. This sounds trite, but from my experience, many jury trials are won or lost with the initial jury selection. It might come down to a simple thing like jurors liking or not liking the attorneys' personalities. We gotta keep the Vietnam War out of this trial—unless it might help."

■ ■ ■

Along with theater, music, wrestling, lumberjack competitions, sports, and politics, criminal trials have always been an American form of entertainment. In the early years of the American experiment, the Massachusetts Assembly outlawed theatrical performances in 1767, ostensibly because they pushed British propaganda. What filled the vacuum was the 1770 murder trial of the British soldiers involved in the Boston Massacre. Boston was riveted by this trial, which had all the essential elements of theatrical entertainment—politics, violence, satire, heroes, villains, histrionics, and more. Americans love a good trial to view from afar as if they are viewing a soap opera dramatically unfold. People v. Mendoza was a microscopic version of this cultural phenomenon. Allen County began to focus on the case, and the publicity it generated went far beyond the Guadalupe Mountains. The valley percolated with idle gossip.

Why did he do it?

Who gets the Allen estate?

Was Mendoza in a satanic cult?

Could others have been involved?

How do they pick the jury?

Why is his brother also helping?

What was in the Indian pouch?

Did Mendoza kill others? How many did he kill in Vietnam?

Was he on drugs?

The court proceedings would be a number one ticket into town. Like those Bostonians of long ago during the Boston Massacre trial, the good folks of Allen County wanted their piece of American justice.

Meanwhile, Sheriff Johnson was discreetly tapping into all his street resources, searching for any leads on the Indian pouch. Nothing. So, if the Mendoza kid took it, why? On the face of it, it was of no value to a kid like him, stoned out of his mind. Maybe he took it because he was stoned and just curious about the contents. He was the only person who could have taken it, and he was playing games with Big Bob for leverage. We'll see how this plays out, he thought, but the sheriff needed to take credit for its destruction to get something from the Original Five, who would make millions from the Allen Trust I. He thought the murder case was solid and that he could probably squeeze Mendoza tighter if he had information. But with those slick attorneys, maybe Mendoza might get off, and he might produce the Indian pouch for a fee.

His other minor problem was Juana Gomez. He had to answer for her brother's injury. He had to convince her it was the bartender's idea. He was familiar with Juana's deadly temper. She had as many street resources as he did and knew all the wrong people in the wrong places. But he also knew she might be mollified if he came into money that would be shared with her. She was a mighty snake, and Big Bob was terrified of snakes—all snakes. He thought of the John Wayne line "Snakes like you usually die of their own poison."

. . .

A week before the preliminary hearing, Curt had a visit from Hank and my father. They knew to avoid discussing the factual specifics of the case since it might compromise them, and they were also cognizant of Sheriff Johnson's set of extra ears—hidden microphones. They tried to keep the conversation light, and it was evident that Curt looked healthier than ever. His skin color, humor, mind, and physical strength had all returned.

Hank was carefully walking them through the preliminary hearing and what to expect and what not to expect. "A preliminary hearing is merely a probable cause hearing, and the judge—the magistrate—will only make a finding that there's probable cause to believe Curt committed the offense charged. Then after the preliminary hearing, Curt will be 'held to answer to the charge, and the case would proceed to a jury trial.'" Hank told them not to expect any surprises, and he almost made it seem like a routine, mundane legal proceeding.

My father briefed Curt on the family. Things at the Mendoza household were fine, considering Curt's situation. They reminisced a great deal about the "old days" when all were younger and times were simpler. Curt missed Mom's cooking and Nana's crude cigarettes. The laughs and sentiments were palliative and soothed their frail nerves. But behind these light sentiments lurked the giant monster facing them.

"Mijo, how have you been sleeping?"

"Good, Pops. All good." Curt knew he couldn't fool them. His vivid nightmares continued every night. His constant visits from Vietnam, Sally, heroin, and Jim Allen's blood kept him up every night. My father understood; the war in the Pacific still visited him too, but not as frequently. The smell of cordite, death, salt water, and rot had been slowly disappearing over the years since 1944.

"That's good, son. You look good and healthy. Keeping yourself healthy will carry you through this."

Curt was quiet, wandering in his thoughts.

"Pops, when this thing is over, you know…I've been reading the news… this Tet thing over there in Nam…it's getting bad over there…I think I wanna go back…I wanna reenlist. I can help."

Hank looked puzzled.

My father looked pissed. "You wanna WHAT?" My father bent forward on his bench as if he couldn't hear Curt.

"Pops, I've thought about this a lot. Ever since I came back, I've been confused. Nothing here makes sense to me. It's like I left something over there and going back might help me get over all this confusion. Look at me…I embarrassed and shamed my family. I have this bullshit case, and I know Hank and Stein will beat it. And I know I didn't kill Mr. Allen. I have this feeling in my gut that I need to go back. That's all."

My father took a deep breath as if he was carefully gathering his thoughts. "When I returned from the Pacific, I had the same thoughts. I thought I left something back there, and I wanted to get it back. I don't know how or why I survived, but I did. It wasn't 'cause I was a great soldier. There were marines who were a lot better who didn't make it. I tried—and still try—to forget that fucking war, but I can't. It's like you have a pot with boiling water, and you put a lid to keep down the steam, but you can't. Eventually, the steam comes out. But you don't want it to come out all at once. All those guys back there—my friends that got killed—I feel guilty…I know I shouldn't, but I do. If it wasn't for your mom, I know I would've never made it back. The thought of coming back to her and my family kept me focused…and I think it brought me luck. And when I came back…shit…I was a fucking mess. Drinking. When I returned, I stayed in San Francisco for about six months, wandering around the streets, doing nothing really. Your mom and nana thought I was somewhere in Japan after the surrender, but I came back. I couldn't come home. Not too sure why…just couldn't. Honestly, there were times when I didn't wanna come back to your mom. I knew I was not the same, and I didn't wanna put her through all my stuff. But eventually I came back. I fought a lot with your mom. Pissed all day. Got into a couple of fights—nothing serious, you know, just bar fights. One guy gave me a hard time in a bar…just teasing. But he pissed me off. I don't even remember what he said to me…or if he even actually said anything to me. I just pounced on him, and before you know it, I was choking him. He started to pass out, and I saw his face real deep, you know? Past his face and deep into his eyes, just looking at me, confused. I seen that look before…over there…in the Pacific. I let him go, but I just wanted to kill him. Just some guy—harmless, joking. But I really wanted to choke him out. When I was beating on him and choking him, it was like I was looking from afar…like someone else was doing it. Hard to explain. I realized I had to come back home. It's where I belong. Your mom and nana could've managed without me. They're stronger than all of us here. They kept our family together while I was away. But I'm glad I returned home. Not an easy adjustment. I know I was difficult…still am. I mostly just wanted to be alone. The job I got was great. Just do my job well. No one bothers me. Clean up the fucking schools…not too bad. Get a steady paycheck. Your mom wanted me to talk about it, but I couldn't. Why? She wouldn't understand. Those things I saw and did over there will always be with me, and I get that. But Curt, you are home. There's nothing you'll find back there in Vietnam. The friends you left are dead, and they'll be just as dead tomorrow and next week and next year. You have nothing over there. All that crap in your brain that's been following you since you got back—that's been nagging you—it won't go away. You're here with your only family. Fight this battle here. Your brother is here. Trust him to help you. Your family is here and will always be here. So cut this shit out about going back. The war is over for you, except those fucked-up memories that followed you here. It's like those awful memories from the war hitched a ride to your mind, and you'll be spending a lot of time trying to get rid of them. Focus on this trial, son. I love you. I let you go to Vietnam because I loved you, and I knew you felt you had to go, but I knew the consequences. Maybe I should've tried to keep you here." He was out of breath. For a few minutes, nothing was said, and they all looked down awkwardly.

"OK, Pops. Sorry I upset you. Just thinking out loud. You're right. Now, how about those fuckin' Dodgers…World Series this year?"

My father blurted out with a laugh and wiped his nose. "Not without Koufax."

∎ ∎ ∎

My parents liked to watch the news. Although they had only ten years of schooling, they were probably more attuned to current events than most "educated" people. I didn't mind too much when my dad abruptly changed the channel to see the news or boxing because it was the only time I would watch TV with him. It was something we always shared. In late February, we were expecting Mr. Stein and Hank to brief us on the upcoming preliminary hearing. My nana and I were lying on our old couch watching *The Twilight Zone*, the one about the astronauts who return from space to a parallel universe. That was kinda how our family had been feeling since Curt was arrested—as if we were in another reality. My father turned the channel to watch Walter Cronkite and the *CBS Evening News* as he did most nights. The Tet Offensive dominated all three channels for those few weeks. We were blitzed with grainy footage of marines defending an embassy, airfields being bombed, and Vietnamese civilians running for cover in anguish. *The Twilight Zone* and Westerns offered a great diversion in those days to avoid the thoughts of the war. Vietnam was all around us, deep and wide.

Cronkite looked somberly into the camera before millions of viewers. The last time he had that look on his face was when he announced President Kennedy's assassination. He proceeded to say:

"It seems now more certain than ever that the bloody experience of Vietnam is to end in a stalemate…It is increasingly clear to this reporter that the only rational way out, then, will be to negotiate, not as victors, but as an honorable people who lived up to their pledge to defend democracy and did the best they could. This is Walter Cronkite. Good night."

My dad turned off the TV, sighed, and left to go his bedroom alone. I could hear him uncap a new bottle of Jim Beam's finest.

Nana only said, "*Dios mio.*"

Mr. Stein arrived later that evening. As he and Hank explained to our family that evening, under most circumstances, a preliminary hearing is a routine, perfunctory proceeding with very few surprises. It's simply a "probable cause hearing."

The prosecution presents a bare-bones case to a magistrate, who has to determine whether there is "sufficient cause" to believe the accused committed the offense or offenses charged. In poker's parlance, the prosecution is not compelled to show all their cards on the table, just enough to demonstrate to the magistrate that they have enough of a case to take it to the final arbiter—the jury. It's a low threshold—nearly hitting the ground—according to most defense attorneys.

Hank and Mr. Stein said not to expect any surprises at this hearing. They said they might be able to elicit some favorable testimony that could be useful at the trial later. All the prosecution trial witnesses did not have to testify—only enough to satisfy the judge that there was "enough evidence" to proceed to a jury trial. When the judge found enough evidence, Curt would be arraigned in the superior court in fifteen days, and the jury trial would commence sixty days thereafter. Our reality was setting in now that we knew what to expect in the following few months. This trial with my brother's life on the line was getting real.

■ ■ ■

Back at school, I kept to myself, avoiding questions or comments about Curt's situation. Except for my three buddies, I tried not to hang around with anyone and focused on algebra, geography, and woodshop.

Back in those days, the boys were assigned to woodshop, and the girls were relegated to "home economics class"—boys being prepared for a skill to bring home the bacon, and girls being groomed as homemakers to cook the fucking bacon. Anyway, I tried with all the God-given talent in my hands to build a kitchen towel rack for my mom to surprise her on her birthday. And building it was cathartic—it took my mind off Curt's case. On paper, the design looked simple. Mr. King, the wood shop instructor, repeatedly reminded us that "even a blind lady with one arm could build it." Unfortunately, dexterity, precision, and patience never entered my DNA. Instead, God blessed me with impatience, hands of stone, and no aesthetic sense. And I couldn't find an armless blind lady to do the project for me. The result was a crooked slab of old pine with hammer marks and nail holes that I never sanded. I could hit a baseball, but not a damn nail head. It looked like an instrument for torture from the Dark Ages. My mom, however, glowed with pride and placed that wooden monstrosity in the kitchen near the sink. Because the rack was so crooked, the towels also hung sadly on the rack, always lopsided. My nana was a little more critical: "Mijo, dos mio. Where's the rest of it?" Over the years, the towel rack mysteriously traveled from the kitchen to the laundry room to a bathroom to the garage, and it finally rested in peace in a basin of scrap wood in the backyard. If I ever encounter an armless blind lady, I'd like to share this anecdote with her.

I also avoided Adela—especially since the winter dance debacle. I no longer sat next to her in math, and we hadn't had lunch together since, but one day she followed me during a class break and told me to follow her to the school library, one of our favorite meeting places. I entered and followed her like a trained puppy toward the book racks, between Roman history and geography.

In my coolest James Dean tone, I asked, "Adela, what's up?"

She whispered, "I now know what you were up to at the dance. I kinda thought you were acting a little weird." She had a strange look as she peered directly up at me, while I tried to avoid eye contact.

"Lemme explain...it was no big deal—"

Before I could offer some specious bullshit explanation, she grabbed both my hands, pulled me toward her, and placed the longest, sweetest, wettest, warmest, juiciest (if I knew of any other adjectives ending with "est," I would include them) kiss on me that still feels moist and sweet fifty years later. The recurring memory still makes my toes tingle. She then casually walked out of the library, and I didn't realize I was already late for my next class.

I think I heard the sweet harmony of the Shirelles.

PART TWENTY

WHEN BLACKNESS EXPLODES

Matt Bradley was near the end of his graveyard shift, maneuvering his off-road Border Patrol pickup along the meandering desert trails in the south end of the county as exhaustion caught up to him. All was quiet. There were no signs of recent encroachments or illegal activity from the border a mile away. Even though a ten-hour shift out in the desert could be exhausting to the mind and body, Matt was looking forward to returning home to an ice-cold beer and TV to keep him company. The sun hovered low on the western horizon, and the mountains turned into shadowy silhouettes.

He turned off the air conditioner, rolled down the windows, and breathed in a deep breath of the heavy desert air, which was musty with a hint of rain. The clouds hovering to the west were pregnant with purple rain. After following the desert trail toward County Highway 15, which ran parallel to the international border, he felt much safer once he was on the highway. Terra firma. Only twenty minutes back to headquarters. The solitary nature of his work with the US Border Patrol gave him time to think while on patrol in the desert—about Vietnam, Willie, high school,

Belinda, sports, and his vague future. Willie and the helicopter were always hovering near the edges of his thoughts.

He also had a growing anxiety about Curt Mendoza's trial and had received a subpoena from the district attorney to testify at his upcoming preliminary hearing. All he could do would be to recount what he observed while tracking Mendoza and two others to the Allen hacienda. Allen was beaten mercilessly and Mendoza could have done it, but he hoped not. From what little he knew, Mendoza had served with distinction, and Matt didn't want to see another Vietnam vet mess up his life. He had already seen too many there in Allen County. Heroin. Drinking. Jail. Failed marriages. Dragging their families into their private abyss. Young lives discarded before they had a chance to reach their tomorrows. The young men and women who experienced Vietnam reflected a generation of lost futures; their elegy of despair and confusion was already being written mostly by those who didn't understand combat vets.

Too many.

He was now just a few miles west of Clarktown. As the sun was setting behind him, he felt a cold sensation inside. Creeping shadows began to crawl along the desert floor like ephemeral ghosts. The wild chorus of nocturnal animals came to life—owls greeting the coyotes, crickets chirping incessantly, and the eagles patiently cruising the sky for food. The nights in the black desert could quickly sink below freezing.

As he passed a row of salt cedar trees to his right, about one hundred meters from the highway, he caught a fleeting glimpse of something out of place, something metallic near the trees. He paused and went off road on the hard sand toward the shiny reflection, instinctively thinking illegal activity might be afoot.

As he approached the object, he realized it was a vehicle; it looked like a nice car. As his eyes focused in the dimming light, he made out a Ford Fairlane 500, probably a '65. Carefully exiting his unit about fifty meters from the car and quietly approaching on foot, he was alert for anything or anyone. Now he could discern its colors—pastel blue with a white top. The chrome on the wheels sparkled from the sun's reflection. He had seen that car before—Tim Shafer's, the neighbor of his high school friend Lucy Bradshaw. He recalled his brief encounter with her not too long ago when she expressed concern about Tim, who had recently returned from Vietnam. She thought he was "not acting right," always inside his bedroom watching cartoons on TV, always keeping to himself. His parents prayed that his "adjustment" from the war would ease over time.

The consensus back in high school was that this Ford "was the most bitchin' ride in the valley." Tim's popularity soared when he parked this mechanical trophy in the high school parking lot. He saved all his summer earnings from bailing hay, cutting lawns, and welding pipes to pay for it, and he showed it off in the school parking lot. He even quit football for a year to work part-time to save money. At school Matt remembered peeking into the car to admire the blood-red upholstery and the shiny stick shift. Man, what a cool car. His parents kept it in their garage like a trophy until Tim returned from Vietnam. The odometer had not moved since he left for Camp Pendleton. The first thing he did upon his return to the world was to install a new sound system in the car: an eight-track tape.

Now on foot, gingerly approaching the Ford, Matt stopped short in his tracks. That smell hit his nose like an invisible punch. He knew it. The sensation released a torrent of mental images. The smell of death can linger in your nostrils, throat, and stomach for days. It's encased in you, deep down.

Hours later, as he was being interviewed by sheriffs and coroners at the scene, he was briefed about what had driven young Timothy Shafer to bring his prized classic Ford Fairlane 500 along with a .38 revolver to the desert. Tim returned from Vietnam with a strong heroin addiction. That stuff was cheap in Vietnam, and the Mexican brown tar heroin was almost as cheap across the border. Matt knew at least two others who had overdosed after they came back to "the world." Tim, like Matt, kept to himself and had no one to talk to about what was going on in his restless mind. Vietnam vet support groups were over a decade away. Heroin kept him company. This liquid anodyne was his only comfort: like sweet nectar, it soothed him. Matt learned later that Tim had sustained a severe concussion when B-52s dropped their payload too close to his marine outpost near the DMZ. His sergeant told him to "just sleep it off." And when he returned stateside, his precious jelly brain that bounced inside his skull from the bombings was irreparably damaged.

Matt wondered what Tim's last thoughts were before he blew his brains out on the beautiful red upholstery of his 1965 Ford Fairlane 500. When blackness exploded, did he think about the horrors he had witnessed? The dying? His parents? His friends? His good times as a kid? The suppressed anguish? Polishing his Ford Fairlane before a quick cruise on a summer day?

What was Timothy Shafer's last image before he placed the .38 onto his temple and blackness exploded?

■ ■ ■

From the *Sonora Desert Review*, March 13, 1968:
Nixon wins the GOP primary in New Hampshire. Eugene McCarthy, the antiwar senator from Minnesota, takes 42 percent in the Democratic vote, shocking experts.

LBJ calls for increased draftees for the war effort. Troop levels are currently over eight hundred thousand, and the US military expressed optimism that the tide is turning.

Westside High's junior class is sponsoring a carwash on Saturday, March 16, in front of Safford Shoe Store from 8 to 1. Proceeds will go to the sponsorship of two talented young girls so they can attend a civic conference this summer at the state capital. The price is only $2 per car and $3 for trucks.

Curt Mendoza's preliminary hearing will start next week at the Allen County Courthouse. The local youth and Vietnam vet is accused in the brutal murder of James Allen Jr. last December. Attorneys familiar with the case could not be reached for comment.

Timothy Shafer of Clarktown was found dead last week of unknown causes. His death remains under investigation by local authorities, and an autopsy is pending. He graduated in 1965 from Westside High and was active in sports and various service clubs before enlisting in the US Marines. He was nineteen at the time of death. He served one tour abroad before being medically discharged. He is survived by his parents, Tom and Nancy Shafer, and a younger sister, Patricia. Services are pending.

■ ■ ■

There is very little legal strategy in criminal preliminary hearings. The prosecutor puts on a skeleton case—just enough for the magistrate to find "sufficient cause to believe the defendant committed the offense or offenses charged." If it were a basketball game, the prosecution would only have to bring the ball to half-court, attempt a half-ass shot near the basket, and the game would then be called in their favor. While some inexperienced prosecutors are prepared for the preliminary hearing and call every potential witness in the case (much to the chagrin of most impatient magistrates), the experienced prosecutors do the opposite—put on the bare minimum, only enough to satisfy the magistrate. The sheer beauty of strategic simplicity was often demonstrated at these hearings. This skeleton hearing provides very little meat for the defense to chew on. Defense attorneys, on the other hand, attempt to squeeze out anything that might help their case for trial. Anything.

In Curt Mendoza's prelim, the prosecutor expected to call only four witnesses:

1. Matthew Bradley, US Border Patrol, who tracked the defendant from the western hills to the Allen hacienda;

2. Sheriff Robert Johnson, who was the first police officer to arrive at the scene of the homicide and initiated the arrest of the defendant a few days later inside a local establishment, Juan's Bar;

3. Rockwood Police Officer James Denny, who investigated another violent episode with the defendant at a local bar when he allegedly assaulted three young men; and finally,

4. Chief Coroner Dr. Samuel Harrison, who conducted the autopsy on James Allen Jr.

Assistant District Attorney William Clyde was set to conduct the preliminary hearing. A seasoned lawyer with twenty years of experience, he had prosecuted two homicides—both convictions. Tall and urbane with thick horn-rimmed glasses, Clyde was the embodiment of a model prosecutor—articulate, calm, ethical, and occasionally empathetic to a defendant. He was about forty with gray hairs popping out on the side. Thick sideburns framed his thin face in his attempt to look hip circa 1968. A dark-blue suit, tailor cut, draped his thin body, with shiny black wingtips completing the package of a smart and committed legal warrior. Stein and he had had a cordial relationship in previous court battles, and they actually had some beers and laughs together after one of their trials ended with a hung jury—a draw on their respective scorecards.

Matt Bradley was relatively brief in describing his military tracking experience and his conclusion that the defendant had guided three others across the international border, through the mountains, and onto the Allen hacienda. He concluded that, for some reason, only Mendoza entered the residence, and the others left toward County Highway 15, where he lost their tracks. During Stein's cross-examination, Bradley also revealed that another person had been inside the Allen bedroom and left. However, he could not provide a clear time of entry and exit of the second individual vis-à-vis Mendoza's entry—only that the defendant entered after the first individual. Bradley surmised that the first person entered "probably within a day of Mendoza's entry." He qualified the estimate of the first person's size as "an educated guess": an adult, about 170–180 pounds, size ten sneakers, and possibly near six feet tall based on the length of the person's gait. Other tire impressions from cars and a bike in and around the hacienda offered nothing of consequence since they were faded impressions in the more compact soil. Thus, the timeline of those impressions was speculative. Bradley did not enter the house since he responded to another emergency but radioed in the information to his office, which relayed the information to the sheriff. He was not even aware that the decedent was in the house.

As he exited the witness stand, Bradley passed by Curt and nodded slightly to him. Respectfully. Curt silently reciprocated.

Sheriff Robert Johnson described the crime scene in the Allen bedroom and the subsequent arrest of the defendant shortly thereafter at Juana's Cuban Bar. Through the sheriff's foundational testimony, People's Exhibits A through K were admitted into evidence without objection by the defense. These exhibits included a photo of James Allen at the scene, the bedroom itself, and the gold coins found on the defendant. Johnson also described the condition of the defendant's fists—red and swollen. There was no mention of the Indian pouch. Stein asked no questions.

Rockwood Police Officer Denny testified regarding Curt's previous detention after a bar fight where he hurt three dove hunters. Stein's cross-exam revealed that the hunters all said "nothing happened, and it was a misunderstanding." They did not pursue a citizens' arrest of the defendant. Stein also laid the foundation for the following piece of evidence: the condition of Curt's fists could have been attributable to the earlier altercation and not the Allen murder. This eventually might prove to be a pyrrhic victory since this incident could arguably be introduced in front of a jury to show Curt's propensity for violence.

Finally, Dr. Harrison described in great detail the decedent's condition. He was bludgeoned to death, sustaining at least twenty blows to his upper body, face, and head. The bruising below the scull in the rear indicated a backward fall onto a piece of furniture, likely the wooden chair depicted in a photo, resulting in a cracked skull. Five photos were submitted as exhibits without objection. Dr. Harrison also concluded that the blows landed mostly on Allen's right side—a logical inference that the attacker was left-handed.

Stein and Hank were fully aware that ultimately the prosecution would be able to establish that Curt was left-handed. At trial, the jail video might be played in front of the jury for that limited purpose since Curt clearly favored his left hand as he was defending himself from the three attackers. No way to sanitize that tape, and the jury would also note Curt's extremely violent reaction to the attack and his deft use of his fists as deadly instruments.

After brief, perfunctory arguments from counsel, the magistrate made the following finding:

"The court finds, based on the testimony, exhibits, and inferences drawn, there is sufficient cause to believe that the defendant committed the crime charged, a violation of PC 187, and accordingly, he will be held to answer. He will be held without bail. Arraignment will be scheduled on April 2 at 9:00 a.m. in Department 8 of the superior court. That is all, gentlemen."

At the conclusion of the hearing, reality began to set in within our family.

■ ■ ■

Curt was arraigned on April 2, and the jury trial was scheduled for August 21. Stein and Hank began to buttress their defense team. Tobias Quinn III was asked to join the defense team to prepare any pretrial and trial motions—motions *in limine*. He graciously allowed the use of his office and secretary to prepare any written pleadings. Quinn was still traveling on his road to redemption and felt he needed to do his part for Curt Mendoza. They anticipated filing a flurry of motions to keep the court and the prosecution busy—change of venue, suppressions of the coins in violation of Curt's Fourth Amendment right, attacking the constitutionality of the death penalty law itself as "cruel and unusual punishment." Hank took a leave of absence from his law firm in Boston. Some of their lawyers with criminal experience also were informally assisting him with suggestions and advising him of any relevant new case laws.

■ ■ ■

"If Bobby Kennedy wins, the damn war might come to an end finally."

Stein folded the newspaper and threw it on the table. He and Hank were in Karina's on a lazy Sunday afternoon, around 6:00 p.m., and they had just ordered their plates—green enchiladas for Stein, and *caldo de res* for Hank. Hank said nothing and politely nodded. They had been brainstorming about the trial since early morning in Quinn's office and were done for the day. The food and a few beers would relax them. Stein said, "Yeah, since Kennedy entered, it's a whole new ballgame.

"Johnson's out, and Kennedy looks like he has a good shot at it in the primaries. I don't think he's a warmonger, and he could beat Nixon, fucker." The calendar on the wall near the kitchen circled April 4, 1968. The lunch crowds were thinning out of the restaurant. All was quiet. The television in the corner was muted, and they both quietly tore into their meal. Hank paused and added, "It might be too late for Kennedy. Nixon's pretty strong." Stein appeared not to listen and was looking at the television set now giving the Sunday evening lineup—*Rowan & Martin's Laugh-In* and a Dean Martin special. That wasn't what caught Stein's attention.

A news bulletin interrupted. Stein turned up the volume that was tuned in to *CBS Evening News* and Walter Cronkite.

Looking somber, like an old relative about to give bad family news, Cronkite turned directly to the camera and to the American public:

"Good evening. Doctor Martin Luther King, the apostle of nonviolence in the civil rights movement, has been shot to death in Memphis, Tennessee. Police have issued an all-points bulletin for a well-dressed, young white man seen running from the scene. Officers also reportedly chased and fired on a radio-equipped car containing two white men. Dr. King was standing on the balcony of a second-floor hotel room tonight when, according to a companion, a shot was fired from across the street. In the friend's words, 'the bullet exploded in his face'…"

Stein clicked off the TV and slowly returned to the dining table. "Oh no, shit…man. Things around this country are getting worse. You know, as shocking as this is, it's still not surprising. I think King knew all along that a white man's bullet would find him, almost like a prophesy. Shit. There will be hell to pay for this."

Both slumped down in their booths and ordered more beers.

■ ■ ■

For the next few weeks, our family was mesmerized by what we saw unfolding on our TV after Dr. King's assassination. Burning buildings in Los Angeles, Philadelphia, South Side Chicago, East Baltimore, Washington, DC—it all seemed the same. National Guard troops patrolling the streets, locked and loaded. Ostensibly they were protecting property, but in reality they were hunting for targets. The images from burning American cities looked not much different from Saigon or Hue during the Tet Offensive. Young, angry Blacks arrested by the hundreds. Anguish. Sirens. Body counts of civilians piling up to shocking numbers. Politicians begging for restraint. Blame the radicals. Blame the police. Blame systemic racism. Blame King himself. America appeared to be spiraling into a black vortex of anarchy. Pundits on TV trying to decipher what all the frightening chaos meant. As a twelve-year-old, I had a hard time understanding these events with some small degree of clarity. All I knew then was that there was some scary, amorphous image that began to shape a murky future for me and for America. Somewhere in that bleak future was my brother Curt.

■ ■ ■

Stein and Hank focused all their waking moments on trial preparation, which was scheduled for late May. Hank studied all he could about California criminal procedure and pestered Stein at all hours of the night with questions. Stein was primarily responsible for the first phase of the jury trial, and Hank would enter the penalty phase—where the jury would then decide whether to impose the death penalty or life without parole (LWOP). A jury might be more sympathetic to a brother literally pleading for his brother's life. With the help of Tobias Quinn III, motions for trial and pretrial were being finalized. Their investigator was pounding the streets of Allen County to look for any potential witnesses and interview those known witnesses. The three persons Curt was smuggling had fallen off the face of the earth and presumably ended up in the interior of Mexico.

Big Bob did not help matters as he covertly directed all sheriffs not to cooperate with the defense. One glimmer of hope was Matt Bradley, who surmised that another person might have entered the home before Curt, but that lead was not solid. The giant gravamen that remained, however, was Curt's undisputed possession of Allen's gold coins. The road to the California gas chamber was paved with those damn gold coins.

And the Indian pouch? Nothing. It soon became an afterthought. Curt didn't help his lawyers very much. He was consistent in his private conversations with them—"I was too stoned to remember much, and I honestly don't know what I did in that house..."—except for a vague recollection of finding the coins and looking for food and water. While Stein was tempted to plant a false narrative in him to fill in the memory gaps, that option was quickly jettisoned. Both Stein and Hank would be guilty of suborning Curt's known perjury if they intentionally planted a false story for him. In a poker game, if you get crappy cards, you have the option of folding, walking away from the deck, and cutting your losses. In a jury trial, that option is not available. You gotta play that hand. In this case, the proverbial hand showed little to play.

While reviewing the case late one evening in Quinn's law office, Hank felt he had absorbed all he could about California criminal law. He closed all the files, notepads, and law books, then sat back alone with his eyes closed and tried to let his thoughts settle. Stein had left an hour before, and they agreed to meet again in the morning. It was three weeks away from jury selection. A tiny seed of an idea in the back of Hank's mind had festered for weeks, and the seed began to sprout. It was a legal strategy that was, on the surface, outlandish, but in Hank's thinking, it was legally sound and logically strong. He quickly took out a legal pad and wrote some rough notes, then called Stein.

"Hey, Stein, you awake?"

"Now I am after the ring…Whatta ya want, Spock?" He sounded groggy and a little annoyed. Hank failed to notice his tone on the other line.

"Stein, let's meet tomorrow early. I'd like to run something by you."

"Sure, but only if you don't call me again before—"

"Seven o'clock, OK?"

"All right, meet you at Karina's at our usual booth. You're gonna buy me a plate of huevos rancheros. You owe me."

"I'll put it on your tab."

Stein didn't know if Hank was joking. Vulcans have no sense of humor.

■ ■ ■

Stein and Hank sat and relaxed. They had just finished their heavy plates of the house specialty—huevos rancheros. The macho Mexican coffee with cinnamon perked them up.

"OK, Spock, tell me your idea."

"All right, I will, but with only one caveat: let me completely run this strategy by you before you dismiss it. That's all I ask."

Stein now looked intrigued. "I'm listening."

"The *Iliad*."

"What about it? Never read it."

"In my final year of undergrad, I took this course in Greek history. It was taught by this brilliant professor, Dr. Raymond Marcote. But his background was not in Greek history or literature. He was a psychiatrist. As a psychiatrist, he has been treating a lot of combat war vets, from World War II, Korea, and Vietnam for combat stress.

"He found that those soldiers in modern wars, like their counterparts in the Greek wars, suffered discernible psychological injuries from the combat stress, and this stress lingered and manifested itself long after their return to so-called normal civilian life. At many points in the *Iliad*, Achilles, for example, falls victim to these stresses.

"Professor Marcote drew a direct line from those ancient wars to modern wars, the American Civil War, World Wars I and II, Korea, and Vietnam. He described references in literature that described combat trauma. He is a vocal critic of his profession for failing to recognize and treat this condition clinically.

"This now brings us to the *Diagnostic and Statistical Manual of Mental Disorders*, the *DSM*. This is the bible, if you will, for all psychology professionals that outlines all the current psychological syndromes and treatment of such syndromes. The *DSM* is updated, and the most recent *DSM-II*, the second edition, was just published. Because of my condition, Asperger syndrome, I have become familiar with the *DSM*. Dr. Marcote is a vocal critic of the *DSM-II* because it does not recognize combat stress as a diagnostic condition.

"I know this is a real phenomenon. Just look at my father. He's someone who appears to have a continuing anxiety directly linked to combat in the Pacific. Alcohol, sporadic episodes of violence, isolation, lack of sleep. He was not like that before he went overseas. He's never been to a psychiatrist, but maybe he should see one. My mom and nana tell me of his odd behavior when he returned from the war. It's a condition that a trained medical professional could diagnose and put in some kind of clinical context to treat. I don't think my father would ever seek treatment. Too proud. Too stubborn. And he just wants to deal with it himself. And my brother Curt exhibits and continues to exhibit some of those same symptoms. Maybe we can select jurors who have had family members with these conditions.

"I don't know what my father went through in the Pacific, nor do I know what Curt went through in Vietnam. You and I cannot fathom— even in our worst nightmares—what they experienced. Heck, I don't even think they can ever understand it either. I do know that no rational human being can survive those traumatic experiences without a profound impact on their long-term psyche.

"Now, this gets us to this trial. The first phase will be the guilty phase— did he do it? Did my brother murder Mr. Allen? Then the next phase is the penalty phase—will the jury vote to condemn him to the gas chamber? The sentencing is just a formality since Curt's life will be decided at trial.

"Here's my final point, and I hope I'm not rambling too much. I've also been reading the pertinent statutes that apply to an insanity defense. Maybe we can convince a jury that, even if Curt killed Allen, they can still consider his combat trauma to grant him life instead of death. Here is the argument: he suffered from a mental disorder caused by his hellish combat experience that caused him to experience a mental episode to the point where his conduct—as horrible as it might be—is legally excusable if he was legally insane. I think a good argument can be made that Curt's mental trauma from combat, like those soldiers before him, might fit within the M'Naghten rule of insanity. The jury might just have enough sympathy for him to acquit or possibly not vote to condemn him to death at the penalty phase."

Stein said nothing and looked away, trying to absorb Hank's presentation.

Stein said, "The problem is this: Curt would either have to admit he killed Allen but argue he was insane when he did it, or Curt would have to argue that he didn't do it, but 'ladies and gentlemen, if you think I did, I was crazy.' Jury will have a hard time buying either scenario. Once they decided he killed Allen, they'll instantly become highly skeptical and outright cynical of any insanity defense."

"I honestly gave much thought to what you just said. And you're right. You've tried many serious cases. I have not tried one case, except a one-day court trial on inverse condemnation. My client prevailed. Anyway…please consider this. As his attorney and as his brother, I think this might be a course of action we can pursue." Hank sat back in the booth as if he were out of breath. Stein was still thinking, looking away into space.

"Spock, this novel theory sounds crazy…but it also sounds logical. You understand that we are entering new territory—a new legal world. Not only is combat trauma not recognized by the majority in the field of psychiatry, I don't think there is any case law or precedent for raising this insanity defense in this context. And we're playing with your brother's life if we raise a novel and untested theory. I don't want him in the gas chamber because we were playing cutesy with the law. The law is a wonderful thing—it's a living, malleable creature that lawyers can manipulate for good and bad. But the law can also kill. Let's get in touch with Dr. Marcote. We have some more work to do, Spock. We might boldly be going where no fucking lawyer has gone before!"

Hank pushed the meal check to Stein and left.

"Damn, Vulcans are also cheap."

PART TWENTY-ONE

INTO THE HEAVENS

Sheriff Johnson left Juana Gomez's ranch in a warm, relaxed mood. After a heated argument about Juana's imbecile brother, they made up with a rough tumble in the bedroom and living room with a climactic ending on the kitchen floor that left the sheriff heavily satisfied. Juana aggressively expanded her sexual repertoire by adding creative positions and moves Nadia Comaneci would envy.

He recognized that he bore some responsibility for her brother's debilitating injury, but he knew Juana would take good care of Rafael. Things were good in Big Bob's life. Although Juana blamed the sheriff for her brother's involvement in the debacle with Curt Mendoza, he thought he convinced her that it wasn't his fault and was the bartender's fault. She appeared to accept his dubious explanation. As he returned to the station, he began to savor the memory of his last heated visit with Juana.

Juana was an entertaining storyteller and often told Big Bob stories from the old country—Cuba. After they lay in bed for a few minutes, she lit a Cohiba, sipped a glass of a thick merlot, and told him the legend of

Matias Perez. Her father often told the story in her youth, and the story always seemed fresh.

Matias Perez had a canopy business in Havana in the nineteenth century. He was fascinated with hot air balloons and made a few ascensions. These balloons became quite popular, and he got the bug to fly. In June 1856, he attempted one such ascension from Havana's Campo de Marte. He went up…and up…and up. Swallowed by the heavens.

He literally disappeared into thin air.

And that tragedy ironically turned him into a Cuban legend. Now when someone disappears, it is said in Cuba that *"volo como* Matias Perez"—he flew away or disappeared like Matias Perez. Or he didn't show up for a doctor's appointment, like Matias Perez. Or the Bautista government might say a dissident volo como Matias Perez—well, "he just disappeared"—to the grieving families. Just fill in any surrounding context to make it fit.

Sheriff Johnson thought this was a funny Cuban anecdote and savored his next visit with Juana. She actually tried to tell her brother not to blame the sheriff. When she spoke to Ramon, she would switch from English to Spanish. Although Big Bob knew little border Spanish, he deciphered a few Cuban idioms from Juana.

One word that stuck out was *despingar*—she mentioned that to Rafael several times. *Despingar*. That word sounded familiar. She told Bob several times in their unstable relationship that *"te voy a despingar,* Bob"—I'm gonna kick your ass, Bob. Or I'm going to fuck you up, Bob. It was often said in jest in the middle of one of Juana's temper tantrums. And when she was most pissed at the sheriff, she switched languages. Why would she use that word with Rafael? Did she mean to threaten Rafael? That she was going to kick, or fuck up, Rafael? Highly unlikely since she shared a deep and unyielding loyalty to him. Plus, the imbecile had already been fucked up completely by that Green Beret. She kept telling Rafael earlier that evening, *"Le voy a despingar."*

As he tried to decipher its meaning, he lost track of his speed—ninety-five miles an hour. This winding country road had a speed limit of fifty miles per hour. Right before he hit one hundred miles per hour, he realized she had told Rafael, "*Le voy a despingar*"—I'm going to fuck <u>him</u> up, not "*te voy a despingar*"—I'm going to fuck <u>you</u> up. Sheriff Robert Johnson's analysis and reflection of Cuban syntax was his last thought on earth.

■ ■ ■

When Juana was being interrogated by Assistant Sheriff Garza about Sheriff Johnson's death along a lonely country road, she convinced him that she knew nothing. Aside from her sultry beauty, her important attribute was her power of persuasion. Apparently, someone tinkered with the sheriff's brakes before he rolled over six times at 105 miles per hour as he "failed to negotiate a sharp curve." He never wore a seat belt since "you never saw John Wayne wearing one"—whatever the hell that meant. He was first catapult-ed through the front windshield, then bounced on his head northbound on Highway 115 a few times and was finally thrust onto a concrete canal headfirst or, more accurately, onto what was left of his head. He probably died between the aforementioned steps two and three. Sheriff Johnson had a long list of enemies, and it finally caught up to him. The investigation narrowed down to twenty possible suspects but never yielded any arrests.

Juana's passing remark to Garza came with a smirk: "*El Big Bob volo como Matias Perez.*"

Garza scratched his head.

PART TWENTY-TWO

"I THOUGHT HE WAS THE PRIME MINISTER"

In 1843 Daniel M'Naghten, a man gifted with delusion and poor judgment, thought the prime minister of England was conspiring to kill him. Thinking he was acting in self-defense, he killed the prime minister's secretary instead, mistaking him for the actual intended target—the prime minister. Oops. The clever and prescient trial barristers raised a novel defense: their client was not guilty since he was insane at the time of the shooting. The trial court thus acquitted him "by reason of insanity."

As a result of the M'Naghten trial, Queen Victoria ordered the high court, the English House of Lords, to develop a standard or consistent legal test of insanity for the courts. Thus, the M'Naghten rule or test was born:

"Every man is to be presumed to be sane, and...that to establish a defense on the ground of insanity, and it must be clearly proved that, at the time of the committing of the act, the party accused was laboring under such a defect of reason, from disease of mind, and not to know the nature and quality of the act he was doing; or if he did know it, that he did not know what he was doing what was wrong." (*Queen v. M'Naghten*, 8 Eng.

Rep. 718 [1843])

This test for insanity was not stillborn; it survived and thrived in the British legal ecosystem. And it was thus transported across the Atlantic to the American courts, a judicial system founded under English common law. The British definition of crazy was also incorporated into the American definition of crazy. (Now, that's insane in itself.) Fast-forward to 1968 in Allen County, and this basic rule still survived and was codified in the California Penal Code.

Stein and Hank had to convince twelve jurors that Curt, like Mr. M'Naghten, was insane when he killed James Allen II. It could be a powerful tool in court. Even if a jury failed to accept this defense, Curt's war trauma could still provide a solid mitigating factor in the penalty phase.

Curt himself was the first person they had to convince that it was a viable legal defense. "You mean, if they think I did it, I was crazy when I did it because the Vietnam War made me insane?" Curt's initial reaction was that the theory itself was insane. He had a deep sense of pride, honor, and devotion to the Green Beret uniform. Blaming his dishonorable conduct on his military experience would be an ugly stain. Curt knew in his heart that he did not commit the murder, and if he did, an insanity defense was not an honorable option.

Hank and Stein spent countless hours persuading Curt to agree, and he finally consented after speaking to my parents. The defense team, lawyers, and their investigator devoted hundreds of hours to preparing for Curt's trial, including holding multiple meetings with Dr. Marcote and other potential witnesses from the sheriff's office. They hired an analyst who they thought might be able to recreate the crime scene to demonstrate Curt could not have killed Mr. Allen. Someone else was in that house and could have killed him. The missing link—the Indian pouch—was never recovered. Curt eventually told Hank and Stein that while his memory was still blurry, he never recalled seeing such a pouch. They found it difficult to contact anyone who had served with Curt in Vietnam. Half of his Special

Forces team was still scattered throughout Vietnam, and others could not be located in the States. Character witnesses were easy. Curt left many close friends in Allen County before he left for Vietnam who could attest to his wonderful character—his humility, his compassion, his humor. And this picture of him could be juxtaposed with the person who returned from Vietnam—isolated, moody, violent. Unfortunately, these juxtaposed images were all too common for the soldiers returning home to "normalcy." These were the only cards that the defense team had received and could play with. They had to make the most of it.

Pretrial hearings and motions would commence May 28, 1968, and jury selection would follow shortly thereafter before the honorable Judge Gates.

■ ■ ■

From the *Sonora Desert Review*, May 11, 1968:

Dodgers lose a tough one to Atlanta, 2–1. Big D, Don Drysdale, took the loss and was outmatched by Ken Johnson, who pitched a complete game at Atlanta Stadium before 13,210 people. The Dodgers' only lone run came with a sacrifice fly by Willie Davis. The Dodgers' dismal season continues with their record at 13 wins and 15 losses, near the bottom of the National League.

Clarktown High School will be hosting a car wash in the parking lot of Oden's Drive-In on Saturday, May 18, from 10 to 5. Tickets are only $1 with a 25-cent discount with proof of purchase from Oden's. According to Sam Gomez, ASB president, "Pull up your car, order your delicious lunch from Oden's, and let us wash your car. Proceeds will go to Boys State sponsorship. Oden's Drive-In: Home of the 'monster burger and the special machaca gran burrito.'"

Allen County Sheriff Robert Johnson was laid to rest last

week in Greenwood Cemetery. He tragically died in a single-car accident, and an investigation is still pending. A public memorial is scheduled for later this month in his honor. Assistant Sheriff Ray Garza has been appointed temporarily until the county board of commissioners elects a new sheriff. Sheriff Garza is the first Mexican American in Allen County to head the department.

Curt Mendoza's murder trial is to start in June. Pretrial motions are scheduled to begin on May 28 before the honorable Tim Gates. Attorneys previously indicated that the trial should last at least two months.

■ ■ ■

"Counsel, we should be ready to start our jury selection by next week. I reviewed your respective trial briefs and motions in limine, which we can handle this week." Judge Gates placed a large stack of trial files on his bench and looked out at his courtroom—not one empty chair. The bench behind the defendant was reserved for his family—his father, mother, and grandmother sat stoically. Curt stood between Stein and Hank, all staring respectfully at the judge. Assistant District Attorney William Clyde and his associate, Deputy District Attorney Lance Holman, were standing on the other side of the attorneys' tables.

Stein gestured to the court, looking like a child in a classroom needing to pee.

"Yes, Mr. Stein, what is it?"

"Your Honor, my client will be modifying his plea. He will now formally enter his plea of not guilty to not guilty by reason of insanity." Stein said nothing further. His eyes slightly squinted like someone expecting a punch in the face.

Clyde and Holman looked at each other with a mixture of surprise, annoyance, and anger. They almost fell off their chairs at the counsel table.

Judge Gates raised both hands, gesturing for all the attorneys to sit down and cautioning spectators from making any audible reaction.

Clyde regained his composure and addressed the court. "Your Honor, we are set for jury trial next week. The defense has not provided any discovery of witnesses in the sanity phase. I demand an offer of proof about this so-called insanity plea. We will not agree to a postponement. I take umbrage with this prank. This, frankly, smells like a typical ploy to force a continuance of the trial. The prosecution has spent a tremendous amount of time and resources preparing. I want the record to reflect in no uncertain terms that we object to this plea at this point in the case. This defendant has no history of mental health issues that we know of."

Judge Gates nodded as he listened to the prosecutor's reaction. "Mr. Stein, you've tried a number of cases in my department. While at times we may have clashed in court, those disagreements, I think, have always involved professional and legal disagreements. I have never seen you engage in tactics or behavior that might arguably undermine the integrity of the court and its process. Having said that, this additional plea smells like a ploy that Mr. Clyde has concerns with. While technically this type of plea may be allowed before jury selection, I'm concerned about trial delays—not to mention legal frivolity."

"Your Honor, we are 100 percent serious about this plea. For the record, we have thoroughly discussed this additional plea and its collateral consequences with our client, and he is prepared to proceed with this plea."

The court: "Mr. Mendoza, have you had enough time to discuss this plea of insanity with your attorneys?"

"Yes, sir, I have. They have explained it to me in detail and all the potential consequences of such a plea." Turning to both attorneys, he added, "I have complete confidence in my attorneys, and I trust them with my life."

"Mr. Mendoza, do you understand that if a jury finds you guilty of the murder but not guilty by reason of insanity, you could spend the rest of your life in a mental facility?"

"Yes, Your Honor."

"And do you understand you may raise this plea of insanity anytime before the jury verdict?"

"Yes, sir."

"Mr. Mendoza, do you understand that the same jury would hear the guilty phase, the sanity phase, and would also be the same jury to determine the death penalty?"

"Yes, sir. My attorneys have explained this to me. I do understand."

"Mr. Mendoza, how much formal education have you had? I have a general idea from reading your file in this case."

"Well, Your Honor, I graduated from high school, and I was a pretty good student. I had plans to finish college and teach later. But…things didn't turn out that way, and I joined the service."

"Special Forces, I understand?"

"Yes, sir."

"And I assume that training required a high level of knowledge from a classroom?"

"Yes, Your Honor. I received extensive training in demolition, weapons, countersurveillance, martial arts, combat first aid, and theories of war."

Deputy DA Holman: "Judge, can we just stipulate he's a trained killer?"

This elicited an audible reaction from the audience, and the judge wasn't pleased.

"Mr. Holman, leave your damn sarcasm at the door, please. Now, Mr. Mendoza, Mr. Curt Mendoza, do you have any questions regarding this additional plea of insanity?"

"No, Your Honor."

"The court is satisfied that this defendant understands the nature and consequences of a plea of insanity. Said plea will be registered and filed herein."

"But, Your Honor—"

"Mr. Clyde, I haven't ignored you. I can anticipate your objections. I wanted to make sure this young man is competent enough to understand what he's doing, and he does. Now, with regard to the factual foundation for this plea.

"The prosecution has not had an opportunity to digest this new plea. My understanding is that the defendant has no concrete history of mental health problems. Mr. Stein and Mr. Mendoza—Mr. Hank Mendoza—I trust you're not going to establish this out of thin air. Please provide the district attorney's office with all…and I mean all…the discovery you have on the issue of defendant's insanity that you intend to use at trial, including any CVs of experts, psychological evaluations, witnesses, reports, etc."

Stein: "Of course, Your Honor. My associate, Tobias Quinn III, has prepared copies of all our discovery we intend to use and will give them to Mr. Clyde before we leave this courtroom."

"Good. We will set a hearing in two days. But let me make something clear, counsel. I need a clear offer of proof about this new plea. And you better have witnesses available in two days for me to make an initial assessment about whether this even gets in front of the jury. You need to show me some meat on those bones because if it's frivolous, you might be precluded from even making this plea. Give me a succinct offer of proof."

"In a nutshell, Your Honor, we believe that Mr. Mendoza's combat experience in Vietnam created a mental episode at the time of the incident that rendered him insane under the M'Naghten rule."

"The war made him crazy…er, insane, which would exonerate him from a murder?"

"As crude as that sounds, I couldn't put it better, Your Honor."

"To my knowledge, counsel, there has never been such a defense recognized in this country." Both Clyde and Holman bobble-headed in unison. "Counsel, we will see you in two days at nine sharp. Be ready. We are adjourned for the day."

■ ■ ■

Day One of Trial: Motion in Limine RE: Offer of Proof of Insanity Plea
　　Courtroom of the Honorable Tim Gates
　　10:00 a.m.

Judge Gates: "Before proceeding with this motion to allow an insanity defense in front of a jury, I just want to outline the framework of this hearing with narrow and clearly defined parameters. I don't want useless commentary or grandstanding. Let's focus on this issue. The defense has raised an insanity defense based on the defendant's military experience, and that experience created some nebulous type of trauma in the defendant, even after returning to the States. I don't know if there's a psychological term for this in the realm of an insanity defense. Trauma? War trauma? Lingering combat fatigue? That is, the defense intends to postulate to a jury that Mr. Mendoza was legally insane at the time of this alleged incident. And the insanity had its genesis in his Vietnam combat experience.

"Further, there is very little, to say the least, of any case law—any known precedence—that would allow an insanity defense in this type of situation. I need to state on the record that the case law and statutory history, both state and federal, offer very little to support of the defense's theory in this context. I realize I have not heard any testimony or evidence, and I will keep an open mind about the issue. But on the face of it, counsel, you have an uphill battle in this court to even allow this plea to be heard in front of the jury. And if this theory is presented to the jury, I will let you know that I will allow the prosecution a great deal of liberty in attacking this defense, because frankly I share their loud skepticism."

Hank unexpectedly stood to address the court. Stein tried to stop him, but it was too late. "Your Honor, this court is absolutely correct…let's be honest. We recognize that our position lacks a great deal of support from the standpoint of precedence. And I can understand the prosecution's—and the court's—reaction in thinking that this might be a threadbare or even a specious argument. But it's not. We would not waste this court's time on a frivolous course of action, especially when my brother's—the defendant's—life is literally at stake. We have the utmost respect for this court and also recognize the difficult job the prosecution has. But we have the same level of respect for our sworn duties as defense attorneys to protect the rights—and the life—of Curtis Mendoza under our constitution. We have an unyielding fealty not only to our client but also to our sworn duty to our cherished legal system.

"At the risk of sounding trite, our laws are living, breathing creatures. They didn't just spring out of thin air. They were born somewhere in the history and shadows of mankind's evolution from the caves to today's civilization. But most laws have their provenance within the basic principles of morality, philosophy, and human nature. All our just laws began somewhere. Just because the state of the law here and now, in 1968, may arguably not recognize an insanity defense for a soldier suffering internally from the vestige of a horrible war, does not mean our fundamental principles of law should turn a blind eye and ignore this awful reality. Insanity can come from many sources—mental illness that one was born with, the long-term effects of alcohol or drugs, child or spousal abuse, the post-trauma one might experience after a car crash…and the effects of exposure to the hellish savagery of war that most of us are lucky enough to never experience.

"We have carefully reviewed the underlying principles of the M'Naghten defense as they apply to this particular case. When those English barristers raised the insanity defense over a hundred years ago, they recognized the novelty of its principle. But their remarkable prescience also recognized the profound strength of this principle as well—one that has survived this long. We also recognize the novelty of this defense in this case, in 1968. And like our English brethren, we also recognize the strength of this defense. It's our firm belief, Your Honor, that this defense should be heard in front of a jury—the people of this community—for them to consider whether Curtis Mendoza was insane. We beg this court not to foreclose this defense, a defense that might block a highway straight to the California gas chamber in San Quinten. Please, just hear us out and hear our witness. And I apologize if I was overly bombastic before Your Honor. Thank you."

Gates clenched his sweaty hands together, looked down as if in prayer, and said, "Call your witness, counsel."

"My name is Dr. Raymond Marcote. Spelled M-A-R-C-O-T-E." Marcote adjusted his witness chair next to the judge and nodded at him respectfully, then turned to the attorneys in front of him. Dr. Marcote was sixty-five years old. His gray wool suit was draped heavily over him as if he had lost weight since he bought it fifteen years ago at a Salvation Army thrift store. A few coffee stains blotched his light-blue tie, which he constantly adjusted, showing his discomfort in the strange surroundings of a courtroom. The stains looked as old as the suit. His thin, white hair showed the outline of a receding hairline slowly creeping to the rear of a large head. A thin nose centered his bearded face, making his high cheekbones more pronounced. His eyes were light blue and intense, and they would shiver like a flickering light bulb. He had a habit of squinting or blinking when questions were being asked—sort of a nervous twitch. In short, if you imagined a nutty professor, Dr. Marcote was straight out of the casting department.

Stein: "Your Honor, before proceeding to the foundational questions, we have previously submitted Dr. Marcote's curriculum vitae to counsel and the court. Would they be willing to stipulate to the doctor's sterling qualifications?" He turned to the prosecution table.

DDA Clyde: "Hell…heck no…no way."

Judge Gates: "I concur. Proceed, Mr. Stein."

"Doctor Marcote, first tell the court about your educational background."

"Certainly counsel," Marcote sank in the witness chair, now more visibly comfortable. "I received my dual undergrad degrees in biology and psychology at Stanford, with a master's also from Stanford in clinical psychology. I then went to med school at Johns Hopkins, where I received my MD in 1938. I continued with my four-year residency at Massachusetts General Hospital. And I have been a practicing psychiatrist since then."

Stein nodded. "Where are you currently employed?"

"I have my sole practice in Boston, and I am still affiliated with Massachusetts General. I worked briefly as a consultant with the Veterans Administration shortly after World War II. I think I found my professional and personal calling after working with returning vets from World War II. In addition, I currently teach an undergrad course in literature at Harvard. Mr. Mendoza was one of my students."

Judge Gates's ears twitched, and he moved closer to the witness, curious.

Stein: "We'll return to your class in a moment. Let me ask you now about the nature of your practice."

"Mr. Stein, Your Honor, in a nutshell, my practice is focused on treating combat veterans. As vets were referred to me after the war, I wanted to explore their combat experience as a form of psychosis—a psychosis that had long-term effects on the individual as they returned to civilian life. Most World War II vets staunchly resisted therapy, much like those returning from Vietnam. And thus, it's difficult to get a large pool of patients to properly assess and form general conclusions from their war experience. But for over twenty years, I've tried to paint a coherent picture of their war experience as related to antisocial behavior. Only when we get a clear picture of the mental and emotional makeup of the vets can we then properly treat them clinically and therapeutically."

Stein: "Can you clarify what you mean by 'antisocial behavior'?"

"Certainly. Compared to the general population, combat vets exhibit much greater percentages of violence, divorce, paranoia, alcoholism, drug usage, depression, and isolation. A case in point is Audie Murphy, the most highly decorated soldier in the war. His combat exploits are well documented and show a soldier, while in the thick of battle, displaying bravery, empathy to his fellow soldiers, and clarity of thought and action that is beyond the belief of most mortals like us. He received the most individual military awards for combat valor. Yet he brought the war home with him. He is a successful actor and adored by most Americans. His autobiography and movie *To Hell and Back* was a small glimpse of his heroism. But the title was incomplete because he brought the hell of the war back with him, except that hell was inside—deep inside. It's documented that he suffered from nightmares and drug addiction and went into detox. He became reclusive and suicidal and lost a lot of money gambling. He tried and is still trying in vain to get the VA to recognize the postwar suffering of the vets. If the war can do that to Audie Murphy, then any combat veteran is at risk." Dr. Marcotte then reached into his breast pocket to retrieve a note. "I brought this note because it's a quote from Audie Murphy. And I quote: 'I remember the experience as I do a nightmare. A demon seemed to have entered my body.'

"I mention case studies from World War II since that's the largest pool—statistically speaking—to draw some observations and conclusions from, from the standpoint of psychiatry. We have a general idea of the term 'combat fatigue,' which was the term in vogue during and after World War II. The army recognized the large scope of the problem. Twenty-five percent of the soldiers that were evacuated from the combat zones weren't evacuated because of physical wounds. Twenty-five percent were evacuated were psychiatric casualties—combat fatigue—twenty-five percent. Depending on the intensity of the fighting, it was probably worse in the Pacific theater of operations. But you have to appreciate the large number of these mentally debilitated casualties. Forty to fifty divisions of soldiers unable to fight. And when they returned to the States, they manifested antisocial behavior that I see in the Vietnam vets—and probably most combat vets throughout history: paranoia, drugs, alcohol, nightmares, brief episodes of violence."

Judge Gates, who appeared to be taking copious notes on the bench, interrupted: "When do we get to the part about this defendant's mental situation in the context of this murder charge?"

Dr. Marcote: "Your Honor, please bear with me. If I sound like I'm rambling, forgive me. But I need to establish some historical context about this since society has certain attitudes toward combat veterans that, I think, are just plain wrong, and this jury needs to be educated on this. Isn't that part of a jury trial? Educating jurors acting as twelve judges to give them the tools to reach a fair decision?"

Gates looked exasperated. "Mr. Stein, please continue…"

Stein: "So how were they treated out in the field?"

Dr. Marcote: "Not very well. The army psychiatrists in the field had no uniform methodology of treatment. The army response at the platoon level varied, to say the least. Some of these traumatized soldiers were labeled 'malingerers' and were quickly sent back into hell. We know of the famous incident involving General Patton. Unfortunately, his reaction to a traumatized soldier was common at many levels.

"One method of treatment that saw success came from an army captain, Captain Frederick Hanson—a neurologist and neurosurgeon. During the campaign in North Africa, he recognized that soldiers exhibiting combat fatigue were simply exhausted. After they were redeployed away from the combat zones, he made it a point to keep them near the combat zones and prescribed sleep-inducing drugs to rest. After rest, they were given showers and fresh clothes and sent back into combat with relative success, usually within a few days. They were kept near the combat zones so they could still hear the sounds of battle as they rested and prepared to return. But I want to emphasize that our society has not figured out what to do with these soldiers once they return to normal society among civilians who could never—never—fathom what these soldiers saw, felt, and smelled from combat."

Stein: "Tell us about the course you teach at Harvard."

Dr. Marcote: "Well, I understand the reactions from some folks when I tell them that I, a practicing psychiatrist, teach a class in literature. I found a profound thread between combat fatigue and references in literature throughout history.

"The first known writings found in cuneiform tablets—clay tablets—

in what is now the Middle East mentioned soldiers suffering, like Audie Murphy, from remnants of the ancient wars. One of the most famous ancient historians, Herodotus, described the Battle of Marathon in 490 BC. Most notable, he wrote about an Athenian soldier who became blind after fighting and witnessing the battle. Homer's description of Achilles shows one of the greatest Greek warriors suffering internally during the Trojan War. Shakespeare describes this phenomenon in *Henry IV, Part 1*, with a combatant's inability to sleep and enjoy life in the aftermath of a battle. In *The Red Badge of Courage*, Stephen Crane describes the horror of a young, inexperienced soldier exposed to his first taste of battle.

"These ancient warriors, like those in our modern wars, all manifested a deep psychosis that stayed with them after they were removed from the field of combat. Achilles and Audie Murphy are like bookends, and in between are thousands of years of war and soldiers traumatized from the inside."

DDA Winston Clyde, looking impatient, said, "Your Honor, while I enjoy this history lesson from the esteemed doctor, can you direct counsel to focus on whether Dr. Marcote's theories and opinions on insanity even have general acceptance in the scientific community? Is this so-called lingering trauma or postcombat fatigue even mentioned in the *DSM*? That's what the court needs to look at in the context of the defense laying a proper foundation for this doctor to testify in front of a jury."

Judge Gates: "OK, Doctor, I think there's no argument against the notion that combat soldiers experience mental trauma after they see the horror of humans slaughtering one another. Maybe that trauma is nebulous and ill-defined to us lay persons. I think what counsel Clyde is alluding to presents a twofold question: One, is this type of combat trauma recognized in the scientific community—the psychiatric community, and two, can this trauma linger even after a soldier returns to civilian life? And I guess there's an extended question arising from the second in terms of this case: Do ex-combat soldiers outwardly manifest antisocial behavior because of their combat experience? I know these are loaded questions, but both this court and the prosecution need some clarity from you before you can serve as an expert witness in the jury trial."

Dr. Marcote: "I will try to be as succinct as I can. The place to start is the *Diagnostic and Statistical Manual of Mental Disorders*—the *DSM*. This is the reference manual for most psychiatric and psychological practitioners in our country. If I were a priest, this would be my bible. It's kind of akin to hornbooks used in law school, which most of you have used and still probably use as reference material. Anyway, the *DSM* outlines the most general categories of mental disorders and serves as a basis for the treatment of these disorders that might, ideally, be used universally by medical practitioners. The *DSM* strongly influences treatment, public health policy, and medical research. The first *DSM*—the *DSM-I*—was produced about sixteen years ago. In relationship to this insanity issue and combat, the *DSM-I* included a diagnosis known as 'gross stress reaction.' It described primarily normal people who had personally experienced a traumatic event, a tragedy, or even combat. Think of your own lives and if you ever saw or experienced something horrible and how that memory lingered in you for a long time. But the *DSM-I* never developed that syndrome into a meaningful mode of therapy. The *DSM-I* treated this 'gross reaction diagnosis' as fleeting and stated that the trauma would disappear over time.

"It's at that starting point where I disagree with most of my profession. If the *DSM-I* had recognized that trauma could linger for years, and victims of this trauma manifest their behaviors in terrible ways—including combat veterans—treatment could have mitigated and ameliorated their behaviors.

"The current *DSM-II* is not much better in my opinion because although it recognizes military combat as a mental trauma and disorder, it offers no guidance in treatment and fails to recognize the severity of the problem."

Judge Gates: "Dr. Marcote, I realize this is all foundational to your ultimate conclusions down the road, but let's get to why Mr. Mendoza's military background and experience might be the basis for an insanity defense. Like my grandchild Emery says, Are we there yet?'"

Dr. Marcote: "Anecdotal evidence from both World War II and Vietnam vets shows an alarming link between their combat trauma and their behavior years after they have returned to society, far removed from the violence and pressure of intense combat. Combat vets typically have higher rates of alcoholism, divorce, suicide, and health issues that are hard to ignore. For example, Jerome Walton. He served two tours with the marines in the Pacific. He saw the worst of it. Leyte and Okinawa. He returned to his wife and family in Omaha, Nebraska. One evening he ventured out to his backyard, saw his neighbors enjoying a barbecue, and stabbed two to death. The witnesses told the police he was heard saying, 'You fuckin' Japs killed my buddy!' The arresting officers described him as being in a 'hallucinatory state of mind as if he was somewhere else.'

"Of course, these are striking examples, and most might manifest abnormal behavior in subtle forms—sleeplessness, not communicating with their family, nightmares, isolation, not holding jobs, fleeting moments of violence directed at neighbors, spouses, children, and coworkers. The returning vets I have treated are reluctant to even talk about their war experience, nor do they even acknowledge it might have affected their behavior. Some kind of warrior's code, I guess. I find this very frustrating as a therapist because I want to treat them. I would say that most families who have lived with combat vets have stories to share about the behavior of these vets. It is a trauma that stays with them inside, and unless we locate more resources to treat them, their tragedies will just be compounded for the next generations. We simply cannot ignore this phenomenon.

"With regard to Curtis Mendoza, I have reviewed the discovery provided to the defense, so I am familiar with the case, at least from the forensic standpoint. I have interviewed Mr. Mendoza, his family, high school classmates, and friends, and what is missing are direct interviews with soldiers he served with."

Stein: "Why?"

Dr. Marcote: "Well, first, you must understand that many of his Special

Forces groups are scattered throughout Vietnam in active war zones. Those who have returned home are difficult to locate. I located one in Texas, and he refused to even acknowledge knowing Mr. Mendoza. His war records are skimpy. You see, Mr. Mendoza's records are highly classified. Within the Special Forces, he was a volunteer with the Special Operations group—a highly secretive operational unit active in unconventional warfare. The army was no help since it does not even acknowledge its existence. However, I can piece together a picture of Mr. Mendoza before, during, and after his deployment to Vietnam from the standpoint of psychoanalysis.

"Everyone familiar with this defendant knows that before he left for Vietnam, he was a popular, respectable young man. A star athlete, a member of the marching band and student government, and popular with class-mates and teachers. He had a part-time job helping his family. I might as well add that he was voted Best All-Around in the 1965 yearbook. He was described as always respectful to all and never had any incidents of fighting or disruptions in school. I heard the worst thing he did in elementary school was chew gum." Laughter in the court. "He was an above-average student who was planning to go to college. We know that tragedy struck when his fiancée was killed in a car accident.

"Mr. Mendoza actually experienced two major traumas—his fiancée's death and Vietnam. Any triggering mechanism can cause psychotic episodes later in life. After his fiancée's death, Mr. Mendoza changed in profound ways. His family and friends saw an utterly different individual—morose, isolated, and short-tempered with increased drinking. His mother and grandmother observed parallels between Curtis Mendoza and his father, who served in the Pacific during World War II. Like his son, the elder Mendoza's personality changed after his return, and he also had some major adjustments. The defendant's mother describes nightmares that her husband still has to this day, although they are not as frequent as before.

"I can piece together snippets of his experience during his two tours in Vietnam. He apparently was in a battle in the A Shau Valley near the

Laos border. The camp was defended by both Special Forces and Montagnards. Mr. Mendoza was slightly wounded by shrapnel—it went through his upper lip. This was the first of two Purple Hearts he received. You can see his scar from here, judge. Two inches one way or another, the shrapnel would have pierced his brain. Three of his team members were killed along with numerous Montagnards with whom the Green Berets enjoyed a close military relationship. After the camp was overrun, Mr. Mendoza and some members of his Special Forces team returned to the camp to retrieve the remains of their comrades, their friends.

"During both tours, he was mostly deployed with the Special Operations groups, but I cannot say precisely what he saw or experienced during those tours—except for what I previously alluded to. I can say, however, that the Special Operations Units are one of the most dangerous assignments in Vietnam, and he volunteered for that assignment. One can only imagine what it might be like to work in small units behind enemy lines. The stress must be enormous—stress that can linger for years.

"The Vietnam War is different from World War II from the standpoint of clinical treatment. In World War II, there were clearly delineated lines separating armies and combat zones. A wounded soldier or a soldier who showed signs of mental fatigue could be removed from the combat zone for recovery. Not in Vietnam. The entire country is a combat zone. And as we can see from recent events of the Tet Offensive, the entire country is unsafe. The American soldiers are not safe even among the civilian population in the cities and countryside. Every single day in the country, an American soldier was exposed to malaria, mosquitos, sabotage, booby traps, deadly snakes, horrible weather, and violent episodes of skirmishes with the enemy. Try eight months of that. It will eat you out from the inside. So, no question, Mr. Mendoza was exposed to these two traumas in his young life.

"And if you compare this man now to the man after the twin traumas, you will find two different human beings. You have his record in this case along with incidents before the homicide—like bar fights, etc."

Stein: "How does this trauma relate to conduct after the trauma has subsided?"

Dr. Marcote: "The key word in your question is 'subsided.' It never disappears from the person's psyche. It lingers and lies dormant just below the psychic surface and can emerge later in many different ways.

"Now, you gentlemen as lawyers are more familiar with the M'Naghten rule than I. But the rule talks about a 'disease of the mind,' when a person acts without knowing the 'nature and quality of the act he was doing.' Those are the more salient portions of the rule. Arguably, if a person has experienced a traumatic event, then that person is at risk of reliving that event—what we call flashbacks. That person actually believes at that specific moment that he is experiencing that moment—a moment and memory that he has tried to suppress. Clinically speaking, these flashbacks are transient dissociative episodes. These episodes involve the person's temporary disconnect from reality and replacing that reality with the traumatic episode. This condition, in my opinion, can arguably fall within the ambit of the M'Naghten rule. A person experiencing this horrible flashback would not know or understand 'the nature and quality of the act' he was committing. I have seen this dozens of times with my patients who are combat vets from World War II and a few from Vietnam. My big gripe, as an aside, is that we are not doing more to treat these vets. What happens when these young vets return home? Society had better be prepared for the next generation and future wars because if it isn't, we all will have a hefty price to pay for not helping these vets more than we should've.

"Now, in this specific case, it appears that Mr. Mendoza indeed entered the Allen bedroom. It appears there was a struggle as, judging from the decedent's hands, there was swelling. He likely punched his assailant several times. The police reports also indicate that the defendant had facial bruises, although they could have been the result of a fight he was involved in a few days before this incident. Also, we know Mr. Mendoza was under the influence of LSD, which would have compounded his sense of not understanding the reality in front of him. If the decedent surprised Mr. Mendoza in the bedroom and hit him, this could have triggered his flashback. Then Mendoza is on automatic pilot, so to speak. He has been trained in close hand-to-hand combat and very likely experienced that in the Shau Valley. You all saw the incident in the jail when he was attacked. He responded as he was trained to respond to a perceived threat. He was trained to kill, and unfortunately, Mr. Jim Allen may have been the victim of Mendoza's dissociative episode." He cleared his throat. "In my opinion, this defendant was legally insane at the time of the homicide, and that is what I am prepared to testify to in front of a jury. Thank you."

Judge Gates: "It's getting late. We will resume tomorrow at ten a.m. sharp with the prosecution's cross-examination. I also will have many follow-up questions. Plus, I need time to conduct more legal research. Gotta hit the books and back to shepardizing counsel. Dr. Marcote, we'll see you in the morning."

PART TWENTY-THREE

RAQUEL

Later, back at his apartment, Stein lounged on his old sofa sleepily watching TV—something mindless, a rerun of *Gilligan's Island*. He daydreamed that he was on the island, stranded and closely snuggled up between Ginger and Mary Ann. He probably would be giving them legal advice on the skipper's tragic negligence before their three-hour tour. The skipper was probably brave and sure but couldn't read a fucking weather report before the weather started getting rough. If it wasn't for the stupidity of the clueless crew, the *Minnow* would not have been lost. An egregious tort if he ever saw one. Stein finished his third beer along with a plate of cold enchiladas—extra salsa and beans.

As he was dozing off around 11:00 p.m., the phone blared. It was Judge Gates. He said, "Mr. Stein, get down here to my chambers in fifteen minutes. My bailiff will let you in. Other counsel on the Mendoza case will be here. Please hurry," and he abruptly hung up before Stein could ask any questions.

Twenty minutes later, Stein entered Gates's chambers. Standing along the wall or seated were DDA Winston Clyde, Hank Mendoza, a court reporter, and newly appointed Sheriff Garza, all looking confused.

Judge Gates: "Counsel, I was contacted by Sheriff Garza one hour ago with information directly linked to the Allen murder case. Mr. Stein and Mr. Mendoza, OK if we have this conversation in your client's absence?"

Stein: "Well, I guess I can waive his presence for now, Judge…as long as there's a record of this chamber's conference. What's this about? I didn't finish *Gilligan's Island*, but OK, as long as we have a court reporter transcribing."

Gates: "Sheriff, it's probably quicker if we just bring her in here."

Garza exited and returned with another person, a woman.

She slowly entered with Sheriff Garza holding on to her elbow. Stein guessed she was about thirty-five, Mexican, lovely olive skin with thick, languid black hair that hung on her shoulders. She was a stark beauty. It was obvious she had not slept in a while. She then gave Sheriff Garza something—a worn Indian pouch with the initials J.A. inscribed. It also looked like it contained some documents. Sheriff Garza announced, "This is Raquel Torres. I'll just let her tell the story. Raquel, go ahead. Start from the beginning."

Judge Gates brought her a chair and handed her a cup of fresh coffee. "Miss Torres, please go ahead."

"I'm very nervous…My name is Raquel Torres, and I have lived in Clarktown most of my life. I used to work for the Allen family. My family worked for the Allens since the old days. It was at the ranch that I met Jimmy…James Allen II. For a long time, we would talk a little as I attended to my work. Then it became something different. We both knew we liked each other…we just knew it. You can feel it deep inside, you know? Well, after a while, we expressed our love to each other. No one else knew that we were seeing each other. A few secret dates here and there. My parents had no idea because they would not permit it…I was only eighteen when I met him. My mom always told me to save myself for the right man, and I knew she would never approve of me with an Allen—they were our family's employers.

"Jimmy and I spent a weekend together in 1955 in San Francisco; I had never been there. I had never been so happy in my life until then. When we returned, we started to make plans for our lives together. I soon realized that I was pregnant. As soon as my parents found out, they sent me to Mexico 'for the shame' they thought I brought to our family. Later I found out my mother and Jimmy's mother made a pact—a deal. No one would never know who the father was. Mrs. Allen warned my mother that if I returned home within five years, she and my father would lose their jobs at the Allen ranch. She told my mom, "My son is not going to marry a little Mexican domestic who trapped him." I think she even paid off my parents to cover expenses for the baby. They also told Jimmy and me a lie—that Jimmy wanted nothing to do with me and that I wanted nothing to do with him. They also told him that I left for Mexico because I found someone else to marry. All a lie. I loved Jimmy so much, and I still do to this day.

"My son was born in December 1955. On the Mexican birth certificate, he was listed as Jaime Torres, twelve pounds with light hair and green eyes. The Mexican birth certificate also listed '*padre desconocido,*' father unknown. By the time I returned to Allen County in 1960, the love between us was already snuffed out. The flame was gone…just ashes of what could have been. I loved him so much, and I know he felt the same way. Jimmy later told me he promised his stepmother that he would never publicly acknowledge he was the father, although he had supported us.

"My son always had an idea of who his father was. Not having a father was a big void in his life, and he felt like he wanted a connection to a father, like all his friends had. I was grateful to the Allens for helping me financially with my son. But that's not what I wanted. My son only wanted the world to know he had a father, that's all. Some kind of acknowledgment from the Allen family. It never came.

"On the morning Jimmy died, my son went to his ranch to ask him and confirm that Mr. Allen was his father. According to my son, they first yelled at each other. Then Mr. Allen took out this legal document in there…a kind of will…and there's a statement that, in fact, Mr. Allen and I are the parents of Jimmy. This document also left a small inheritance for my son. My son didn't believe he was included in Allen's document and began to hit Mr. Allen, who did his best to protect himself. My son is only thirteen years old, but he's the size of a grown man. Well, he kept hitting Jimmy until he knocked him down, and he hit his head on a metal bed frame and bled to death. My son took the will and ran. I never knew… until this afternoon when I cleaned Jimmy's closet. I found the Indian pouch everyone's been talking about. The document is still there, and the dried blood didn't damage it. I also found Jimmy's clothes with blood in our shed in the backyard. I approached Jimmy, and he told me everything. All he wanted was for the world to know who his father was. Then I called Sheriff Garza. He's a good friend of mine, and I trust him. I'm so sorry that Curtis was arrested and had to endure all this. He's a good boy. My son's a good boy too." She took a sip of the coffee, shaking, sniffling.

Sheriff Garza: "We detained the boy today, and he's being held in the juvenile detention facility."

DAA Clyde: "Judge, once we confirm this, I will speak to my boss. We can formally dismiss the case today in court, and Sheriff Garza can cut him loose then."

Stein turned to Hank. The somber ambiance of Judge Gates's chamber was dark and eerily quiet—broken only by Hank's soft cries.

EPILOGUE

As I write this fifty years later, I am constantly reminded that those two years shaped and defined my life, and the lives of others, in a deeply profound way. My parents passed away ten years ago, two days apart. My nana passed away in her sleep in the summer of 1995 during a quiet morning. She's buried next to Tata, but she's still next to my heart. Curt returned to school and teaches history at Rockwood High. He never married and lost a kidney to Agent Orange. Hank's kidney was compatible, and he gave it to Curt. Now they are truly blood brothers. Hank remained in Boston but visits every Christmas. Hank is also on the board of directors of the Allen II Charitable Trust Foundation. I was one of its recipients and was given a full scholarship to college. I am now a writer for the *Los Angeles Tribune*.

Sammy Williams, the guy who allegedly plastered the Vulture, became the first African American mayor of Clarktown in 2004. He ran on a platform of law and order. Sheriff Garza retired as sheriff after forty years of loyal service in 1990. Matt Bradshaw became a good friend of the family, especially to Curt, over the years. Karina's Restaurant closed in 1995, and now a giant Walmart sits there. I can still smell a waft of chile colorado at times as I pass the Walmart greeter. Jimmy Torres spent one year in a juvenile facility and moved out of Allen County with his mom in 1970, and I never heard from him.

Attorney Robert Stein returned to Berkeley and is now the assistant public defender in San Francisco. He has sought investors to start a kosher Mexican fusion restaurant in the Mission District. Sometime around 1980, he ran into Judge Gates at a legal seminar. After Gates's fifth vodka/tonic, he confided to Stein that he would have allowed the insanity defense for what we now know as PTSD. American jurisprudence has finally recognized this as well. My crew—Stinky, Skip It, and Moe—still live in the valley, growing old and fat with their wives and kids. I see them often during my visits from Los Angeles. They still argue about the best music of the 1960s.

Tobias Quinn III was appointed to the municipal court in 1990, but he still counsels lawyers with alcoholism. He finally arrived at his destination on his path to redemption.

Juana Gomes disappeared completely with her damaged brother. There's a new saying in Allen County: "Juana la Cubana Volo Como Matias Perez."

My name is Samuel Mendoza, and this is my story.